UNKNOWN TO HISTORY

UNKNOWN TO HISTORY

Is it true? Was the girl about whom Charlotte Yonge wove this famous romance a real figure, who was deliberately allowed to slip out of history's pages? Miss Yonge, basing her story on some old references, believed it might be so.

The tale begins on a blustery day in 1568, when Mistress Talbot is waiting anxiously for her sailor husband's return. After the fearful storm of the previous night, she is relieved to hear his firm tread on the stair. He appears, carrying a baby girl in his arms.

The child was the sole survivor from the wreck of a Scottish ship. The only clues to her identity were a little gold cross, a curious mark branded on her shoulder-blade and a scroll of paper bearing a message in some indecipherable code.

Nobody claimed the child, so they named her Cicely and she was brought up with the three Talbot boys at their home near Sheffield Park, where the Earl of Shrewsbury, a kinsman of theirs, stood keeper over that most unhappy lady, Mary Queen of Scots.

It was not unnatural, perhaps, that Mary grew fond of the cheerful carefree children, and Mrs. Talbot and Cicely became a part of that strange court circle. Cicely, in turn, adored the romantic Queen— but was stunned when she discovered the truth about herself.

From then on, her life was in constant danger, and they were all surrounded by web upon web of intrigue. Walsingham, Queen Elizabeth's spy master, was determined that Mary must be destroyed; and when the axe fell, she might not be the only one to die. For Cicely and the man she loved there was just one way of escape. They must vanish from history . . .

How much is true? We shall never know. What matters is that Charlotte Yonge took these tenuous threads from the past and, with them, made a timeless, wonderfully appealing, historical novel.

"His mother's foot was on the rocker."

UNKNOWN TO HISTORY

A STORY OF THE
CAPTIVITY OF MARY OF SCOTLAND

"They that parted from her meant to know her again."—P. 14.

ILLUSTRATED BY W. HENNESSY

TOM STACEY

First Published in Great Britain 1883

This edition published 1972 by
Tom Stacey Reprints Ltd.
28–29 Maiden Lane, London, WC2E 7JP,
England.

ISBN 085468 173 6

Printed in Great Britain by
C. Tinling & Co. Ltd, Prescot and London.

PREFACE.

In p. 58 of vol. ii. of the second edition of Miss Strickland's *Life of Mary Queen of Scots*, or p. 100, vol. v. of Burton's *History of Scotland*, will be found the report on which this tale is founded.

If circumstances regarding the Queen's captivity and Babington's plot have been found to be omitted, as well as many interesting personages in the suite of the captive Queen, it must be remembered that the art of the story-teller makes it needful to curtail some of the incidents which would render the narrative too complicated to be interesting to those who wish more for a view of noted characters in remarkable situations, than for a minute and accurate sifting of facts and evidence.

C. M. YONGE.

February 27, 1882.

CONTENTS.

A*

CHAPTER VIII.

CHAPTER IX.

CHAPTER X.

CHAPTER XI.

CHAPTER XII.

CHAPTER XIII.

CHAPTER XIV.

CHAPTER XV.

CHAPTER XVI.

CHAPTER XVII.

CHAPTER XVIII.

CHAPTER XIX.

CHAPTER XX.

CHAPTER XXI.

CHAPTER XXII.

CHAPTER XXIII.

CHAPTER XXIV.

CHAPTER XXV.

CHAPTER XXVI.

CHAPTER XXVII.

CHAPTER XXXVIII.

CHAPTER XXXIX.

CHAPTER XL.

CHAPTER XLI.

CHAPTER XLII.

CHAPTER XLIII.

CHAPTER XLIV.

CHAPTER XLV.

UNKNOWN TO HISTORY.

CHAPTER I.

THE LITTLE WAIF.

On a spring day, in the year 1568, Mistress Talbot sat in her lodging at Hull, an upper chamber, with a large latticed window, glazed with the circle and diamond leading perpetuated in Dutch pictures, and opening on a carved balcony, whence, had she been so minded, she could have shaken hands with her opposite neighbour. There was a richly carved mantel-piece, with a sea-coal fire burning in it, for though it was May, the sea winds blew cold, and there was a fishy odour about the town, such as it was well to counteract. The floor was of slippery polished oak, the walls hung with leather, gilded in some places and depending from cornices, whose ornaments proved to an initiated eye, that this had once been the refectory of a small priory, or cell, broken up at the Reformation.

Of furniture there was not much, only an open cupboard, displaying two silver cups and tankards, a sauce-pan of the same metal, a few tall, slender, Venetian glasses, a little pewter, and some rare shells. A few high - backed chairs were ranged against the wall; there was a tall "armory," *i.e.* a linen-press of dark oak, guarded on each side by the twisted weapons of the sea unicorn, and in the middle of the room stood a large, solid-looking table, adorned with a brown earthenware beau-pot, containing a stiff posy of roses, southernwood, gillyflowers, pinks and pansies, of small dimensions. On hooks, against the wall, hung a pair of spurs, a shield, a breastplate, and other pieces of armour, with an open helmet bearing the dog, the well-known crest of the Talbots of the Shrewsbury line.

On the polished floor, near the window, were a child's cart, a little boat, some whelks and limpets. Their owner, a stout boy of three years old, in a tight, borderless, round cap, and home-spun, madder-dyed frock, lay fast asleep in a big wooden cradle, scarcely large enough, however, to contain him, as he lay curled up, sucking his thumb, and hugging to his breast the soft fragment of a sea-bird's downy breast. If he stirred, his mother's foot was on the rocker, as she sat spinning, but her spindle danced languidly on the floor, as if "feeble was her hand, and silly her thread;" while she listened anxiously for every sound in the street below. She wore a dark blue dress, with a small lace ruff opening in front, deep cuffs to match, and a white apron likewise edged with lace, and a coif, bent down in the centre, over a sweet countenance, matronly, though youthful, and now full of wistful expectancy, not untinged with anxiety and sorrow.

Susan Hardwicke was a distant kinswoman of the famous Bess of Hardwicke, and had formed one of the little court of gentlewomen with whom great ladies were wont to surround themselves. There she met Richard Talbot, the second son of a relative of the Earl of Shrewsbury, a young man who, with the in-

difference of those days to service by land or sea, had
been at one time a gentleman pensioner of Queen
Mary; at another had sailed under some of the great
mariners of the western main. There he had acquired
substance enough to make the offer of his hand to the
dowerless Susan no great imprudence; and as neither
could be a subject for ambitious plans, no obstacle
was raised to their wedding.

He took his wife home to his old father's house in
the precincts of Sheffield Park, where she was kindly
welcomed; but wealth did not so abound in the family
but that, when opportunity offered, he was thankful
to accept the command of the *Mastiff*, a vessel commissioned by Queen Elizabeth, but built, manned, and
maintained at the expense of the Earl of Shrewsbury.
It formed part of a small squadron which was cruising
on the eastern coast to watch over the intercourse
between France and Scotland, whether in the interest
of the imprisoned Mary, or of the Lords of the Congregation. He had obtained lodgings for Mistress Susan
at Hull, so that he might be with her when he put
into harbour, and she was expecting him for the first
time since the loss of their second child, a daughter
whom he had scarcely seen during her little life of a
few months.

Moreover, there had been a sharp storm a few days
previously, and experience had not hardened her to
the anxieties of a sailor's wife. She had been down
once already to the quay, and learnt all that the old
sailors could tell her of chances and conjectures; and
when her boy began to fret from hunger and weariness,
she had left her serving-man, Gervas, to watch for
further tidings. Yet, so does one trouble drive out
another, that whereas she had a few days ago dreaded

the sorrow of his return, she would now have given worlds to hear his step.

Hark, what is that in the street? Oh, folly! If the *Mastiff* were in, would not Gervas have long ago brought her the tidings? Should she look over the balcony only to be disappointed again? Ah! she had been prudent, for the sounds were dying away. Nay, there was a foot at the door! Gervas with ill news! No, no, it bounded as never did Gervas's step! It was coming up. She started from the chair, quivering with eagerness, as the door opened and in hurried her sun-tanned sailor! She was in his arms in a trance of joy. That was all she knew for a moment, and then, it was as if something else were given back to her. No, it was not a dream! It was substance. In her arms was a little swaddled baby, in her ears its feeble wail, mingled with the glad shout of little Humfrey, as he scrambled from the cradle to be uplifted in his father's arms.

"What is this?" she asked, gazing at the infant between terror and tenderness, as its weak cry and exhausted state forcibly recalled the last hours of her own child.

"It is the only thing we could save from a wreck off the Spurn," said her husband. "Scottish as I take it. The rogues seem to have taken to their boats, leaving behind them a poor woman and her child. I trust they met their deserts and were swamped. We saw the fluttering of her coats as we made for the Humber, and I sent Goatley and Jaques in the boat to see if anything lived. The poor wench had gone before they could lift her up, but the little one cried lustily, though it has waxen weaker since. We had no milk on board, and could only give it bits of soft bread soaked in beer, and I misdoubt me whether it did not all run out at the corners of its mouth."

This was interspersed with little Humfrey's eager outcries that little sister was come again, and Mrs. Talbot, the tears running down her cheeks, hastened to summon her one woman-servant, Colet, to bring the porringer of milk.

Captain Talbot had only hurried ashore to bring the infant, and show himself to his wife. He was forced instantly to return to the wharf, but he promised to come back as soon as he should have taken order for his men, and for the *Mastiff*, which had suffered considerably in the storm, and would need to be refitted.

Colet hastily put a manchet of fresh bread, a pasty, and a stoup of wine into a basket, and sent it by her husband, Gervas, after their master ; and then eagerly assisted her mistress in coaxing the infant to swallow food, and in removing the soaked swaddling clothes which the captain and his crew had not dared to meddle with.

When Captain Talbot returned, as the rays of the setting sun glanced high on the roofs and chimneys, little Humfrey stood peeping through the tracery of the balcony, watching for him, and shrieking with joy at the first glimpse of the sea-bird's feather in his cap. The spotless home-spun cloth and the trenchers were laid for supper, a festive capon was prepared by the choicest skill of Mistress Susan, and the little ship-wrecked stranger lay fast asleep in the cradle.

All was well with it now, Mrs. Talbot said. Nothing had ailed it but cold and hunger, and when it had been fed, warmed, and dressed, it had fallen sweetly asleep in her arms, appeasing her heartache for her

own little Sue, while Humfrey fully believed that
father had brought his little sister back again.

The child was in truth a girl, apparently three or
four months old. She had been rolled up in Mrs.
Talbot's baby's clothes, and her own long swaddling
bands hung over the back of a chair, where they had
been dried before the fire. They were of the finest
woollen below, and cambric above, and the outermost
were edged with lace, whose quality Mrs. Talbot esti-
mated very highly.

"See," she added, "what we found within. A
Popish relic, is it not? Colet and Mistress Gale were
for making away with it at once, but it seemed to me
that it was a token whereby the poor babe's friends may
know her again, if she have any kindred not lost at sea."

The token was a small gold cross, of peculiar work-
manship, with a crystal in the middle, through which
might be seen some mysterious object neither husband
nor wife could make out, but which they agreed must
be carefully preserved for the identification of their
little waif. Mrs. Talbot also produced a strip of writing
which she had found sewn to the inmost band wrapped
round the little body, but it had no superscription, and
she believed it to be either French, Latin, or High
Dutch, for she could make nothing of it. Indeed, the
good lady's education had only included reading, writing, needlework and cookery, and she knew no language
but her own. Her husband had been taught Latin,
but his acquaintance with modern tongues was of
the nautical order, and entirely oral and vernacular.
However, it enabled him to aver that the letter—if
such it were—was neither Scottish, French, Spanish,
nor High or Low Dutch. He looked at it in all directions, and shook his head over it.

"Who can read it for us?" asked Mrs. Talbot. "Shall we ask Master Heatherthwayte? he is a scholar, and he said he would look in to see how you fared."

"At supper-time, I trow," said Richard, rather grimly, "the smell of thy stew will bring him down in good time."

"Nay, dear sir, I thought you would be fain to see the good man, and he lives but poorly in his garret."

"Scarce while he hath good wives like thee to boil his pot for him," said Richard, smiling. "Tell me, hath he heard aught of this gear? thou hast not laid this scroll before him?"

"No, Colet brought it to me only now, having found it when washing the swaddling-bands, stitched into one of them."

"Then hark thee, good wife, not one word to him of the writing."

"Might he not interpret it?"

"Not he! I must know more about it ere I let it pass forth from mine hands, or any strange eye fall upon it—Ha, in good time! I hear his step on the stair."

The captain hastily rolled up the scroll and put it into his pouch, while Mistress Susan felt as if she had made a mistake in her hospitality, yet almost as if her husband were unjust towards the good man who had been such a comfort to her in her sorrow; but there was no lack of cordiality or courtesy in Richard's manner when, after a short, quick knock, there entered a figure in hat, cassock, gown, and bands, with a pleasant, though grave countenance, the complexion showing that it had been tanned and sunburnt in early youth, although it wore later traces of a sedentary student life, and, it might be, of less genial living than had nourished the up-growth of that sturdily-built frame

Master Joseph Heatherthwayte was the greatly underpaid curate of a small parish on the outskirts of Hull. He contrived to live on some £10 per annum in the attic of the house where the Talbots lodged,—and not only to live, but to be full of charitable deeds, mostly at the expense of his own appetite. The square cut of his bands, and the uncompromising roundness of the hat which he doffed on his entrance, marked him as inclined to the Puritan party, which, being that of apparent progress, attracted most of the ardent spirits of the time.

Captain Talbot's inclinations did not lie that way, but he respected and liked his fellow-lodger, and his vexation had been merely the momentary disinclination of a man to be interrupted, especially on his first evening at home. He responded heartily to Master Heatherthwayte's warm pressure of the hand and piously expressed congratulation on his safety, mixed with condolence on the grief that had befallen him.

"And you have been a good friend to my poor wife in her sorrow," said Richard, "for the which I thank you heartily, sir."

"Truly, sir, I could have been her scholar, with such edifying resignation did she submit to the dispensation," returned the clergyman, uttering these long words in a broad northern accent which had nothing incongruous in it to Richard's ears, and taking advantage of the lady's absence on "hospitable tasks intent" to speak in her praise.

Little Humfrey, on his father's knee, comprehending that they were speaking of the recent sorrow, put in his piece of information that "father had brought little sister back from the sea."

"Ah, child!" said Master Heatherthwayte, in the ponderous tone of one unused to children, "thou hast yet to learn the words of the holy David, ' I shall go to him, but he shall not return to me.' "

"Bring not that thought forward, Master Heather-thwayte," said Richard, " I am well pleased that my poor wife and this little lad can take the poor little one as a solace sent them by God, as she assuredly is."

" Mean you, then, to adopt her into your family ?" asked the minister.

" We know not if she hath any kin," said Richard, and at that moment Susan entered, followed by the man and maid, each bearing a portion of the meal, which was consumed by the captain and the clergy-man as thoroughly hungry men eat; and there was silence till the capon's bones were bare and two large tankards had been filled with Xeres sack, captured in a Spanish ship, " the only good thing that ever came from Spain," quoth the sailor.

Then he began to tell how he had weathered the storm on the Berwickshire coast; but he was inter-rupted by another knock, followed by the entrance of a small, pale, spare man, with the lightest possible hair, very short, and almost invisible eyebrows; he had a round ruff round his neck, and a black, scholarly gown, belted round his waist with a girdle, in which he carried writing tools.

" Ha, Cuthbert Langston, art thou there ? " said the captain, rising. " Thou art kindly welcome. Sit down and crush a cup of sack with Master Heatherthwayte and me."

" Thanks, cousin," returned the visitor, " I heard that the *Mastiff* was come in, and I came to see whether all was well."

" It was kindly done, lad," said Richard, while the others did their part of the welcome, though scarcely

so willingly.   Cuthbert Langston was a distant relation
on the mother's side of Richard, a young scholar who,
after his education at Oxford, had gone abroad with a
nobleman's son as his pupil, and on his return, instead
of taking Holy Orders, as was expected, had obtained
employment in a merchant's counting-house at Hull,
for which his knowledge of languages eminently fitted
him.   Though he possessed none of the noble blood of
the Talbots, the employment was thought by Mistress
Susan somewhat derogatory to the family dignity, and
there was a strong suspicion both in her mind and
that of Master Heatherthwayte that his change of
purpose was due to the change of religion in England,
although he was a perfectly regular church - goer.
Captain Talbot, however, laughed at all this, and,
though he had not much in common with his kinsman,
always treated him in a cousinly fashion.   He too had
heard a rumour of the foundling, and made inquiry for
it, upon which Richard told his story in greater detail,
and his wife asked what the poor mother was like.

"I saw her not," he answered, "but Goatley
thought the poor woman to whom she was bound
more like to be nurse than mother, judging by her
years and her garments."

"The mother may have been washed off before," said
Susan, lifting the little one from the cradle, and hushing
it. "Weep not, poor babe, thou hast found a mother here."

"Saw you no sign of the crew?" asked Master
Heatherthwayte.

"None at all.   The vessel I knew of old as the
brig *Bride of Dunbar*, one of the craft that ply between
Dunbar and the French ports."

"And how think you? Were none like to be saved?"

"I mean to ride along the coast to-morrow, to see

whether aught can be heard of them, but even if their boats could live in such a sea, they would have evil hap among the wreckers if they came ashore. I would not desire to be a shipwrecked man in these parts, and if I had a Scottish or a French tongue in my head so much the worse for me."

" Ah, Master Heatherthwayte," said Susan, " should not a man give up the sea when he is a husband and father ? "

" Tush, dame ! With God's blessing the good ship *Mastiff* will ride out many another such gale. Tell thy mother, little Numpy, that an English sailor is worth a dozen French or Scottish lubbers."

" Sir," said Master Heatherthwayte, " the pious trust of the former part of your discourse is contradicted by the boast of the latter end."

" Nay, Sir Minister, what doth a sailor put his trust in but his God foremost, and then his good ship and his brave men ? "

It should be observed that all the three men wore their hats, and each made a reverent gesture of touching them. The clergyman seemed satisfied by the answer, and presently added that it would be well, if Master and Mistress Talbot meant to adopt the child, that she should be baptized.

" How now ? " said Richard, " we are not so near any coast of Turks or Infidels that we should deem her sprung of heathen folk."

" Assuredly not," said Cuthbert Langston, whose quick, light-coloured eyes had spied the reliquary in Mistress Susan's work-basket, " if this belongs to her. By your leave, kinswoman," and he lifted it in his hand with evident veneration, and began examining it.

" It is Babylonish gold, an accursed thing !" ex-

claimed Master Heatherthwayte. "Beware, Master
Talbot, and cast it from thee."

"Nay," said Richard, "that shall I not do. It may
lead to the discovery of the child's kindred. Why,
my master, what harm think you it will do to us in
my dame's casket? Or what right have we to make
away with the little one's property?"

His common sense was equally far removed from
the horror of the one visitor as from the reverence of
the other, and so it pleased neither   Master Langston
was the first to speak, observing that the relic made it
evident that the child must have been baptized.

"A Popish baptism," said Master Heatherthwayte,
"with chrism and taper and words and gestures to
destroy the pure simplicity of the sacrament."

Controversy here seemed to be setting in, and the
infant cause of it here setting up a cry, Susan escaped
under pretext of putting Humfrey to bed in the next
room, and carried off both the little ones. The conversation then fell upon the voyage, and the captain
described the impregnable aspect of the castle of
Dumbarton, which was held for Queen Mary by her
faithful partisan, Lord Flemyng. On this, Cuthbert
Langston asked whether he had heard any tidings of
the imprisoned Queen, and he answered that it was reported at Leith that she had well-nigh escaped from Lochleven, in the disguise of a lavender or washerwoman.
She was actually in the boat, and about to cross the lake,
when a rude oarsman attempted to pull aside her muffler,
and the whiteness of the hand she raised in self-protec-
tion betrayed her, so that she was carried back. "If she
had reached Dumbarton," he said, "she might have
mocked at the Lords of the Congregation. Nay, she
might have been in that very brig, whose wreck I beheld."

"And well would it have been for Scotland and England had it been the will of Heaven that so it should fall out," observed the Puritan.

"Or it may be," said the merchant, "that the poor lady's escape was frustrated by Providence, that she might be saved from the rocks of the Spurn."

"The poor lady, truly! Say rather the murtheress," quoth Heatherthwayte.

"Say rather the victim and scapegoat of other men's plots," protested Langston.

"Come, come, sirs," says Talbot, "we'll have no high words here on what Heaven only knoweth. Poor lady she is, in all sooth, if sackless; poorer still if guilty; so I know not what matter there is for falling out about. In any sort, I will not have it at my table." He spoke with the authority of the captain of a ship, and the two visitors, scarce knowing it, submitted to his decision of manner, but the harmony of the evening seemed ended. Cuthbert Langston soon rose to bid good-night, first asking his cousin at what hour he proposed to set forth for the Spurn, to which Richard briefly replied that it depended on what had to be done as to the repairs of the ship.

The clergyman tarried behind him to say, "Master Talbot, I marvel that so godly a man as you have ever been should be willing to harbour one so popishly affected, and whom many suspect of being a seminary priest."

"Master Heatherthwayte," returned the captain, "my kinsman is my kinsman, and my house is my house. No offence, sir, but I brook not meddling."

The clergyman protested that no offence was intended, only caution, and betook himself to his own bare chamber, high above. No sooner was he gone than Captain Talbot again became absorbed in the

endeavour to spell out the mystery of the scroll, with
his elbows on the table and his hands over his ears, nor
did he look up till he was touched by his wife, when
he uttered an impatient demand what she wanted now.

She had the little waif in her arms undressed, and
with only a woollen coverlet loosely wrapped round
her, and without speaking she pointed to the little

shoulder - blades,   where   two   marks

had been indelibly made—on one side the crowned
monogram of the Blessed Virgin, on the other a device

like the Labarum,      only that the up-

right was surmounted by a *fleur-de-lis*.

Richard Talbot gave a sort of perplexed grunt of
annoyance to acknowledge that he saw them.

"Poor little maid! how could they be so cruel?
They have been branded with a hot iron," said the
lady.

"They that parted from her meant to know her
again," returned Talbot.

"Surely they are Popish marks," added Mistress
Susan.

"Look you here, Dame Sue, I know you for a dis-

creet woman. Keep this gear to yourself, both the
letter and the marks. Who hath seen them?"

"I doubt me whether even Colet has seen this mark."

"That is well. Keep all out of sight. Many a
man has been brought into trouble for a less matter
swelled by prating tongues."

"Have you made it out?"

"Not I. It may be only the child's horoscope, or
some old wife's charm that is here sewn up, and these
marks may be naught but some sailor's freak; but, on
the other hand, they may be concerned with perilous
matter, so the less said the better."

"Should they not be shown to my lord, or to her
Grace's Council?"

"I'm not going to run my head into trouble for making a coil about what may be naught. That's what
befell honest Mark Walton. He thought he had seized
matter of State, and went up to Master Walsingham,
swelling like an Indian turkey-cock, with his secret
letters, and behold they turned out to be a Dutch fish-
wife's charm to bring the herrings. I can tell you he
has rued the work he made about it ever since. On the
other hand, let it get abroad through yonder prating fellow, Heatherthwayte, or any other, that Master Richard
Talbot had in his house a child with, I know not what
Popish tokens, and a scroll in an unknown tongue, and
I should be had up in gyves for suspicion of treason,
or may be harbouring the Prince of Scotland himself,
when it is only some poor Scottish archer's babe."

"You would not have me part with the poor little
one?"

"Am I a Turk or a Pagan? No. Only hold thy
peace, as I shall hold mine, until such time as I can
meet some one whom I can trust to read this riddle.

Tell me—what like is the child? Wouldst guess it to be of gentle, or of clownish blood, if women can tell such things?"

"Of gentle blood, assuredly," cried the lady, so that he smiled and said, "I might have known that so thou wouldst answer."

"Nay, but see her little hands and fingers, and the mould of her dainty limbs. No Scottish fisher clown was her father, I dare be sworn. Her skin is as fair and fine as my Humfrey's, and moreover she has always been in hands that knew how a babe should be tended. Any woman can tell you that!"

"And what like is she in your woman's eyes? What complexion doth she promise?"

"Her hair, what she has of it, is dark; her eyes—bless them—are of a deep blue, or purple, such as most babes have till they take their true tint. There is no guessing. Humfrey's eyes were once like to be brown, now are they as blue as thine own."

"I understand all that," said Captain Talbot, smiling. "If she have kindred, they will know her better by the sign manual on her tender flesh than by her face."

"And who are they?"

"Who are they?" echoed the captain, rolling up the scroll in despair. "Here, take it, Susan, and keep it safe from all eyes. Whatever it may be, it may serve thereafter to prove her true name. And above all, not a word or breath to Heatherthwayte, or any of thy gossips, wear they coif or bands."

"Ah, sir! that you will mistrust the good man."

"I said not I mistrust any one; only that I will have no word of all this go forth! Not one! Thou heedest me, wife?"

"Verily I do, sir; I will be mute."

CHAPTER II.

EVIL TIDINGS.

AFTER giving orders for the repairs of the *Mastiff*, and the disposal of her crew, Master Richard Talbot purveyed himself of a horse at the hostel, and set forth for Spurn Head to make inquiries along the coast respecting the wreck of the *Bride of Dunbar*, and he was joined by Cuthbert Langston, who said his house had had dealings with her owners, and that he must ascertain the fate of her wares. His good lady remained in charge of the mysterious little waif, over whom her tender heart yearned more and more, while her little boy hovered about in serene contemplation of the treasure he thought he had recovered. To him the babe seemed really his little sister; to his mother, if she sometimes awakened pangs of keen regret, yet she filled up much of the dreary void of the last few weeks.

Mrs. Talbot was a quiet, reserved woman, not prone to gadding abroad, and she had made few acquaintances during her sojourn at Hull; but every creature she knew, or might have known, seemed to her to drop in that day, and bring at least two friends to inspect the orphan of the wreck, and demand all particulars.

The little girl was clad in the swaddling garments of Mrs. Talbot's own children, and the mysterious marks were suspected by no one, far less the letter which Susan, for security's sake, had locked up in her nearly empty, steel-bound, money casket. The opinions of the gossips varied, some thinking the babe might belong to some of the Queen of Scotland's party fleeing to France, others fathering her on the refugees from the persecutions in Flanders, a third party believing her a mere fisherman's child, and one lean, lantern-jawed old crone, Mistress Rotherford, observing, " Take my word, Mrs. Talbot, and keep her not with you. They that are cast up by the sea never bring good with them."

The court of female inquiry was still sitting when a heavy tread was heard, and Colet announced " a serving-man from Bridgefield had ridden post haste to speak with madam," and the messenger, booted and spurred, with the mastiff badge on his sleeve, and the hat he held in his hand, followed closely.

" What news, Nathanael ?" she asked, as she responded to his greeting.

" Ill enough news, mistress," was the answer. " Master Richard's ship be in, they tell me."

" Yea, but he is rid out to make inquiry for a wreck," said the lady. " Is all well with my good father-in-law ?"

" He ails less in body than in mind, so please you. Being that Master Humfrey was thrown by Blackfoot, the beast being scared by a flash of lightning, and never spoke again."

" Master Humfrey !"

" Ay, mistress. Pitched on his head against the south gate-post. I saw how it was with him when we took him up, and he never so much as lifted an eyelid, but died at the turn of the night. Heaven rest his soul !"

"Heaven rest his soul!" echoed Susan, and the ladies around chimed in. They had come for one excitement, and here was another.

"There! See but what I said!" quoth Mrs. Rotherford, uplifting a skinny finger to emphasise that the poor little flotsome had already brought evil.

"Nay," said the portly wife of a merchant, "begging your pardon, this may be a fat instead of a lean sorrow. Leaves the poor gentleman heirs, Mrs. Talbot?"

"Oh no!" said Susan, with tears in her eyes. "His wife died two years back, and her chrisom babe with her. He loved her too well to turn his mind to wed again, and now he is with her for aye." And she covered her face and sobbed, regardless of the congratulations of the merchant's wife, and exclaiming, "Oh! the poor old lady!"

"In sooth, mistress," said Nathanael, who had stood all this time as if he had by no means emptied his budget of ill news, "poor old madam fell down all of a heap on the floor, and when the wenches lifted her, they found she was stricken with the dead palsy, and she has not spoken, and there's no one knows what to do, for the poor old squire is like one distraught, sitting by her bed like an image on a monument, with the tears flowing down his old cheeks. 'But,' says he to me, 'get you to Hull, Nat, and take madam's palfrey and a couple of sumpter beasts, and bring my good daughter Talbot back with you as fast as she and the babes may brook.' I made bold to say, 'And Master Richard, your worship?' then he groaned somewhat, and said, 'If my son's ship be come in, he must do as her Grace's service permits, but meantime he must spare us his wife, for she is sorely needed here.' And he looked at the bed so as it would break

B

your heart to see, for since old Nurse Tooke hath been doited, there's not been a wench about the house that can do a hand's turn for a sick body."

Susan knew this was true, for her mother-in-law had been one of those bustling, managing housewives, who prefer doing everything themselves to training others, and she was appalled at the idea of the probable desolation and helplessness of the bereaved household.

It was far too late to start that day, even had her husband been at home, for the horses sent for her had to rest. The visitors would fain have extracted some more particulars about the old squire's age, his kindred to the great Earl, and the amount of estate to which her husband had become heir. There were those among them who could not understand Susan's genuine grief, and there were others whose consolations were no less distressing to one of her reserved character. She made brief answer that the squire was threescore and fifteen years old, his wife nigh about his age; that her husband was now their only child; that he was descended from a son of the great Earl John, killed at the Bridge of Chatillon; that he held the estate of Bridgefield in fief on tenure of military service to the head of his family. She did not know how much it was worth by the year, but she must pray the good ladies to excuse her, as she had many preparations to make. Volunteers to assist her in packing her mails were made, but she declined them all, and rejoiced when left alone with Colet to arrange for what would be probably her final departure from Hull.

It was a blow to find that she must part from her servant-woman, who, as well as her husband Gervas, was a native of Hull. Not only were they both unwilling to leave, but the inland country was to their imagination a wild unexplored desert. Indeed, Colet had only entered Mrs. Talbot's service to supply the place of a maid who had sickened with fever and ague, and had to be sent back to her native Hallamshire.

Ere long Mr. Heatherthwayte came down to offer his consolation, and still more his advice, that the little foundling should be at once baptized—conditionally, if the lady preferred it.

The Reformed of imperfect theological training, and as such Joseph Heatherthwayte must be classed, were apt to view the ceremonial of the old baptismal form, symbolical and beautiful as it was, as almost destroying the efficacy of the rite. Moreover, there was a further impression that the Church by which the child was baptized, had a right to bring it up, and thus the clergyman was urgent with the lady that she should seize this opportunity for the little one's baptism.

"Not without my husband's consent and knowledge," she said resolutely.

"Master Talbot is a good man, but somewhat careless of sound doctrine, as be the most of seafaring men."

Susan had been a little nettled by her husband's implied belief that she was influenced by the minister, so there was double resolution, as well as some offence in her reply, that she knew her duty as a wife too well to consent to such a thing without him. As to his being careless, he was a true and God-fearing man, and Mr. Heatherthwayte should know better than to speak thus of him to his wife.

Mr. Heatherthwayte's real piety and goodness had made him a great comfort to Susan in her lonely grief, but he had not the delicate tact of gentle blood, and

had not known where to stop, and as he stood half
apologising and half exhorting, she felt that her Richard
was quite right, and that he could be both meddling
and presuming.   He was exceedingly in the way of
her packing too, and she was at her wit's end to get rid
of him, when suddenly Humfrey managed to pinch his
fingers in a box, and set up such a yell, as, seconded by
the frightened baby, was more than any masculine ears
could endure, and drove Master Heatherthwayte to
beat a retreat.

Mistress Susan was well on in her work when her
husband returned, and as she expected, was greatly
overcome by the tidings of his brother's death.   He
closely questioned Nathanael on every detail, and could
think of nothing but the happy days he had shared
with his brother, and of the grief of his parents.   He
approved of all that his wife had done ; and as the
damage sustained by the *Mastiff* could not be repaired
under a month, he had no doubt about leaving his crew
in the charge of his lieutenant while he took his family
home.

So busy were both, and so full of needful cares, the
one in giving up her lodging, the other in leaving his
men, that it was impossible to inquire into the result
of his researches, for the captain was in that mood of
suppressed grief and vehement haste in which irrele-
vant inquiry is perfectly unbearable.

It was not till late in the evening that Richard
told his wife of his want of success in his investiga-
tions.   He had found witnesses of the destruction of
the ship, but he did not give them full credit.   " The
fellows say the ship drove on the rock, and that they
saw her boats go down with every soul on board, and
that they would not lie to an officer of her Grace.

Heaven pardon me if I do them injustice in believing
they would lie to him sooner than to any one else.
They are rogues enough to take good care that no poor
wretch should survive even if he did chance to come
to land."

"Then if there be no one to claim her, we may
bring up as our own the sweet babe whom Heaven
hath sent us."

"Not so fast, dame. Thou wert wont to be more
discreet. I said not so, but for the nonce, till I can
come by the rights of that scroll, there's no need to
make a coil. Let no one know of it, or of the trinket
—Thou hast them safe ?"

"Laid up with the Indian gold chain, thy wedding
gift, dear sir."

"'Tis well. My mother!—ah me," he added,
catching himself up; "little like is she to ask questions,
poor soul."

Then Susan diffidently told of Master Heatherthwayte's earnest wish to christen the child, and, what
certainly biassed her a good deal, the suggestion that
this would secure her to their own religion.

"There is something in that," said Richard,
"specially after what Cuthbert said as to the golden
toy yonder. If times changed again—which Heaven
forfend—that fellow might give us trouble about the
matter."

"You doubt him then, sir !" she asked.

"I relished not his ways on our ride to-day," said
Richard. "Sure I am that he had some secret cause
for being so curious about the wreck. I suspect him
of some secret commerce with the Queen of Scots' folk."

"Yet you were on his side against Mr. Heatherthwayte," said Susan.

"I would not have my kinsman browbeaten at mine own table by the self-conceited son of a dalesman, even if he have got a round hat and Geneva band! Ah, well! one good thing is we shall leave both of them well behind us, though I would it were for another cause."

Something in the remonstrance had, however, so worked on Richard Talbot, that before morning he declared that, hap what hap, if he and his wife were to bring up the child, she should be made a good Protestant Christian before they left the house, and there should be no more ado about it.

It was altogether illogical and untheological; but Master Heatherthwayte was delighted when in the very early morning his devotions were interrupted, and he was summoned by the captain himself to christen the child.

Richard and his wife were sponsors, but the question of name had never occurred to any one. However, in the pause of perplexity, when the response lagged to "Name this child," little Humfrey, a delighted spectator, broke out again with "Little Sis."

And forthwith, "Cicely, if thou art not already baptized," was uttered over the child, and Cicely became her name. It cost Susan a pang, as it had been that of her own little daughter, but it was too late to object, and she uttered no regret, but took the child to her heart, as sent instead of her who had been taken from her.

Master Heatherthwayte bade them good speed, and Master Langston stood at the door of his office and waved them a farewell, both alike unconscious of the rejoicing with which they were left behind. Mistress Talbot rode on the palfrey sent for her use, with the

little stranger slung to her neck for security's sake.
Her boy rode "a cock-horse" before his father, but
a resting-place was provided for him on a sort of
pannier on one of the sumpter beasts. What these
animals could not carry of the household stuff was left
in Colet's charge to be despatched by carriers; and the
travellers jogged slowly on through deep Yorkshire
lanes, often halting to refresh the horses and supply
the wants of the little children at homely wayside inns,
their entrance usually garnished with an archway
formed of the jawbones of whales, which often served
for gate-posts in that eastern part of Yorkshire. And
thus they journeyed, with frequent halts, until they
came to the Derbyshire borders.

Bridgefield House stood on the top of a steep slope
leading to the river Dun, with a high arched bridge
and a mill below it. From the bridge proceeded one
of the magnificent avenues of oak-trees which led up
to the lordly lodge, full four miles off, right across
Sheffield Park.

The Bridgefield estate had been a younger son's
portion, and its owners had always been regarded as
gentlemen retainers of the head of their name, the Earl
of Shrewsbury. Tudor jealousy had forbidden the
marshalling of such a *meiné* as the old feudal lords
had loved to assemble, and each generation of the
Bridgefield Talbots had become more independent than
the former one. The father had spent his younger
days as esquire to the late Earl, but had since become
a justice of the peace, and took rank with the substan-
tial landowners of the country. Humfrey, his eldest
son, had been a gentleman pensioner of the Queen till
his marriage, and Richard, though beginning his career
as page to the present Earl's first wife, had likewise

entered the service of her Majesty, though still it was
understood that the head of their name had a claim to
their immediate service, and had he been called to
take up arms, they would have been the first to follow
his banner.   Indeed, a pair of spurs was all the annual
rent they paid for their estate, which they held on
this tenure, as well as on paying the heriard horse
on the death of the head of the family, and other con-
tributions to their lord's splendour when he knighted
his son or married his daughter.   In fact, they stood
on the borderland of that feudal retainership which
was being rapidly extinguished.   The estate, carved
out of the great Sheffield property, was sufficient to
maintain the owner in the dignities of an English
gentleman, and to portion off the daughters, provided
that the superfluous sons shifted for themselves, as
Richard had hitherto done.   The house had been
ruined in the time of the Wars of the Roses, and rebuilt in the later fashion, with a friendly-looking front,
containing two large windows, and a porch projecting
between them.   The hall reached to the top of the
house, and had a waggon ceiling, with mastiffs alternat-
ing with roses on portcullises at the intersections of
the timbers.   This was the family sitting and dining
room, and had a huge chimney never devoid of a wood
fire.   One end had a buttery-hatch communicating
with the kitchen and offices; at the other was a small
room, sacred to the master of the house, niched under
the broad staircase that led to the upper rooms, which
opened on a gallery running round three sides of the
hall.

Outside, on the southern side of the house, was a
garden of potherbs, with the green walks edged by a
few bright flowers for beau-pots and posies.   This had

stone walls separating it from the paddock, which sloped down to the river, and was a good deal broken by ivy-covered rocks. Adjoining the stables were farm-buildings and barns, for there were several fields for tillage along the river-side, and the mill and two more farms were the property of the Bridgefield squire, so that the inheritance was a very fair one, wedged in, as it were, between the river and the great Chase of Sheffield, up whose stately avenue the riding party looked as they crossed the bridge, Richard having become more silent than ever as he came among the familiar rocks and trees of his boyhood, and knew he should not meet that hearty welcome from his brother which had never hitherto failed to greet his return. The house had that strange air of forlornness which seems to proclaim sorrow within. The great court doors stood open, and a big, rough deer-hound, at the sound of the approaching hoofs, rose slowly up, and began a series of long, deep-mouthed barks, with pauses between, sounding like a knell. One or two men and maids ran out at the sound, and as the travellers rode up to the horse-block, an old gray-bearded serving-man came stumbling forth with " Oh! Master Diccon, woe worth the day!"

"How does my mother?" asked Richard, as he sprang off and set his boy on his feet.

" No worse, sir, but she hath not yet spoken a word —back, Thunder—ah! sir, the poor dog knows you."

For the great hound had sprung up to Richard in eager greeting, but then, as soon as he heard his voice, the creature drooped his ears and tail, and instead of continuing his demonstrations of joy, stood quietly by, only now and then poking his long, rough nose into Richard's hand, knowing as well as possible that

B*

though not his dear lost master, he was the next thing!

Mistress Susan and the infant were lifted down— a hurried question and answer assured them that the funeral was over yesterday. My Lady Countess had come down and would have it so; my lord was at Court, and Sir Gilbert and his brothers had been present, but the old servants thought it hard that none nearer in blood should be there to lay their young squire in his grave, nor to support his father, who, poor old man, had tottered, and been so like to swoon as he passed the hall door, that Sir Gilbert and old Diggory could but help him back again, fearing lest he, too, might have a stroke.

It was a great grief to Richard, who had longed to look on his brother's face again, but he could say nothing, only he gave one hand to his wife and the other to his son, and led them into the hall, which was in an indescribable state of confusion. The trestles which had supported the coffin were still at one end of the room, the long tables were still covered with cloths, trenchers, knives, cups, and the remains of the funeral baked meats, and there were overthrown tankards and stains of wine on the cloth, as though, whatever else were lacking, the Talbot retainers had not missed their revel.

One of the dishevelled rough-looking maidens began some hurried muttering about being so distraught, and not looking for madam so early, but Susan could not listen to her, and merely putting the babe into her arms, came with her husband up the stairs, leaving little Humfrey with Nathanael.

Richard knocked at the bedroom door, and, receiving no answer, opened it. There in the tapestry-hung chamber was the huge old bedstead with its solid posts. In it lay something motionless, but the first thing the husband and wife saw was the bent head which was lifted up by the burly but broken figure in the chair beside it.

The two knotted old hands clasped the arms of the chair, and the squire prepared to rise, his lip trembling under his white beard, and emotion working in his dejected features. They were beforehand with him. Ere he could rise both were on their knees before him, while Richard in a broken voice cried, " Father, O father !"

" Thank God that thou art come, my son," said the old man, laying his hands on his shoulders, with a gleam of joy, for as they afterwards knew, he had sorely feared for Richard's ship in the storm that had caused Humfrey's death. " I looked for thee, my daughter," he added, stretching out one hand to Susan, who kissed it. " Now it may go better with her ! Speak to thy mother, Richard, she may know thy voice."

Alas ! no ; the recently active, ready old lady was utterly stricken, and as yet held in the deadly grasp of paralysis, unconscious of all that passed around her.

Susan found herself obliged at once to take up the reins, and become head nurse and housekeeper. The old squire trusted implicitly to her, and helplessly put the keys into her hands, and the serving-men and maids, in some shame at the condition in which the hall had been found, bestirred themselves to set it in order, so that there was a chance of the ordinary appearance of things being restored by supper-time, when Richard hoped to persuade his father to come down to his usual place.

Long before this, however, a trampling had been heard in the court, and a shrill voice, well known to Richard and Susan, was heard demanding, "Come home, is she——Master Diccon too? More shame for you, you sluttish queans and lazy lubbers, never to have let me know; but none of you have any respect——"

A visit from my Lady Countess was a greater favour to such a household as that of Bridgefield than it would be to a cottage of the present day; Richard was hurrying downstairs, and Susan only tarried to throw off the housewifely apron in which she had been compounding a cooling drink for the poor old lady, and to wash her hands, while Humfrey, rushing up to her, exclaimed "Mother, mother, is it the Queen?"

Queen Elizabeth herself was not inaptly represented by her namesake of Hardwicke, the Queen of Hallamshire, sitting on her great white mule at the door, sideways, with her feet on a board, as little children now ride, and attended by a whole troop of gentlemen ushers, maidens, prickers, and running footmen. She was a woman of the same type as the Queen, which was of course enough to stamp her as a celebrated beauty, and though she had reached middle age, her pale, clear complexion and delicate features were well preserved. Her chin was too sharp, and there was something too thin and keen about her nose and lips to promise good temper. She was small of stature, but she made up for it in dignity of presence, and as she sat there, with her rich embroidered green satin farthingale spreading out over the mule, her tall ruff standing up fanlike on her shoulders, her riding-rod in her hand, and her master of the horse standing at her rein, while a gentleman usher wielded an enormous, long-handled, green fan, to keep the sun from incommoding her, she was, perhaps, even more magnificent than the maiden queen herself might have been in her more private expeditions. Indeed, she was new to her dignity as Countess, having been only a few weeks married to the Earl, her fourth husband. Captain Talbot did not feel it derogatory to his dignity as a gentleman to advance with his hat in his hand to kiss her hand, and put a knee to the ground as he invited her to alight, an invitation his wife heard with dismay as she reached the door, for things were by no means yet as they should be in the hall. She curtsied low, and advanced with her son holding her hand, but shrinking behind her.

"Ha, kinswoman, is it thou!" was her greeting, as she, too, kissed the small, shapely, white, but exceedingly strong hand that was extended to her; "So thou art come, and high time too. Thou shouldst never have gone a-gadding to Hull, living in lodgings, awaiting thine husband, forsooth. Thou art over young a matron for such gear, and so I told Diccon Talbot long ago."

"Yea, madam," said Richard, somewhat hotly, "and I made answer that my Susan was to be trusted, and truly no harm has come thereof."

"Ho! and you reckon it no harm that thy father and mother were left to a set of feckless, brainless, idle serving-men and maids in their trouble? Why, none would so much as have seen to thy brother's poor body being laid in a decent grave had not I been at hand to take order for it as became a distant kinsman of my lord. I tell thee, Richard, there must be no more of these vagabond seafaring ways. Thou must serve my lord, as a true retainer and kinsman is bound —Nay," in reply to a gesture, "I will not come in, I

know too well in what ill order the house is like to
be. I did but take my ride this way to ask how it
fared with the mistress, and try if I could shake the
squire from his lethargy, if Mrs. Susan had not had
the grace yet to be here. How do they?" Then in
answer, "Thou must waken him, Diccon—rouse him,
and tell him that I and my lord expect it of him that
he should bear his loss as a true and honest Christian
man, and not pule and moan, since he has a son left—
ay, and a grandson. You should breed your boy up
to know his manners, Susan Talbot," as Humfrey resisted an attempt to make him do his reverence to my
lady; "that stout knave of yours wants the rod.
Methought I heard you'd borne another, Susan! Ay!
as I said it would be," as her eye fell on the swaddled
babe in a maid's arms. "No lack of fools to eat up
the poor old squire's substance. A maid, is it? Be-
shrew me, if your voyages will find portions for all
your wenches! Has the leech let blood to thy good-
mother, Susan? There! not one amongst you all
bears any brains. Knew you not how to send up to
the castle for Master Drewitt? Farewell! Thou
wilt be at the lodge to-morrow to let me know how it
fares with thy mother, when her brain is cleared by
further blood-letting. And for the squire, let him
know that I expect it of him that he shall eat, and
show himself a man!"

So saying, the great lady departed, escorted as far
as the avenue gate by Richard Talbot, and leaving the
family gratified by her condescension, and not allowing
to themselves how much their feelings were chafed.

CHAPTER III.

THE CAPTIVE.

DEATH and sorrow seemed to have marked the house of Bridgefield, for the old lady never rallied after the blood-letting enjoined by the Countess's medical science, and her husband, though for some months able to creep about the house, and even sometimes to visit the fields, had lost his memory, and became more childish week by week.

Richard Talbot was obliged to return to his ship at the end of the month, but as soon as she was laid up for the winter he resigned his command, and returned home, where he was needed to assume the part of master. In truth he became actually master before the next spring, for his father took to his bed with the first winter frosts, and in spite of the duteous cares lavished upon him by his son and daughter-in-law, passed from his bed to his grave at the Christmas feast. Richard Talbot inherited house and lands, with the undefined sense of feudal obligation to the head of his name, and ere long he was called upon to fulfil those obligations by service to his lord.

There had been another act in the great Scottish tragedy. Queen Mary had effected her escape from Lochleven, but only to be at once defeated, and then to

cross the Solway and throw herself into the hands of
the English Queen.

Bolton Castle had been proved to be too perilously
near the Border to serve as her residence, and the
inquiry at York, and afterwards at Westminster, having
proved unsatisfactory, Elizabeth had decided on detain-
ing her in the kingdom, and committed her to the
charge of the Earl of Shrewsbury.

To go into the history of that ill-managed investigation is not the purpose of this tale.   It is probable
that Elizabeth believed her cousin guilty, and wished
to shield that guilt from being proclaimed, while her
councillors, in their dread of the captive, wished to
enhance the crime in Elizabeth's eyes, and were by no
means scrupulous as to the kind of evidence they
adduced.   However, this lies outside our story; all
that concerns it is that Lord Shrewsbury sent a summons to his trusty and well-beloved cousin, Richard
Talbot of Bridgefield, to come and form part of the
guard of honour which was to escort the Queen of
Scots to Tutbury Castle, and there attend upon her.

All this time no hint had been given that the little
Cicely was of alien blood.   The old squire and his
lady had been in no state to hear of the death of their
own grandchild, or of the adoption of the orphan, and
Susan was too reserved a woman to speak needlessly of
her griefs to one so unsympathising as the Countess or so
flighty as the daughters at the great house.   The men
who had brought the summons to Hull had not been
lodged in the house, but at an inn, where they either
had heard nothing of Master Richard's adventure or had
drowned their memory in ale, for they said nothing;
and thus, without any formed intention of secrecy,
the child's parentage had never come into question.

Indeed, though without doubt Mrs. Talbot was very loyal in heart to her noble kinsfolk, it is not to be denied that she was a good deal more at peace when they were not at the lodge. She tried devoutly to follow out the directions of my Lady Countess, and thought herself in fault when things went amiss, but she prospered far more when free from such dictation.

She had nothing to wish except that her husband could be more often at home, but it was better to have him only a few hours' ride from her, at Chatsworth or Tutbury, than to know him exposed to the perils of the sea. He rode over as often as he could be spared, to see his family and look after his property; but his attendance was close, and my Lord and my Lady were exacting with one whom they could thoroughly trust, and it was well that in her quiet way Mistress Susan proved capable of ruling men and maids, farm and stable as well as house, servants and children, to whom another boy was added in the course of the year after her return to Bridgefield.

In the autumn, notice was sent that the Queen of Scots was to be lodged at Sheffield, and long trains of waggons and sumpter horses and mules began to arrive, bringing her plenishing and household stuff in advance. Servants without number were sent on, both by her and by the Earl, to make preparations, and on a November day, tidings came that the arrival might be expected in the afternoon. Commands were sent that the inhabitants of the little town at the park gate should keep within doors, and not come forth to give any show of welcome to their lord and lady, lest it should be taken as homage to the captive queen; but at the Manor-house there was a little family gathering to hail the Earl and Countess. It

chiefly consisted of ladies with their children, the
husbands of most being in the suite of the Earl acting
as escort or guard to the Queen.   Susan Talbot, being
akin to the family on both sides, was there with the
two elder children ; Humfrey, both that he might
greet his father the sooner, and that he might be able
to remember the memorable arrival of the captive
queen, and Cicely, because he had clamoured loudly
for her company.   Lady Talbot, of the Herbert blood,
wife to the heir, was present with two young sisters-
in-law, Lady Grace, daughter to the Earl, and Mary,
daughter to the Countess, who had been respectively
married to Sir Henry Cavendish and Sir Gilbert Talbot, a few weeks before their respective parents were
wedded, when the brides were only twelve and fourteen
years old.   There, too, was Mrs. Babington of Dethick,
the recent widow of a kinsman of Lord Shrewsbury, to
whom had been granted the wardship of her son, and
the little party waiting in the hall also numbered
Elizabeth and William Cavendish, the Countess's
youngest children, and many dependants mustered in
the background, ready for the reception.   Indeed, the
castle and manor-house, with their offices, lodges, and
outbuildings, were an absolute little city in themselves.
The castle was still kept in perfect repair, for the
battle of Bosworth was not quite beyond the memory
of living men's fathers ; and besides, who could tell
whether any day England might not have to be cor-
tested inch by inch with the Spaniard ?   So the
gray walls stood on the tongue of land in the valley,
formed by the junction of the rivers Sheaf and Dun,
with towers at all the gateways, enclosing a space of
no less than eight acres, and with the actual fortress,
crisp, strong, hard, and unmouldered in the midst, its

tallest square tower serving as a look-out place for those who watched to give the first intimation of the arrival.

The castle had its population, but chiefly of grooms, warders, and their families. The state-rooms high up in that square tower were so exceedingly confined, so stern and grim, that the grandfather of the present earl had built a manor-house for his family residence on the sloping ground on the farther side of the Dun.

This house, built of stone, timber, and brick, with two large courts, two gardens, and three yards, covered nearly as much space as the castle itself. A pleasant, smooth, grass lawn lay in front, and on it converged the avenues of oaks and walnuts, stretching towards the gates of the park, narrowing to the eye into single lines, then going absolutely out of sight, and the sea of foliage presenting the utmost variety of beautiful tints of orange, yellow, brown, and red. There was a great gateway between two new octagon towers of red brick, with battlements and dressings of stone, and from this porch a staircase led upwards to the great stone-paved hall, with a huge fire burning on the open hearth. Around it had gathered the ladies of the Talbot family waiting for the reception. The warder on the tower had blown his horn as a signal that the master and his royal guest were within the park, and the banner of the Talbots had been raised to announce their coming, but nearly half an hour must pass while the party came along the avenue from the drawbridge over the Sheaf ere they could arrive at the lodge.

So the ladies, in full state dresses, hovered over the fire, while the children played in the window seat near at hand.

Gilbert Talbot's wife, a thin, yellow-haired, young creature, promising to be like her mother, the Countess, had a tongue which loved to run, and with the precocity and importance of wifehood at sixteen, she dilated to her companions on her mother's constant attendance on the Queen, and the perpetual plots for that lady's escape. "She is as shifty and active as any cat-a-mount; and at Chatsworth she had a scheme for being off out of her bedchamber window to meet a traitor fellow named Roll; but my husband smelt it out in good time, and had the guard beneath my lady's window, and the fellows are in gyves, and to see the lady the day it was found out! Not a wry face did she make. Oh no! 'Twas all my good lord, and my sweet sir with her. I promise you butter would not melt in her mouth, for my Lord Treasurer Cecil hath been to see her, and he has promised to bring her to speech of her Majesty. May I be there to see. I promise you 'twill be diamond cut diamond between them."

"How did she and my Lord Treasurer fare together?" asked Mrs. Babington.

"Well, you know there's not a man of them all that is proof against her blandishments. Her Majesty should have women warders for her. 'Twas good sport to see the furrows in his old brow smoothing out against his will as it were, while she plied him with her tongue. I never saw the Queen herself win such a smile as came on his lips, but then he is always a sort of master, or tutor, as it were, to the Queen. Ay," on some exclamation from Lady Talbot, "she heeds him like no one else. She may fling out, and run counter to him for the very pleasure of feeling that she has the power, but she will come round at last, and 'tis his will that is done in the long run. If this lady

could beguile him indeed, she might be a free woman
in the end."

"And think you that she did?"

"Not she! The Lord Treasurer is too long-headed,
and has too strong a hate to all Papistry, to be beguiled
more than for the very moment he was before her. He
cannot help the being a man, you see, and they are all
alike when once in her presence—your lord and father,
like the rest of them, sister Grace. Mark me if there
be not tempests brewing, an we be not the sooner rid
of this guest of ours. My mother is not the woman
to bear it long."

Dame Mary's tongue was apt to run on too fast,
and Lady Talbot interrupted its career with an amused
gesture towards the children.

For the little Cis, babe as she was, had all the three
boys at her service. Humfrey, with a paternal air, was
holding her on the window-seat; Antony Babington
was standing to receive the ball that was being tossed
to and fro between them, but as she never caught it,
Will Cavendish was content to pick it up every time
and return it to her, appearing amply rewarded by her
laugh of delight.

The two mothers could not but laugh, and Mrs.
Babington said the brave lads were learning their
knightly courtesy early, while Mary Talbot began
observing on the want of likeness between Cis and
either the Talbot or Hardwicke race. The little girl
was much darker in colouring than any of the boys, and
had a pair of black, dark, heavy brows, that prevented
her from being a pretty child. Her adopted mother
shrank from such observations, and was rejoiced that a
winding of horns, and a shout from the boys, announced
that the expected arrival was about to take place. The

ladies darted to the window, and beholding the avenue
full of horsemen and horsewomen, their accoutrements
and those of their escort gleaming in the sun, each
mother gathered her own chicks to herself, smoothed
the plumage somewhat ruffled by sport, and advanced
to the head of the stone steps, William Cavendish, the
eldest of the boys, being sent down to take his stepfather's rein and hold his stirrup, page fashion.

Clattering and jingling the troop arrived. The
Earl, a stout, square man, with a long narrow face,
lengthened out farther by a light-coloured, silky beard,
which fell below his ruff, descended from his steed,
gave his hat to Richard Talbot, and handed from her
horse a hooded and veiled lady of slender proportions,
who leant on his arm as she ascended the steps.

The ladies knelt, whether in respect to the heads of
the family, or to the royal guest, may be doubtful.

The Queen came up the stairs with rheumatic steps,
declaring, however, as she did so, that she felt the
better for her ride, and was less fatigued than when
she set forth. She had the soft, low, sweet Scottish
voice, and a thorough Scottish accent and language,
tempered, however, by French tones, and as, coming
into the warmer air of the hall, she withdrew her
veil, her countenance was seen. Mary Stuart was
only thirty-one at this time, and her face was still
youthful, though worn and wearied, and bearing tokens
of illness. The features were far from being regularly
beautiful; there was a decided cast in one of the
eyes, and in spite of all that Mary Talbot's detracting
tongue had said, Susan's first impression was disappointment. But, as the Queen greeted the lady
whom she already knew, and the Earl presented his
daughter, Lady Grace, his stepdaughter, Elizabeth

Cavendish, and his kinswoman, Mistress Susan Talbot, the extraordinary magic of her eye and lip beamed on them, the queenly grace and dignity joined with a wonderful sweetness impressed them all, and each in measure felt the fascination.

The Earl led the Queen to the fire to obtain a little warmth before mounting the stairs to her own apartments, and likewise while Lady Shrewsbury was dismounting, and being handed up the stairs by her second stepson, Gilbert. The ladies likewise knelt on one knee to greet this mighty dame, and the children should have done so too, but little Cis, catching sight of Captain Richard, who had come up bearing the Earl's hat, in immediate attendance on him, broke out with an exulting cry of "Father! father! father!" trotted with outspread arms right in front of the royal lady, embraced the booted leg in ecstasy, and then stretching out, exclaimed "Up! up!"

"How now, malapert poppet!" exclaimed the Countess, and though at some distance, uplifted her riding-rod. Susan was ready to sink into the earth with confusion at the great lady's displeasure, but Richard had stooped and lifted the little maid in his arms, while Queen Mary turned, her face lit up as by a sunbeam, and said, "Ah, bonnibell, art thou fain to see thy father? Wilt thou give me one of thy kisses, sweet bairnie?" and as Richard held her up to the kind face, "A goodly child, brave sir. Thou must let me have her at times for a playfellow. Wilt come and comfort a poor prisoner, little sweeting?"

The child responded with "Poor poor," stroking the soft delicate cheek, but the Countess interfered, still wrathful. "Master Richard, I marvel that you should let her Grace be beset by a child, who, if she cannot

demean herself decorously, should have been left at
home.   Susan Hardwicke, I thought I had schooled
you better."

"Nay, madam, may not a babe's gentle deed of
pity be pardoned?" said Mary.

"Oh! if it pleasures you, madam, so be it," said
Lady Shrewsbury, deferentially; "but there be children
here more worthy of your notice than yonder little
black-browed wench, who hath been allowed to thrust
herself forward, while others have been kept back
from importuning your Grace."

"No child can importune a mother who is cut off
from her own," said Mary, eager to make up for the
jealousy she had excited.   "Is this bonnie laddie yours,
madam?   Ah! I should have known it by the
resemblance."

She held her white hand to receive the kisses of
the boys: William Cavendish, under his mother's eye,
knelt obediently; Antony Babington, a fair, pretty lad,
of eight or nine, of a beautiful pink and white complexion, pressed forward with an eager devotion which
made the Queen smile and press her delicate hand on
his curled locks; as for Humfrey, he retreated behind
the shelter of his mother's farthingale, where his
presence was forgotten by every one else, and, after
the rebuff just administered to Cicely, there was no
inclination to bring him to light, or combat with his
bashfulness.

The introductions over, Mary gave her hand to the
Earl to be conducted from the hall up the broad staircase, and along the great western gallery to the south
front, where for many days her properties had been in
course of being arranged.

Lady Shrewsbury followed as mistress of the house,

and behind, in order of precedence, came the Scottish
Queen's household, in which the dark, keen features of
the French, and the rufous hues of the Scots, were
nearly equally divided. Lady Livingstone and Mistress
Seaton, two of the Queen's Maries of the same age
with herself, came next, the one led by Lord Talbot,
the other by Lord Livingstone. There was also the
faithful French Marie de Courcelles, paired with Master
Beatoun, comptroller of the household, and Jean
Kennedy, a stiff Scotswoman, whose hard outlines
did not do justice to her tenderness and fidelity, and
with her was a tall, active, keen-faced stripling, looked
on with special suspicion by the English, as Willie
Douglas, the contriver of the Queen's flight from Lochleven. Two secretaries, French and Scottish, were
shrewdly suspected of being priests, and there were
besides, a physician, surgeon, apothecary, with per-
fumers, cooks, pantlers, scullions, lacqueys, to the
number of thirty, besides their wives and attendants,
these last being " permitted of my lord's benevolence."

They were all eyed askance by the sturdy, north
country English, who naturally hated all strangers,
above all French and Scotch, and viewed the band of
captives much like a caged herd of wild beasts.

When on the way home Mistress Susan asked her
little boy why he would not make his obeisance to the
pretty lady, he sturdily answered, " She is no pretty
lady of mine. She is an evil woman who slew her
husband."

" Poor lady ! tongues have been busy with her," said
his father.

" How, sir ?" asked Susan, amazed, " do you think
her guiltless in the matter ?"

" I cannot tell," returned Richard. " All I know is

that many who have no mercy on her would change their minds if they beheld her patient and kindly demeanour to all."

This was a sort of shock to Susan, as it seemed to her to prove the truth of little Lady Talbot's words, that no one was proof against Queen Mary's wiles; but she was happy in having her husband at home once more, though, as he told her, he would be occupied most of each alternate day at Sheffield, he and another relation having been appointed "gentlemen porters," which meant that they were to wait in a chamber at the foot of the stairs, and keep watch over whatever went in or out of the apartments of the captive and her suite.

" And," said Richard, " who think you came to see me at Wingfield ? None other than Cuthbert Langston."

" Hath he left his merchandise at Hull ?"

" Ay, so he saith. He would fain have had my good word to my lord for a post in the household, as comptroller of accounts, clerk, or the like. It seemed as though there were no office he would not take so that he might hang about the neighbourhood of this queen."

" Then you would not grant him your recommendation ?"

" Nay, truly. I could not answer for him, and his very anxiety made me the more bent on not bringing him hither. I'd fain serve in no ship where I know not the honesty of all the crew, and Cuthbert hath ever had a hankering after the old profession."

" Verily then it were not well to bring him hither."

" Moreover, he is a lover of mysteries and schemes," said Richard. " He would never be content to let alone the question of our little wench's birth, and would be fretting us for ever about the matter."

"Did he speak of it?"

"Yea. He would have me to wit that a nurse and babe had been put on board at Dumbarton. Well, said I, and so they must have been, since on board they were. Is that all thou hast to tell me? And mighty as was the work he would have made of it, this was all he seemed to know. I asked, in my turn, how he came to know thus much about a vessel sailing from a port in arms against the Lords of the Congregation, the allies of her Majesty?"

"What said he?"

"That his house had dealings with the owners of the *Bride of Dunbar*. I like not such dealings, and so long as this lady and her train are near us, I would by no means have him whispering here and there that she is a Scottish orphan."

"It would chafe my Lady Countess!" said Susan, to whom this was a serious matter. "Yet doth it not behove us to endeavour to find out her parentage?"

"I tell you I proved to myself that he knew nothing, and all that we have to do is to hinder him from making mischief ou. of that little," returned Richard impatiently.

The honest captain could scarcely have told the cause of his distrust or of his secrecy, but he had a general feeling that to let an intriguer like Cuthbert Langston rake up any tale that could be connected with the party of the captive queen, could only lead to danger and trouble.

CHAPTER IV.

THE OAK AND THE OAKEN HALL.

THE oaks of Sheffield Park were one of the greatest glories of the place. Giants of the forest stretched their huge arms over the turf, kept smooth and velvety by the creatures, wild and tame, that browsed on it, and made their covert in the deep glades of fern and copsewood that formed the background.

There were not a few whose huge trunks, of such girth that two men together could not encompass them with outstretched arms, rose to a height of more than sixty feet before throwing out a horizontal branch, and these branches, almost trees in themselves, spread forty-eight feet on each side of the bole, lifting a mountain of rich verdure above them, and casting a delicious shade upon the ground beneath them. Beneath one of these noble trees, some years after the arrival of the hapless Mary Stuart, a party of children were playing, much to the amusement of an audience of which they were utterly unaware, namely, of sundry members of a deer-hunting party; a lady and gentleman who, having become separated from the rest, were standing in the deep bracken, which rose nearly as high as their heads, and were further sheltered by a rock, looking and listening.

"Now then, Cis, bravely done! Show how she treats her ladies——"

"Who will be her lady? Thou must, Humfrey!"

"No, no, I'll never be a lady," said Humfrey, gruffly.

"Thou then, Diccon."

"No, no," and the little fellow shrank back, "thou wilt hurt me, Cis."

"Come then, do thou, Tony! I'll not strike too hard!"

"As if a wench could strike too hard."

"He might have turned that more chivalrously," whispered the lady to her companion. "What are they about to represent? *Mort de ma vie*, the profane little imps! I believe it is my sacred cousin, the Majesty of England herself! Truly the little maid hath a bearing that might serve a queen, though she be all too black and beetle-browed for Queen Elizabeth. Who is she, Master Gilbert?"

"She is Cicely Talbot, daughter to the gentleman porter of your Majesty's lodge."

"See to her—mark her little dignity with her heather and bluebell crown as she sits on the rock, as stately as jewels could make her! See her gesture with her hands, to mark where the standing ruff ought to be. She hath the true spirit of the comedy —ah! and here cometh young Antony with mincing pace, with a dock-leaf for a fan, and a mantle for a farthingale! She speaks! now hark!"

"Good morrow to you, my young mistress," began a voice pitched two notes higher than its actual childlike key. "Thou hast a new farthingale, I see! O Antony, that's not the way to curtsey—do it like this. No no! thou clumsy fellow—back and knees together."

"Never mind, Cis," interposed one of the boys—
"we shall lose all our play time if you try to make
him do it with a grace. Curtsies are women's work
—go on."

"Where was I? O——" (resuming her dignity after
these asides) "Thou hast a new farthingale, I see."

"To do my poor honour to your Grace's birthday."

"Oh ho! Is it so? Methought it had been to do
honour to my fair mistress's own taper waist. And
pray how much an ell was yonder broidered stuff?"

"Two crowns, an't please your Grace," returned
the supposed lady, making a wild conjecture.

"Two crowns! thou foolish Antony!" Then
recollecting herself, "two crowns! what, when mine
costs but half! Thou presumptuous, lavish varlet—
no, no, wench! what right hast thou to wear gowns
finer than thy liege?—I'll teach you." Wherewith,
erecting all her talons, and clawing frightfully with
them in the air, the supposed Queen Bess leapt at the
unfortunate maid of honour, appeared to tear the
imaginary robe, and drove her victim off the stage
with a great air of violence, amid peals of laughter
from the other children, loud enough to drown those
of the elders, who could hardly restrain their merriment. Gilbert Talbot, however, had been looking
about him anxiously all the time, and would fain have
moved away; but a sign from Queen Mary withheld
him, as one of the children cried,

"Now! show us how she serves her lords."

The play seemed well understood between them,
for the mimic queen again settled herself on her
throne, while Will Cavendish, calling out, "Now I'm
Master Hatton," began to tread a stately measure on
the grass, while the queen exclaimed, "Who is this

new star of my court ?   What stalwart limbs, what
graceful tread !   Who art thou, sir ?"

"Madam, I am—I am.   What is it? An ef—ef——"

"A daddy-long-legs," mischievously suggested another of the group.

"No, it's Latin.   Is it Ephraim ?   No ; it's a fly,
something like a gnat" (then at an impatient gesture
from her Majesty) "disporting itself in the beams of
the noontide sun."

"Blood-sucking," whispered the real Queen behind
the fern.   "He is not so far out there.   See ! see !
with what a grace the child holds out her little hand
for him to kiss.   I doubt me if Elizabeth herself could
be more stately.   But who comes here ?"

"I'm Sir Philip Sydney."

"No, no," shouted Humfrey, "Sir Philip shall not
come into this fooling.   My father says he's the best
knight in England."

"He is as bad as the rest in flattery to the Queen,"
returned young Cavendish.

"I'll not have it, I say.   You may be Lord Leicester an you will !   He's but Robin Dudley."

"Ah !" began the lad, now advancing and shading
his eyes.   "What burnished splendour dazzles my
weak sight ?   Is it a second Juno that I behold, or
lovely Venus herself ?   Nay, there is a wisdom in her
that can only belong to the great Minerva herself !
So youthful too.   Is it Hebe descended to this earth ?"

Cis smirked, and held out a hand, saying in an
affected tone, "Lord Earl, are thy wits astray ?"

"Whose wits would not be perturbed at the mere
sight of such exquisite beauty ?"

"Come and sit at our feet, and we will try to restore
them," said the stage queen ; but here little Diccon,

the youngest of the party, eager for more action, called out, "Show us how she treats her lords and ladies together."

On which young Babington, as the lady, and Humfrey, made demonstrations of love-making and betrothal, upon which their sovereign lady descended on them with furious tokens of indignation, abusing them right and left, until in the midst the great castle bell pealed forth, and caused a flight general, being, in fact, the summons to the school kept in one of the castle chambers by one Master Snigg, or Sniggius, for the children of the numerous colony who peopled the castle.   Girls, as well as boys, were taught there, and thus Cis accompanied Humfrey and Diccon, and consorted with their companions.

Queen Mary was allowed to hunt and take out-of-door exercise in the park whenever she pleased, but Lord Shrewsbury, or one of his sons, Gilbert and Francis, never was absent from her for a moment when she went beyond the door of the lesser lodge, which the Earl had erected for her, with a flat, leaded, and parapeted roof, where she could take the air, and with only one entrance, where was stationed a "gentleman porter," with two subordinates, whose business it was to keep a close watch over every person or thing that went in or out.   If she had any purpose of losing herself in the thickets of fern, or copsewood, in the park, or holding unperceived conference under shelter of the chase, these plans were rendered impossible by the pertinacious presence of one or other of the Talbots, who acted completely up to their name.

Thus it was that the Queen, with Gilbert in close attendance, had found herself an unseen spectator of the children's performance, which she watched with the keen enjoyment that sometimes made her forget her troubles for the moment.

"How got the imps such knowledge?" mused Gilbert Talbot, as he led the Queen out on the sward which had been the theatre of their mimicry.

"Do *you* ask that, Sir Gilbert?" said the Queen with emphasis, for indeed it was his wife who had been the chief retailer of scandal about Queen Elizabeth, to the not unwilling ears of herself and his mother; and Antony Babington, as my lady's page, had but used his opportunities.

"They are insolent varlets and deserve the rod," continued Gilbert.

"You are too ready with the rod, you English," returned Mary. "You flog all that is clever and spirited out of your poor children!"

"That is the question, madam. Have the English been found so deficient in spirit compared with other nations?"

"Ah! we all know what you English can say for yourselves," returned the Queen. "See what Master John Coke hath made of the herald's argument before Dame Renown, in his translation. He hath twisted all the other way."

"Yea, madam, but the French herald had it all his own way before. So it was but just we should have our turn."

Here a cry from the other hunters greeted them, and they found Lord Shrewsbury, some of the ladies, and a number of prickers, looking anxiously for them.

"Here we are, good my lord," said the Queen, who, when free from rheumatism, was a most active walker. "We have only been stalking my sister Queen's court

c

in small, the prettiest and drollest pastime I have seen
for many a long day."

Much had happened in the course of the past years.
The intrigues with Northumberland and Norfolk, and
the secret efforts of the unfortunate Queen to obtain
friends, and stir up enemies against Elizabeth, had
resulted in her bonds being drawn closer and closer.
The Rising of the North had taken place, and Cuthbert Langston had been heard of as taking a prominent
part beneath the sacred banner, but he had been
wounded and not since heard of, and his kindred knew
not whether he were among the unnamed dead who
loaded the trees in the rear of the army of Sussex, or
whether he had escaped beyond seas.   Richard Talbot
still remained as one of the trusted kinsmen of Lord
Shrewsbury, on whom that nobleman depended for the
execution of the charge which yearly became more wearisome and onerous, as hope decayed and plots thickened.

Though resident in the new lodge with her train,
it was greatly diminished by the dismissal from time
to time of persons who were regarded as suspicious;
Mary still continued on intimate terms with Lady
Shrewsbury and her daughters, specially distinguishing
with her favour Bessie Pierrepoint, the eldest grandchild
of the Countess, who slept with her, and was her plaything and her pupil in French and needlework.   The
fiction of her being guest and not prisoner had not
entirely passed away ; visitors were admitted, and she
went in and out of the lodge, walked or rode at will,
only under pretext of courtesy.   She never was un-
accompanied by the Earl or one of his sons, and they
endeavoured to make all private conversation with
strangers, or persons unauthorised from Court, impossible to her.

The invitation given to little Cicely on the arrival had not been followed up. The Countess wished to reserve to her own family all the favours of one who might at any moment become the Queen of England, and she kept Susan Talbot and her children in what she called their meet place, in which that good lady thoroughly acquiesced, having her hands much too full of household affairs to run after queens.

There was a good deal of talk about this child's play, a thing which had much better have been left where it was; but in a seclusion like that of Sheffield subjects of conversation were not over numerous, and every topic which occurred was apt to be worried to shreds. So Lady Shrewsbury and her daughters heard the Queen's arch description of the children's mimicry, and instantly conceived a desire to see the scene repeated. The gentlemen did not like it at all: their loyalty was offended at the insult to her gracious Majesty, and besides, what might not happen if such sports ever came to her ears? However, the Countess ruled Sheffield; and Mary Talbot and Bessie Cavendish ruled the Countess, and they were bent on their own way. So the representation was to take place in the great hall of the manor-house, and the actors were to be dressed in character from my lady's stores.

"They will ruin it, these clumsy English, after their own fashion," said Queen Mary, among her ladies. "It was the unpremeditated grace and innocent audacity of the little ones that gave the charm. Now it will be a mere broad farce, worthy of Bess of Hardwicke. *Mais que voulez vous ?*"

The performance was, however, laid under a great disadvantage by the absolute refusal of Richard and Susan Talbot to allow their Cicely to assume the part of Queen Elizabeth. They had been dismayed at her doing so in child's play, and since she could read fluently, write pretty well, and cipher a little, the good mother had decided to put a stop to this free association with the boys at the castle, and to keep her at home to study needlework and housewifery. As to her acting with boys before the assembled households, the proposal seemed to them absolutely insulting to any daughter of the Talbot line, and they had by this time forgotten that she was no such thing. Bess Cavendish, the special spoilt child of the house, even rode down, armed with her mother's commands, but her feudal feeling did not here sway Mistress Susan.

Public acting was esteemed an indignity for women, and, though Cis was a mere child, all Susan's womanhood awoke, and she made answer firmly that she could not obey my Lady Countess in this.

Bess flounced out of the house, indignantly telling her she should rue the day, and Cis herself cried passionately, longing after the fine robes and jewels, and the presentation of herself as a queen before the whole company of the castle. The harsh system of the time made the good mother think it her duty to requite this rebellion with the rod, and to set the child down to her seam in the corner, and there sat Cis, pouting and brooding over what Antony Babington had told her of what he had picked up when in his page's capacity, attending his lady, of Queen Mary's admiration of the pretty ways and airs of the little mimic Queen Bess, till she felt as if she were defrauded of her due. The captive Queen was her dream, and to hear her commendations, perhaps be kissed by her, would be supreme bliss. Nay, she still hoped that

there would be an interference of the higher powers
on her behalf, which would give her a triumph.

No! Captain Talbot came home, saying, "So,
Mistress Sue, thou art a steadfast woman, to have
resisted my lady's will!"

"I knew, my good husband, that thou wouldst
never see our Cis even in sport a player!"

"Assuredly not, and thou hadst the best of it, for
when Mistress Bess came in as full of wrath as a
petard of powder, and made your refusal known, my
lord himself cried out, 'And she's in the right o't!
What a child may do in sport is not fit for a gentlewoman in earnest.'"

"Then, hath not my lord put a stop to the whole?"

"Fain would he do so, but the Countess and her
daughters are set on carrying out the sport. They
have set Master Sniggius to indite the speeches, and
the boys of the school are to take the parts for their
autumn interlude."

"Surely that is perilous, should it come to the
knowledge of those at Court."

"Oh, I promise you, Sniggius hath a device for
disguising all that could give offence. The Queen
will become Semiramis or Zenobia, I know not which,
and my Lord of Leicester, Master Hatton, and the
others, will be called Ninus or Longinus, or some
such heathenish long-tailed terms, and speak speeches
of mighty length. Are they to be in Latin, Humfrey?"

"Oh no, sir," said Humfrey, with a shudder.
"Master Sniggius would have had them so, but the
young ladies said they would have nothing to do with
the affair if there were one word of Latin uttered. It
is bad enough as it is. I am to be Philidaspes, an

Assyrian knight, and have some speeches to learn, at least one is twenty-five lines, and not one is less than five!"

"A right requital for thy presumptuous and treasonable game, my son," said his father, teasing him.

"And who is to be the Queen?" asked the mother.

"Antony Babington," said Humfrey, "because he can amble and mince more like a wench than any of us. The worse luck for him. He will have more speeches than any one of us to learn."

The report of the number of speeches to be learnt took off the sting of Cis's disappointment, though she would not allow that it did so, declaring with truth that she could learn by hearing faster than any of the boys. Indeed, she did learn all Humfrey's speeches, and Antony's to boot, and assisted both of them with all her might in committing them to memory.

As Captain Talbot had foretold, the boys' sport was quite sufficiently punished by being made into earnest. Master Sniggius was far from merciful as to length, and his satire was so extremely remote that Queen Elizabeth herself could hardly have found out that Zenobia's fine moral lecture on the vanities of too aspiring ruffs was founded on the box on the ear which rewarded poor Lady Mary Howard's display of her rich petticoat, nor would her cheeks have tingled when the Queen of the East—by a bold adaptation—played the part of Lion in interrupting the interview of our old friends Pyramus and Thisbe, who, by an awful anachronism, were carried to Palmyra. It was no plagiarism from "Midsummer Night's Dream," only drawn from the common stock of playwrights.

So, shorn of all that was perilous, and only understood by the initiated, the play took place in the Castle

Hall, the largest available place, with Queen Mary seated upon the dais, with a canopy of State over her head, Lady Shrewsbury on a chair nearly as high, the Earl, the gentlemen and ladies of their suites drawn up in a circle, the servants where they could, the Earl's musicians thundering with drums, tooting with fifes, twanging on fiddles, overhead in a gallery. Cis and Diccon, on either side of Susan Talbot, gazing on the stage, where, much encumbered by hoop and farthingale, and arrayed in a yellow curled wig, strutted forth Antony Babington, declaiming—

> "Great Queen Zenobia am I,
> The Roman Power I defy.
> At my Palmyra, in the East,
> I rule o'er every man and beast."

Here was an allusion couched in the Roman power, which Master Antony had missed, or he would hardly have uttered it, since he was of a Roman Catholic family, though, while in the Earl's household, he had to conform outwardly.

A slender, scholarly lad, with a pretty, innocent face, and a voice that could "speak small, like a woman," came in and announced himself thus—

> "I'm Thisbe, an Assyrian maid,
> My robe's with jewels overlaid."

The stiff colloquy between the two boys, encumbered with their dresses, shy and awkward, and rehearsing their lines like a task, was no small contrast to the merry impromptu under the oak, and the gay, free grace of the children.

Poor Philidaspes acquitted himself worst of all, for when done up in a glittering suit of sham armour, with

a sword and dagger of lath, his entire speech, though
well conned, deserted him, and he stood red-faced,
hesitating, and ready to cry, when suddenly from the
midst of the spectators there issued a childish voice,
" Go on, Humfrey !

> " Philidaspes am I, most valorous knight,
> Ever ready for Church and Queen to fight.

"Go on, I say !" and she gave a little stamp of
impatience, to the extreme confusion of the mother and
the great amusement of the assembled company.
Humfrey, once started, delivered himself of the rest of
his oration in a glum and droning voice, occasioning
fits of laughter, such as by no means added to his self-
possession.

The excellent Sniggius and his company of boys
had certainly, whether intentionally or not, deprived
the performance of all its personal sting, and most
likewise of its interest.   Such diversion as the spectators derived was such as Hippolyta seems to have found
in listening to Wall, Lion, Moonshine and Co.; but,
like Theseus, Lord Shrewsbury was very courteous, and
complimented both playwright and actors, relieved and
thankful, no doubt, that Queen Zenobia was so unlike
his royal mistress.

There was nothing so much enforced by Queen
Elizabeth as that strangers should not have resort to
Sheffield Castle.   No spectators, except those attached
to the household, and actually forming part of the
colony within the park, were therefore supposed to be
admitted, and all of them were carefully kept at a distant part of the hall, where they could have no access
to the now much reduced train of the Scottish Queen,
with whom all intercourse was forbidden.

Humfrey was therefore surprised when, just as he had come out of the tiring-room, glad to divest himself of his encumbering and gaudy equipments, a man touched him on the arm and humbly said, "Sir, I have a humble entreaty to make of you. If you would convey my petition to the Queen of Scots!"

"I have nothing to do with the Queen of Scots," said the ex-Philidaspes, glancing suspiciously at the man's sleeve, where, however, he saw the silver dog, the family badge.

"She is a charitable lady," continued the man, who looked like a groom, "and if she only knew that my poor old aunt is lying famishing, she would aid her. Pray you, good my lord, help me to let this scroll reach to her."

"I'm no lord, and I have naught to do with the Queen," repeated Humfrey, while at the same moment Antony, who had been rather longer in getting out of his female attire, presented himself; and Humfrey, pitying the man's distress, said, "This young gentleman is the Countess's page. He sometimes sees the Queen."

The man eagerly told his story, how his aunt, the widow of a huckster, had gone on with the trade till she had been cruelly robbed and beaten, and now was utterly destitute, needing aid to set herself up again. The Queen of Scots was noted for her beneficent alms-giving, and a few silver pieces from her would be quite sufficient to replenish her basket.

Neither boy doubted a moment. Antony had the *entrée* to the presence chamber, where on this festival night the Earl and Countess were sure to be with the Queen. He went straightway thither, and trained as he was in the usages of the place, told his business to the Earl, who was seated near the Queen. Lord

c*.

Shrewsbury took the petition from him, glanced it over, and asked, "Who knew the Guy Norman who sent it?" Frank Talbot answered for him, that he was a yeoman pricker, and the Earl permitted the paper to be carried to Mary, watching her carefully as she read it, when Antony had presented it on one knee.

"Poor woman!" she said, "it is a piteous case. Master Beatoun, hast thou my purse? Here, Master Babington, wilt thou be the bearer of this angel for me, since I know that the delight of being the bearer will be a reward to thy kind heart."

Antony gracefully kissed the fair hand, and ran off joyously with the Queen's bounty. Little did any one guess what the career thus begun would bring that fair boy.

CHAPTER V.

THE HUCKSTERING WOMAN.

THE huckstering woman, Tibbott by name, was tended by Queen Mary's apothecary, and in due time was sent off well provided, to the great fair of York, whence she returned with a basket of needles, pins (such as they were), bodkins, and the like articles, wherewith to circulate about Hallamshire, but the gate-wards would not relax their rules so far as to admit her into the park. She was permitted, however, to bring her wares to the town of Sheffield, and to Bridgefield, but she might come no farther.

Thither Antony Babington came down to lay out the crown which had been given to him on his birth-day, and indeed half Master Sniggius's scholars dis-covered needs, and came down either to spend, or to give advice to the happy owners of groats and testers. So far so good; but the huckster-woman soon made Bridgefield part of her regular rounds, and took little commissions which she executed for the household of Sheffield, who were, as the Cavendish sisters often said in their spleen, almost as much prisoners as the Queen of Scots. Antony Babington was always her special patron, and being Humfrey's great companion and play-fellow, he was allowed to come in and out of the gates

unquestioned, to play with him and with Cis, who no
longer went to school, but was trained at home in
needlework and housewifery.

Match-making began at so early an age, that when
Mistress Susan had twice found her and Antony
Babington with their heads together over the lament-
able ballad of the cold fish that had been a lady, and
which sang its own history "forty thousand fathom
above water," she began to question whether the girl
were the attraction. He was now an orphan, and his
wardship and marriage had been granted to the Earl,
who, having disposed of all his daughters and step-
daughters, except Bessie Cavendish, might very fairly
bestow on the daughter of his kinsman so good a
match as the young squire of Dethick.

"Then should we have to consider of her parentage,"
said Richard, when his wife had propounded her views.

"I never can bear in mind that the dear wench is
none of ours," said Susan. "Thou didst say thou
wouldst portion her as if she were our own little maid,
and I have nine webs ready for her household linen.
Must we speak of her as a stranger?"

"It would scarce be just towards another family to
let them deem her of true Talbot blood, if she were to
enter among them," said Richard; "though I look on
the little merry maid as if she were mine own child.
But there is no need yet to begin upon any such coil;
and, indeed, I would wager that my lady hath other
views for young Babington."

After all, parents often know very little of what
passes in children's minds, and Cis never hinted to her
mother that the bond of union between her and Antony
was devotion to the captive Queen. Cis had only had a
glimpse or two of her, riding by when hunting or hawk-

ing, or when, on festive occasions, all who were privileged
to enter the park were mustered together, among whom
the Talbots ranked high as kindred to both Earl and
Countess; but those glimpses had been enough to fill
the young heart with romance, such as the matter-of-
fact elders never guessed at. Antony Babington, who
was often actually in the gracious presence, and received
occasional smiles, and even greetings, was immeasur-
ably devoted to the Queen, and maintained Cicely's
admiration by his vivid descriptions of the kindness,
the grace, the charms of the royal captive, in contrast with the innate vulgarity of their own Countess.

Willie Douglas (the real Roland Græme of the
escape from Lochleven) had long ago been dismissed
from Mary's train, with all the other servants who were
deemed superfluous; but Antony had heard the details
of the story from Jean Kennedy (Mrs. Kennett, as the
English were pleased to call her), and Willie was the
hero of his emulative imagination.

"What would I not do to be like him!" he fervently
exclaimed when he had narrated the story to Humfrey
and Cis, as they lay on a nest in the fern one fine
autumn day, resting after an expedition to gather
blackberries for the mother's preserving.

"I would not be him for anything," said Humfrey.

"Fie, Humfrey," cried Cis; "would not you dare
exile or anything else in a good cause?"

"For a good cause, ay," said Humfrey in his stolid
way.

"And what can be a better cause than that of the
fairest of captive queens?" exclaimed Antony, hotly.

"I would not be a traitor," returned Humfrey, as
he lay on his back, looking up through the chequer-
work of the branches of the trees towards the sky.

"Who dares link the word traitor with my name?" said Babington, feeling for the imaginary handle of a sword.

"Not I; but you'll get it linked if you go on in this sort."

"For shame, Humfrey," again cried Cis, passionately. "Why, delivering imprisoned princesses always was the work of a true knight."

"Yea; but they first defied the giant openly," said Humfrey.

"What of that?" said Antony.

"They did not do it under trust," said Humfrey.

"I am not under trust," said Antony. "Your father may be a sworn servant of the Earl and the Queen—Queen Elizabeth, I mean; but I have taken no oaths—nobody asked me if I would come here."

"No," said Humfrey, knitting his brows; "but you see we are all trusted to go in and out as we please, on the understanding that we do nought that can be unfaithful to the Earl; and I suppose it was thus with this same Willie Douglas."

"She was his own true and lawful Queen," cried Cis. "His first duty was to her."

Humfrey sat up and looked perplexed, but with a sudden thought exclaimed, "No Scots are we, thanks be to Heaven! and what might be loyalty in him would be rank treason in us."

"How know you that?" said Antony. "I have heard those who say that our lawful Queen is there," and he pointed towards the walls that rose in the distance above the woods.

Humfrey rose wrathful. "Then truly you are no better than a traitor, and a Spaniard, and a Papist," and fists were clenched on both sides, while Cis flew between, pulling down Humfrey's uplifted hand, and crying, " No, no ; he did not say he thought so, only he had heard it."

" Let him say it again ! " growled Antony, his arm bared.

" No, don't, Humfrey ! " as if she saw it between his clenched teeth. " You know you only meant if Tony thought so, and he didn't. Now how can you two be so foolish and unkind to me, to bring me out for a holiday to eat blackberries and make heather crowns, and then go and spoil it all with folly about Papists, and Spaniards, and grown-up people's nonsense that nobody cares about ! "

Cis had a rare power over both her comrades, and her piteous appeal actually disarmed them, since there was no one present to make them ashamed of their own placability. Grown - up people's follies were avoided by mutual consent through the rest of the walk, and the three children parted amicably when Antony had to return to fulfil his page's duties at my lord's supper, and Humfrey and Cis carried home their big basket of blackberries.

When they entered their own hall they found their mother engaged in conversation with a tall, stout, and weather-beaten man, whom she announced—" See here, my children, here is a good friend of your father's, Master Goatley, who was his chief mate in all his voyages, and hath now come over all the way from Hull to see him ! He will be here anon, sir, so soon as the guard is changed at the Queen's lodge. Meantime, here are the elder children."

Diccon, who had been kept at home by some temporary damage to his foot, and little Edward were devouring the sailor with their eyes ; and Humfrey

and Cis were equally delighted with the introduction,
especially as Master Goatley was just returned from
the Western Main, and from a curious grass-woven
basket which he carried slung to his side, produced
sundry curiosities in the way of beads, shell-work,
feather-work, and a hatchet of stone, and even a curious
armlet of soft, dull gold, with pearls set in it. This
he had, with great difficulty, obtained on purpose for
Mistress Talbot, who had once cured him of a bad
festering hurt received on board ship.

The children clustered round in ecstasies of admiration and wonder as they heard of the dark brown
natives, the curious expedients by which barter was
carried on ; also of cruel Spaniards, and of savage
fishes, with all the marvels of flying-fish, corals, palm-
trees, humming birds—all that is lesson work to our
modern youth, but was the most brilliant of living
fairy tales at this Elizabethan period. Humfrey and
Diccon were ready to rush off to voyage that instant,
and even little Ned cried imitatively in his imperfect
language that he would be " a tailor."

Then their father came home, and joyfully welcomed and clasped hands with his faithful mate,
declaring that the sight did him good ; and they sat
down to supper and talked of voyages, till the boys'
eyes' glowed, and they beat upon their own knees with
the enthusiasm that their strict manners bade them
repress ; while their mother kept back her sighs as
she saw them becoming infected with that sea fever so
dreaded by parents. Nay, she saw it in her husband
himself. She knew him to be grievously weary of a
charge most monotonously dull, and only varied by
suspicions and petty detections ; and that he was
hungering and thirsting for his good ship and to be

facing winds and waves. She could hear his longing in
the very sound of the "Ays?" and brief inquiries by
which he encouraged Goatley to proceed in the story
of voyages and adventures, and she could not wonder
when Goatley said, "Your heart is in it still, sir.
Not one of us all but says it is a pity such a noble
captain should be lost as a landsman, with nothing to
do but to lock the door on a lady."

"Speak not of it, my good Goatley," said Richard,
hastily, "or you will set me dreaming and make me
mad."

"Then it is indeed so," returned Goatley. "Wherefore then come you not, sir, where a crew is waiting for
you of as good fellows as ever stepped on a deck, and
who, one and all, are longing after such a captain
as you are, sir? Wherefore hold back while still in
your prime?"

"Ask the mistress, there," said Richard, as he saw
his Susan's white face and trembling fingers, though
she kept her eyes on her work to prevent them from
betraying their tears and their wistfulness.

"O sweet father," burst forth Humfrey, "do but
go, and take me. I am quite old enough."

"Nay, Humfrey, 'tis no matter of liking," said his
father, not wishing to prolong his wife's suspense.
"Look you here, boy, my Lord Earl is captain of all
of his name by right of birth, and so long as he needs
my services, I have no right to take them from him.
Dost see, my boy?"

Humfrey reluctantly did see. It was a great favour
to be thus argued with, and admitted of no reply.

Mrs. Talbot's heart rejoiced, but she was not sorry
that it was time for her to carry off Diccon and Ned to
their beds, away from the fascinating narrative, and she

would give no respite, though Diccon pleaded hard.
In fact, the danger might be the greatest to him, since
Humfrey, though born within the smell of the sea,
might be retained by the call of duty like his father.   To
Cis, at least, she thought the sailor's conversation could
do no harm, little foreboding the words that presently
ensued.   "And, sir, what befell the babe we found in
our last voyage off the Spurn ?   It would methinks be
about the age of this pretty mistress."

Richard Talbot endeavoured to telegraph a look
both of assent and warning, but though Master
Goatley would have been sharp to detect the least
token of a Spanish galleon on the most distant horizon,
the signal fell utterly short.   "Ay, sir.   What, is it
so ?   Bless me !   The very maiden !   And you have
bred her up for your own."

"Sir !   Father ! " cried Cis, looking from one to the
other, with eyes and mouth wide open.

"Soh ! " cried the sailor, " what have I done ?   I
beg your pardon, sir, if I have overhauled what
should have been let alone.   But," continued the
honest, but tactless man, " who could have thought of
the like of that, and that the pretty maid never knew
it ?   Ay, ay, dear heart.   Never fear but that the
captain will be good father to you all the same."

For Richard Talbot had held out his arm, and,
as Cis ran up to him, he had seated her on his
knee, and held her close to him.   Humfrey likewise
started up with an impulse to contradict, which was
suddenly cut short by a strange flash of memory, so
all he did was to come up to his father, and grasp
one of the girl's hands as fast as he could.   She
trembled and shivered, but there was something in the
presence of this strange man which choked back all

inquiry, and the silence, the vehement grasp, and the shuddering, alarmed the captain, lest she might suddenly go off into a fit upon his hands.

"This is gear for mother," said he, and taking her up like a baby, carried her off, followed closely by Humfrey. He met Susan coming down, asking anxiously, "Is she sick?"

"I hope not, mother," he said, "but honest Goatley, thinking no harm, hath blurted out that which we had never meant her to know, at least not yet awhile, and it hath wrought strangely with her."

"Then it is true, father?" said Humfrey, in rather an awe-stricken voice, while Cis still buried her face on the captain's breast.

"Yes," he said, "yea, my children, it is true that God sent us a daughter from the sea and the wreck when He had taken our own little maid to His rest. But we have ever loved our Cis as well, and hope ever to do so while she is our good child. Take her, mother, and tell the children how it befell; if I go not down, the fellow will spread it all over the house, and happily none were present save Humfrey and the little maiden."

Susan put the child down on her own bed, and there, with Humfrey standing by, told the history of the father carrying in the little shipwrecked babe. They both listened with eyes devouring her, but they were as yet too young to ask questions about evidences, and Susan did not volunteer these, only when the girl asked, "Then, have I no name?" she answered, "A godly minister, Master Heatherthwayte, gave thee the name of Cicely when he christened thee."

"I marvel who I am?" said Cis, gazing round her, as if the world were all new to her.

"It does not matter," said Humfrey, "you are just the same to us, is she not, mother?"

"She is our dear Heaven-sent child," said the mother tenderly.

"But thou art not my true mother, nor Humfrey nor Diccon my brethren," she said, stretching out her hands like one in the dark.

"If I'm not your brother, Cis, I'll be your husband, and then you will have a real right to be called Talbot. That's better than if you were my sister, for then you would go away, I don't know where, and now you will always be mine—mine—mine very own."

And as he gave Cis a hug in assurance of his intentions, his father, who was uneasy about the matter, looked in again, and as Susan, with tears in her eyes, pointed to the children, the good man said, "By my faith, the boy has found the way to cut the knot—or rather to tie it.   What say you, dame? If we do not get a portion for him, we do not have to give one with her, so it is as broad as it is long, and she remains our dear child.   Only listen, children, you are both old enough to keep a secret.   Not one word of all this matter is to be breathed to any soul till I bid you."

"Not to Diccon," said Humfrey decidedly.

"Nor to Antony?" asked Cis wistfully.

"To Antony? No, indeed! What has he to do with it?   Now, to your beds, children, and forget all about this tale."

"There, Humfrey," broke out Cis, as soon as they were alone together, "Huckstress Tibbott *is* a wise woman, whatever thou mayest say."

"How?" said Humfrey.

"Mindst thou not the day when I crossed her hand with the tester father gave me?"

"When mother whipped thee for listening to for-
tune-tellers, and wasting thy substance. Ay, I mind
it well," said Humfrey, "and how thou didst stand
simpering at her pack of lies, ere mother made thee
sing another tune."

"Nay, Humfrey, they were no lies, though I thought
them so then. She said I was not what I seemed,
and that the Talbots' kennel would not always hold
one of the noble northern eagles. So Humfrey, sweet
Humfrey, thou must not make too sure of wedding
me."

"I'll wed thee though all the lying old gipsy-wives
in England wore their false throats out in screeching
out that I shall not," cried Humfrey.

"But she must have known," said Cis, in an awestruck voice; "the spirits must have spoken with her,
and said that I am none of the Talbots."

"Hath mother heard this?" asked Humfrey, re-
coiling a little, but never thinking of the more plau-
sible explanation.

"Oh no, no! tell her not, Humfrey, tell her not.
She said she would whip me again if ever I talked
again of the follies that the fortune-telling woman had
gulled me with, for if they were not deceits, they were
worse. And, thou seest, they are worse, Humfrey!"

With which awe-stricken conclusion the children
went off to bed.

CHAPTER VI.

THE BEWITCHED WHISTLE.

A CHILD'S point of view is so different from that of a
grown person, that the discovery did not make half
so much difference to Cis as her adopted parents
expected. In fact it was like a dream to her. She
found her daily life and her surroundings the same,
and her chief interest was—at least apparently—how
soon she could escape from psalter and seam, to play
with little Ned, and look out for the elder boys returning, or watch for the Scottish Queen taking her daily
ride. Once, prompted by Antony, Cis had made a
beautiful nosegay of lilies and held it up to the Queen
when she rode in at the gate on her return from
Buxton. She had been rewarded by the sweetest of
smiles, but Captain Talbot had said it must never
happen again, or he should be accused of letting billets
pass in posies. The whole place was pervaded, in
fact, by an atmosphere of suspicion, and the vigilance,
which might have been endurable for a few months, was
wearing the spirits and temper of all concerned, now
that it had already lasted for seven or eight years, and
there seemed no end to it. Moreover, in spite of all
care, it every now and then became apparent that
Queen Mary had some communication with the outer

world which no one could trace, though the effects endangered the life of Queen Elizabeth, the peace of the kingdom, and the existence of the English Church. The blame always fell upon Lord Shrewsbury; and who could wonder that he was becoming captiously suspicious, and soured in temper, so that even such faithful kinsmen as Richard Talbot could sometimes hardly bear with him, and became punctiliously anxious that there should not be the smallest loophole for censure of the conduct of himself and his family?

The person on whom Master Goatley's visit had left the most impression seemed to be Humfrey. On the one hand, his father's words had made him enter into his situation of trust and loyalty, and perceive something of the constant sacrifice of self to duty that it required, and, on the other hand, he had assumed a position towards Cis of which he in some degree felt the force. There was nothing in the opinions of the time to render their semi-betrothal ridiculous. At the Manor-house itself, Gilbert Talbot and Mary Cavendish had been married when no older than he was; half their contemporaries were already plighted, and the only difference was that in the present harassing state of surveillance in which every one lived, the parents thought that to avow the secret so long kept might bring about inquiry and suspicion, and they therefore wished it to be guarded till the marriage could be contracted. As Cis developed, she had looks and tones which so curiously harmonised, now with the Scotch, now with the French element in the royal captive's suite, and which made Captain Richard believe that she must belong to some of the families who seemed amphibious between the two courts; and her identification as a Seaton, a Flemyng, a Beatoun, or as a mem-

ber of any of the families attached to the losing cause,
would only involve her in exile and disgrace. Besides,
there was every reason to think her an orphan, and a
distant kinsman was scarcely likely to give her such a
home as she had at Bridgefield, where she had always
been looked on as a daughter, and was now regarded
as doubly their own in right of their son. So Humfrey was permitted to consider her as peculiarly his
own, and he exerted this right of property by a
certain jealousy of Antony Babington which amused
his parents, and teased the young lady. Nor was
he wholly actuated by the jealousy of proprietor-
ship, for he knew the devotion with which Antony
regarded Queen Mary, and did not wholly trust him.
His sense of honour and duty to his father's trust was
one thing, Antony's knight-errantry to the beautiful
captive was another; each boy thought himself strictly
honourable, while they moved in parallel lines and
could not understand one another; yet, with the
reserve of childhood, all that passed between them
was a secret, till one afternoon when loud angry
sounds and suppressed sobs attracted Mistress Susan
to the garden, where she found Cis crying bitterly,
and little Diccon staring eagerly, while a pitched
battle was going on between her eldest son and young
Antony Babington, who were pommelling each other
too furiously to perceive her approach.

"Boys! boys! fie for shame," she cried, with a
hand on the shoulder of each, and they stood apart
at her touch, though still fiercely looking at one
another.

"See what spectacles you have made of yourselves!"
she continued. "Is this your treatment of your guest,
Humfrey? How is my Lord's page to show himself at

Chatsworth to-morrow with such an eye?   What is it all about?"

Both combatants eyed each other in sullen silence.

"Tell me, Cis.   Tell me, Diccon.   I will know, or you shall have the rod as well as Humfrey."

Diccon, who was still in the era of timidity, instead of secretiveness, spoke out.   "He," indicating his brother, "wanted the packet."

"What packet?" exclaimed the mother, alarmed.

"The packet that *he* (another nod towards Antony) wanted Cis to give that witch in case she came while he is at Chatsworth."

"It was the dog-whistle," said Cis.   "It hath no sound in it, and Antony would have me change it for him, because Huckster Tibbott may not come within the gates.   I did not want to do so; I fear Tibbott, and when Humfrey found me crying he fell on Antony.   So blame him not, mother."

"If Humfrey is a jealous churl, and Cis a little fool, there's no help for it," said Antony, disdainfully turning his back on his late adversary.

"Then let me take charge of this whistle," returned the lady, moved by the universal habit of caution, but Antony sprang hastily to intercept her as she was taking from the little girl a small paper packet tied round with coloured yarn, but he was not in time, and could only exclaim, "Nay, nay, madam, I will not trouble you.   It is nothing."

"Master Babington," said Susan firmly, "you know as well as I do that no packet may pass out of the park unopened.   If you wished to have the whistle changed you should have brought it uncovered.   I am sorry for the discourtesy, and ask your pardon, but this parcel may not pass."

"Then," said Antony, with difficulty repressing something much more passionate and disrespectful, "let me have it again."

"Nay, Master Babington, that would not suit with my duty."

The boy altogether lost his temper. "Duty! duty!" he cried. "I am sick of the word. All it means is a mere feigned excuse for prying and spying, and besetting the most beautiful and unhappy princess in the world for her true faith and true right!"

"Master Antony Babington," said Susan gravely, "you had better take care what you are about. If those words of yours had been spoken in my Lord's hearing, they would bring you worse than the rod or bread and water."

"What care I what I suffer for such a Queen?" exclaimed Antony.

"Suffering is a different matter from saying 'What care I,'" returned the lady, "as I fear you will learn, Master Antony."

"O mother! sweet mother," said Cis, "you will not tell of him!"——but mother shook her head.

"Prithee, dear mother," added Humfrey, seeing no relenting in her countenance, "I did but mean to hinder Cis from being maltreated and a go-between in this traffic with an old witch, not to bring Tony into trouble."

"His face is a tell-tale, Humfrey," said Susan. "I meant ere now to have put a piece of beef on it. Come in, Antony, and let me wash it."

"Thank you, madam, I need nothing here," said Antony, stalking proudly off; while Humfrey, exclaiming "Don't be an ass, Tony!——Mother, no one would care to ask what we had given one another black eyes for in a friendly way," tried to hold him back, and he

did linger when Cis added her persuasions to him not
to return the spectacle he was at present.

"If this lady will promise not to betray an unfortunate Queen," he said, as if permission to deal with
his bruises were a great reward.

"Oh! you foolish boy!" exclaimed Mistress Talbot,
"you were never meant for a plotter! you have yourself betrayed that you are her messenger."

"And I am not ashamed of it," said Antony, holding his head high. "Madam, madam, if you have
surprised this from me, you are the more bound not to
betray her. Think, lady, if you were shut up from
your children and friends, would you not seek to send
tidings to them?"

"Child, child! Heaven knows I am not blaming
the poor lady within there. I am only thinking what
is right."

"Well," said Antony, somewhat hopefully, "if that
be all, give me back the packet, or tear it up, if you
will, and there can be no harm done."

"Oh, do so, sweet mother," entreated Cis, earnestly;
"he will never bid me go to Tibbott again."

"Ay," said Humfrey, "then no tales will be told."
For even he, with all his trustworthiness, or indeed
because of it, could not bear to bring a comrade to
disgrace; but the dilemma was put an end to by the
sudden appearance on the scene of Captain Richard
himself, demanding the cause of the disturbance, and
whether his sons had been misbehaving to their guest.

"Dear sir, sweet father, do not ask," entreated Cis,
springing to him, and taking his hand, as she was
privileged to do; "mother has come, and it is all made
up and over now."

Richard Talbot, however, had seen the packet

which his wife was holding, and her anxious, perplexed countenance, and the perilous atmosphere of suspicion around him made it incumbent on him to turn to her and say, "What means this, mother? Is it as Cis would have me believe, a mere childish quarrel that I may pass over? or what is this packet?"

"Master Babington saith it is a dog-whistle which he was leaving in charge with Cis to exchange for another with Huckstress Tibbott," she answered.

"Feel,—nay, open it, and see if it be not, sir," cried Antony.

"I doubt not that so it is," said the captain; "but you know, Master Babington, that it is the duty of all here in charge to let no packet pass the gate which has not been viewed by my lord's officers."

"Then, sir, I will take it back again," said Antony, with a vain attempt at making his brow frank and clear.

Instead of answering, Captain Talbot took the knife from his girdle, and cut in twain the yarn that bound the packet. There was no doubt about the whistle being there, nor was there anything written on the wrapper; but perhaps the anxiety in Antony's eye, or even the old association with boatswains, incited Mr. Talbot to put the whistle to his lips. Not a sound would come forth. He looked in, and saw what led him to blow with all his force, when a white roll of paper protruded, and on another blast fell out into his hand.

He held it up as he found it, and looked full at Antony, who exclaimed in much agitation, "To keep out the dust. Only to keep out the dust. It is all gibberish—from my old writing-books."

"That will we see," said Richard very gravely.

"Mistress, be pleased to give this young gentleman some water to wash his face, and attend to his bruises, keeping him in the guest-chamber without speech from any one until I return. Master Babington, I counsel you to submit quietly. I wish, and my Lord will wish, to spare his ward as much scandal as possible, and if this be what you say it is, mere gibberish from your exercise-books, you will be quit for chastisement for a forbidden act, which has brought you into suspicion. If not, it must be as my Lord thinks good."

Antony made no entreaties. Perhaps he trusted that what was unintelligible to himself might pass for gibberish with others; perhaps the headache caused by Humfrey's fists was assisting to produce a state of sullen indifference after his burst of eager chivalry; at any rate he let Mistress Talbot lead him away without resistance. The other children would have followed, but their father detained them to hear the particulars of the commission and the capture. Richard desired to know from his son whether he had any reason for suspecting underhand measures; and when Humfrey looked down and hesitated, added, "On your obedience, boy; this is no slight matter."

"You will not beat Cis, father?" said Humfrey.

"Wherefore should I beat her, save for doing errands that yonder lad should have known better than to thrust on her?"

"Nay, sir, 'tis not for that; but my mother said she should be beaten if ever she spake of the fortune yonder Tibbott told her, and we are sure that she— Tibbott I mean—is a witch, and knows more than she ought."

"What mean'st thou? Tell me, children;" and Cis, nothing loath, since she was secured from the beating, related the augury which had left so deep an impression on her, Humfrey bearing witness that it was before they knew themselves of Cicely's history.

"But that is not all," added Cicely, seeing Mr. Talbot less impressed than she expected by these supernatural powers of divination. "She can change from a woman to a man!"

"In sooth!" exclaimed Richard, startled enough by this information.

"Yea, father," said Cicely, "Faithful Ekins, the carrier's boy, saw her, in doublet and hose, and a tawny cloak, going along the road to Chesterfield. He knew her by the halt in her left leg."

"Ha!" said Richard, "and how long hast thou known this?"

"Only yestermorn," said Cis; "it was that which made me so much afraid to have any dealings with her."

"She shall trouble thee no more, my little wench," said Richard in a tone that made Humfrey cry out joyously,

"O father! sweet father! wilt thou duck her for a witch? Sink or swim! that will be rare!"

"Hush, hush! foolish lad," said Richard, "and thou, Cicely, take good heed that not a word of all this gets abroad. Go to thy mother, child,—nay, I am not wroth with thee, little one. Thou hast not done amiss, but bear in mind that nought is ever taken out of the park without knowledge of me or of thy mother."

CHAPTER VII.

THE BLAST OF THE WHISTLE

RICHARD TALBOT was of course convinced that witch-craft was not likely to be the most serious part of the misdeeds of Tibbott the huckstress. Committing Antony Babington to the custody of his wife, he sped on his way back to the Manor-house, where Lord Shrewsbury was at present residing, the Countess being gone to view her buildings at Chatsworth, tak-ing her daughter Bessie with her. He sent in a message desiring to speak to my lord in his privy chamber.

Francis Talbot came to him. " Is it matter of great moment, Dick ?" he said, " for my father is so fretted and chafed, I would fain not vex him further to-night. —What ! know you not ? Here are tidings that my lady hath married Bess—yes, Bess Cavendish, in secret to my young Lord Lennox, the brother of this Queen's unlucky husband ! How he is to clear himself before her Grace of being concerned in it, I know not, for though Heaven wots that he is as innocent as the child unborn, she will suspect him !"

" I knew she flew high for Mistress Bess," returned Richard.

" High ! nothing would serve her save royal blood !

My poor father says as sure as the lions and *fleur-de-lis* have come into a family, the headsman's axe has come after them."

" However it is not our family."

" So I tell him, but it gives him small comfort," said Frank, " looking as he doth on the Cavendish brood as his own, and knowing that there will be a mighty coil at once with my lady and these two queens. He is sore vexed to-night, and saith that never was Earl, not to say man, so baited by woman as he, and he bade me see whether yours be a matter of such moment that it may not wait till morning or be despatched by me."

" That is for you to say, Master Francis. What think you of this for a toy?" as he produced the parcel with the whistle and its contents. " I went home betimes to-day, as you know, and found my boy Humfrey had just made young Master Babington taste of his fists for trying to make our little wench pass this packet to yonder huckster-woman who was succoured some months back by the Queen of Scots."

Francis Talbot silently took the whistle and unrolled the long narrow strip of paper. " This is the cipher," said he, " the cipher used in corresponding with her French kin ; Phillipps the decipherer showed me the trick of it when he was at Tutbury in the time of the Duke of Norfolk's business. Soh! your son hath done good service, Richard. That lad hath been tampered with then, I thought he was over thick with the lady in the lodge. Where is he, the young traitor ?"

" At Bridgefield, under my wife's ward, having his bruises attended to. I would not bring him up here till I knew what my Lord would have done with him. He is but a child, and no doubt was wrought with by sweet looks, and I trust my Lord will not be hard with him."

" If my father had hearkened to me, he should never have been here," said Francis. " His father was an honest man, but his mother was, I find, a secret recusant, and when she died, young Antony was quite old enough to have sucked in the poison. You did well to keep him, Richard; he ought not to return hither again, either in ward or at liberty."

" If he were mine, I would send him to school," said Richard, " where the masters and the lads would soon drive out of him all dreams about captive princesses and seminary priests to boot. For, Cousin Francis, I would have you to know that my children say there is a rumour that this woman Tibbott the huckstress hath been seen in a doublet and hose near Chesterfield."

" The villain ! When is she looked for here again ?"

" Anon, I should suppose, judging by the boy leaving this charge with Cis in case she should come while he is gone to Chatsworth."

" We will take order as to that," said Francis, compressing his lips; " I know you will take heed, cousin, that she, or he, gets no breath of warning. I should not wonder if it were Parsons himself !" and he unfolded the scroll with the air of a man seeking to confirm his triumph.

" Can you make anything of it ?" asked Richard, struck by its resemblance to another scroll laid up among his wife's treasures.

" I cannot tell, they are not matters to be read in an hour," said Francis Talbot, " moreover, there is one in use for the English traitors, her friends, and another for the French. This looks like the French sort. Let

D

me see, they are read by taking the third letter in each
second word." Francis Talbot, somewhat proud of his
proficiency, and perfectly certain of the trustworthiness
of his cousin Richard, went on puzzling out the ciphered
letters, making Richard set each letter down as he
picked it out, and trying whether they would make
sense in French or English. Both understood French,
having learned it in their page days, and kept it up by
intercourse with the French suite. Francis, however,
had to try two or three methods, which, being a young
man, perhaps he was pleased to display, and at last
he hit upon the right, which interpreted the apparent
gibberish of the scroll—excepting that the names of
persons were concealed under soubriquets which
Francis Talbot could not always understand—but
the following sentence by and by became clear :—
"*Quand le matelot vient des marais, un feu peut
eclater dans la meute et dans la melée*"—" When the
sailor lands from the fens, a fire might easily break
out in the dog-kennel, and in the confusion"
(name could not be read) " could carry off the tercel
gentle."

"*La meute*," said Francis, " that is their term for
the home of us Talbots, and the sailor in the fens is
this Don John of Austria, who means, after conquering
the Dutchmen, to come and set free this tercel gentle,
as she calls herself, and play the inquisitor upon us.
On my honour, Dick, your boy has played the man in
making this discovery. Keep the young traitor fast,
and take down a couple of yeomen to lay hands on
this same Tibbott as she calls herself."

"If I remember right," said Richard, "she was
said to be the sister or aunt to one of the grooms or
prickers."

"So it was, Guy Norman, methinks. Belike he was the very fellow to set fire to our kennel. Yea, we must secure him. I'll see to that, and you shall lay this scroll before my father meantime, Dick. Why, to fall on such a trail will restore his spirits, and win back her Grace to believe in his honesty, if my lady's tricks should have made her doubtful."

Off went Francis with great alacrity, and ere long the Earl was present with Richard. The long light beard was now tinged with gray, and there were deep lines round the mouth and temples, betraying how the long anxiety was telling on him, and rendering him suspicious and querulous. "Soh! Richard Talbot," was his salutation, "what's the coil now? Can a man never be left in peace in his own house, between queens and ladies, plots and follies, but his own kins-folk and retainers must come to him on every petty broil among the lads! I should have thought your boy and young Babington might fight out their quarrels alone without vexing a man that is near driven dis-tracted as it is."

"I grieve to vex your lordship," said Richard, standing bareheaded, "but Master Francis thought this scroll worthy of your attention. This is the manner in which he deciphered it."

"Scrolls, I am sick of scrolls," said the Earl testily. "What! is it some order for saying mass,—or to get some new Popish image or a skein of silk? I wear my eyes out reading such as that, and racking my brains for some hidden meaning!"

And falling on Francis's first attempt at copying, he was scornful of the whole, and had nearly thrown the matter aside, but when he lit at last on the sen-tence about burning the *meute* and carrying off the

tercel gentle, his brow grew dark indeed, and his
inquiries came thickly one upon the other, both as to
Antony Babington and the huckstering woman.

In the midst, Frank Talbot returned with the
tidings that the pricker Guy Norman was nowhere
to be found. He had last been seen by his comrades
about the time that Captain Richard had returned to
the Manor-house. Probably he had taken alarm on
seeing him come back at that unusual hour, and had
gone to carry the warning to his supposed aunt. This
last intelligence made the Earl decide on going down at
once to Bridgefield to examine young Babington before
there was time to miss his presence at the lodge, or
to hold any communication with him. Frank caused
horses to be brought round, and the Earl rode down with
Richard by a shaded alley in an ordinary cloak and hat.

My Lord's appearance at Bridgefield was a rarer
and more awful event than was my Lady's, and if
Mistress Susan had been warned beforehand, there is
no saying how at the head of her men and maids she
would have scrubbed and polished the floors, and
brushed the hangings and cushions. What then were
her feelings when the rider, who dismounted from his
little hackney as unpretendingly as did her husband
in the twilight court, proved to have my Lord's long
beard and narrow face !

Curtseying her lowest, and with a feeling of consternation and pity as she thought of the orphan boy,
she accepted his greeting with duteous welcome as he
said, " Kinswoman, I am come to cumber you, whilst
I inquire into this matter. I give your son thanks
for the honesty and faithfulness he hath shown in the
matter, as befitted his father's son. I should wish
myself to examine the springald."

Humfrey was accordingly called, and, privately
admonished by his father that he must not allow any
scruples about bringing his playmate into trouble to
lead him to withhold his evidence, or shrink from
telling the whole truth as he knew it, Humfrey.
accordingly stood before the Earl and made his replies
a little sullenly but quite straightforwardly. He had
prevented the whistle from being given to his sister
for the huckstress because the woman was a witch,
who frightened her, and moreover he knew it was
against rules. Did he suspect that the whistle came
from the Queen of Scots ?

He looked startled, and asked if it were so indeed,
and when again commanded to say why he had
thought it possible, he replied that he knew Antony
thought the Queen of Scots a fair and gracious lady.

Did he believe that Antony ever had communication with her or her people unheard by others ?

"Assuredly ! Wherefore not, when he carried my
Lady Countess's messages ?"

Lord Shrewsbury bent his brow, but did not further
pursue this branch of the subject, but demanded of
Humfrey a description of Tibbott, huckster or witch,
man or woman.

"She wears a big black hood and muffler," said
Humfrey, "and hath a long hooked stick."

"I asked thee not of her muffler, boy, but of her
person."

"She hath pouncet boxes and hawks' bells, and
dog-whistles in her basket," proceeded Humfrey, but
as the Earl waxed impatient, and demanded whether
no one could give him a clearer account, Richard bade
Humfrey call his mother.

She, however, could say nothing as to the woman's

appearance. She had gone to Norman's cottage to offer
her services after the supposed accident, but had been
told that the potticary of the Queen of Scots had
undertaken her cure, and had only seen her huddled
up in a heap of rags, asleep. Since her recovery the
woman had been several times at Bridgefield, but it
had struck the mistress of the house that there was
a certain avoidance of direct communication with her,
and a preference for the servants and children. This
Susan had ascribed to fear that she should be warned
off for her fortune-telling propensities, or the children's
little bargains interfered with. All she could answer
for was that she had once seen a huge pair of grizzled
eyebrows, with light eyes under them, and that the
woman, if woman she were, was tall, and bent a good
deal upon a hooked stick, which supported her limping
steps. Cicely could say little more, except that the
witch had a deep awesome voice, like a man, and a
long nose terrible to look at. Indeed, there seemed to
have been a sort of awful fascination about her to all
the children, who feared her yet ran after her.

Antony was then sent for. It was not easy to
judge of the expression of his disfigured countenance,
but when thus brought to bay he threw off all tokens
of compunction, and stood boldly before the Earl.

"So, Master Babington, I find you have been betraying the trust I placed in you——"

"What trust, my Lord?" said Antony, his bright
blue eyes looking back into those of the nobleman.

"The cockerel crows loud," said the Earl. "What
trust, quotha! Is there no trust implied in the coming and going of one of my household, when such a
charge is committed to me and mine?"

"No one ever gave me any charge," said Antony.

"Dost thou bandy words, thou froward imp?" said the Earl. "Thou hast not the conscience to deny that there was no honesty in smuggling forth a letter thus hidden. Deny it not. The treasonable cipher hath been read!"

"I knew nought of what was in it," said the boy.

"I believe thee there, but thou didst know that it was foully disloyal to me and to her Majesty to bear forth secret letters to disguised traitors. I am willing to believe that the smooth tongue which hath deluded many a better man than thou hath led thee astray, and I am willing to deal as lightly with thee as may be, so thou wilt tell me openly all thou knowest of this infamous plot."

"I know of no plot, sir."

"They would scarce commit the knowledge to the like of him," said Richard Talbot.

"May be not," said Lord Shrewsbury, looking at him with a glance that Antony thought contemptuous, and which prompted him to exclaim, "And if I did know of one, you may be assured I would never betray it were I torn with wild horses."

"Betray, sayest thou!" returned the Earl. "Thou hast betrayed my confidence, Antony, and hast gone as far as in thee lies to betray thy Queen."

"My Queen is Mary, the lawful Queen of us all," replied Antony, boldly.

"Ho! Sayest thou so? It is then as thou didst trow, cousin, the foolish lad hath been tampered with by the honeyed tongue. I need not ask thee from whom thou hadst this letter, boy. We have read it and know the foul treason therein. Thou wilt never return to the castle again, but for thy father's sake thou shalt be dealt with less sternly, if thou wilt tell who this

woman is, and how many of these toys thou hast given
to her, if thou knowest who she is."

But Antony closed his lips resolutely. In fact,
Richard suspected him of being somewhat flattered by
being the cause of such a commotion, and actually
accused of so grand and manly a crime as high treason.
The Earl could extract no word, and finally sentenced
him to remain at Bridgefield, shut up in his own
chamber till he could be dealt with. The lad walked
away in a dignified manner, and the Earl, holding up
his hands, half amused, half vexed, said, " So the spell
is on that poor lad likewise. What shall I do with
him ? An orphan boy too, and mine old friend's son."

" With your favour, my Lord," said Richard, " I
should say, send him to a grammar school, where
among lads of his own age, the dreams about captive
princesses might be driven from him by hard blows
and merry games."

"That may scarce serve," said the Earl rather severely,
for public schools were then held beneath the dignity of
both the nobility and higher gentry. " I may, however,
send him to study at Cambridge under some trusty
pedagogue. Back at the castle I cannot have him, so
must I cumber you with him, my good kinswoman,
until his face have recovered your son's lusty chastisement. Also it may be well to keep him here till we
can lay hands on this same huckster-woman, since
there may be need to confront him with her. It were
best if you did scour the country toward Chesterfield
for her, while Frank went to York."

Having thus issued his orders, the Earl took a
gracious leave of the lady, mounted his horse, and
rode back to Sheffield, dispensing with the attendance
of his kinsman, who had indeed to prepare for an early

start the next morning, when he meant to take
Humfrey with him, as not unlikely to recognise the
woman, though he could not describe her.

"The boy merits well to go forth with me," said
he. "He hath done yeoman's service, and proved
himself staunch and faithful."

"Was there matter in that scroll?" asked Susan.

"Only such slight matter as burning down the
Talbots' kennel, while Don John of Austria is landing
on the coast."

"God forgive them, and defend us!" sighed Susan,
turning pale. "Was that in the cipher?"

"Ay, in sooth, but fear not, good wife. Much is
purposed that ne'er comes to pass. I doubt me if the
ship be built that is to carry the Don hither."

"I trust that Antony knew not of the wickedness?"

"Not he. His is only a dream out of the romances
the lads love so well, of beauteous princesses to be
freed, and the like."

"But the woman!"

"Yea, that lies deeper. What didst thou say of
her? Wherefore do the children call her a witch? Is
it only that she is grim and ugly?"

"I trow there is more cause than that," said Susan.
"It may be that I should have taken more heed to
their babble at first; but I have questioned Cis while
you were at the lodge, and I find that even before
Mate Goatley spake here, this Tibbott had told the
child of her being of lofty race in the north, alien to
the Talbots' kennel, holding out to her presages of
some princely destiny."

"That bodeth ill!" said Richard, thoughtfully.
"Wife, my soul misgives me that the hand of
Cuthbert Langston is in this."

D*

Susan started. The idea chimed in with Tibbott's avoidance of her scrutiny, and also with a certain vague sense she had had of having seen those eyes before. So light-complexioned a man would be easily disguised, and the halt was accounted for by a report that he had had a bad fall when riding to join in the Rising in the North. Nor could there now be any doubt that he was an ardent partisan of the imprisoned Mary, while Richard had always known his inclination to intrigue. She could only agree with her husband's opinion, and ask what he would do.

"My duty must be done, kin or no kin," said Richard, "that is if I find him; but I look not to do that, since Norman is no doubt off to warn him."

"I marvel whether he hath really learnt who our Cis can be?"

"Belike not! The hint would only have been thrown out to gain power over her."

"Said you that you read the cipher?"

"Master Frank did so."

"Would it serve you to read our scroll?"

"Ah, woman! woman! Why can thy kind never let well alone? I have sufficient on my hands without reading of scrolls!"

Humfrey's delight was extreme when he found that he was to ride forth with his father, and half-a-dozen of the earl's yeomen, in search of the supposed witch. They traced her as far as Chesterfield; but having met the carrier's waggon on the way, they carefully examined Faithful Ekins on his report, but all the youth was clear about was the halt and the orange tawny cloak, and after entering Chesterfield, no one knew anything of these tokens. There was a large village belonging to a family of recusants, not far off,

where the pursuers generally did lose sight of suspicious
persons; and, perhaps, Richard was relieved, though
his son was greatly chagrined.

The good captain had a sufficient regard for his
kinsman to be unwilling to have to unmask him as a
traitor, and to be glad that he should have effected an
escape, so that, at least, it should be others who should
detect him—if Langston indeed it were.

His next charge was to escort young Babington to
Cambridge, and deliver him up to a tutor of his lordship's selection, who might draw the Popish fancies out
of him.

Meantime, Antony had been kept close to the
house and garden, and not allowed any intercourse
with any of the young people, save Humfrey, except
when the master or mistress of the house was present;
but he did not want for occupation, for Master Sniggius came down, and gave him a long chapter of the
Book of Proverbs—chiefly upon loyalty, in the Septua-
gint, to learn by heart, and translate into Latin and
English as his Saturday's and Sunday's occupation,
under pain of a flogging, which was no light thing from
the hands of that redoubted dominie.

Young Babington was half-flattered and half-
frightened at the commotion he had excited. "Am I
going to the Tower?" he asked, in a low voice, awe-
stricken, yet not without a certain ring of self-importance, when he saw his mails brought down, and was
bidden to put on his boots and his travelling dress.

And Captain Talbot had a cruel satisfaction in
replying, "No, Master Babington; the Tower is not
for refractory boys. You are going to your school-
master."

But where the school was to be Richard kept an

absolute secret by special desire, in order that no communication should be kept up through any of the household. He was to avoid Chatsworth, and to return as soon as possible to endeavour to trace the supposed huckster-woman at Chesterfield.

When once away from home, he ceased to treat young Babington as a criminal, but rode in a friendly manner with him through lanes and over moors, till the young fellow began to thaw towards him, and even went so far as to volunteer one day that he would not have brought Mistress Cicely into the matter if there had been any other sure way of getting the letter delivered in his absence.

" Ah, boy !" returned Richard, " when once we swerve from the open and direct paths, there is no saying into what tangles we may bring ourselves and others."

Antony winced a little, and said, " Whoever says I lied, lies in *his* throat."

" No one hath said thou wert false in word, but how as to thy deed ? "

" Sir," said Antony, " surely when a high emprise and great right is to be done, there is no need to halt over such petty quibbles."

" Master Babington, no great right was ever done through a little wrong. Depend on it, if you cannot aid without a breach of trust, it is the sure sign that it is not the will of God that you should be the one to do it."

Captain Talbot mused whether he should convince or only weary the lad by an argument he had once heard in a sermon, that the force of Satan's temptation to our blessed Lord, when showing Him all the kingdoms of the world, must have been the absolute and immediate vanishing of all kinds of evil, by a voluntary abdication on the part of the Prince of this world, instead not only of the coming anguish of the strife, but of the long, long, often losing, battle which has been waging ever since. Yet for this great achievement He would not commit the moment's sin. He was just about to begin when Antony broke in, " Then, sir, you do deem it a great wrong ?"

" That I leave to wiser heads than mine," returned the sailor. " My duty is to obey my Lord, his duty is to obey her Grace. That is all a plain man needs to see."

" But an if the true Queen be thus mewed up, sir ?" asked Antony. Richard was too wise a man to threaten the suggestion down as rank treason, well knowing that thus he should never root it out.

" Look you here, Antony," he said ; " who ought to reign is a question of birth, such as neither of us can understand nor judge. But we know thus much, that her Grace, Queen Elizabeth, hath been crowned and anointed and received oaths of fealty as her due, and that is quite enough for any honest man."

" Even when she keeps in durance the Queen, who came as her guest in dire distress ?"

" Nay, Master Antony, you are not old enough to remember that the durance began not until the Queen of Scots tried to form a party for herself among the English liegemen. And didst thou know, thou simple lad, what the letter bore, which thou didst carry, and what it would bring on this peaceful land ?"

Antony looked a little startled when he heard of the burning of the kennel, but he averred that Don John was a gallant prince.

" I have seen more than one gallant Spaniard under whose power I should grieve to see any friend of mine."

All the rest of the way Richard Talbot entertained the young gentleman with stories of his own voyages and adventures, into which he managed to bring traits of Spanish cruelty and barbarity as shown in the Low Countries, such as, without actually drawing the moral every time, might show what was to be expected if Mary of Scotland and Don John of Austria were to reign over England, armed with the Inquisition.

Antony asked a good many questions, and when he found that the captain had actually been an eye-witness of the state of a country harried by the Spaniards, he seemed a good deal struck.

" I think if I had the training of him I could make a loyal Englishman of him yet," said Richard Talbot to his wife on his return.   " But I fear me there is that in his heart and his conscience which will only grow, while yonder sour-faced doctor, with whom I had to leave him at Cambridge, preaches to him of the perdition of Pope and Papists."

" If his mother were indeed a concealed Papist," said Susan, " such sermons will only revolt the poor child."

" Yea, truly. If my Lord wanted to make a plotter and a Papist of the boy he could scarce find a better means.   I myself never could away with yonder lady's blandishments.   But when he thinks of her in contrast to yonder divine, it would take a stronger head than his not to be led away.   The best chance for him is that the stir of the world about him may put captive princesses out of his head."

CHAPTER VIII.

THE KEY OF THE CIPHER.

WHERE is the man who does not persuade himself that when he gratifies his own curiosity he does so for the sake of his womankind? So Richard Talbot, having made his protest, waited two days, but when next he had any leisure moments before him, on a Sunday evening, he said to his wife, " Sue, what hast thou done with that scroll of Cissy's ? I trow thou wilt not rest till thou art convinced it is but some lying horoscope or Popish charm."

Susan had in truth been resting in perfect quietness, being extremely busy over her spinning, so as to be ready for the weaver who came round periodically to direct the more artistic portions of domestic work. However, she joyfully produced the scroll from the depths of the casket where she kept her chief treasures, and her spindle often paused in its dance as she watched her husband over it, with his elbows on the table and his hands in his hair, from whence he only removed them now and then to set down a letter or two by way of experiment. She had to be patient, for she heard nothing that night but that he believed it was French, that the father of deceits himself might be puzzled with the thing, and that she might as well ask him

for his head at once as propose his consulting Master
Francis.

The next night he unfolded it with many a groan,
and would say nothing at all; but he sat up late and
waked in early dawn to pore over it again, and on the
third day of study he uttered a loud exclamation of
dismay, but he ordered Susan off to bed in the midst,
and did not utter anything but a perplexed groan or
two when he followed her much later.

It was not till the next night that she heard anything, and then, in the darkness, he began, " Susan,
thou art a good wife and a discreet woman."

Perhaps her heart leapt as she thought to herself,
" At last it is coming, I knew it would!" but she only
made some innocent note of attention.

" Thou hast asked no questions, nor tried to pry
into this unhappy mystery," he went on.

" I knew you would tell me what was fit for me to
hear," she replied.

" Fit! It is fit for no one to hear! Yet I needs
must take counsel with thee, and thou hast shown thou
canst keep a close mouth so far."

" Concerns it our Cissy, husband?"

" Ay does it. Our Cissy, indeed! What wouldst
say, Sue, to hear she was daughter to the lady
yonder."

" To the Queen of Scots?"

" Hush! hush!" fairly grasping her to hinder the
words from being uttered above her breath.

" And her father?"

" That villain, Bothwell, of course. Poor lassie,
she is ill fathered!"

" You may say so. Is it in the scroll?"

" Ay! so far as I can unravel it; but besides the

cipher no doubt much was left for the poor woman to tell that was lost in the wreck."

And he went on to explain that the scroll was a letter to the Abbess of Soissons, who was aunt to Queen Mary, as was well known, since an open correspondence was kept up through the French ambassador. This letter said that " our trusty Alison Hepburn " would tell how in secrecy and distress Queen Mary had given birth to this poor child in Lochleven, and how she had been conveyed across the lake while only a few hours old, after being hastily baptized by the name of Bride, one of the patron saints of Scotland. She had been nursed in a cottage for a few weeks till the Queen had made her first vain attempt to escape, after which Mary had decided on sending her with her nurse to Dumbarton Castle, whence Lord Flemyng would despatch her to France. The Abbess was implored to shelter her, in complete ignorance of her birth, until such time as her mother should resume her liberty and her throne. " Or if," the poor Queen said, " I perish in the hands of my enemies, you will deal with her as my uncles of Guise and Lorraine think fit, since, should her unhappy little brother die in the rude hands of yonder traitors, she may bring the true faith back to both realms."

"Ah !" cried Susan, with a sudden gasp of dismay, as she bethought her that the child was indeed heiress to both realms after the young King of Scots. " But has there been no quest after her? Do they deem her lost?"

" No doubt they do. Either all hands were lost in the *Bride of Dunbar*, or if any of the crew escaped, they would report the loss of nurse and child. The few who know that the little one was born believe her to have perished. None will ever ask for her. They deem that she has been at the bottom of the sea these twelve years or more."

" And you would still keep the knowledge to our-selves ?" asked his wife, in a tone of relief.

" I would I knew it not myself ! " sighed Richard. " Would that I could blot it out of my mind."

" It were far happier for the poor maid herself to remain no one's child but ours," said Susan.

" In sooth it is !   A drop of royal blood is in these days a mere drop of poison to them that have the ill luck to inherit it.   As my lord said the other day, it brings the headsman's axe after it."

" And our boy Humfrey calls himself contracted to her ! "

" So long as we let the secret die with us that can do her no ill.   Happily the wench favours not her mother, save sometimes in a certain lordly carriage of the head and shoulders.   She is like enough to some of the Scots retinue to make me think she must take her face from her father, the villain, who, some one told me, was beetle-browed and swarthy."

" Lives he still ? "

" So 'tis thought, but somewhere in prison in the north.   There have been no tidings of his death ; but my Lady Queen, you'll remember, treats the marriage as nought, and has made offer of herself for the misfortune of the Duke of Norfolk, ay, and of this Don John, and I know not whom besides."

" She would not have done that had she known that our Cis was alive."

" Mayhap she would, mayhap not.   I believe my-self she would do anything short of disowning her Popery to get out of prison ; but as matters stand I doubt me whether Cis———."

" The Lady Bride Hepburn," suggested Susan.

" Pshaw, poor child, I misdoubt me whether they would own her claim even to that name."

" And they might put her in prison if they did," said Susan.

" They would be sure to do so, sooner or later. Here has my lord been recounting in his trouble about my lady's fine match for her Bess, all that hath come of mating with royal blood, the very least disaster being poor Lady Mary Grey's ! Kept in ward for life ! It is a cruel matter. I would that I had known the cipher at first. Then she might either have been disposed of at the Queen's will, or have been sent safe to this nunnery at Soissons."

" To be bred a Papist ! Oh fie, husband ! "

" And to breed dissension in the kingdoms ! " added her husband. " It is best so far for the poor maiden herself to have thy tender hand over her than that of any queen or abbess of them all."

" Shall we then keep all things as they are, and lock this knowledge in our own hearts ?" asked Susan hopefully.

" To that am I mightily inclined," said Richard. " Were it blazed abroad at once, thou and I might be made out guilty of I know not what for concealing it ; and as to the maiden, she would either be put in close ward with her mother, or, what would be more likely, had up to court to be watched, and flouted, and spied upon, as were the two poor ladies—sisters to the Lady Jane—ere they made their lot hopeless by marrying. Nay, I have seen those who told me that poor Lady Katherine was scarce worse bested in the Tower than she was while at court."

" My poor Cis ! No, no ! The only cause for which

I could bear to yield her up would be the thought that she would bring comfort to the heart of the poor captive mother who hath the best right to her."

"Forsooth! I suspect her poor captive mother would scarce be pleased to find this witness to her ill-advised marriage in existence."

"Nor would she be permitted to be with her."

"Assuredly not. Moreover, what could she do with the poor child?"

"Rear her in Popery," exclaimed Susan, to whom the word was terrible.

"Yea, and make her hand secure as the bait to some foreign prince or some English traitor, who would fain overthrow Queen and Church."

Susan shuddered. "Oh yes! let us keep the poor child to ourselves. I *could* not give her up to such a lot as that. And it might imperil you too, my husband. I should like to get up instantly and burn the scroll."

"I doubt me whether that were expedient," said Richard. "Suppose it were in the course of providence that the young King of Scots should not live, then would this maid be the means of uniting the two kingdoms in the true and Reformed faith! Heaven forefend that he should be cut off, but meseemeth that we have no right to destroy the evidence that may one day be a precious thing to the kingdom at large."

"No chance eye could read it even were it discovered?" said Susan.

"No, indeed. Thou knowest how I strove in vain to read it at first, and even now, when Frank Talbot unwittingly gave me the key, it was days before I could fully read it. It will tell no tales, sweet wife, that can prejudice any one, so we will let it be, even with

the baby clouts. So now to sleep, with no more
thoughts on the matter."

That was easy to say, but Susan lay awake long,
pondering over the wonder, and only slept to dream
strange dreams of queens and princesses, ay, and
worse, for she finally awoke with a scream, thinking
her husband was on the scaffold, and that Humfrey
and Cis were walking up the ladder, hand in hand
with their necks bared, to follow him!

There was no need to bid her hold her tongue.
She regarded the secret with dread and horror, and a
sense of something amiss which she could not quite
define, though she told herself she was only acting
in obedience to her husband, and indeed her judgment
went along with his.

Often she looked at the unconscious Cis, studying
whether the child's parentage could be detected in her
features.   But she gave promise of being of larger
frame than her mother, who had the fine limbs and
contour of her Lorraine ancestry, whereas Cis did,
as Richard said, seem to have the sturdy outlines of
the Borderer race from whom her father came.   She
was round-faced too, and sunburnt, with deep gray
eyes under black straight brows, capable of frowning
heavily.   She did not look likely ever to be the
fascinating beauty which all declared her mother to
be—though those who saw the captive at Sheffield,
believed the charm to be more in indefinable grace
than in actual features,—in a certain wonderful
smile and sparkle, a mixed pathos and archness which
seldom failed of its momentary effect, even upon
those who most rebelled against it.   Poor little Cis, a
sturdy girl of twelve or thirteen, playing at ball with
little Ned on the terrace, and coming with tardy steps

tc her daily task of spinning, had little of the princess about her; and yet when she sat down, and the management of distaff and thread threw her shoulders back, there was something in the poise of her small head and the gesture of her hand that forcibly recalled the Queen. Moreover, all the boys around were at her beck and call, not only Humfrey and poor Antony Babington, but Cavendishes, Pierrepoints, all the young pages and grandsons who dwelt at castle or lodge, and attended Master Sniggius's school. Nay, the dominie himself, though owning that Mistress Cicely promoted idleness and inattention among his pupils, had actually volunteered to come down to Bridgefield twice a week himself to prevent her from forgetting her Lilly's grammar and her Cæsar's Commentaries, an attention with which this young lady would willingly have dispensed.

Stewart, Lorraine, Hepburn, the blood of all combined was a perilous inheritance, and good Susan Talbot's instinct was that the young girl whom she loved truly like her own daughter would need all the more careful and tender watchfulness and training to overcome any tendencies that might descend to her. Pity increased her affection, and even while in ordinary household life it was easy to forget who and what the girl really was, yet Cis was conscious that she was admitted to the intimacy and privileges of an elder daughter, and made a companion and friend, while her contemporaries at the Manor-house were treated as children, and rated roundly, their fingers tapped with fans, their shoulders even whipped, whenever they transgressed. Cis did indeed live under equal restraint, but it was the wise and gentle restraint of firm influence and constant watchfulness, which took from her the wish to resist.

CHAPTER IX.

UNQUIET.

BRIDGEFIELD was a peaceable household, and the castle
and manor beyond might envy its calm.

From the time of the marriage of Elizabeth Cavendish with the young Earl of Lennox all the shreds
of comfort which had remained to the unfortunate
Earl had vanished.   First he had to clear himself
before Queen Elizabeth from having been a consenting party, and then he found his wife furious with
him at his displeasure at her daughter's aggrandise-
ment.   Moreover, whereas she had formerly been
on terms of friendly gossiphood with the Scottish
Queen, she now went over to the Lennox side because
her favourite daughter had married among them ; and
it was evident that from that moment all amity
between her and the prisoner was at an end.

She was enraged that her husband would not at once
change his whole treatment of the Queen, and treat her
as such guilt deserved ; and with the illogical dulness
of a passionate woman, she utterly scouted and failed to
comprehend the argument that the unhappy Mary was,
to say the least of it, no more guilty now than when
she came into their keeping, and that to alter their demeanour towards her would be unjust and unreasonable.

"My Lady is altogether beyond reason," said Captain Talbot, returning one evening to his wife; "neither my Lord nor her daughter can do ought with her; so puffed up is she with this marriage! Moreover, she is hotly angered that young Babington should have been sent away from her retinue without notice to her, and demands our Humfrey in his stead as a page."

"He is surely too old for a page!" said his mother, thinking of her tall well-grown son of fifteen.

"So said I," returned Richard. "I had sooner it were Diccon, and so I told his lordship."

Before Richard could speak for them, the two boys came in, eager and breathless. "Father!" cried Humfrey, "who think you is at Hull? Why, none other than your old friend and shipmate, Captain Frobisher!"

"Ha! Martin Frobisher! Who told thee, Humfrey?"

"Faithful Ekins, sir, who had it from the Doncaster carrier, who saw Captain Frobisher himself, and was asked by him if you, sir, were not somewhere in Yorkshire, and if so, to let you know that he will be in Hull till May-day, getting men together for a voyage to the northwards, where there is gold to be had for the picking—and if you had a likely son or two, now was the time to make their fortunes, and show them the world. He said, any way you might ride to see an old comrade."

"A long message for two carriers," said Richard Talbot, smiling, "but Martin never was a scribe!"

"But, sir, you will let me go," cried Humfrey, eagerly. "I mean, I pray you to let me go. Dear mother, say nought against it," entreated the youth. "Cis, think of my bringing thee home a gold bracelet like mother's."

"What," said his father, "when my Lady has just craved thee for a page."

"A page!" said Humfrey, with infinite contempt— "to hear all their tales and bickerings, hold skeins of silk, amble mincingly along galleries, be begged to bear messages that may have more in them than one knows, and be noted for a bear if one refuses."

The father and Cis laughed, the mother looked unhappy.

"So Martin is at Hull, is he?" said Richard, musingly. "If my Lord can give me leave for a week or fortnight, methinks I must ride to see the stout old knave."

"And oh, sweet father! prithee take me with you," entreated Humfrey, "if it be only to come back again. I have not seen the sea since we came here, and yet the sound is in my ears as I fall asleep. I entreat of you to let me come, good my father."

"And, good father, let me come," exclaimed Diccon; "I have never even seen the sea!"

"And dear, sweet father, take me," entreated little Ned.

"Nay," cried Cis, "what should I do? Here is Antony Babington borne off to Cambridge, and you all wanting to leave me."

"I'll come home better worth than he!" muttered Humfrey, who thought he saw consent on his father's brow, and drew her aside into the deep window.

"You'll come back a rude sailor, smelling of pitch and tar, and Antony will be a well-bred, point-device scholar, who will know how to give a lady his hand," said the teasing girl.

And so the playful war was carried on, while the father, having silenced and dismissed the two younger

lads, expressed his intention of obtaining leave of
absence, if possible, from the Earl."

"Yea," he added to his wife, "I shall even let
Humfrey go with me. It is time he looked beyond
the walls of this place, which is little better than a
prison."

"And will you let him go on this strange voyage?"
she asked wistfully, "he, our first-born, and our heir."

"For that, dame, remember his namesake, my
poor brother, was the one who stayed at home, I the one
to go forth, and here am I now!" The lad's words
may have set before thee weightier perils in yonder
park than he is like to meet among seals and bears
under honest old Martin."

"Yet here he has your guidance," said Susan.

"Who knows how they might play on his honour
as to talebearing? Nay, good wife, when thou hast
thought it over, thou wilt see that far fouler shoals
and straits lie up yonder, than in the free open sea that
God Almighty made. Martin is a devout and godly
man, who hath matins and evensong on board each
day when the weather is not too foul, and looks well
that there be no ill-doings in his ship; and if he have
a berth for thy lad, it will be a better school for him
than where two-thirds of the household are raging
against one another, and the third ever striving to
corrupt and outwit the rest. I am weary of it all!
Would that I could once get into blue water again,
and leave it all behind!"

"You will not! Oh! you will not!" implored
Susan. "Remember, my dear, good lord, how you said
all your duties lay at home."

"I remember, my good housewife. Thou needst
not fear for me. But there is little time to spare. If

I am to see mine old friend, I must get speech of my
Lord to-night, so as to be on horseback to-morrow.
Saddle me Brown Dumpling, boys."

And as the boys went off, persuading Cis, who went
coyly protesting that the paddock was damp, yet still
following after them, he added, " Yea, Sue, considering
all, it is better those two were apart for a year or so,
till we see better what is this strange nestling that we
have reared. Ay, thou art like the mother sparrow
that hath bred up a cuckoo and doteth on it, yet it
mateth not with her brood."

" It casteth them out," said Susan, " as thou art
doing now, by your leave, husband."

" Only for a flight, gentle mother," he answered,
" only for a flight, to prove meanwhile whether there
be the making of a simple household bird, or of a
hawk that might tear her mate to pieces, in yonder
nestling."

Susan was too dutiful a wife to say more, though
her motherly heart was wrung almost as much at the
implied distrust of her adopted daughter as by the
sudden parting with her first-born to the dangers of
the northern seas. She could better enter into her
husband's fears of the temptations of page life at Sheffield, and being altogether a wife, " bonner and bough-
some," as her marriage vow held it, she applied herself
and Cis to the choosing of the shirts and the crimping
of the ruffs that were to appear in Hull, if, for there
was this hope at the bottom of her heart, my Lord might
refuse leave of absence to his " gentleman porter."

The hope was fallacious ; Richard reported that my
Lord was so much relieved to find that he had detected
no fresh conspiracy, as to be willing to grant him a
fortnight's leave, and even had said with a sigh that

he was in the right on't about his son, for Sheffield was more of a school for plotting than for chivalry.

It was a point of honour with every good house-wife to have a store of linen equal to any emergency, and, indeed, as there were no washing days in the winter, the stock of personal body-linen was at all times nearly a sufficient outfit; so the main of Hum-frey's shirts were to be despatched by a carrier, in the trust that they would reach him before the expedition should sail.

There was then little to delay the father and son, after the mother, with fast-gathering tears resolutely forced back, had packed and strapped their mails, with Cis's help, Humfrey standing by, booted and spurred, and talking fast of the wonders he should see, and the gold and ivory he should bring home, to hide the qualms of home-sickness, and mother-sickness, he was already beginning to feel; and maybe to get Cis to pronounce that *then* she should think more of him than of Antony Babington with his airs and graces. Wist-fully did the lad watch for some such tender assurance, but Cis seemed all provoking brilliancy and teasing. "She knew he would be back over soon. Oh no, *he* would never go to sea! She feared not. Mr. Frobisher would have none of such awkward lubbers. More's the pity. There would be some peace to get to do her broidery, and leave to play on the virginals when he was gone."

But when the horsemen had disappeared down the avenue, Cis hid herself in a corner and cried as if her heart would break.

She cried again behind the back of the tall settle when the father came back alone, full of praises of Captain Frobisher, his ship, and his company, and his assurances that he would watch over Humfrey like his own son.

Meantime the domestic storms at the park were such that Master Richard and his wife were not sorry that the boy was not growing up in the midst of them, though the Countess rated Susan severely for her ingratitude.

Queen Elizabeth was of course much angered at the Lennox match, and the Earl had to write letter after letter to clear himself from any participation in bringing it about. Queen Mary also wrote to clear herself of it, and to show that she absolutely regretted it, as she had small esteem for Bess Cavendish. Moreover, though Lady Shrewsbury's friendship might not be a very pleasant thing, it was at least better than her hostility. However, she was not much at Sheffield. Not only was she very angry with her husband, but Queen Elizabeth had strictly forbidden the young Lord Lennox from coming under the same roof with his royal sister-in-law. He was a weakly youth, and his wife's health failed immediately after her marriage, so that Lady Shrewsbury remained almost constantly at Chatsworth with her darling.

Gilbert Talbot, who was the chief peacemaker of the family, went to and fro, wrote letters and did his best, which would have been more effective but for Mary, his wife, who, no doubt, detailed all the gossip of Sheffield at Chatsworth, as she certainly amused Sheffield with stories of her sister Bess as a royal countess full of airs and humours, and her mother treating her, if not as a queen, at least on the high road to become one, and how the haughty dame of Shrewsbury ran willingly to pick up her daughter's kerchief, and stood over the fire stirring the posset, rather than let it fail to tempt the appetite which became more dainty by being cossetted.

The difference made between Lady Lennox and her elder sisters was not a little nettling to Dame Mary Talbot, who held that some consideration was her due, as the proud mother of the only grandson of the house of Shrewsbury, little George, who was just able to be put on horseback in the court, and say he was riding to see "Lady Danmode," and to drink the health of "Lady Danmode" at his meals.

Alas! the little hope of the Talbots suddenly faded. One evening after supper a message came down in haste to beg for the aid of Mistress Susan, who, though much left to the seclusion of Bridgefield in prosperous days, was always a resource in trouble or difficulty. Little George, then two and a half years old, had been taken suddenly ill after a supper on marchpane and plum broth, washed down by Christmas ale. Convulsions had come on, and the skill of Queen Mary's apothecary had only gone so far as to bleed him. Susan arrived only just in time to see the child breathe his last sigh, and to have his mother, wild with tumultuous clamorous grief, put into her hands for such soothing and comforting as might be possible, and the good and tender woman did her best to turn the mother's thoughts to something higher and better than the bewailing at one moment "her pretty boy," with a sort of animal sense of bereavement, and the next with lamentations over the honours to which he would have succeeded. It was of little use to speak to her of the eternal glories of which he was now secure, for Mary Talbot's sorrow was chiefly selfish, and was connected with the loss of her pre-eminence as parent to the heir-male.

However, the grief of those times was apt to expend itself quickly, and when little George's coffin, smothered under heraldic devices and funeral escutcheons, had been bestowed in the family vault, Dame Mary soon revived enough to take a warm interest in the lords who were next afterwards sent down to hold conferences with the captive; and her criticism of the fashion of their ruffs and doublets was as animated as ever. Another grief, however, soon fell upon the family. Lady Lennox's ailments proved to be no such trifles as her sisters and sisters-in-law had been pleased to suppose, and before the year was out, she had passed away from all her ambitious hopes, leaving a little daughter. The Earl took a brief leave of absence to visit his lady in her affliction at Chatsworth, and to stand godfather to the motherless infant.

" She will soon be fatherless, too," said Richard Talbot on his return to Bridgefield, after attending his lord on this expedition. " My young Lord Lennox, poor youth, is far gone in the wasting sickness, as well as distraught with grief, and he could scarcely stand to receive my Lord."

" Our poor lady ! " said Susan, " it pities me to think what hopes she had fixed upon that young couple whom she had mated together."

" I doubt me whether her hopes be ended now," quoth Richard. " What think you she hath fixed on as the name of the poor puling babe yonder ? They have called her Arbel or Arabella."

" Arabella, say you ? I never heard such a name. It is scarce Christian. Is it out of a romaunt ? "

" Better that it were. It is out of a pedigree. They have got the whole genealogy of the house of Lennox blazoned fair, with crowns and coronets and coats of arms hung up in the hall at Chatsworth, going up on the one hand through Sir Æneas of Troy, and on the other hand through Woden to Adam and Eve! Pass for all before the Stewart line became Kings of Scots! Well, it seems that these Lennox Stewarts sprang from one Walter, who was son to King Robert II., and that the mother of this same Walter was called Arnhild, or as the Scots here call it Annaple, but the scholars have made it into Arabella, and so my young lady is to be called. They say it was a special fancy of the young Countess's."

" So I should guess. My lady would fill her head with such thoughts, and of this poor youth being next of kin to the young Scottish king, and to our own Queen."

" He is not next heir to Scotland even, barring a little one we wot of, Dame Sue. The Hamiltons stand between, being descended from a daughter of King James I."

" So methought I had heard. Are they not Papists?"

" Yea! Ah ha, sweetheart, there is another of the house of Hardwicke as fain to dreams of greatness for her child as ever was the Countess, though she may be more discreet in the telling of them."

" Ah me, dear sir, I dreamt not of greatness for splendour's sake—'twere scarce for the dear child's happiness. I only thought of what you once said, that she may be the instrument of preserving the true religion."

" And if so, it can only be at a mighty cost!" said her husband.

" Verily," said Susan, " glad am I that you sent our Humfrey from her. Would that nought had ever passed between the children!"

"They were but children," said Richard ; "and there was no contract between them."

"I fear me there was what Humfrey will hold to, or know good reason why," said his mother.

"And were the young King of Scots married and father to a goodly heir, there is no reason he should not hold to it," rejoined Richard.

However Richard was still anxious to keep his son engaged at a distance from Sheffield. There was great rejoicing and thankfulness when one of the many messengers constantly passing between London and Sheffield brought a packet from Humfrey, whose ship had put into the Thames instead of the Humber.

The packet contained one of the black stones which the science of the time expected to transmute into gold, also some Esquimaux trinkets made of bone, and a few shells. These were for the mother and Cis, and there were also the tusks of a sea-elephant which Humfrey would lay up at my Lord's London lodgings till his father sent tidings what should be done with them, and whether he should come home at once by sea to Hull, or if, as he much desired to do, he might join an expedition which was fitting out for the Spanish Main, where he was assured that much more both of gold and honour was to be acquired than in the cold northern seas, where nothing was to be seen for the fog at most times, and when it cleared only pigmies, with their dogs, white bears, and seals, also mountains of ice bigger than any church, blue as my lady's best sapphires, green as her emeralds, sparkling as her diamonds, but ready to be the destruction of the ships.

"One there was," wrote Humfrey, "that I could have thought was no other than the City that the blessed St. John saw descending from Heaven, so fair

E

was it to look on, but they cried out that it was rather
a City of Destruction, and when we had got out of the
current where it was bearing down on us, our noble
captain piped all hands up to prayers, and gave thanks
for our happy deliverance therefrom."

Susan breathed a thanksgiving as her husband read,
and he forbore to tell her of the sharks, the tornadoes,
and the fevers which might make the tropical seas more
perilous than the Arctic.   No Elizabethan mariner had
any scruples respecting piracy, and so long as the captain was a godly man who kept up strict discipline on
board, Master Richard held the quarterdeck to be a
much more wholesome place than the Manor-house,
and much preferred the humours of the ship to those
of any other feminine creature; for, as to his Susan, he
always declared that she was the only woman who had
none.

So she accepted his decision, and saw the wisdom
of it, though her tender heart deeply felt the disappointment.   Tenderly she packed up the shirts which
she and Cis had finished, and bestrewed them with
lavender, which, as she said, while a tear dropped with
the gray blossoms, would bring the scent of home to
the boy.

Cis affected to be indifferent and offended.   "Master Humfrey might do as he chose.   She did not care
if he did prefer pitch and tar, and whale blubber and
grease, to hawks and hounds, and lords and ladies.   She
was sure she wanted no more great lubberly lads—with
a sly cut at Diccon—to tangle her silk, and torment
her to bait their hooks.   She was well quit of any one
of them.

When Diccon proposed that she should write a
letter to Humfrey, she declared that she should do no

such thing, since he had never attempted to write to her. In truth Diccon may have made the proposal in order to obtain a companion in misfortune, since Master Sniggius, emulous of the success of other tutors, insisted on his writing to his brother in Latin, and the unfortunate epistle of Ricardus to Onofredus was revised and corrected to the last extremity, and as it was allowed to contain no word unknown to Virgilius Maro, it could not have afforded much delectation to the recipient.

But when Mrs. Susan had bestowed all the shirts as neatly as possible, on returning to settle them for the last time before wrapping them up for the messenger, she felt something hard among them. It was a tiny parcel wrapped in a piece of a fine kerchief, tied round with a tress of dark hair, and within, Susan knew by the feeling, a certain chess rook which had been won by Cis when shooting at the butts a week or two before.

CHAPTER X.

THE LADY ARBELL.

AFTER several weary months of languishing, Charles
Stewart was saved from the miseries which seemed
the natural inheritance of his name by sinking into
his grave.   His funeral was conducted with the
utmost magnificence, though the Earl of Shrewsbury
declined to be present at it, and shortly after, the
Countess intimated her purpose of returning to Sheffield,
bringing with her the little orphan, Lady Arabella
Stewart.   Orders came that the best presence chamber in
the Manor-house should be prepared, the same indeed
where Queen Mary had been quartered before the
lodge had been built for her use.   The Earl was
greatly perturbed.   "Whom can she intend to bring ?"
he went about asking.   "If it were the Lady Margaret,
it were as much as my head were worth to admit her
within the same grounds as this Queen."

"There is no love lost between the mother-in-law
and daughter-in-law," observed his son Gilbert in a
consolatory tone.

"Little good would that do to me, if once it came
to the ears of her Grace and the Lord Treasurer that
both had been my guests !   And if I had to close the
gates—though in no other way could I save my life

and honour—your mother would never forget it. It
would be cast up to me for ever. What think you,
daughter Talbot ? "

"Mayhap," said Dame Mary, "my lady mother
has had a hint to make ready for her Majesty herself,
who hath so often spoken of seeing the Queen of
Scots, and might think well to take her unawares."

This was a formidable suggestion. "Say you so,"
cried the poor Earl, with an alarm his eye would never
have betrayed had Parma himself been within a march
of Sheffield, "then were we fairly spent. I am an
impoverished man, eaten out of house and lands as it
is, and were the Queen herself to come, I might take
at once to the beggar's bowl."

"But think of the honour, good my lord," cried
Mary. "Think of all Hallamshire coming to do her
homage. Oh, how I should laugh to hear the Mayor
stumbling over his address."

"Laugh, ay," growled the Earl; "and how will
you laugh when there is not a deer left in the park,
nor an ox in the stalls ? "

"Nay, my Lord," interposed Gilbert, "there is no
fear of her Majesty's coming. That post from M. de
la Mauvissière reported her at Greenwich only five
days back, and it would take her Majesty a far longer
time to make her progress than yonder fellow, who
will tell you himself that she had no thoughts of
moving."

"That might only be a feint to be the more sudden
with us," said his wife, actuated in part by the diversion
of alarming her father-in-law, and in part really fired
by the hope of such an effectual enlivenment of the
dulness of Sheffield.

They were all in full family conclave drawn up in

the hall for the reception, and Mistress Susan, who could not bear to see the Earl so perplexed and anxious, ventured to say that she was quite sure that my Lady Countess would have sent warning forward if indeed she were bringing home such a guest, and at that moment the blare of trumpets announced that the cavalcade was approaching. The start which the Earl gave showed how much his nerves had become affected by his years of custody. Up the long avenue they came, with all the state with which the Earl had conducted Queen Mary to the lodge before she was absolutely termed a prisoner. Halberdiers led the procession, horse and foot seemed to form it. The home party stood on the top of the steps watching with much anxiety. There was a closed litter visible, beside which Lady Shrewsbury, in a mourning dress and hood, could be seen riding her favourite bay palfrey. No doubt it contained the Lady Margaret, Countess of Lennox; and the unfortunate Earl, forgetting all his stately dignity, stood uneasily moving from leg to leg, and pulling his long beard, torn between the instincts of hospitality and of loyal obedience, between fear of his wife and fear of the Queen.

The litter halted at the foot of the steps, the Earl descended. All he saw was the round face of an infant in its nurse's arms, and he turned to help his wife from the saddle, but she waved him aside. " My son Gilbert will aid me, my Lord," said she, " your *devoir* is to the princess."

Poor Lord Shrewsbury, his apologies on his tongue, looked into the litter, where he saw the well-known and withered countenance of the family nurse. He also beheld a buxom young female, whose dress marked her as a peasant, but before he had time to seek further for

the princess, the tightly rolled chrysalis of a child was
thrust into his astonished arms, while the round face
puckered up instantly with terror at sight of his
bearded countenance, and he was greeted with a loud
yell.   He looked helplessly round, and his lady was
ready at once to relieve him.   "My precious ! My
sweetheart ! My jewel ! Did he look sour at her and
frighten her with his ugsome beard ?" and the like
endearments common to grandmothers in all ages.

"But where is the princess ?"

"Where ?   Where should she be but here ?   Her
grandame's own precious, royal, queenly little darling !"
and as a fresh cry broke out, "Yes, yes ; she shall to
her presence chamber.   Usher her, Gilbert."

"Bess's brat !" muttered Dame Mary, in ineffable
disappointment.

Curiosity and the habit of obedience to the Countess
carried the entire troop on to the grand apartments on
the south side, where Queen Mary had been lodged while
the fiction of her guestship had been kept up.   Lady
Shrewsbury was all the time trying to hush the child,
who was quite old enough to be terrified by new faces
and new scenes, and who was besides tired and restless
in her swaddling bands, for which she was so nearly
too old that she had only been kept in them for greater
security upon the rough and dangerous roads.   Great
was my lady's indignation on reaching the state
rooms on finding that no nursery preparations had
been made, and her daughter Mary, with a giggle
hardly repressed by awe of her mother, stood forth and
said, "Why, verily, my lady, we expected some great
dame, my Lady Margaret or my Lady Hunsdon at the
very least, when you spoke of a princess."

"And who should it be but one who has both the

royal blood of England and Scotland in her veins?"
You have not saluted the child to whom you have the
honour to be akin, Mary! On your knee, minion; I
tell you she hath as good or a better chance of wearing
a crown as any woman in England."

"She hath a far better chance of a prison,"
muttered the Earl, "if all this foolery goes on."

"What! What is that? What are you calling
these honours to my orphan princess?" cried the lady,
but the princess herself here broke in with the lustiest
of squalls, and Susan, who was sorry for the child,
contrived to insert an entreaty that my lady would
permit her to be taken at once to the nursery chamber
that had been made ready for her, and let her there be
fed, warmed, and undressed at once.

There was something in the quality of Susan's voice
to which people listened, and the present necessity
overcame the Countess's desire to assert the dignity of
her granddaughter, so she marched out of the room
attended by the women, while the Earl and his sons
were only too glad to slink away—there is no other word
for it, their relief as to the expected visitor having been
exchanged for consternation of another description.

There was a blazing fire ready, and all the baby
comforts of the time provided, and poor little Lady
Arbell was relieved from her swathing bands, and
allowed to stretch her little limbs on her nurse's lap,
the one rest really precious to babes of all periods and
conditions—but the troubles were not yet over, for the
grandmother, glancing round, demanded, "Where is the
cradle inlaid with pearl? Why was it not provided?
Bring it here."

Now this cradle, carved in cedar wood and inlaid
with mother-of-pearl, had been a sponsor's gift to poor

little George, the first male heir of the Talbots, and it
was regarded as a special treasure by his mother, who
was both wounded and resentful at the demand, and
stood pouting and saying, "It was my son's. It is
mine."

"It belongs to the family. You," to two of the
servants, "fetch it here instantly!"

The ladies of Hardwicke race were not guarded in
temper or language, and Mary burst into passionate
tears and exclamations that Bess's brat should not
have her lost George's cradle, and flounced away to get
before the servants and lock it up. Lady Shrewsbury
would have sprung after her, and have made no scruple
of using her fists and nails even on her married
daughter, but that she was impeded by a heavy table,
and this gave time for Susan to throw herself before
her, and entreat her to pause.

"You, you, Susan Talbot! You should know better
than to take the part of an undutiful, foul-tongued
vixen like that. Out of my way, I say!" and as
Susan, still on her knees, held the riding-dress, she
received a stinging box on the ear. But in her maiden
days she had known the weight of my lady's hand, and
without relaxing her hold, she only entreated: "Hear
me, hear me for a little space, my lady. Did you but
know how sore her heart is, and how she loved little
Master George!"

"That is no reason she should flout and miscall
her dead sister, of whom she was always jealous!"

"O madam, she wept with all her heart for poor
Lady Lennox. It is not any evil, but she sets such
store by that cradle in which her child died — she
keeps it by her bed even now, and her woman told
me how, for all she seems gay and blithe by day,

E*

she weeps over it at night, as if her heart would
break."

Lady Shrewsbury was a little softened. " The
child died in it ?" she asked.

" Yea, madam. He had been on his father's knee,
and had seemed a little easier, and as if he might
sleep, so Sir Gilbert laid him down, and he did but
stretch himself out, shiver all over, draw a long breath,
and the pretty lamb was gone to Paradise!"

" You saw him, Susan ?"

" Yea, madam. Dame Mary sent for me, but none
could be of any aid where it was the will of Heaven
to take him."

" If I had been there," said the Countess, " I who
have brought up eight children and lost none, I should
have saved him ! So he died in yonder cedar cradle !
Well, e'en let Mary keep it. It may be that there is
infection in the smell of the cedar wood, and that the
child will sleep better out of it. It is too late to do
aught this evening, but to-morrow the child shall be
lodged as befits her birth, in the presence chamber."

" Ah, madam !" said Susan, " would it be well for
the sweet babe if her Majesty's messengers, who be so
often at the castle, were to report her so lodged ?"

" I have a right to lodge my grandchild where and
how I please in my own house."

" Yea, madam, that is most true, but you wot how
the Queen treats all who may have any claim to the
throne in future times ; and were it reported by any of
the spies that are ever about us, how royal honours
were paid to the little Lady Arbell, might she not be
taken from your ladyship's wardship, and bestowed with
those who would not show her such loving care ?"

The Countess would not show whether this had

any effect on her, or else some sound made by the child attracted her. It was a puny little thing, and she had a true grandmother's affection for it, apart from her absurd pride and ambition, so that she was glad to hold counsel over it with Susan, who had done such justice to her training as to be, in her eyes, a mother who had sense enough not to let her children waste and die; a rare merit in those days, and one that Susan could not disclaim, though she knew that it did not properly belong to her.

Cis had stood by all the time like a little statue, for no one, not even young Lady Talbot, durst sit down uninvited in the presence of Earl or Countess; but her black brows were bent, her gray eyes intent.

"Mother," she said, as they went home on their quiet mules, "are great ladies always so rudely spoken to one another?"

"I have not seen many great ladies, Cis, and my Lady Countess has always been good to me."

"Antony said that the Scots Queen and her ladies never storm at one another like my lady and her daughters."

"Open words do not always go deep, Cis," said the mother. "I had rather know and hear the worst at once." And then her heart smote her as she recollected that she might be implying censure of the girl's true mother, as well as defending wrath and passion, and she added, "Be that as it may, it is a happy thing to learn to refrain the tongue."

CHAPTER XI.

QUEEN MARY'S PRESENCE CHAMBER.

THE storm that followed on the instalment of the Lady
Arbell at Sheffield was the precursor of many more.
Her grandmother did sufficiently awake to the danger
of alarming the jealousy of Queen Elizabeth to submit
to leave her in the ordinary chambers of the children
of the house, and to exact no extraordinary marks of
respect towards the unconscious infant; but there was
no abatement in the Countess's firm belief that an
English-born, English-bred child, would have more
right to the crown than any "foreign princes," as she
contemptuously termed the Scottish Queen and her
son.

Moreover, in her two years' intercourse with the
elder Countess of Lennox, who was a gentle-tempered
but commonplace woman, she had adopted to the full
that unfortunate princess's entire belief in the guilt of
Queen Mary, and entertained no doubt that she had
been the murderer of Darnley. Old Lady Lennox
had seen no real evidence, and merely believed what
she was told by her lord, whose impeachment of Bothwell had been baffled by the Queen in a most
suspicious manner. Conversations with this lady had
entirely changed Lady Shrewsbury from the friendly

hostess of her illustrious captive, to be her enemy and
persecutor, partly as being convinced of her guilt,
partly as regarding her as an obstacle in the path of
little Arbell to the throne.   So she not only refused
to pay her respects as usual to " that murtheress," but
she insisted that her husband should tighten the bonds
of restraint, and cut off all indulgences.

The Countess was one of the women to whom
argument and reason are impossible, and who was entirely swayed by her predilections, as well as of so
imperious a nature as to brook no opposition, and to
be almost always able to sweep every one along with
her.

Her own sons always were of her mind, and her
daughters might fret and chafe, but were sure to take
part with her against every one else outside the Cavendish family.   The idea of being kinsfolk to the future
Queen excited them all, and even Mary forgot her
offence about the cradle, and her jealousy of Bess, and
ranked herself against her stepfather, influencing her
husband, Gilbert, on whom the unfortunate Earl had
hitherto leant.   On his refusal to persecute his unfortunate captive beyond the orders from the Court,
Bess of Hardwicke, emboldened by the support she
had gathered from her children, passionately declared
that it could only be because he was himself in love
with the murtheress.   Lord Shrewsbury could not
help laughing a little at the absurdity of the idea,
whereupon my lady rose up in virtuous indignation,
calling her sons and daughters to follow her.

All that night, lights might have been seen flitting
about at the Manor-house, and early in the morning
bugles sounded to horse.   A huge procession, consisting of the Countess herself, and all her sons and

daughters then at Sheffield, little Lady Arbell, and the whole of their attendants, swept out of the gates of the park on the way to Hardwicke. When Richard Talbot went up to fulfil his duties as gentleman porter at the lodge the courts seemed well-nigh deserted, and a messenger summoned him at once to the Earl, whom he found in his bed-chamber in his morning gown terribly perturbed.

"For Heaven's sake send for your wife, Richard Talbot!" he said. "It is her Majesty's charge that some of mine household, or I myself, see this unhappy Queen of Scots each day for not less than two hours, as you well know. My lady has broken away, and all her daughters, on this accursed fancy—yea, and Gilbert too, Gilbert whom I always looked to to stand by me; I have no one to send. If I go and attend upon her alone, as I have done a thousand times to my sorrow, it will but give colour to the monstrous tale; but if your good wife, an honourable lady of the Hardwicke kin, against whom none ever breathed a word, will go and give the daily attendance, then can not the Queen herself find fault, and my wife's heated fancy can coin nothing suspicious. You must all come up, and lodge here in the Manor-house till this tempest be overpast. Oh, Richard, Richard! will it last out my life? My very children are turned against me. Go you down and fetch your good Susan, and take order for bringing up your children and gear. Benthall shall take your turn at the lodge. What are you tarrying for? Do you doubt whether your wife have rank enough to wait on the Queen? She should have been a knight's lady long ago, but that I deemed you would be glad to be quit of herald's fees; your service and estate have merited it, and I will crave license by

to-day's courier from her Majesty to lay knighthood
on your shoulder."

"That was not what I thought of, my Lord, though
I humbly thank you, and would be whatever was best
for your Lordship's service, though, if it would serve
you as well, I would rather be squire than knight;
but I was bethinking me how we should bestow our
small family. We have a young damsel at an age not
to be left to herself."

"The black-browed maid—I recollect her. Let
her e'en follow her mother. Queen Mary likes a young
face, and is kindly disposed to little maids. She
taught Bess Pierrepoint to speak French and work
with her needle, and I cannot see that she did the lass
any harm, nay, she is the only one of them all that
can rule her tongue to give a soft answer if things
go not after her will, and a maid might learn worse
things. Besides, your wife will be there to look
after the maiden, so you need have no fears. And
for your sons, they will be at school, and can eat
with us."

Richard's doubts being thus silenced he could not
but bring his wife to his lord's rescue, though he well
knew that Susan would be greatly disturbed on all
accounts, and indeed he found her deep in the ironing
that followed the great spring wash, and her housewifely
mind was as much exercised as to the effects of her
desertion, as was her maternal prudence at the plunge
which her unconscious adopted child was about to
make. However, there was no denying the request,
backed as it was by her husband, looking at her
proudly, and declaring she was by general consent
the only discreet woman in Sheffield. She was very
sorry for the Earl's perplexity, and had a loyal pity

for the Countess's vexation and folly, and she was
consoled by the assurance that she would have a free
time between dinner and supper to go home and
attend to her wash, and finish her preparations. Cis,
who had been left in a state of great curiosity, to
continue compounding pickle while the mother was
called away, was summoned to don her holiday kirtle,
for she was to join in attendance on the Queen of
Scots while Lady Shrewsbury and her daughters were
absent.

It was unmixed delight to the girl, and she was not
long in fresh-binding up her hair—black with a little
rust-coloured tinge—under her stiff little cap, smoothing down the front, which was alone visible, putting
on the well-stiffened ruff with the dainty little lace
edge and close-fitting tucker, and then the gray home-
spun kirtle, with the puffs at the top of the tight
sleeves, and the slashes into which she had persuaded
mother to insert some old pink satin, for was not she
sixteen now, and almost a woman ?   There was a pink
breast-knot to match, and Humfrey's owch just above it,
gray stockings, home-spun and worked with elaborate
pink clocks, but knitted by Cis herself; and a pair of
shoes with pink roses to match were put into a bag, to
be assumed when she arrived at the lodge. Out of
this simple finery beamed a face, bright in spite of the
straight, almost bushy, black brows. There was a light
of youth, joy, and intelligence, about her gray eyes
which made them sparkle all the more under their
dark setting, and though her complexion had no
brilliancy, only the clearness of health, and her
features would not endure criticism, there was a
wonderful lively sweetness about her fresh, innocent
young mouth ; and she had a tall lithe figure, sur-

passing that of her stepmother. She would have been
a sonsie Border lass in appearance but for the remarkable carriage of her small head and shoulders, which
was assuredly derived from her royal ancestry, and
indeed her air and manner of walking were such that
Diccon had more than once accused her of sailing
about ambling like the Queen of Scots, an accusation
which she hotly denied. Her hands had likewise a
slender form and fine texture, such as none of the
ladies of the houses of Talbot or Hardwicke could
rival, but she was on the whole viewed as far from
being a beauty. The taste of the day was altogether
for light, sandy-haired, small-featured women, like
Queen Elizabeth or her namesake of Hardwicke, so that
Cis was looked on as a sort of crow, and her supposed
parents were pitied for having so ill-favoured a
daughter, so unlike all their families, except one black-
a-vised Talbot grandmother, whose portrait had been
discovered on a pedigree.

Much did Susan marvel what impression the
daughter would make on the true mother as they
jogged up on their sober ponies through the long
avenues, whose branches were beginning to wear the
purple shades of coming spring.

Lord Shrewsbury himself met them in front of the
lodge, where, in spite of all his dignity, he had
evidently been impatiently awaiting them. He
thanked Susan for coming, as if he had not had a
right to order, gave her his ungloved hand when she
had dismounted, then at the single doorway of the
lodge caused his gentleman to go through the form of
requesting admission for himself and Mistress Talbot,
his dear kinswoman, to the presence of the Queen. It
was a ceremony daily observed as an acknowledgment

of Mary's royalty, and the Earl was far too courteous
ever to omit it.

Queen Mary's willingness to admit him was notified
by Sir Andrew Melville, a tall, worn man, with the
typical Scottish countenance and a keen steadfast gray
eye.   He marshalled the trio up a circular staircase,
made as easy as possible, but necessarily narrow, since
it wound up through a brick turret at the corner, to
the third and uppermost story of the lodge.

There, however, was a very handsome anteroom,
with tapestry hangings, a richly moulded ceiling, and
wide carved stone chimneypiece, where a bright fire was
burning, around which sat several Scottish and French
gentlemen, who rose at the Earl's entrance.   Another
wide doorway with a tapestry curtain over the folding
leaves led to the presence chamber, and Sir Andrew
announced in as full style as if he had been marshalling an English ambassador to the Court of Holyrood,
the most high and mighty Earl of Shrewsbury.   The
room was full of March sunshine, and a great wood
fire blazed on the hearth.   Part of the floor was
carpeted, and overhung with a canopy, proceeding from
the tapestried wall, and here was a cross-legged velvet
chair on which sat Queen Mary.   This was all that
Cis saw at first, while the Earl advanced, knelt on
one step of the dais, with bared head, exchanging
greetings with the Queen.   He then added, that his
wife, the Countess, and her daughter, having been
called away from Sheffield, he would entreat her
Grace to accept for a few days in their stead the
attendance of his good kinswoman, Mrs. Talbot, and
her daughter, Mistress Cicely.

Mary graciously intimated her consent, and extended
her hand for each to kiss as they knelt in turn on the

step; Susan either fancied, or really saw a wonderful likeness in that taper hand to the little one whose stitches she had so often guided. Cis, on her part, felt the thrill of girlhood in the actual touch of the subject of her. dreams. She stood, scarcely hearing what passed, but taking in, from under her black brows, all the surroundings, and recognising the persons from her former glimpses, and from Antony Babington's descriptions. The presence chamber was ample for the suite of the Queen, which had been reduced on every fresh suspicion. There was in it, besides the Queen's four ladies, an elderly one, with a close black silk hood——Jean Kennedy, or Mrs. Kennett as the English called her; another, a thin slight figure, with a worn face, as if a great sorrow had passed over her, making her look older than her mistress, was the Queen's last remaining Mary, otherwise Mrs. Seaton. The gossip of Sheffield had not failed to tell how the chamberlain, Beatoun, had been her suitor, and she had half consented to accept him when he was sent on a mission to France, and there died. The dark-complexioned bright-eyed little lady, on a smaller scale than the rest, was Marie de Courcelles, who, like the two others, had been the Queen's companion in all her adventures; and the fourth, younger and prettier than the rest, was already known to Cis and her mother, since she was the Barbara Mowbray who was affianced to Gilbert Curll, the Queen's Scottish secretary, recently taken into her service. Both these were Protestants, and, like the Bridgefield family, attended service in the castle chapel. They were all at work, as was like-wise their royal lady, to whom the girl, with the youth-ful coyness that halts in the fulfilment of its dreams, did not at first raise her eyes, having first taken in all

the ladies, the several portions of one great coverlet
which they were all embroidering in separate pieces,
and the gentleman who was reading aloud to them from
a large book placed on a desk at which he was standing.

When she did look up, as the Queen was graciously
requesting her mother to be seated, and the Earl excusing
himself from remaining longer, her first impression was
one of disappointment. Either the Queen of Scots was
less lovely seen leisurely close at hand than Antony
Babington and Cis's own fancy had painted her, or the
last two or three years had lessened her charms, as well
they might, for she had struggled and suffered much
in the interval, had undergone many bitter disappointments, and had besides endured much from rheumatism every winter, indeed, even now she could not
ride, and could only go out in a carriage in the park
on the finest days, looking forward to her annual visit
to Buxton to set her up for the summer. Her face
was longer and more pointed than in former days, her
complexion had faded, or perhaps in these private
moments it had not been worth while to enhance it ;
though there was no carelessness in the general attire,
the black velvet gown, and delicate lace of the cap,
and open ruff always characteristic of her. The small
curls of hair at her temples had their auburn tint
softened by far more white than suited one who was
only just over forty, but the delicate pencilling of the
eyebrows was as marked as ever ; and the eyes, on
whose colour no one ever agreed, melted and sparkled
as of old. Cis had heard debates as to their hue, and
furtively tried to form her own opinion, but could not
decide on anything but that they had a dark effect,
and a wonderful power of expression, seeming to look
at every one at once, and to rebuke, encourage, plead,

or smile, from moment to moment. The slight cast in one of them really added to their force of expression rather than detracted from their beauty, and the delicate lips were ready to second the glances with wondrous smiles. Cis had not felt the magic of her mere presence five minutes without being convinced that Antony Babington was right; the Lord Treasurer and all the rest utterly wrong, and that she beheld the most innocent and persecuted of princesses.

Meantime, all due formalities having been gone through, Lord Shrewsbury bowed himself out backwards with a dexterity that Cis breathlessly admired in one so stately and so stiff, forgetting that he had daily practice in the art. Then Queen Mary courteously entreated her visitors to be seated, near herself, asking with a smile if this were not the little maiden who had queened it so prettily in the brake some few years since. Cis blushed and drew back her head with a pretty gesture of dignified shyness as Susan made answer for her that she was the same.

"I should have known it," said the Queen, smiling, "by the port of her head alone. 'Tis strange," she said, musing, "that maiden hath the bearing of head and neck that I have never seen save in my own mother, the saints rest her soul, and in her sisters, and which we always held to be their inheritance from the blood of Charlemagne."

"Your grace does her too much honour," Susan contrived to say, thankful that no less remote resemblance had been detected.

"It was a sad farce when they tried to repeat your pretty comedy with the chief performer omitted," proceeded the Queen, directing her words to the girl, but the mother replied for her.

" Your Grace will pardon me, I could not permit
her to play in public, before all the *menié* of the castle."

" Madame is a discreet and prudent mother," said
the Queen. " The mistake was in repeating the representation at all, not in abstaining from appearing in
it. I should be very sorry that this young lady should
have been concerned in a spectacle *à la comtesse.*"

There was something in the intonation of " this
young lady " that won Cis's heart on the spot, something in the concluding words that hurt Susan's faithful loyalty towards her kinswoman, in spite of the
compliment to herself. However Mary did not pursue
the subject, perceiving with ready tact that it was dis-
tasteful, and proceeded to ask Dame Susan's opinion
of her work, which was intended as a gift to her good
aunt, the Abbess of Soissons. How strangely the
name fell upon Susan's ear. It was a pale blue satin
coverlet, worked in large separate squares, innumerable
shields and heraldic devices of Lorraine, Bourbon,
France, Scotland, etc., round the border, and beautiful
meandering patterns of branches, with natural flowers
and leaves growing from them covering the whole with
a fascinating regular irregularity. Cis could not repress
an exclamation of delight, which brought the most
charming glance of the winning eyes upon her. There
was stitchery here that she did not understand, but
when she looked at some of the flowers, she could not
help uttering the sentiment that the eyes of the daisies
were not as mother could make them.

So, as a great favour, Queen Mary entreated to be
shown Mrs. Talbot's mode of dealing with the eyes of
the daisies. No, her good Seaton would not learn so
well as she should ; Madame must come and sit by
her and show her. Meantime here was her poor little

Bijou whimpering to be taken on her lap. Would not he find a comforter in sweet Mistress—ah, what was her name?

"We named her Cicely, so please your Grace," said Susan, unable to help blushing.

"Cécile, a fair name. Ah! so the poor Antoine called her. I see my Bijou has found a friend in you, Mistress Cécile"—as the girl's idle hands were only too happy to caress the pretty little shivering Italian greyhound rather than to be busy with a needle. "Do you ever hear of that young Babington, your play-fellow?" she added.

"No, madam," said Cis, looking up, "he hath never been here!"

"I thought not," said Queen Mary, sighing. "Take heed to manifest no pity for me, maiden, if you should ever chance to be inspired with it for a poor worn-out old prisoner. It is the sure sentence of misfortune and banishment."

"In his sex, madam," here put in Marie de Cour-celles. "If it were so in ours, woe to some of us."

"That is true, my dear friends," said Mary, her eyes glistening with dew. "It is the women who are the most fearless, the most faithful, and whom the saints therefore shield."

"Alas, there are some who are faithful but who are not shielded!"

It was merely a soft low murmur, but the tender-hearted Queen had caught it, and rising impulsively, crossed the room and gathered Mary Seaton's hands into hers, no longer the queen but the loving friend of equal years, soothing her in a low fond voice, and pre-sently sending her to the inner chamber to compose herself. Then as the Queen returned slowly to her

seat it would be seen how lame she was from rheumatism.   Mrs. Kennedy hurried to assist her, with a
nurse-like word of remonstrance, to which she replied
with a bewitching look of sweetness that she could not
but forget her aches and pains when she saw her dear
Mary Seaton in trouble.

Most politely she then asked whether her visitors
would object to listening to the conclusion of her day's
portion of reading.   There was no refusing, of course,
though, as Susan glanced at the reader and knew him
to be strongly suspected of being in Holy Orders conferred abroad, she had her fears for her child's Protestant
principles.   The book, however, proved to be a translation of St. Austin on the Psalms, and, of course, she
could detect nothing that she disapproved, even if
Cis had not been far too much absorbed by the little
dog and its mistress to have any comprehending ears
for theology.   Queen Mary confidentially observed as
much to her after the reading, having, no doubt, detected her uneasy glance.

" You need not fear for your child, madam," she
said ; " St. Augustine is respected by your own Queen
and her Bishops.   At the readings with which my good
Mr. Belton favours me, I take care to have nothing you
Protestants dispute when I know it."   She added,
smiling, " Heaven knows that I have endeavoured to
understand your faith, and many a minister has argued
with me.   I have done my best to comprehend them, but
they agreed in nothing but in their abuse of the Pope.
At least so it seemed to my poor weak mind.   But
you are satisfied, madam, I see it in your calm eyes
and gentle voice.   If I see much of you, I shall learn
to think well of your religion."

Susan made an obeisance without answering.   She

had heard Sir Gilbert Talbot say, " If she tries to persuade you that you can convert her, be sure that she
means mischief," but she could not bear to believe it
anything but a libel while the sweet sad face was gazing
into hers.

Queen Mary changed the subject by asking a few
questions about the Countess's sudden departure. There
was a sort of guarded irony suppressed in her tone—she
was evidently feeling her way with the stranger, and
when she found that Susan would only own to causes
Lord Shrewsbury had adduced on the spur of the
moment, she was much too wary to continue the
examination, though Susan could not help thinking
that she knew full well the disturbance which had
taken place.

A short walk on the roof above followed.   The sun
was shining brilliantly, and lame as she was, the Queen's
strong craving for free air led her to climb her stairs
and creep to and fro on Sir Andrew Melville's arm,
gazing out over the noble prospect of the park close
below, divided by the winding vales of the three rivers,
which could be traced up into the woods and the moors
beyond, purple with spring freshness and glory.   Mary
made her visitors point out Bridgefield, and asked
questions about all that could be seen of the house
and pleasance, which, in truth, was little enough,
but she contrived to set Cis off into a girl's chatter
about her home occupations, and would not let her be
hushed.

" You little know the good it does a captive to take
part, only in fancy, in a free harmless life," returned
Mary, with the wistful look that made her eyes so
pathetic.   " There is no refreshment to me like a child's
prattle."

Susan's heart smote her as she thought of the true relations in which these two stood to one another, and she forbore from further interference; but she greatly rejoiced when the great bell of the castle gave notice of noon, and of her own release.   When Queen Mary's dinner was served, the Talbot ladies in attendance left her and repaired to the general family meal in the hall.

CHAPTER XII.

A FURIOUS LETTER.

A PERIOD now began of daily penance to Mrs. Talbot, of daily excitement and delight to Cis. Two hours or more had to be spent in attendance on Queen Mary. Even on Sundays there was no exemption, the visit only took place later in the day, so as not to interfere with going to church.

Nothing could be more courteous or more friendly than the manner in which the elder lady was always received. She was always made welcome by the Queen herself, who generally entered into conversation with her almost as with an equal. Or when Mary herself was engaged in her privy chamber in dictating to her secretaries, the ladies of the suite showed themselves equally friendly, and told her of their mistress's satisfaction in having a companion free from all the rude and unaccountable humours and caprices of my Lady Countess and her daughters. And if Susan was favoured, Cis was petted. Queen Mary always liked to have young girls about her. Their fresh, spontaneous, enthusiastic homage was pleasant to one who loved above all to attract, and it was a pleasure to a prisoner to have a fresh face about her.

Was it only this, or was it the maternal instinct

that made her face light up when the young girl
entered the room and return the shy reverential kiss
of the hand with a tender kiss on the forehead, that
made her encourage the chatter, give little touches to
the deportment, and present little keepsakes, which increased in value till Sir Richard began to look grave,
and to say there must be no more jewels of price
brought from the lodge ?   And as his wife uttered a
word that sounded like remonstrance, he added, " Not
while she passes for *my* daughter."

Cis, who had begun by putting on a pouting face,
burst into tears.   Her adopted parents had always
been more tolerant and indulgent to her than if she
had been a child over whom they felt entire rights,
and instead of rewarding her petulance with such a
blow as would have fallen to the lot of a veritable
Talbot, Richard shrugged his shoulders and left the
room—the chamber which had been allotted to Dame
Susan at the Manor-house, while Susan endeavoured
to cheer the girl by telling her not to grieve, for her
father was not angry with her.

" Why—why may not the dear good Queen give me
her dainty gifts ? " sobbed Cis.

" See, dear child," said Susan, " while she only gave
thee an orange stuck with cloves, or an embroidery
needle, or even a puppy dog, it is all very well ; but
when it comes to Spanish gloves and coral clasps, the
next time there is an outcry about a plot, some evil-
disposed person would be sure to say that Master Richard
Talbot had been taking bribes through his daughter."

" It would be vilely false ! " cried Cis with flashing
eyes.

" It would not be the less believed," said Susan.
" My Lord would say we had betrayed our trust, and

there never has been one stain on my husband's
honour."

" You are wroth with me too, mother!" said Cis.

" Not if you are a good child, and guard the honour
of the name you bear."

" I will, I will!" said Cis.   " Never will I take
another gift from the Queen if only you and he will
call me your child, and be—good to me——" The rest
was lost in tears and in the tender caresses that Susan
lavished on her; all the more as she caught the
broken words, " Humfrey, too, he would never forgive
me."

Susan told her husband what had passed, adding,
" She will keep her word."

" She must, or she shall go no more to the lodge,"
he said.

" You would not have doubted had you seen her
eye flash at the thought of bringing your honour into
question.   There spoke her kingly blood."

" Well, we shall see," sighed Richard, " if it be
blood that makes the nature.   I fear me hers is but
that of a Scottish thief!   Scorn not warning, mother,
but watch thy stranger nestling well."

" Nay, mine husband.   While we own her as our
child, she will do anything to be one with us.   It is
when we seem to put her from us that we wound her
so that I know not what she might do, fondled as she
is—by—by her who—has the best right to the dear
child."

Richard uttered a certain exclamation of disgust
which silenced his discreet wife.

Neither of them had quite anticipated the result,
namely, that the next morning, Cis, after kissing the
Queen's hand as usual, remained kneeling, her bosom

heaving, and a little stammering on her tongue, while tears rose to her eyes.

" What is it, mignonne," said Mary, kindly ; " is the whelp dead ? or is the clasp broken ? "

" No, madam ; but—but I pray you give me no more gifts. My father says it touches his honour, and I have promised him—Oh, madam, be not displeased with me, but let me give you back your last beauteous gift."

Mary was standing by the fire. She took the ivory and coral trinket from the hand of the kneeling girl, and dashed it into the hottest glow. There was passion in the action, and in the kindling eye, but it was but for a moment. Before Cis could speak or Susan begin her excuses, the delicate hand was laid on the girl's head, and a calm voice said, " Fear not, child. Queens take not back their gifts. I ought to have borne in mind that I am balked of the pleasure of giving—the best of all the joys they have robbed me of. But tremble not, sweetheart, I am not chafed with thee. I will vex thy father no more. Better thou shouldst go without a trinket or two than deprive me of the light of that silly little face of thine, so long as they will leave me that sunbeam."

She stooped and kissed the drooping brow, and Susan could not but feel as if the voice of nature were indeed speaking.

A few words of apology in her character of mother for the maiden's abrupt proceeding were met by the Queen most graciously. " Spare thy words, good madam. We understand and reverence Mr. Talbot's point of honour. Would that all who approached us had held his scruples ! "

Perhaps Mary was after this more distant and

dignified towards the matron, but especially tender and caressing towards the maiden, as if to make up by kindness for the absence of little gifts.

Storms, however, were brewing without. Lady Shrewsbury made open complaints of her husband having become one of Mary's many victims, representing herself as an injured wife driven out of her house. She actually in her rage carried the complaint to Queen Elizabeth, who sent down two commissioners to inquire into the matter. They sat in the castle hall, and examined all the attendants, including Richard and his wife. The investigation was extremely painful and distressing, but it was proved that nothing could have been more correct and guarded than the whole intercourse between the Earl and his prisoner. If he had erred, it had been on the side of caution and severity, though he had always preserved the courteous demeanour of a gentleman, and had been rejoiced to permit whatever indulgences could be granted. If there had been any transgressions of the strict rules, they had been made by the Countess herself and her daughters in the days of their intimacy with the Queen; and the aspersions on the unfortunate Earl were, it was soon evident, merely due to the violent and unscrupulous tongues of the Countess and her daughter Mary. No wonder that Lord Shrewsbury wrote letters in which he termed the lady "his wicked and malicious wife," and expressed his conviction that his son Gilbert's mind had been perverted by her daughter.

The indignation of the captive Queen was fully equal to his, as one after another of her little court returned and was made to detail the points on which he or she had been interrogated. Susan found her pacing up and down the floor like a caged tigress, her

cap and veil thrown back, so that her hair—far whiter
than what was usually displayed——was hanging dishevelled, her ruff torn open, as if it choked back the
swelling passion in her throat.

"Never, never content with persecuting me, they
must insult me! Is it not enough that I am stripped
of my crown, deprived of my friends; that I cannot
take a step beyond this chamber, queen as I am, without my warder? Must they attaint me as a woman?
Oh, why, why did the doom spare me that took my
little brothers? Why did I live to be the most
wretched, not of sovereigns alone, but of women?"

"Madam," entreated Marie de Courcelles, "dearest
madam, take courage. All these horrible charges
refute themselves."

"Ah, Marie! you have said so ten thousand times,
and what charge has ever been dropped?"

"This one is dropped!" exclaimed Susan, coming
forward. "Yes, your Grace, indeed it is! The Com-
missioner himself told my husband that no one believed
it for a moment."

"Then why should these men have been sent but
to sting and gall me, and make me feel that I am in
their power?" cried the Queen.

"They came," said the Secretary Curll, "because
thus alone could the Countess be silenced."

"The Countess!" exclaimed Mary. "So my cousin
hath listened to her tongue!"

"Backed by her daughter's," added Jean Kennedy.

"It were well that she knew what those two dames
can say of her Majesty herself, when it serves them,"
added Marie de Courcelles.

"That shall she!" exclaimed Mary. "She shall
have it from mine own hand! Ha! ha! Elizabeth

shall know the choice tales wherewith Mary Talbot
hath regaled us, and then shall she judge how far anything that comes from my young lady is worth heeding
for a moment. Remember you all the tales of the
nips and the pinches? Ay, and of all the endearments to Leicester and to Hatton? She shall have it
all, and try how she likes the dish of scandal of Mary
Talbot's cookery, sauced by Bess of Hardwicke. Here,
nurse, come and set this head-gear of mine in order,
and do you, my good Curll, have pen, ink, and paper
in readiness for me."

The Queen did little but write that morning. The
next day, on coming out from morning prayers, which
the Protestants of her suite attended, with the rest of
the Shrewsbury household, Barbara Mowbray contrived to draw Mrs. Talbot apart as they went towards
the lodge.

"Madam," she said, "they all talk of your power to
persuade. Now is the time you could do what would
be no small service to this poor Queen, ay, and it may
be to your own children."

"I may not meddle in any matters of the Queen's,"
returned Susan, rather stiffly.

"Nay, but hear me, madam. It is only to hinder
the sending of a letter."

"That letter which her Grace was about to write
yesterday?"

"Even so. 'Tis no secret, for she read fragments
of it aloud, and all her women applauded it with all
their might, and laughed over the stings that it would
give, but Mr. Curll, who had to copy it, saith that there
is a bitterness in it that can do nothing but make her
Majesty of England the more inflamed, not only
against my Lady Shrewsbury, but against her who writ

F

the letter, and all concerned. Why, she hath even
brought in the comedy that your children acted in the
woodland, and that was afterwards repeated in the
hall !"

"You say not so, Mistress Barbara ?"

"Indeed I do. Mr. Curll and Sir Andrew Melville are both of them sore vexed, and would fain
have her withdraw it; but Master Nau and all the
French part of the household know not how to rejoice
enough at such an exposure of my Lady, which gives a
hard fling at Queen Elizabeth at the same time ! Nay,
I cannot but tell you that there are things in it that
Dame Mary Talbot might indeed say, but I know
not how Queen Mary could bring herself to set
down——"

Barbara Mowbray ventured no more, and Susan felt
hopeless of her task, since how was she by any means
to betray knowledge of the contents of the letter ? Yet
much that she had heard made her feel very uneasy
on all accounts. She had too much strong family
regard for the Countess and for Gilbert Talbot and his
wife to hear willingly of what might imperil them,
and though royal indignation would probably fly over
the heads of the children, no one was too obscure in
those Tudor times to stand in danger from a sovereign
who might think herself insulted. Yet as a Hardwicke, and the wife of a Talbot, it was most unlikely
that she would have any opening for remonstrance
given to her.

However, it was possible that Curll wished to give
her an opening, for no sooner were the ladies settled at
work than he bowed himself forward and offered his
mistress his copy of the letter.

"Is it fair engrossed, good Curll ?" asked Mary.

"Thanks. Then will we keep your copy, and you shall fold and prepare our own for our sealing."

"Will not your Majesty hear it read over ere it pass out of your hands?" asked Curll.

"Even so," returned Mary, who really was delighted with the pungency of her own composition. "Mayhap we may have a point or two to add."

After what Mistress Barbara had said, Susan was on thorns that Cis should hear the letter; but that good young lady, hating the expressions therein herself, and hating it still more for the girl, bethought her of asking permission to take Mistress Cicely to her own chamber, there to assist her in the folding of some of her laces, and Mary consented. It was well, for there was much that made the English-bred Susan's cheeks glow and her ears tingle.

But, at least, it gave her a great opportunity. When the letter was finished, she advanced and knelt on the step of the canopied chair, saying, "Madam, pardon me, if in the name of my unfortunate children, I entreat you not to accuse them to the Queen."

"Your children, lady! How have I included them in what I have told her Majesty of our sweet Countess?"

"Your Grace will remember that the foremost parts in yonder farce were allotted to my son Humfrey and to young Master Babington. Nay, that the whole arose from the woodland sport of little Cis, which your Grace was pleased to admire."

"Sooth enough, my good gossip, but none could suspect the poor children of the malice my Lady Countess contrived to put into the matter."

"Ah, madam! these are times when it is convenient to shift the blame on one who can be securely punished."

"Certes," said Mary, thoughtfully, "the Countess is capable of making her escape by denouncing some one else, especially those within her own reach."

"Your Grace, who can speak such truth of my poor Lady," said Susan, "will also remember that though my Lord did yield to the persuasions of the young ladies, he so heedfully caused Master Sniggius to omit all perilous matter, that no one not informed would have guèssed at the import of the piece, as it was played in the hall."

"Most assuredly not," said Mary, laughing a little at the recollection. "It might have been played in Westminster Hall without putting my gracious cousin, ay, or Leicester and Hatton themselves, to the blush."

"Thus, if the Queen should take the matter up and trace it home, it could not but be brought to my poor innocent children! Humfrey is for the nonce out of reach, but the maiden——I wis verily that your Highness would be loath to do her any hurt!"

"Thou art a good pleader, madam," said the queen. "Verily I should not like to bring the bonnie lassie into trouble. It will give Master Curll a little more toil, ay and myself likewise, for the matter must stand in mine own hand; but we will leave out yonder unlucky farce."

"Your Highness is very good," said Susan earnestly.

"Yet you look not yet content, my good lady. What more would you have of me?"

"What your Majesty will scarce grant," said Susan.

"Ha! thou art of the same house thyself. I had forgotten it; thou art so unlike to them. I wager that it is not to send this same letter at all."

"Your Highness hath guessed my mind. Nay, madam, though assuredly I do desire it because the

Countess hath been ever my good lady, and bred me
up ever since I was an orphan, it is not solely for her
sake that I would fain pray you, but fully as much for
your Majesty's own."

"Madame Talbot sees the matter as I do," said Sir
Andrew Melville. "The English Queen is as like to
be irate with the reporter of the scandal as with the
author of it, even as the wolf bites the barb that pierces
him when he cannot reach the archer."

"She is welcome to read the letter," said Mary,
smiling; "thy semblance falleth short, my good friend."

"Nay, madam, that was not the whole of my purport," said Susan, standing with folded hands, looking
from one to another. "Pardon me. My thought was
that to take part in all this repeating of thoughtless,
idle words, spoken foolishly indeed, but scarce so much
in malice as to amuse your Grace with Court news,
and treasured up so long, your Majesty descends from
being the patient and suffering princess, meek, generous,
and uncomplaining, to be—to be——"

"No better than one of them, wouldst thou add?"
asked Mary, somewhat sharply, as Susan paused.

"Your Highness has said it," answered Susan;
then, as there was a moment's pause, she looked up,
and with clasped hands added, "Oh, madam! would
it not be more worthy, more noble, more queenly, more
Christian, to refrain from stinging with this repetition
of these vain and foolish slanders?"

"Most Christian treatment have I met with," returned Mary; but after a pause she turned to her
almoner, Master Belton, saying, "What say you, sir?"

"I say that Mrs. Talbot speaks more Christian
words than are often heard in these parts," returned
he. "The thankworthiness of suffering is lost by

those who return the revilings upon those who utter them."

"Then be it so," returned the Queen. "Elizabeth shall be spared the knowledge that some ladies' tongues can be as busy with her as with her poor cousin."

With her own hands Mary tore up her own letter, but Curll's copy unfortunately escaped destruction, to be discovered in after times. Lord and Lady Shrewsbury never knew the service Susan had rendered them by causing it to be suppressed.

CHAPTER XIII.

BEADS AND BRACELETS.

THE Countess was by no means pacified by the investigation, and both she and her family remained at Court, maligning her husband and his captive. As the season advanced, bringing the time for the Queen's annual resort to the waters of Buxton, Lord Shrewsbury was obliged to entreat Mrs. Talbot again to be her companion, declaring that he had never known so much peace as with that lady in the Queen's chambers.

The journey to Buxton was always the great holiday of the imprisoned Court. The place was part of the Shrewsbury property, and the Earl had a great house there, but there were no conveniences for exercising so strict a watch as at Sheffield, and there was altogether a relaxation of discipline. Exercise was considered an essential part of the treatment, and recreations were there provided.

Cis had heard so much of the charms of the expedition, that she was enraptured to hear that she was to share it, together with Mrs. Talbot. The only drawback was that Humfrey had promised to come home after this present voyage, to see whether his little Cis were ready for him; and his father was much disposed to remain at home, receive him first, and

communicate to him the obstacles in the way of
wedding the young lady.   However, my Lord refused
to dispense with the attendance of his most trustworthy kinsman, and leaving Ned at school under
charge of the learned Sniggius, the elder and the
younger Richard Talbot rode forth with the retinue
of the Queen and her warder.

Neither Cicely nor Diccon had ever left home before, and they were in raptures which would have
made any journey delightful to them, far more a ride
through some of the wildest and loveliest glades that
England can display.   Nay, it may be that they
would better have enjoyed something less like Sheffield Park than the rocks, glens, and woods, through
which they rode.   Their real delight was in the towns
and villages at which there was a halt, and every
traveller they saw was such a wonder to them, that at
the end of the first day they were almost as full of
exultation in their experiences, as if, with Humfrey,
they had been far on the way to America.

The delight of sleeping at Tideswell was in their
eyes extreme, though the hostel was so crowded that
Cis had to share a mattress with Mrs. Talbot, and
Diccon had to sleep in his cloak on the floor, which he
persuaded himself was high preferment.   He woke,
however, much sooner than was his wont, and finding
it useless to try to fall asleep again, he made his way
out among the sleeping figures on the floor and hall,
and finding the fountain in the midst of the court,
produced his soap and comb from his pocket, and
made his morning toilet in the open air with considerable satisfaction at his own alertness.   Presently there
was a tap at the window above, and he saw Cicely
making signals to him to wait for her, and in a few

minutes she skipped out from the door into the sun-
light of the early summer morning.

"No one is awake yet," she said. "Even the guard
before the Queen's door is fast asleep. I only heard
a wench or two stirring. We can have a run in the
fields and gather May dew before any one is afoot."

"'Tis not May, 'tis June," said matter-of-fact
Diccon. "But yonder is a guard at the yard gate;
will he let us past?"

"See, here's a little wicket into a garden of potherbs," said Cis. "No doubt we can get out that
way, and it will bring us the sooner into the fields.
I have a cake in my wallet that mother gave me for
the journey, so we shall not fast. How sweet the
herbs smell in the dew——and see how silvery it lies
on the strawberry leaves. Ah! thou naughty lad,
think not whether the fruit be ripe. Mayhap we shall
find some wild ones beyond."

The gate of the garden was likewise guarded, but
by a yeoman who well knew the young Talbots, and
made no difficulty about letting them out into the
broken ground beyond the garden, sloping up into a
little hill. Up bounded the boy and girl, like young
mountaineers, through gorse and fern, and presently
had gained a sufficient height to look over the country,
marking the valleys whence still were rising "fragrant
clouds of dewy steam" under the influence of the sun-
beams, gazing up at the purple heights of the Peak,
where a few lines of snow still lingered in the crevices,
trying to track their past journey from their own
Sheffield, and with still more interest to guess which
wooded valley before them contained Buxton.

"Have you lost your way, my pretty mistress?"
said a voice close to them, and turning round hastily

F*

they saw a peasant woman with a large basket on her arm.

"No," said Cicely courteously, "we have only come out to take the air before breakfast."

"I crave pardon," said the woman, curtseying, "the pretty lady belongs to the great folk down yonder. Would she look at my poor wares? Here are beads and trinkets of the goodly stones, pins and collars, bracelets and eardrops, white, yellow, and purple," she said, uncovering her basket, where were arranged various ornaments made of Derbyshire spar.

"We have no money, good woman," said Cicely, rising to return, vaguely uncomfortable at the woman's eye, which awoke some remembrance of Tibbott the huckster, and the troubles connected with her.

"Yea, but if my young mistress would only bring me in to the Great Lady there, I know she would buy of me my beads and bracelets, or give me an alms for my poor children. I have five of them, good young lady, and they lie naked and hungry till I can sell my few poor wares, and the yeomen are so rough and hard. They would break and trample every poor bead I have in pieces rather than even let my Lord hear of them. But if even my basket could be carried in and shown, and if the good Earl heard my sad tale, I am sure he would give license."

"He never does!" said Diccon, roughly; "hold off, woman, do not hang on us, or I'll get thee branded for a vagabond."

The woman put her knuckles into her eyes, and wailed out that it was all for her poor children, and Cicely reproved him for his roughness, and as the woman kept close behind them, wailing, moaning, and persuading, the boy and girl were wrought upon at last to give her leave to wait outside the gate of the inn garden, while they saw whether it was possible to admit her or her basket.

But before they reached the gate, they saw a figure beyond it, scanning the hill eagerly. They knew him for their father even before he shouted to them, and, as they approached, his voice was displeased : " How now, children ; what manners are these ? "

" We have only been on the hillside, sweet father," said Cis, " Diccon and I together. We thought no harm."

" This is not Sheffield Chace, Cis, and thou art no more a child, but a maiden who needs to be discreet, above all in these times. Whom did I see following you ? "

" A poor woman, whom — Ha, where is she ? " exclaimed Cis, suddenly perceiving that the woman seemed to have vanished.

" A troublesome begging woman who beset us with her wares," said Diccon, " and would give us no peace, praying that we would get them carried in to the Queen and her ladies, whining about her children till she made Cis soft-hearted. Where can she have hidden herself ? "

The man who was stationed as sentry at the gate said he had seen the woman come over the brow of the hill with Master Diccon and Mistress Cicely, but that as they ran forward to meet Captain Talbot she had disappeared amid the rocks and brushwood.

" Poor woman, she was afraid of our father," said Cicely ; " I would we could see her again."

" So would not I," said Richard. " It looks not well, and heed me well, children, there must be no more of these pranks, nor of wandering out of bounds, or babbling with strangers. Go thou in to thy mother, Cis, she hath been in much trouble for thee."

Mistress Susan was unusually severe with the girl
on the indiscretion of gadding in strange places with
no better escort than Diccon, and of entering into conversation with unknown persons.   Moreover, Cicely's
hair, her shoes, and camlet riding skirt were all so
dank with dew that she was with difficulty made presentable by the time the horses were brought round.
The Queen, who had not seen the girl that morning,
made her come and ride near her, asking questions on
the escapade, and giving one of her bewitching pathetic
smiles as she said how she envied the power of thus
dancing out on the greensward, and breathing the free
and fresh morning air.   " My Scottish blood loves the
mountains, and bounds the more freely in the fresh
breeze," she said, gazing towards the Peak.   " I love
the scent of the dew.   Didst get into trouble, child ?
Methought I heard sounds of chiding ? "

" It was no fault of mine," said Cis, inclined to
complain when she found sympathy, " the woman
would speak to us."

" What woman ? " asked the Queen.

" A poor woman with a basket of wares, who
prayed hard to be allowed to show them to your
Grace or some of the ladies.   She said she had five
sorely hungered children, and that she heard your
Grace was a compassionate lady."

" Woe is me, compassion is full all that I am
permitted to give," said the Queen, sadly; " she brought
trinkets to sell.   What were her wares, saidst thou ? "

" I had no time to see many," said Cis, " something
pure and white like a new-laid egg, I saw, and a
necklet, clouded with beauteous purple."

" Ay, beads and bracelets, no doubt," said the
Queen.

"Yes, beads and bracelets," returned Cicely, the soft chime of the Queen's Scottish accent bringing back to her that the woman had twice pressed on her beads and bracelets.

"She dwelt on them," said the Queen lightly. "Ay, I know the chant of the poor folk who ever hover about our outskirts in hopes to sell their country gewgaws, beads and bracelets, collars and pins, little guessing that she whom they seek is poorer than themselves. Mayhap, our Argus-eyed lord may yet let the poor dame within his fence, and we may be able to gratify thy longing for those same purple and white beads and bracelets."

Meantime the party were riding on, intending to dine at Buxton, which meant to reach it by noonday. The tall roof of the great hall erected by the Earl over the baths was already coming in sight, and by and by they would look into the valley. The Wye, after coming down one of those lovely deep ravines to be found in all mountainous countries, here flowed through a more open space, part of which had been artificially levelled, but which was covered with buildings, rising out amongst the rocks and trees.

Most conspicuous among them was a large freshly-built erection in Tudor architecture, with a wide portal arch, and five separate gables starting from one central building, which bore a large clock-tower, and was decorated at every corner with the Talbots' stout and sturdy form. This was the great hall, built by the present Earl George, and containing five baths, intended to serve separately for each sex, gentle and simple, with one special bath reserved for the sole use of the more distinguished visitors. Besides this, at no great distance, was the Earl's own mansion, "a very goodly house, four

square, four stories high," with stables, offices, and all
the requisites of a nobleman's establishment, and this
was to be the lodging of the Scottish Queen.

Farther off was another house, which had been
built by permission of the Earl, under the auspices of
Dr. Jones, probably one of the first of the long series
of physicians who have made it their business to
enhance the fame of the watering-places where they
have set up their staff. This was the great hostel or
lodging-house for the patients of condition who resorted to the healing springs, and nestled here and
there among the rocks were cottages which accom-
modated, after a fashion, the poorer sort, who might
drag themselves to the spot in the hope of washing
away their rheumatic pains and other infirmities. In
a distant and magnificent way, like some of the lesser
German potentates, the mighty Lord of Shrewsbury
took toll from the visitors to his baths, and this con-
tributed to repair the ravages to his fortune caused by
the maintenance of his royal captive.

Arriving just at noontide, the Queen and her escort
beheld a motley crowd dispersed about the sward on
the banks of the river, some playing at ball, others
resting on benches or walking up and down in groups,
exercise being recommended as part of the cure. All
thronged together to watch the Earl and his captive
ride in with their suite, the household turning out to
meet them, while foremost stood a dapper little figure
with a short black cloak, a stiff round ruff, and a
square barrett cap, with a gold-headed cane in one
hand and a paper in the other.

"Prepare thy patience, Cis," whispered Barbara
Mowbray, "now shall we not be allowed to alight
from our palfreys till we have heard his full welcome

to my Lord, and all his plans for this place, how it is
to be made a sanctuary for the sick during their abode
there, for all causes saving sacrilege, treason, murder,
burglary, and highway robbery, with a license to eat
flesh on a Friday, as long as they are drinking the
waters!"

It was as Mistress Mowbray said.　Dr. Jones's
harangue on the progress of Buxton and its prospects
had always to be endured before any one was allowed
to dismount; but royalty and nobility were inured to
listening with a good grace, and Mary, though wearied
and aching, sat patiently in the hot sunshine, and was
ready to declare that Buxton put her in good humour.
In fact the grandees and their immediate attendants
endured with all the grace of good breeding; but the
farther from the scene of action, the less was the
patience, and the more restless and confused the
movements of the retinue.

Diccon Talbot, hungry and eager, had let his
equally restless pony convey him, he scarce knew
where, from his father's side, when he saw, making her
way among the horses, the very woman with the basket
whom he had encountered at Tideswell in the early
morning.　How could she have gone such a distance
in the time? thought the boy, and he presently caught
the words addressed to one of the grooms of the Scottish Queen's suite.　"Let me show my poor *beads and
bracelets.*"　The Scotsman instantly made way for her,
and she advanced to a wizened thin old Frenchman,
Maître Gorion, the Queen's surgeon, who jumped down
from his horse, and was soon bending over her basket
exchanging whispers in the lowest possible tones; but
a surge among those in the rear drove Diccon up so
near that he was absolutely certain that they were

speaking French, as indeed he well knew that M. Gorion never could succeed in making himself understood in English.

The boy, bred up in the perpetual caution and suspicion of Sheffield, was eager to denounce one who he was sure was a conspirator; but he was hemmed in among horses and men, so that he could not make his way out or see what was passing, till suddenly there was a scattering to the right and left, and a simultaneous shriek from the ladies in front.

When Diccon could see anything, his father was pressing forward to a group round some one prostrate on the ground before the house, and there were exclamations, " The poor young lady! The chirurgeon! To the front, the Queen is asking for you, sir," and Cicely's horse with loose bridle passed before his eyes.

" Let me through! let me through!" cried the boy; " it is my sister."

He threw his bridle to a groom, and, squeezing between horses and under elbows, succeeded in seeing Cis lying on the ground with her eyes shut and her head in his mother's lap, and the French surgeon bending over her. She gave a cry when he touched her arm, and he said something in his mixture of French and English, which Diccon could not hear. The Queen stood close by, a good deal agitated, anxiously asking questions, and throwing out her hands in her French fashion. Diccon, much frightened, struggled on, but only reached the party just as his father had gathered Cicely up in his arms to carry her upstairs. Diccon followed as closely as he could, but blindly in the crowd in the strange house, until he found himself in a long gallery, shut out, among various others of both sexes. " Come, my masters and mistresses all," said the voice of the seneschal, "you had best to your chambers, there is naught for you to do here."

However, he allowed Diccon to remain leaning against the balustrade of the stairs which led up out-side the house, and in another minute his father came out. "Ha, Diccon, that is well," said he. "No, thou canst not enter. They are about to undress poor little Cis. Nay, it seemed not to me that she was more hurt than thy mother could well have dealt with, but the French surgeon would thrust in, and the Queen would have it so. We will walk here in the court till we hear what he saith of her. How befell it, dost thou ask? Truly I can hardly tell, but I believe one of the Frenchmen's horses got restless, either with a fly or with standing so long to hear yonder leech's discourse. He must needs cut the beast with his rod, and so managed to hit White Posy, who starts aside, and Cis, sitting unheedfully on that new-fangled French saddle, was thrown in an instant."

"I shall laugh at her well for letting herself be thrown by a Frenchman with his switch," said Diccon.

"I hope the damage hath not been great," said his father, anxiously looking up the stair. "Where wast thou, Dick? I had lost sight of thee."

"I was seeking you, sir, for I had seen a strange sight," said Dick. "That woman who spoke with us at Tideswell was here again; yea, and she talked with the little old Frenchman that they call Gorion, the same that is with Cis now."

"She did! Folly, boy! The fellow can hardly comprehend five words of plain English together, long as he hath been here! One of the Queen's women is gone in even now to interpret for him."

" That do I wot, sir. Therefore did I marvel, and sought to tell you."

" What like was the woman ? " demanded Richard.

Diccon's description was lame, and his father bade him hasten out of the court, and fetch the woman if he could find her displaying her trinkets to the water-drinkers, instructing him not to alarm her by peremptory commands, but to give her hopes of a purchaser for her spars. Proud of the commission entrusted to him, the boy sallied forth, but though he wandered through all the groups on the sward, and encountered two tumblers and one puppet show, besides a bear and monkey, he utterly failed in finding the vendor of the beads and bracelets.

CHAPTER XIV.

THE MONOGRAMS.

WHEN Cicely had been carried into a chamber
by Master Talbot, and laid half - conscious and
moaning on the grand carved bed, Mrs. Talbot by
word and gesture expelled all superfluous spectators.
She would have preferred examining alone into the
injury sustained by the maiden, which she did not
think beyond her own management ; but there was no
refusing the services of Maître Gorion, or of Mrs.
Kennedy, who indeed treated her authoritatively,
assuming the direction of the sick-room.   She found
herself acting under their orders as she undid the
boddice, while Mrs. Kennedy ripped up the tight
sleeve of the riding dress, and laid bare the arm and
shoulder, which had been severely bruised and twisted,
but neither broken nor dislocated, as Mrs. Kennedy
informed her, after a few rapid words from the Frenchman, unintelligible to the English lady, who felt somewhat impatient of this invasion of her privileges, and
was ready to say she had never supposed any such
thing.

The chirurgeon skipped to the door, and for a
moment she hoped that she was rid of him, but he had
only gone to bring in a neat case with which his

groom was in waiting outside, whence he extracted a
lotion and sponge, speaking rapidly as he did so.

"Now, madam," said Jean Kennedy, "lift the
lassie, there, turn back her boddice, and we will bathe
her shouther.   So!   By my halidome!"

"Ah!   *Mort de ma vie!*"

The two exclamations darted simultaneously from
the lips of the Scottish nurse and the French doctor.
Susan beheld what she had at the moment forgotten,
the curious mark branded on her nursling's shoulder,
which indeed she had not seen since Cicely had been
of an age to have the care of her own person, and
which was out of the girl's own sight.   No more
was said at the moment, for Cis was reviving fast,
and was so much bewildered and frightened that she
required all the attention and soothing that the two
women could give, but when they removed the rest of
her clothing, so that she might be laid down comfortably to rest, Mrs. Kennedy by another dexterous movement uncovered enough of the other shoulder to obtain
a glimpse of the monogram upon it.

Nothing was spoken.   Those two had not been so
many years attendants on a suspected and imprisoned
queen without being prudent and cautious; but when
they quitted the apartment after administering a febri-
fuge, Susan felt a pang of wonder, whether they were
about to communicate their discovery to their mistress.
For the next quarter of an hour, the patient needed all
her attention, and there was no possibility of obeying the
summons of a great clanging bell which announced dinner.
When, however, Cis had fallen asleep it became possible
to think over the situation.   She foresaw an inquiry
and would have given much for a few words with her
husband; but reflection showed her that the one point

essential to his safety was not to betray that he and
she had any previous knowledge of the rank of their
nursling. The existence of the scroll might have to
be acknowledged, but to show that Richard had deciphered it would put him in danger on all hands.

She had just made up her mind on this point when
there was a knock at the door, and Mrs. Kennedy bore
in a salver with a cup of wine, and took from an
attendant, who remained outside, a tray with some
more solid food, which she placed on the broad edge
of the deep-set window, and coming to the bedside,
invited Mrs. Talbot to eat, while she watched the girl.
Susan complied, though with little appetite, and Mrs.
Kennedy, after standing for a few minutes in contemplation, came to the window. She was a tall woman,
her yellow hair softened by an admixture of gray, her
eyes keen and shrewd, yet capable of great tenderness
at times, her features certainly not youthful, but not
a whit more aged than they had been when Susan had
first seen her fourteen years ago. It was a quiet mouth,
and one that gave a sense of trust both in its firmness,
secrecy, and kindness.

"Madam," said she, in her soft Scotch voice,
lowered considerably, but not whispering, and with
her keen eyes fixed on Susan—"Madam, what garred
ye gie your bit lassie yonder marks? Ye need not
fear, that draught of Maister Gorion's will keep her
sleeping fast for a good hour or two longer, and it
behoves me to ken how she cam by yonder brands."

"She had them when she came to us," said Susan.

"Ye'll no persuade me that they are birth marks,"
returned Mistress Jean. "Such a thing would be a
miracle in a loyal Scottish Catholic's wean, let alone an
English heretic's."

" No," said Susan, who had in fact only made the
answer to give herself time to think whether it were
possible to summon her husband. "They never seemed
to me birth marks."

"Woman," said Jean Kennedy, laying a strong,
though soft hand, on her wrist, "this is not gear for
trifling. Is the lass your ain bairn? Ha! I always
thought she had mair of the kindly Scot than of the
Southron about her. Hech! so they made the puir
wean captive! Wha gave her till you to keep? Your
lord, I trow."

" The Lord of heaven and earth," replied Susan.
" My husband took her, the only living thing left on a
wreck off the Spurn Head."

" Hech, sirs !" exclaimed Mrs. Kennedy, evidently
much struck, but still exercising great self-command.
" And when fell this out ?"

" Two days after Low Sunday, in the year of grace
1568," returned Susan.

" My halidome !" again ejaculated Jean, in a low
voice, crossing herself. " And what became of honest
Ailie—I mean," catching herself up, " what befell those
that went with her ?"

" Not one lived," said Susan, gravely. " The mate
of my husband's ship took the little one from the arms
of her nurse, who seemed to have been left alone with
her by the crew, lashed to the wreck, and to have had
her life freshly beaten out by the winds and waves, for
she was still warm. I was then lying, at Hull, and
they brought the babe to me, while there was still time
to save her life, with God's blessing."

" And the vessel ?" asked Jean.

" My husband held it to be the *Bride of Dunbar*,
plying between that port and Harfleur."

"Ay! ay! Blessed St. Bride!" muttered Jean Kennedy, with an awe-stricken look; then, collecting herself, she added, "Were there no tokens, save these, about the little one, by which she could be known?"

"There was a gold chain with a cross, and what you call a reliquary about her little neck, and a scroll written in cipher among her swaddling bands; but they are laid up at home, at Bridgefield."

It was a perplexing situation for this simple-hearted and truthful woman, and, on the other hand, Jean Kennedy was no less devoted and loyal in her own line, a good and conscientious woman, but shrewder, and, by nature and breeding, far less scrupulous as to absolute truth.

The one idea that Susan, in her confusion, could keep hold of was that any admission of knowledge as to who her Cis really was, would be a betrayal of her husband's secret; and on the other hand she saw that Mrs. Kennedy, though most keen to discover everything, and no doubt convinced that the maiden was her Queen's child, was bent on not disclosing that fact to the foster-mother.

She asked anxiously whether Mistress Cicely knew of her being only an adopted child, and Susan replied that they had intended that she never should learn that she was of alien birth; but that it had been revealed by the old sailor who had brought her on board the *Mastiff*, though no one had heard him save young Humfrey and the girl herself, and they had been, so far as she knew, perfectly reserved on the subject.

Jean Kennedy then inquired how the name of Cicely had been given, and whether the child had been so baptized by Protestant rites.

"Wot you who the maid may be, madam?" Susan

took courage to ask; but the Scotswoman would not
be disconcerted, and replied,

"How suld I ken without a sight of the tokens?
Gin I had them, maybe I might give a guess, but there
was mony a leal Scot sairly bestead, wife and wean
and all, in her Majesty's cause that wearie spring."

Here Cis stirred in her sleep, and both women were
at her side in a moment, but she did not wake.

Jean Kennedy stood gazing at the girl with eagerness that she did not attempt to conceal, studying each
feature in detail; but Cis showed in her sleep very
little of her royal lineage, which betrayed itself far
more in her gait and bearing than in her features.
Susan could not help demanding of the nurse whether
she saw any resemblance that could show the maiden's
parentage.

The old lady gave a kind of Scotch guttural sound
expressive of disappointment, and said, "I'll no say
but I've seen the like beetle-broo. But we'll waken
the bairn with our clavers. I'll away the noo. Maister
Gorion will see her again ere night, but it were ill to
break her sleep, the puir lassie!"

Nevertheless, she could not resist bending over and
kissing the sleeper, so gently that there was no movement. Then she left the room, and Susan stood with
clasped hands.

"My child! my child! Oh, is it coming on thee?
Wilt thou be taken from me! Oh, and to what a fate!
And to what hands! They will never never love thee as
we have done! O God, protect her, and be her Father."

And Susan knelt by the bed in such a paroxysm of
grief that her husband, coming in unshod that he might
not disturb the girl, apprehended that she had become
seriously worse.

However, his entrance awoke her, and she found herself much better, and was inclined to talk, so he sat down on a chest by the bed, and related what Diccon had told him of the reappearance of the woman with the basket of spar trinkets.

"Beads and bracelets," said Cicely.

"Ay ?" said he. "What knowest thou of them ?"

"Only that she spake the words so often ; and the Queen, just ere that doctor began his speech, asked of me whether she did not sell beads and bracelets."

" 'Tis a password, no doubt, and we must be on our guard," said Richard, while his wife demanded with whom Diccon had seen her speaking.

"With Gorion," returned he. "That was what made the lad suspect something, knowing that the chirurgeon can barely speak three sentences in any tongue but his own, and those are in their barbarous Scotch. I took the boy with me and inquired here, there, and everywhere this afternoon, but could find no one who had ever seen or heard of any one like her."

"Tell me, Cis," exclaimed Susan, with a sudden conviction, "was she like in any fashion to Tibbott the huckster-woman who brought young Babington into trouble three years agone ?"

"Women's heads all run on one notion," said Richard. "Can there be no secret agents save poor Cuthbert, whom I believe to be beyond seas ?"

"Nay, but hear what saith the child ?" asked Susan.

"This woman was not nearly so old as Tibbott," said Cis, "nor did she walk with a staff, nor had she those grizzled black brows that were wont to frighten me."

"But was she tall ?" asked Susan.

" Oh yes, mother. She was very tall—she came after Diccon and me with long strides—yet it could never have been Tibbott!"

Susan had reasons for thinking otherwise, but she could not pursue the subject at that time, as she had to go down to supper with her husband, and privacy was impossible. Even at night, nobody enjoyed extensive quarters, and but for Cicely's accident she would have slept with Dyot, the tirewoman, who had arrived with the baggage, which included a pallet bed for them. However, the young lady had been carried to a chamber intended for one of Queen Mary's suite; and there it was decreed that she should remain for the night, the mother sleeping with her, while the father and son betook themselves to the room previously allotted to the family. Only on the excuse of going to take out her husband's gear from the mails was Susan able to secure a few words with him, and then by ordering out Diccon, Dyot, and the serving-man. Then she could succeed in saying, " Mine husband, all will soon out—Mistress Kennedy and Master Gorion have seen the brands on the child's shoulders. It is my belief that she of the ' beads and bracelets ' bade the chirurgeon look for them. Else, why should he have thrust himself in for a hurt that women-folk had far better have tended? Now, that kinsman of yours knew that poor Cis was none of ours, and gave her a hint of it long ago—that is, if Tibbott were he, and not something worse."

Richard shook his head. " Give a woman a hint of a seminary priest in disguise, and she would take a new-born baby for one. I tell thee I heard that Cuthbert was safe in Paris. But, be that as it may, I trust thou hast been discreet."

" So I strove to be," said Susan. " Mrs. Kennedy questioned me, and I told her."

" What ?" sharply demanded her husband.

" Nought but truth," she answered, " save that I showed no knowledge who the maid really is, nor let her guess that you had read the scroll."

" That is well. Frank Talbot was scarce within his duty when he gave me the key, and it were as much as my head were worth to be known to have been aware of the matter." To this Susan could only assent, as they were interrupted by the serving-man coming to ask directions about the bestowal of the goods.

She was relieved by this short colloquy, but it was a sad and wakeful night for her as Cicely slept by her side. Her love was too truly motherly not to be deeply troubled at the claim of one of differing religion and nation, and who had so uncertain and perilous a lot in which to place her child. There was also the sense that all her dearest, including her eldest son, were involved in the web of intrigue with persons far mightier and more unscrupulous than themselves ; and that, however they might strive to preserve their integrity, it would be very hard to avoid suspicion and danger.

In this temporary abode, the household of the Queen and of the Earl ate together, in the great hall, and thus while breaking their fast in the morning Jean Kennedy found opportunity to examine Richard Talbot on all the circumstances of the wreck of the *Bride of Dunbar*, and the finding of the babe. She was much more on her guard than the day before, and said that she had a shrewd suspicion as to who the babe's parents might be, but that she could not be certain without

seeing the reliquary and the scroll. Richard replied
that they were at home, but made no offer of sending
for them. "Nor will I do so," said he to his wife,
"unless I am dealt plainly with, and the lady herself
asks for them. Then should I have no right to detain
them."

M. Gorion would not allow his patient to leave
her room that day, and she had to remain there while
Susan was in attendance on the Queen, who did not
appear to her yet to have heard of the discovery, and
who was entering with zest into the routine of the
place, where Dr. Jones might be regarded as the
supreme legislator.

Each division of the great bath hall was fitted with
drying and dressing room, arranged commodiously according to the degree of those who were to use them. Royalty,
of course, enjoyed a monopoly, and after the hot bath,
which the Queen took immediately after rising, she
breakfasted in her own apartments, and then came
forth, according to the regimen of the place, by playing
at *Trowle Madame*. A board with arches cut in, just
big enough to permit the entrance of the balls used in
playing at bowls was placed on the turf at a convenient
distance from the player. Each arch was numbered,
from one to thirteen, but the numbers were irregularly
arranged, and the game consisted in rolling bowls into
the holes in succession, each player taking a single
turn, and the winner reaching the highest number
first,—being, in fact, a sort of lawn bagatelle. Dr.
Jones recommended it as good to stretch the rheumatic
joints of his patients, and Queen Mary, an adept at all
out-of-door games, delighted in it, though she had refused
an offer to have the lawn arranged for it at Sheffield,
saying that it would only spoil a Buxton delight. She

was still too stiff to play herself, but found infinite
amusement in teaching the new-comers the game, and
poor Susan, with her thoughts far away, was scarcely
so apt a pupil as befitted a royal mistress, especially
as she missed Mrs. Kennedy.

When she came back, she found that the dame had
been sitting with the patient, and had made herself
very agreeable to the girl by drawing out from her all
she knew of her own story from beginning to end,
having first shown that she knew of the wreck of the
Bride of Dunbar.

"And, mother," said Cis, "she says she is nearly
certain that she knows who my true parents were, and
that she could be certain if she saw the swaddling
clothes and tokens you had with me. Have you,
mother? I never knew of them."

"Yes, child, I have. We did not wish to trouble
and perturb your mind, little one, while you were content to be our daughter."

"Ah, mother, I would fain be yours and father's
still. They must not take me from you. But suppose I was some great and noble lord's daughter, and
had a great inheritance and lordship to give Humfrey!"

"Alas, child! Scottish inheritances are wont to
bring more strife than wealth."

Nevertheless, Cis went on supposing and building
castles that were pain and grief to her foreboding
auditor. That evening, however, Richard called his
wife. It was late, but the northern sunset was only
just over, and Susan could wander out with him on
the greensward in front of the Earl's house.

"So this is the tale we are to be put off with," he
said, "from the Queen herself, ay, herself, and told
with such an air of truth that it would almost make

me discredit the scroll.   She told me with one of her
sweetest smiles how a favourite kinswoman of hers
wedded in secret with a faithful follower of hers, of the
clan Hepburn.   Oh, I assure you it might have been
a ballad sung by a harper for its sadness.   Well, this
fellow ventured too far in her service, and had to flee
to France to become an archer of the guard, while the
wife remained and died at Lochleven Castle, having
given birth to our Cis, whom the Queen in due time
despatched to her father, he being minded to have her
bred up in a French nunnery, sending her to Dunbar
to be there embarked in the *Bride of Dunbar*."

"And the father?"

"Oh, forsooth, the father!   It cost her as little to
dispose of him as of the mother.   He was killed in
some brawl with the Huguenots; so that the poor child
is altogether an orphan, beholden to our care, for which
she thanked me with tears in her eyes, that were more
true than mayhap the poor woman could help."

"Poor lady," said Susan.   "Yet can it not be sooth
indeed?"

"Nay, dame, that may not be.   The cipher is not
one that would be used in simply sending a letter to
the father."

"Might not the occasion have been used for corresponding in secret with French friends?"

"I tell thee, wife, if I read one word of that letter,
I read that the child was her own, and confided to the
Abbess of Soissons!   I will read it to thee once more
ere I yield it up, that is if I ever do.   Wherefore
cannot the woman speak truth to me?   I would be
true and faithful were I trusted, but to be thus put
off with lies makes a man ready at once to ride off
with the whole to the Queen in council."

"Think, but think, dear sir," pleaded Susan, "how the poor lady is pressed, and how much she has to fear on all sides."

"Ay, because lies have been meat and drink to her, till she cannot speak a soothfast word nor know an honest man when she sees him."

"What would she have?"

"That Cis should remain with us as before, and still pass for our daughter, till such time as these negotiations are over, and she recover her kingdom. That is—so far as I see—like not to be till latter Lammas—but meantime what sayest thou, Susan? Ah! I knew, anything to keep the child with thee! Well, be it so—though if I had known the web we were to be wound into, I'd have sailed for the Indies with Humfrey long ago!"

CHAPTER XV.

MOTHER AND CHILD.

CICELY was well enough the next day to leave her room and come out on the summer's evening to enjoy the novel spectacle of Trowle Madame, in which she burned to participate, so soon as her shoulder should be well. It was with a foreboding heart that her adopted mother fell with her into the rear of the suite who were attending Queen Mary, as she went downstairs to walk on the lawn, and sit under a canopy whence she could watch either that game, or the shooting at the butts which was being carried on a little farther off.

"So, our bonnie maiden," said Mary, brightening as she caught sight of the young girl, "thou art come forth once more to rejoice mine eyes, a sight for sair een, as they say in Scotland," and she kissed the fresh cheeks with a tenderness that gave Susan a strange pang. Then she asked kindly after the hurt, and bade Cis sit at her feet, while she watched a match in archery between some of the younger attendants, now and then laying a caressing hand upon the slender figure.

"Little one," she said, "I would fain have thee to share my pillow. I have had no young bed-fellow

since Bess Pierrepoint left us. Wilt thou stoop to
come and cheer the poor old caged bird ?"

" Oh, madam, how gladly will I do so if I may!"
cried Cicely, delighted.

" We will take good care of her, Mistress Talbot,"
said Mary, " and deliver her up to you whole and sain
in the morning," and there was a quivering playfulness
in her voice.

" Your Grace is the mistress," answered Susan, with
a sadness not quite controlled.

" Ah! you mock me, madam. Would that I were !"
returned the Queen. " It is my Lord's consent that
we must ask. How say you, my Lord, may I have
this maiden for my warder at night ?"

Lord Shrewsbury was far from seeing any objection,
and the promise was given that Cis should repair to
the Queen's chamber for at least that night. She was
full of excitement at the prospect.

" Why look you so sadly at me, sweet mother ?" she
cried, as Susan made ready her hair, and assisted her in
all the arrangements for which her shoulder was still
too stiff; " you do not fear that they will hurt my arm ?"

" No, truly, my child. They have tender and skilful hands."

" May be they will tell me the story of my parents,"
said Cis; " but you need never doubt me, mother.
Though I were to prove to be ever so great a lady, no
one could ever be mine own mother like you !"

" Scarcely in love, my child," said Susan, as she
wrapped the little figure in a loose gown, and gave her
such a kiss as parents seldom permitted themselves, in
the fear of " cockering" their children, which was considered to be a most reprehensible practice. Nor could
she refrain from closely pressing Cicely's hand as they

G

passed through the corridor to the Queen's apartments,
gave the word to the two yeomen who were on guard
for the night at the head of the stairs, and tapped at
the outmost door of the royal suite of rooms.   It was
opened by a French valet ; but Mrs. Kennedy instantly advanced, took the maiden by the hand, and
with a significant smile said : " Gramercy, madam, we
will take unco gude tent of the lassie.   A fair gude
nicht to ye."   And Mrs. Talbot felt, as she put the little
hand into that of the nurse, and saw the door shut on
them, as if she had virtually given up her daughter,
and, oh ! was it for her good ?

Cis was led into the bedchamber, bright with
wax tapers, though the sky was not yet dark.   She
heard a sound as of closing and locking double
doors, while some one drew back a crimson, gold-edged
velvet curtain, which she had seen several times, and
which it was whispered concealed the shrine where
Queen Mary performed her devotions.   She had just
risen from before it, at the sound of Cis's entrance,
and two of her ladies, Mary Seaton and Marie de
Courcelles, seemed to have been kneeling with her.
She was made ready for bed, with a dark-blue velvet
gown corded round her, and her hair, now very gray,
braided beneath a little round cap, but a square of soft
cambric drapery had been thrown over her head, so as
to form a perfectly graceful veil, and shelter the features
that were aging.   Indeed, when Queen Mary wore the
exquisite smile that now lit up her face as she held out
her arms, no one ever paused to think what those
lineaments really were.   She held out her arms as
Cis advanced bashfully, and said : " Welcome, my
sweet bed-fellow, my little Scot—one more loyal subject come to me in my bondage."

Cis's impulse was to put a knee to the ground and kiss the hands that received her. "Thou art our patient," continued Mary. "I will see thee in bed ere I settle myself there." The bed was a tall, large, carved erection, with sweeping green and silver curtains, and a huge bank of lace-bordered pillows. A flight of low steps facilitated the ascent; and Cis, passive in this new scene, was made to throw off her dressing-gown and climb up.

"And now," said the Queen, "let me see the poor little shoulder that hath suffered so much."

"My arm is still bound, madam," said Cis. But she was not listened to; and Mrs. Kennedy, much to her discomfiture, turned back her under-garment. The marks were, in fact, so placed as to be entirely out of her own view, and Mrs. Susan had kept them from the knowledge or remark of any one. They were also high enough up to be quite clear from the bandages, and thus she was amazed to hear the exclamation, "There! sooth enough."

"Monsieur Gorion could swear to them instantly."

"What is it? Oh, what is it, madam?" cried Cis, affrighted; "is there anything on my back? No plague spot, I hope;" and her eyes grew round with terror.

The Queen laughed. "No plague spot, sweet one, save, perhaps, in the eyes of you Protestants, but to me they are a gladsome sight—a token I never hoped to see."

And the bewildered girl felt a pair of soft lips kiss each mark in turn, and then the covering was quickly and caressingly restored, and Mary added, "Lie down, my child, and now to bed, to bed, my maids. Put out the lights." Then, making the sign of the cross, as

Cis had seen poor Antony Babington do, the Queen, just as all the lights save one were extinguished, was divested of her wrapper and veil, and took her place beside Cis on the pillows. The two Maries left the chamber, and Jean Kennedy disposed herself on a pallet at the foot of the bed.

" And so," said the Queen, in a low voice, tender, but with a sort of banter, " she thought she had the plague spot on her little white shoulders. Didst thou really not know what marks thou bearest, little one ?"

" No, madam," said Cis. " Is it what I have felt with my fingers ?"

" Listen, child," said Mary. " Art thou at thine ease ; thy poor shoulder resting well ? There, then, give me thine hand, and I will tell thee a tale. There was a lonely castle in a lake, grim, cold, and northerly ; and thither there was brought by angry men a captive woman. They had dealt with her strangely and sub- tilly ; they had laid on her the guilt of the crimes them- selves had wrought ; and when she clung to the one man whom at least she thought honest, they had forced and driven her into wedding him, only that all the world might cry out upon her, forsake her, and deliver her up into those cruel hands."

There was something irresistibly pathetic in Mary's voice, and the maiden lay gazing at her with swimming eyes.

" Thou dost pity that poor lady, sweet one ? There was little pity for her then ! She had looked her last on her lad - bairn ; ay, and they had said she had striven to poison him, and they were breeding him up to loathe the very name of his mother ; yea, and to hate and persecute the Church of his father and his mother both. And so it was, that the lady vowed that if another babe was granted to her, sprung of that last strange miserable wedlock, these foes of hers should have no part in it, nor knowledge of its very existence, but that it should be bred up beyond their ken—safe out of their reach. Ah! child; good Nurse Kennedy can best tell thee how the jealous eyes and ears were disconcerted, and in secrecy and sorrow that birth took place."

Cis's heart was beating too fast for speech, but there was a tight close pressure of the hand that Mary had placed within hers.

"The poor mother," went on the Queen in a low trembling voice, "durst have scarce one hour's joy of her first and only daughter, ere the trusty Gorion took the little one from her, to be nursed in a hut on the other side of the lake. There," continued Mary, forgetting the third person, "I hoped to have joined her, so soon as I was afoot again. The faithful lavender lent me her garments, and I was already in the boat, but the men-at-arms were rude and would have pulled down my muffler; I raised my hand to protect myself, and it was all too white. They had not let me stain it, because the dye would not befit a washerwoman. So there was I dragged back to ward again, and all our plans overthrown. And it seemed safer and meeter to put my little one out of reach of all my foes, even if it were far away from her mother's aching heart. Not one more embrace could I be granted, but my good chaplain Ross—whom the saints rest—baptized her in secret, and Gorion had set two marks on the soft flesh, which he said could never be blotted out in after years, and then her father's clanswoman, Alison Hepburn, undertook to carry her to France, with a letter of mine bound up in her swathing clothes, committing

her to the charge of my good aunt, the Abbess of
Soissons, in utter secrecy, until better days should
come. Alas! I thought them not so far off. I
deemed that were I once beyond the clutches of
Morton, Ruthven, and the rest, the loyal would rally
once more round my standard, and my crown would
be mine own, mine enemies and those of my Church
beneath my feet. Little did I guess that my escape
would only be to see them slain and routed, and that
when I threw myself on the hospitality of my cousin,
her tender mercies would prove such as I have found
them. '*Libera me, Domine, libera me.*'"

Cis began dimly to understand, but she was still
too much awed to make any demonstration, save a
convulsive pressure of the Queen's hand, and the
murmuring of the Latin prayer distressed her.

Presently Mary resumed. "Long, long did I hope
my little one was safely sheltered from all my troubles
in the dear old cloisters of Soissons, and that it was
caution in my good aunt the abbess that prevented my
hearing of her; but through my faithful servants, my
Lord Flemyng, who had been charged to speed her from
Scotland, at length let me know that the ship in which
she sailed, the *Bride of Dunbar*, had been never heard
of more, and was thought to have been cast away in a
tempest that raged two days after she quitted Dunbar. And I——I shed some tears, but I could well
believe that the innocent babe had been safely welcomed among the saints, and I could not grieve that
she was, as I thought, spared from the doom that
rests upon the race of Stewart. Till one week back,
I gave thanks for that child of sorrow as cradled in
Paradise."

Then followed a pause, and then Cis said in a low

trembling voice, "And it was from the wreck of the *Bride of Dunbar* that I was taken?"

"Thou hast said it, child! My bairn, my bonnie bairn!" and the girl was absorbed in a passionate embrace and strained convulsively to a bosom which heaved with the sobs of tempestuous emotion, and the caresses were redoubled upon her again and again with increasing fervour that almost frightened her.

"Speak to me! Speak to me! Let me hear my child's voice."

"Oh, madam——"

"Call me mother! Never have I heard that sound from my child's lips. I have borne two children, two living children, only to be stripped of both. Speak, child—let me hear thee."

Cis contrived to say "Mother, my mother," but scarcely with effusion. It was all so strange, and she could not help feeling as if Susan were the mother she knew and was at ease with. All this was much too like a dream, from which she longed to awake. And there was Mrs. Kennedy too, rising up and crying quite indignantly—"Mother indeed! Is that all thou hast to say, as though it were a task under the rod, when thou art owned for her own bairn by the fairest and most ill-used queen in Christendom? Out on thee! Have the Southron loons chilled thine heart and made thee no leal to thine ain mother that hath hungered for thee?"

The angry tones, and her sense of her own short-comings, could only make Cis burst into tears.

"Hush, hush, nurse! thou shalt not chide my new-found bairn. She will learn to ken us better in time if they will leave her with us," said Mary. "There, there; greet not so sair, mine ain. I ask

thee not to share my sorrows and my woes. That
Heaven forefend. I ask thee but to come from time
to time and cheer my nights, and lie on my weary
bosom to still its ache and yearning, and let me feel
that I have indeed a child."

"Oh, mother, mother!" Cis cried again in a stifled
voice, as one who could not utter her feelings, but not
in the cold dry tone that had called forth Mrs.
Kennedy's wrath. "Pardon me, I know not—I
cannot say what I would. But oh! I would do anything for—for your Grace."

"All that I would ask of thee is to hold thy peace
and keep our counsel. Be Cicely Talbot by day as
ever. Only at night be mine—my child, my Bride,
for so wast thou named after our Scottish patroness.
It was a relic of her sandals that was hung about thy
neck, and her ship in which thou didst sail; and lo, she
heard and guarded thee, and not merely saved thee from
death, but provided thee a happy joyous home and
well-nurtured childhood. We must render her our
thanks, my child. *Beata Brigitta, ora pro nobis.*"

"It was the good God Almighty who saved me,
madam," said Cis bluntly.

"Alack! I forgot that yonder good lady could
not fail to rear thee in the outer darkness of her
heresy; but thou wilt come back to us, my ain wee
thing! Heaven forbid that I should deny Whose Hand
it was that saved thee, but it was at the blessed
Bride's intercession. No doubt she reserved for me,
who had turned to her in my distress, this precious
consolation! But I will not vex thy little heart with
debate this first night. To be mother and child is
enough for us. What art thou pondering?"

"Only, madam, who was it that told your Grace
that I was a stranger?"

"The marks, bairnie, the marks," said Mary. "They told their own tale to good Nurse Jeanie; ay, and to Gorion, whom we blamed for his cruelty in branding my poor little lammie."

"Ah! but," said Cicely, "did not yonder woman with the beads and bracelets bid him look?"

If it had been lighter, Cicely would have seen that the Queen was not pleased at the inquiry, but she only heard the answer from Jean's bed, "Hout no, I wad she knew nought of thae brands. How should she?"

"Nay," said Cicely, "she—no, it was Tibbott the huckster-woman told me long ago that I was not what I seemed, and that I came from the north—I cannot understand! Were they the same?"

"The bairn kens too much," said Jean. "Dinna ye deave her Grace with your speirings, my lammie. Ye'll have to learn to keep a quiet sough, and to see mickle ye canna understand here."

"Silence her not, good nurse," said the Queen, "it imports us to know this matter. What saidst thou of Tibbott?"

"She was the woman who got Antony Babington into trouble," explained Cicely. "I deemed her a witch, for she would hint strange things concerning me, but my father always believed she was a kinsman of his, who was concerned in the Rising of the North, and who, he said, had seen me brought in to Hull from the wreck."

"Ay?" said the Queen, as a sign to her to continue.

"And meseemed," added Cicely timidly, "that the strange woman at Tideswell who talked of beads and bracelets minded me of Tibbott, though she was

G*

younger, and had not her grizzled brows; but father says that cannot be, for Master Cuthbert Langston is beyond seas at Paris."

"Soh! that is well," returned Mary, in a tone of relief. "See, child. That Langston of whom you speak· was a true friend of mine. He has done much for me under many disguises, and at the time of thy birth he lived as a merchant at Hull, trading with Scotland. Thus it may have become known to him that the babe he had seen rescued from the wreck was one who had been embarked at Dunbar. But no more doth he know. The secret of thy birth, my poor bairn, was entrusted to none save a few of those about me, and all of those who are still living thou hast already seen. Lord Flemyng, who put thee on board, believed thee the child of James Hepburn of Lillieburn, the archer, and of my poor Mary Stewart, a kinswoman of mine ain; and it was in that belief doubtless that he, or Tibbott, as thou call'st him, would have spoken with thee."

"But the woman at Tideswell," said Cis, who was getting bewildered—"Diccon said that she spake to Master Gorion."

"That did she, and pointed thee out to him. It is true. She is another faithful friend of mine, and no doubt she had the secret from him. But no more questions, child. Enough that we sleep in each other's arms."

It was a strange night. Cis was more conscious of wonder, excitement, and a certain exultation, than of actual affection. She had not been bred up so as to hunger and crave for love. Indeed she had been treated with more tenderness and indulgence than was usual with people's own daughters, and her adopted parents had absorbed her undoubting love and respect.

Queen Mary's fervent caresses were at least as embarrassing as they were gratifying, because she did not know what response to make, and the novelty and wonder of the situation were absolutely distressing.

They would have been more so but for the Queen's tact. She soon saw that she was overwhelming the girl, and that time must be given for her to become accustomed to the idea. So, saying tenderly something about rest, she lay quietly, leaving Cis, as she supposed, to sleep. This, however, was impossible to the girl, except in snatches which made her have to prove to herself again and again that it was not all a dream. The last of these wakenings was by daylight, as full as the heavy curtains would admit, and she looked up into a face that was watching her with such tender wistfulness that it drew from her perforce the word " Mother."

" Ah! that is the tone with the true ring in it. I thank thee and I bless thee, my bairn," said Mary, making over her the sign of the cross, at which the maiden winced as at an incantation. Then she added, " My little maid, we must be up and stirring. Mind, no word of all this. Thou art Cicely Talbot by day, as ever, and only my child, my Bride, mine ain wee thing, my princess by night. Canst keep counsel?"

" Surely, madam," said Cis, " I have known for five years that I was a foundling on the wreck, and I never uttered a word."

Mary smiled. " This is either a very simple child or a very canny one," she said to Jean Kennedy. " Either she sees no boast in being of royal blood, or she deems that to have the mother she has found is worse than the. being the nameless foundling."

" Oh! madam, mother, not so! I meant but that I had held my tongue when I had something to tell!"

"Let thy secrecy stand thee in good stead, child,"
said the Queen. "Remember that did the bruit once
get abroad, thou wouldest assuredly be torn from
me, to be mewed up where the English Queen could
hinder thee from ever wedding living man. Ay, and
it might bring the head of thy foster-father to the
block, if he were thought to have concealed the matter.
I fear me thou art too young for such a weighty secret."

"I am seventeen years old, madam," returned Cis,
with dignity; "I have kept the other secret since I
was twelve."

"Then thou wilt, I trust, have the wisdom not to
take the princess on thee, nor to give any suspicion that
we are more to one another than the caged bird and
the bright linnet that comes to sing on the bars of
her cage. Only, child, thou must get from Master
Talbot these tokens that I hear of. Hast seen them?"

"Never, madam; indeed I knew not of them."

"I need them not to know thee for mine own, but
it is not well that they should be in stranger hands.
Thou canst say—But hush, we must be mum for the
present."

For it became necessary to admit the Queen's
morning draught of spiced milk, borne in by one of
her suite who had to remain uninitiated; and from
that moment no more confidences could be exchanged,
until the time that Cis had to leave the Queen's
chamber to join the rest of the household in the daily
prayers offered in the chapel. Her dress and hair had,
according to promise, been carefully attended to, but
she was only finished and completed just in time to
join her adopted parents on the way down the stairs.
She knelt in the hall for their blessing—an action as
regular and as mechanical as the morning kiss and

greeting now are between parent and child; but there
was something in her face that made Susan say to
herself, " She knows all."

They could not speak to one another till not only
matins but breakfast were ended, and then—after the
somewhat solid meal—the ladies had to put on their
out-of-door gear to attend Queen Mary in her daily
exercise.   The dress was not much, high summer as it
was, only a loose veil over the stiff cap, and a fan in
the gloved hand to act as parasol.   However the
retirement gave Cicely an interval in which to say,
" O mother, she has told me," and as Susan sat holding
out her arms, the adopted child threw herself on her
knees, hiding her face on that bosom where she had
found comfort all her life, and where, her emotion at
last finding full outlet, she sobbed without knowing
why for some moments, till she started nervously at
the entrance of Richard, saying, " The Queen is asking
for you both.   But how now ?   Is all told ?"

" Ay," whispered his wife.

" So!   And why these tears ?   Tell me, my maid,
was not she good to thee ?   Doth she seek to take thee
into her own keeping ?"

" Oh no, sir, no," said Cis, still kneeling against the
motherly knee and struggling with her sobs.   " No one
is to guess.   I am to be Cicely Talbot all the same,
till better days come to her."

" The safer and the happier for thee, child.   Here
are two honest hearts that will not cast thee off, even
if, as I suspect, yonder lady would fain be quit of thee."

" Oh no!" burst from Cicely, then, shocked at
having committed the offence of interrupting him, she
added, "Dear sir, I crave your pardon, but, indeed, she
is all fondness and love."

" Then what means this passion ?" he asked, looking from one to the other.

" It means only that the child's senses and spirits are overcome," said Susan, " and that she scarce knows how to take this discovery.   Is it not so, sweetheart ?"

" Oh, sweet mother, yes in sooth.   You will ever be mother to me indeed !"

" Well said, little maid !" said Richard.   " Thou mightest search the world over and never hap upon such another."

" But she oweth duty to the true mother," said Susan, with her hand on the girl's neck.

" We wot well of that," answered her husband, " and I trow the first is to be secret."

" Yea, sir," said Cis, recovering herself, " none save the very few who tended her, the Queen at Lochleven, know who I verily am.   Such as were aware of the babe being put on board ship at Dunbar, thought me the daughter of a Scottish archer, a Hepburn, and she, the Queen my mother, would have me pass as such to those who needs must know I am not myself."

" Trust her for making a double web when a single one would do," muttered Richard, but so that the girl could not hear.

" There is no need for any to know at present," said Susan hastily, moved perhaps by the same dislike to deception ; " but ah, there's that fortune-telling woman."

Cis, proud of her secret information, here explained that Tibbott was indeed Cuthbert Langston, but not the person whose password was " beads and bracelets," and that both alike could know no more than the story of the Scottish archer and his young wife ; but they were here interrupted by the appearance of Diccon, who had been sent by my Lord himself to hasten them.

at the instance of the Queen. Master Richard sent the boy on with his mother, saying he would wait and bring Cis, as she had still to compose her hair and coif, which had become somewhat disordered.

"My maiden," he said, gravely, "I have somewhat to say unto thee. Thou art in a stranger case than any woman of thy years between the four seas; nay, it may be in Christendom. It is woeful hard for thee not to be a traitor through mere lapse of tongue to thine own mother, or else to thy Queen. So I tell thee this once for all. See as little, hear as little, and, above all, say as little as thou canst."

"Not to mother?" asked Cis.

"No, not to her, above all not to me; and, my girl, pray God daily to keep thee true and loyal, and guard thee and the rest of us from snares. Now have with thee. We may tarry no longer!"

All went as usual for the rest of the day, so that the last night was like a dream, until it became plain that Cicely was again to share the royal apartment.

"Ah, I have thirsted for this hour!" said Mary, holding out her arms and drawing her daughter to her bosom. "Thou art a canny lassie, mine ain wee thing. None could have guessed from thy bearing that there was aught betwixt us."

"In sooth, madam," said the girl, "it seems that I am two maidens in one—Cis Talbot by day, and Bride of Scotland by night."

"That is well! Be all Cis Talbot by day. When there is need to dissemble, believe in thine own feigning. 'Tis for want of that art that these clumsy Southrons make themselves but a laughing-stock whenever they have a secret."

Cis did not understand the maxim, and submitted

in silence to some caresses before she said, "My father
will give your Grace the tokens when we return."

"Thy father, child?"

"I crave your pardon, madam, it comes too trip-
pingly to my tongue thus to term Master Talbot."

"So much the better. Thy tongue must not lose
the trick. I did but feel a moment's fear lest thou
hadst not been guarded enough with yonder sailor
man, and had let him infer over much."

"O, surely, madam, you never meant me to withhold the truth from father and mother," cried Cis, in
astonishment and dismay.

"Tush! silly maid!" said the Queen, really angered.
"Father and mother, forsooth! Now shall we have a
fresh coil! I should have known better than to have
trusted thy word."

"Never would I have given my word to deceive
them," cried Cis, hotly.

"Lassie!" exclaimed Jean Kennedy, "ye forget to
whom ye speak."

"Nay," said Mary, recovering herself, or rather seeing how best to punish, "'tis the poor bairn who will
be the sufferer. Our state cannot be worse than it is
already, save that I shall lose her presence, but it
pities me to think of her."

"The secret is safe with them," repeated Cis. "O
madam, none are to be trusted like them."

"Tell me not," said the Queen. "The sailor's
blundering loyalty will not suffer him to hold his
tongue. I would lay my two lost crowns that he is
down on his honest knees before my Lord craving pardon for having unwittingly fostered one of the viper
brood. Then, *via!* off goes a post——boots and spurs are
no doubt already on——and by and by comes Knollys,

or Carey, or Walsingham, to bear off the perilous
maiden to walk in Queen Bess's train, and have her
ears boxed when her Majesty is out of humour, or
when she gets weary of dressing St. Katherine's hair,
and weds the man of her choice, she begins to taste
of prison walls, and is a captive for the rest of her
days."

Cis was reduced to tears, and assurances that if
the Queen would only broach the subject to Master
Richard, she would perceive that he regarded as sacred,
secrets that were not his own ; and to show that he
meant no betrayal, she repeated his advice as to seeing,
hearing, and saying as little as possible.

"Wholesome counsel !" said Mary. "Cheer thee,
lassie mine, I will credit whatever thou wilt of this
foster-father of thine until I see it disproved ; and for
the good lady his wife, she hath more inward, if less
outward, grace than any dame of the mastiff brood
which guards our prison .court ! I should have
warned thee that they were not excepted from those
who may deem thee my poor Mary's child."

Cicely did not bethink herself that, in point of fact,
she had not communicated her royal birth to her
adopted parents, but that it had been assumed between
them, as, indeed, they had not mentioned their previous
knowledge. Mary presently proceeded—" After all,
we may not have to lay too heavy a burden on their
discretion. Better days are coming. One day shall
our faithful lieges open the way to freedom and royalty,
and thou shalt have whatever boon thou wouldst ask,
even were it pardon for my Lady Shrewsbury."

"There is one question I would fain ask, Madam
mother : Doth my real father yet live ? The Earl
of——"

Jean Kennedy made a sound of indignant warning
and consternation, cutting her short in dismay; but
the Queen gripped her hand tightly for some moments,
and then said : " 'Tis not a thing to speir of me, child,
of me, the most woefully deceived and forlorn of ladies.
Never have I seen nor heard from him since the parting at Carbery Hill, when he left me to bear the
brunt! Folk say that he took ship for the north.
Believe him dead, child. So were it best for us both ;
but never name him to me more."

Jean Kennedy knew, though the girl did not, what
these words conveyed. If Bothwell no longer lived,
there would be no need to declare the marriage null
and void, and thus sacrifice his daughter's position ;
but supposing him to be in existence, Mary had
already shown herself resolved to cancel the very
irregular bonds which had united them,—a most
easy matter for a member of her Church, since they
had been married by a Reformed minister, and Bothwell had a living wife at the time. Of all this Cicely
was absolutely ignorant, and was soon eagerly listening
as the Queen spoke of her hopes of speedy deliverance.
" My son, my Jamie, is working for me !" she said.
" Nay, dost not ken what is in view for me ?"

" No, madam, my good father, Master Richard, I
mean, never tells aught that he hears in my Lord's
closet."

" That is to assure me of his discretion, I trow !
But this is no secret ! No treason against our well-
beloved cousin Bess ! Oh no ! But thy brother, mine
ain lad-bairn, hath come to years of manhood, and
hath shaken himself free of the fetters of Knox and
Morton and Buchanan, and all their clamjamfrie.
The Stewart lion hath been too strong for them. The

puir laddie hath true men about him, at last,— the
Master of Gray, as they call him, and Esmé Stewart of
Aubigny, a Scot polished as the French know how
to brighten Scottish steel.　Nor will the lad bide
that his mother should pine longer in durance.　He
yearns for her, and hath writ to her and to Elizabeth
offering her a share in his throne.　Poor laddie, what
would be *outrecuidance* in another is but duteousness
in him.　What will he say when we bring him a
sister as well as a mother?　They tell me that he is
an unco scholar, but uncouth in his speech and manners, and how should it be otherwise with no woman
near him save my old Lady Mar?　We shall have to
take him in hand to teach him fair courtesy."

"Sure he will be an old pupil!" said Cis, "if he be
more than two years my elder."

"Never fear, if we can find a winsome young bride
for him, trust mother, wife, and sister for moulding
him to kingly bearing.　We will make our home in
Stirling or Linlithgow, we two, and leave Holyrood to
him.　I have seen too much there ever to thole the
sight of those chambers, far less of the High Street of
Edinburgh; but Stirling, bonnie Stirling, ay, I would
fain ride a hawking there once more.　Methinks a
Highland breeze would put life and youth into me
again.　There's a little chamber opening into mine,
where I will bestow thee, my Lady Bride of Scotland, for so long as I may keep thee.　Ah! it will not
be for long.　They will be seeking thee, my brave
courtly faithful kindred of Lorraine, and Scottish
nobles and English lords will vie for this little hand
of thine, where courses the royal blood of both realms."

"So please you, madam, my mother——"

"Eh?　What is it?　Who is it?　I deemed that

yonder honourable dame had kept thee from all the
frolics and foibles of the poor old profession. Fear
not to tell me, little one. Remember thine own
mother hath a heart for such matters. I guess
already. *C'etait un beau garçon, ce pauvre Antoine.*"

"Oh no, madam," exclaimed Cicely. "When the
sailor Goatley disclosed that I was no child of my
father's, of Master Richard I mean, and was a nameless
creature belonging to no one, Humfrey Talbot stood
forth and pledged himself to wed me so soon as we
were old enough."

"And what said the squire and dame?"

"That I should then be indeed their daughter."

"And hath the contract gone no farther?"

"No, madam. He hath been to the North with
Captain Frobisher, and since that to the Western Main,
and we look for his return even now."

"How long is it since this pledge, as thou callest
it, was given?"

"Five years next Lammas tide, madam."

"Was it by ring or token?"

"No, madam. Our mother said we were too young,
but Humfrey meant it with all his heart."

"Humfrey! That was the urchin who must
needs traverse the correspondence through the seeming
Tibbott, and so got Antony removed from about us.
A stout lubberly Yorkshire lad, fed on beef and pudding, a true Talbot, a mere English bull-dog who will
have lost all the little breeding he had, while committing spulzie and piracy at sea on his Catholic Majesty's
ships. Bah, *mon enfant*, I am glad of it. Had he
been a graceful young courtly page like the poor
Antony, it might have been a little difficult, but a
great English carle like that, whom thou hast not seen

for five years——" She made a gesture with her graceful hands as if casting away a piece of thistledown.

"Humfrey is my very good—my very good brother,
madam," cried Cicely, casting about for words to
defend him, and not seizing the most appropriate.

"Brother, quotha? Yea, and as good brother he shall
be to thee, and welcome, so long as thou art Cis Talbot
by day—but no more, child. Princesses mate not with
Yorkshire esquires. When the Lady Bride takes her
place in the halls of her forefathers, she will be the
property of Scotland, and her hand will be sought by
princes. Ah, lassie! let it not grieve thee. One thing
thy mother can tell thee from her own experience.
There is more bliss in mating with our equals, by the
choice of others, than in following our own wild will.
Thou gazest at me in wonder, but verily my happy
days were with my gentle young king—and so will
thine be, I pray the saints happier and more endur-
ing than ever were mine. Nothing has ever lasted
with me but captivity, *O libera me.*"

And in the murmured repetition the mother fell
asleep, and the daughter, who had slumbered little the
night before, could not but likewise drop into the
world of soothing oblivion, though with a dull feeling
of aching and yearning towards the friendly kindly
Humfrey, yet with a certain exultation in the fate
that seemed to be carrying her on inevitably beyond
his reach.

CHAPTER XVI.

THE PEAK CAVERN.

IT was quite true that at this period Queen Mary had good hope of liberation in the most satisfactory manner possible——short of being hailed as English Queen. Negotiations were actually on foot with James VI. and Elizabeth for her release. James had written to her with his own hand, and she had for the first time consented to give him the title of King of Scotland. The project of her reigning jointly with him had been mooted, and each party was showing how enormous a condescension it would be in his or her eyes! Thus there was no great unlikelihood that there would be a recognition of the Lady Bride, and that she would take her position as the daughter of a queen. Therefore, when Mary contrived to speak to Master Richard Talbot and his wife in private, she was able to thank them with gracious condescension for the care they had bestowed in rearing her daughter, much as if she had voluntarily entrusted the maiden to them, saying she trusted to be in condition to reward them.

Mistress Susan's heart swelled high with pain, as though she had been thanked for her care of Humfrey or Diccon, and her husband answered, " We seek

no reward, madam. The damsel herself, while she
was ours, was reward enough."

"And I must still entreat, that of your goodness
you will let her remain yours for a little longer," said
Mary, with a touch of imperious grace, "until this
treaty is over, and I am free, it is better that she con-
tinues to pass for your daughter. The child herself
has sworn to me by her great gods," said Mary, smiling with complimentary grace, "that you will preserve her secret—nay, she becomes a little fury when
I express my fears lest you should have scruples."

"No, madam, this is no state secret; such as I
might not with honour conceal," returned Richard.

"There is true English sense!" exclaimed Mary.
"I may then count on your giving my daughter the
protection of your name and your home until I can
reclaim her and place her in her true position. Yea,
and if your concealment should give offence, and bring
you under any displeasure of my good sister, those who
have so saved and tended my daughter will have the
first claim to whatever I can give when restored to
my kingdom."

"We are much beholden for your Grace's favour,"
said Richard, somewhat stiffly, "but I trust never to
serve any land save mine own."

"Ah! there is your *fièreté*," cried Mary. "Happy
is my sister to have subjects with such a point of
honour. Happy is my child to have been bred up by
such parents!"

Richard bowed. It was all a man could do at such
a speech, and Mary further added, "She has told me
to what bounds went your goodness to her. It is well
that you acted so prudently that the children's hearts
were not engaged; for, as we all know but too well,
royal blood should have no heart."

"I am quite aware of it, madam," returned Richard, and there for the time the conversation ended. The Queen had been most charming, full of gratitude, and perfectly reasonable in her requests, and yet there was some flaw in the gratification of both, even while neither thought the disappointment would go very hard with their son. Richard could never divest himself of the instinctive prejudice with which soft words inspire men of his nature, and Susan's maternal heart was all in revolt against the inevitable, not merely grieving over the wrench to her affections, but full of forebodings and misgivings as to the future welfare of her adopted child. Even if the brightest hopes should be fulfilled; the destiny of a Scottish princess did not seem to Southern eyes very brilliant at the best, and whether poor Bride Hepburn might be owned as a princess at all was a doubtful matter, since, if her father lived (and he had certainly been living in 1577 in Norway), both the Queen and the Scottish people would be agreed in repudiating the marriage. Any way, Susan saw every reason to fear for the happiness and the religion alike of the child to whom she had given a mother's love. Under her grave, self-contained placid demeanour, perhaps Dame Susan was the most dejected of those at Buxton. The captive Queen had her hopes of freedom and her newly found daughter, who was as yet only a pleasure, and not an encumbrance to her, the Earl had been assured that his wife's slanders had been forgotten. He was secure of his sovereign's favour, and permitted to see the term of his weary jailorship, and thus there was an unusual liveliness and cheerfulness about the whole sojourn at Buxton, where, indeed, there was always more or less of a holiday time.

To Cis herself, her nights were like a perpetual fairy tale, and so indeed were all times when she was alone with the initiated, who were indeed all those original members of her mother's suite who had known of her birth at Lochleven, people who had kept too many perilous secrets not to be safely entrusted with this one, and whose finished habits of caution, in a moment, on the approach of a stranger, would change their manner from the deferential courtesy due to their princess, to the good-natured civility of court ladies to little Cicely Talbot.

Dame Susan had been gratified at first by the young girl's sincere assurances of unchanging affection and allegiance, and, in truth, Cis had clung the most to her with the confidence of a whole life's daughterhood, but as the days went on, and every caress and token of affection imaginable was lavished upon the maiden, every splendid augury held out to her of the future, and every story of the past detailed the charms of Mary's court life in France, seen through the vista of nearly twenty sadly contrasted years, it was in the very nature of things that Cis should regard the time spent perforce with Mistress Talbot much as a petted child views its return to the strict nurse or governess from the delights of the drawing-room. She liked to dazzle the homely housewife with the wonderful tales of French gaieties, or the splendid castles in the air she had heard in the Queen's rooms, but she resented the doubt and disapproval they sometimes excited; she was petulant and fractious at any exercise of authority from her foster-mother, and once or twice went near to betray herself by lapsing into a tone towards her which would have brought down severe personal chastisement on any real daughter even of seventeen.

It was well that the Countess and her sharp-eyed daughter Mary were out of sight, as the sight of such " cockering of a malapert maiden " would have led to interference that might have brought matters to extremity.   Yet, with all the forbearance thus exercised, Susan could not but feel that the girl's love was being weaned from her; and, after all, how could she complain, since it was by the true mother ?   If only she could have hoped it was for the dear child's good, it would not have been so hard !   But the trial was a bitter one, and not even her husband guessed how bitter it was.

The Queen meantime improved daily in health and vigour in the splendid summer weather.   The rheumatism had quitted her, and she daily rode and played at Trowle Madame for hours after supper in the long bright July evenings.   Cis, whose shoulder was quite well, played with great delight on the greensward, where one evening she made acquaintance with a young esquire and his sisters from the neighbourhood, who had come with their father to pay their respects to my Lord Earl, as the head of all Hallamshire.   The Earl, though it was not quite according to the recent stricter rules, ventured to invite them to stay to sup with the household, and afterwards they came out with the rest upon the lawn.

Cis was walking between the young lad and his sister, laughing and talking with much animation, for she had not for some time enjoyed the pleasure of free intercourse with any of her fellow-denizens in the happy land of youth.

Dame Susan watched her with some uneasiness, and presently saw her taking them where she herself was privileged to go, but strangers were never permitted

to approach, on the Trowle Madame sward reserved
for the Queen, on which she was even now entering.

"Cicely!" she called, but the young lady either
did not or would not hear, and she was obliged to walk
hastily forward, meet the party, and with courteous
excuses turn them back from the forbidden ground.
They submitted at once, apologising, but Cis, with a
red spot on her cheek, cried, "The Queen would take
no offence."

"That is not the matter in point, Cicely," said
Dame Susan gravely. "Master and Mistress Eyre
understand that we are bound to obedience to the Earl."

Master Eyre, a well-bred young gentleman, made
reply that he well knew that no discourtesy was
intended, but Cis pouted and muttered, evidently to
the extreme amazement of Mistress Alice Eyre; and
Dame Susan, to divert her attention, began to ask
about the length of their ride, and the way to their
home.

Cis's ill humour never lasted long, and she suddenly
broke in, "O mother, Master Eyre saith there is a
marvellous cavern near his father's house, all full of
pendants from the roof like a minster, and great
sheeted tables and statues standing up, all grand and
ghostly on the floor, far better than in this Pool's Hole.
He says his father will have it lighted up if we will
ride over and see it."

"We are much beholden to Master Eyre," said
Susan, but Cis read refusal in her tone, and began to
urge her to consent.

"It must be as my husband wills," was the grave
answer, and at the same time, courteously, but very
decidedly, she bade the strangers farewell, and made
her daughter do the same, though Cis was inclined to

resistance, and in a somewhat defiant tone added, " I shall not forget your promise, sir. I long to see the cave."

" Child, child," entreated Susan, as soon as they were out of hearing, " be on thy guard. Thou wilt betray thyself by such conduct towards me."

" But, mother, they did so long to see the Queen, and there would have been no harm in it. They are well affected, and the young gentleman is a friend of poor Master Babington."

" Nay, Cis, that is further cause that I should not let them pass onward. I marvel not at thee, my maid, but thou and thy mother queen must bear in mind that while thou passest for our daughter, and hast trust placed in thee, thou must do nothing to forfeit it or bring thy fa——, Master Richard I mean, into trouble."

" I meant no harm," said Cis, rather crossly.

" Thou didst not, but harm may be done by such as mean it the least."

" Only, mother, sweet mother," cried the girl, child-like, set upon her pleasure, " I will be as good as can be. I will transgress in nought if only thou wilt get my father to take me to see Master Eyre's cavern."

She was altogether the home daughter again in her eagerness, entreating and promising by turns with the eager curiosity of a young girl bent on an expedition, but Richard was not to be prevailed on. He had little or no acquaintance with the Eyre family, and to let them go to the cost and trouble of lighting up the cavern for the young lady's amusement would be like the encouragement of a possible suit, which would have been a most inconvenient matter. Richard did not believe the young gentleman had warrant from his

father in giving this invitation, and if he had, that was
the more reason for declining it.   The Eyres, then holding the royal castle of the Peak, were suspected of being
secretly Roman Catholics, and though the Earl could
not avoid hospitably bidding them to supper, the less
any Talbot had to do with them the better, and for the
present Cis must be contented to be reckoned as one.

So she had to put up with her disappointment, and
she did not do so with as good a grace as she would
have shown a year ago.   Nay, she carried it to Queen
Mary, who at night heard her gorgeous description of
the wonders of the cavern, which grew in her estima-
tion in proportion to the difficulty of seeing them, and
sympathised with her disappointment at the denial.

"Nay, thou shalt not be balked," said Mary, with
the old queenly habit of having her own way.
"Prisoner as I am, I will accomplish this.   My
daughter shall have her wish."

So on the ensuing morning, when the Earl came to
pay his respects, Mary assailed him with, "There is a
marvellous cavern in these parts, my Lord, of which I
hear great wonders."

"Does your grace mean Pool's Hole?"

"Nay, nay, my Lord.   Have I not been conducted
through it by Dr. Jones, and there writ my name for
his delectation?   This is, I hear, as a palace compared
therewith."

"The Peak Cavern, Madam!" said Lord Shrewsbury,
with the distaste of middle age for underground expeditions, " is four leagues hence, and a dark, damp, doleful
den, most noxious for your Grace's rheumatism."

"Have you ever seen it, my Lord?"

"No, verily," returned his lordship with a shudder.

"Then you will be edified yourself, my Lord, if you

will do me the grace to escort me thither," said Mary,
with the imperious suavity she well knew how to
adopt.

"Madam, madam," cried the unfortunate Earl, "do
but consult your physicians. They will tell you that all
the benefits of the Buxton waters will be annulled by
an hour in yonder subterranean hole."

"I have heard of it from several of my suite," replied Mary, "and they tell me that the work of nature
on the lime-droppings is so marvellous that I shall not
rest without a sight of it. Many have been instant
with me to go and behold the wondrous place."

This was not untrue, but she had never thought of
gratifying them in her many previous visits to Buxton.
The Earl found himself obliged either to utter a harsh
and unreasonable refusal, or to organise an expedition
which he personally disliked extremely, and moreover
distrusted, for he did not in the least believe that
Queen Mary would be so set upon gratifying her curiosity about stalactites without some ulterior motive.
He tried to set on Dr. Jones to persuade Messieurs
Gorion and Bourgoin, her medical attendants, that
the cave would be fatal to her rheumatism, but it so
happened that the Peak Cavern was Dr. Jones's
favourite lion, the very pride of his heart. Pool's Hole
was dear to him, but the Peak Cave was far more
precious, and the very idea of the Queen of Scots
honouring it with her presence, and leaving behind her
the flavour of her name, was so exhilarating to the
little man that if the place had been ten times more
damp he would have vouched for its salubrity. Moreover, he undertook that fumigations of fragrant woods
should remove all peril of noxious exhalations, so that
the Earl was obliged to give his orders that Mr.

Eyre should be requested to light up the cave, and heartily did he grumble and pour forth his suspicions and annoyance to his cousin Richard.

"And I," said the good sailor, "felt it hard not to be able to tell him that all was for the freak of a silly damsel."

Mistress Cicely laughed a little triumphantly. It was something like being a Queen's daughter to have been the cause of making my Lord himself bestir himself against his will. She had her own way, and might well be good-humoured. "Come, dear sir father," she said, coming up to him in a coaxing, patronising way, which once would have been quite alien to them both, "be not angered. You know nobody means treason! And, after all, 'tis not I but you that are the cause of all the turmoil. If you would but have ridden soberly out with your poor little Cis, there would have been no coil, but my Lord might have paced stately and slow up and down the terrace-walk undisturbed."

"Ah, child, child!" said Susan, vexed, though her husband could not help smiling at the arch drollery of the girl's tone and manner, "do not thou learn light mockery of all that should be honoured."

"I am not bound to honour the Earl," said Cis, proudly.

"Hush, hush!" said Richard. "I have allowed thee unchecked too long, maiden. Wert thou ten times what thou art, it would not give thee the right to mock at the gray-haired, highly-trusted noble, the head of the name thou dost bear."

"And the torment of her whom I am most bound to love," broke from Cicely petulantly.

Richard's response to this sally was to rise up,

make the young lady the lowest possible reverence,
with extreme and displeased gravity, and then to quit
the room.   It brought the girl to her bearings at once.
" Oh, mother, mother, how have I displeased him ?"

" I trow thou canst not help it, child," said Susan,
sadly ; " but it is hard that thou shouldst bring home
to us how thine heart and thine obedience are parted
from us."

The maiden was in a passion of tears at once,
vowing that she meant no such thing, that she loved
and obeyed them as much as ever, and that if only
her father would forgive her she would never wish to
go near the cavern.   She would beg the Queen to give
up the plan at once, if only Sir Richard would be her
good father as before.

Susan looked at her sadly and tenderly, but smiled,
and said that what had been lightly begun could not
now be dropped, and that she trusted Cis would be
happy in the day's enjoyment, and remember to be-
have herself as a discreet maiden.   " For truly," said
she, " so far from discretion being to be despised by
Queen's daughters, the higher the estate the greater the
need thereof."

This little breeze did not prevent Cicely from setting
off in high spirits, as she rode near the Queen, who
declared that she wanted to enjoy *through* the merry
maiden, and who was herself in a gay and joyous mood,
believing that the term of her captivity was in sight,
delighted with her daughter, exhilarated by the fresh
breezes and rapid motion, and so mirthful that she
could not help teasing and bantering the Earl a little,
though all in the way of good-humoured grace.

The ride was long, about eight miles ; but though the
Peak Castle was a royal one, the Earl preferred not to

enter it, but, according to previous arrangement, caused
the company to dismount in the valley, or rather ravine,
which terminates in the cavern, where a repast was
spread on the grass.   It was a wonderful place, cool and
refreshing, for the huge rocks on either side cast a deep
shadow, seldom pierced by the rays of the sun.   Lofty,
solemn, and rich in dark reds and purples, rose the walls
of rock, here and there softened by tapestry of ivy or
projecting bushes of sycamore, mountain ash, or with
fruit already assuming its brilliant tints, and jack-
daws flying in and out of their holes above.   Deep
beds of rich ferns clothed the lower slopes, and sheets
of that delicate flower, the enchanter's nightshade,
reared its white blossoms down to the bank of a little
clear stream that came flowing from out of the mighty
yawning arch of the cavern, while above the precipice
rose sheer the keep of Peak Castle.

The banquet was gracefully arranged to suit the
scene, and comprised, besides more solid viands, large
bowls of milk, with strawberries or cranberries floating
in them.   Mr. Eyre, the keeper of the castle, and his
daughter did the honours, while his son superintended
the lighting and fumigation of the cavern, assisted, if
not directed by Dr. Jones, whose short black cloak and
gold-headed cane were to be seen almost everywhere
at once.

Presently clouds of smoke began to issue from the
vast archway that closed the ravine.   "Beware, my
maidens," said the Queen, merrily, "we have roused
the dragon in his den, and we shall see him come forth
anon, curling his tail and belching flame."

"With a marvellous stomach for a dainty maiden
or two," added Gilbert Curll, falling into her humour.

"Hark!   Good lack!" cried the Queen, with an

H

affectation of terror, as a most extraordinary noise proceeded from the bowels of the cavern, making Cis start and Marie de Courcelles give a genuine shriek.

" Your Majesty is pleased to be merry," said the Earl, ponderously.   " The sound is only the coughing of the torchbearers from the damp whereof I warned your Majesty."

" By my faith," said Mary, " I believe my Lord Earl himself fears the monster of the cavern, to whom he gives the name of Damp.   Dread nothing, my Lord ; the valorous knight Sir Jones is even now in conflict with the foul worm, as those cries assure me, being in fact caused by his fumigations."

The jest was duly received, and in the midst of the laughter, young Eyre came forward, bowing low, and holding his jewelled hat in his hand, while his eyes betrayed that he had recently been sneezing violently.

" So please your Majesty," he said, " the odour hath rolled away, and all is ready if you will vouchsafe to accept my poor guidance."

" How say you, my Lord ?" said Mary.   " Will you dare the lair of the conquered foe, or fear you to be pinched with aches and pains by his lurking hobgoblins ?   If so, we dispense with your attendance."

" Your Majesty knows that where she goes thither I am bound to attend her," said the rueful Earl.

" Even into the abyss ! " said Mary.   " Valiantly spoken, for have not Ariosto and his fellows sung of captive princesses for whom every cave held an enchanter who could spirit them away into vapour thin as air, and leave their guardians questing in vain for them ?"

" Your Majesty jests with edged tools," sighed the Earl.

Old Mr. Eyre was too feeble to act as exhibitor of

the cave, and his son was deputed to lead the Queen
forward. This was, of course, Lord Shrewsbury's privi-
lege, but he was in truth beholden to her fingers for
aid, as she walked eagerly forward, now and then
accepting a little help from John Eyre, but in general
sure-footed and exploring eagerly by the light of the
numerous torches held by yeomen in the Eyre livery,
one of whom was stationed wherever there was a
dangerous pass or a freak of nature worth studying.

The magnificent vaulted roof grew lower, and presently it became necessary to descend a staircase, which
led to a deep hollow chamber, shaped like a bell, and
echoing like one. A pool of intensely black water
filled it, reflecting the lights on its surface, that only
enhanced its darkness, while there moved on a mysterious flat-bottomed boat, breaking them into shim-
mering sparks, and John Eyre intimated that the
visitors must lie down flat in it to be ferried one by
one over a space of about fourteen yards.

"Your Majesty will surely not attempt it," said the
Earl, with a shudder.

"Wherefore not? It is but a foretaste of Charon's
boat!" said Mary, who was one of those people whose
spirit of enterprise rises with the occasion, and she
murmured to Mary Seaton the line of Dante—

> "Quando noi fermerem li nostri passi
> Su la triste riviera a' Acheronte."

"Will your Majesty enter?" asked John Eyre.
"Dr. Jones and some gentlemen wait on the other side
to receive you."

"Some gentlemen?" repeated Mary. "You are sure
they are not Minos and Rhadamanthus, sir? My
obolus is ready; shall I put it in my mouth?"

"Nay, madam, pardon me," said the Earl, spurred

by a miserable sense of his duties; "since you will thus venture, far be it from me to let you pass over until I have reached the other side to see that it is fit for your Majesty!"

"Even as you will, most devoted cavalier," said Mary, drawing back; "we will be content to play the part of the pale ghosts of the unburied dead a little longer. See, Mary, the boat sinks down with him and his mortal flesh! We shall have Charon complaining of him anon."

"Your Highness gars my flesh grue," was the answer of her faithful Mary.

"Ah, *ma mie!* we have not left all hope behind. We can afford to smile at the doleful knight, ferried o'er on his back, in duteous and loyal submission to his task mistress. Child, Cicely, where art thou? Art afraid to dare the black river?"

"No, madam, not with you on the other side, and my father to follow me."

"Well said. Let the maiden follow next after me. Or mayhap Master Eyre should come next, then the young lady. For you, my ladies, and you, good sirs, you are free to follow or not, as the fancy strikes you. So—here is Charon once more—must I lie down?"

"Ay, madam," said Eyre, "if you would not strike your head against yonder projecting rock."

Mary lay down, her cloak drawn about her, and saying, "Now then, for Acheron. Ah! would that it were Lethe!"

"Her Grace saith well," muttered faithful Jean Kennedy, unversed in classic lore, "would that we were once more at bonnie Leith. Soft there now, 'tis you that follow her next, my fair mistress."

Cicely, not without trepidation, obeyed, laid herself

flat, and was soon midway, feeling the passage so grim and awful, that she could think of nothing but the dark passages of the grave, and was shuddering all over, when she was helped out on the other side by the Queen's own hand.

Some of those in the rear did not seem to be similarly affected, or else braved their feelings of awe by shouts and songs, which echoed fearfully through the subterranean vaults. Indeed Diccon, following the example of one or two young pages and grooms of the Earl's, began to get so daring and wild in the strange scene, that his father became anxious, and tarried for him on the other side, in the dread of his wandering away and getting lost, or falling into some of the fearful dark rivers that could be heard—not seen —rushing along. By this means, Master Richard was entirely separated from Cicely, to whom, before crossing the water, he had been watchfully attending, but he knew her to be with the Queen and her ladies, and considered her natural timidity the best safeguard against the chief peril of the cave, namely, wandering away.

Cicely did, however, miss his care, for the Queen could not but be engrossed by her various cicerones and attendants, and it was no one's especial business to look after the young girl over the rough descent to the dripping well called Roger Rain's House, and the grand cathedral-like gallery, with splendid pillars of stalagmite, and pendants above. By the time the steps beyond were reached, a toilsome descent, the Queen had had enough of the expedition, and declined to go any farther, but she good-naturedly yielded to the wish of Master John Eyre and Dr. Jones, that she would inscribe her name on the farthest column that she had reached.

There was a little confusion while this was being
done, as some of the more enterprising wished to
penetrate as far as possible into the recesses of the
cave, and these were allowed to pass forward—Diccon
and his father among them. In the passing and re-
passing, Cicely entirely lost sight of all who had any
special care of her, and went stumbling on alone,
weary, frightened, and repenting of the wilfulness with
which she had urged on the expedition. Each of
the other ladies had some cavalier to help her, but
none had fallen to Cicely's lot, and though, to an
active girl, there was no real danger where the torch-
bearers lined the way, still there was so much difficulty that she was a laggard in reaching the likeness
of Acheron, and could see no father near as she laid
herself down in Charon's dismal boat, dimly rejoicing
that this time it was to return to the realms of day,
and yet feeling as if she should never reach them. A
hand was given to assist her from the boat by one of
the torchbearers, a voice strangely familiar was in her
ears, saying, " Mistress Cicely ! " and she knew the
eager eyes, and exclaimed under her breath, " Antony,
you here ? In hiding ? What have you done ? "

" Nothing," he answered, smiling, and holding her
hand, as he helped her forward. " I only put on this
garb that I might gaze once more on the most divine
and persecuted of queens, and with some hope likewise
that I might win a word with her who deigned once
to be my playmate. Lady, I know the truth respecting
you."

" Do you in very deed ? " demanded Cicely, considerably startled.

" I know your true name, and that you are none of
the mastiff race," said Antony.

"Did—did Tibbott tell you, sir ?" asked Cicely.

"You are one of us," said Antony; "bound by natural allegiance in the land of your birth to this lady."

"Even so," said Cis, here becoming secure of what she had before doubted, that Babington only knew half the truth he referred to.

"And you see and speak with her privily," he added.

"As Bess Pierrepoint did," said she.

These words passed during the ascent, and were much interrupted by the difficulties of the way, in which Antony rendered such aid that she was each moment more impelled to trust to him, and relieved to find herself in such familiar hands. On reaching the summit the light of day could be seen glimmering in the extreme distance, and the maiden's heart bounded at the sight of it; but she found herself led somewhat aside, where in a sort of side aisle of the great bell chamber were standing together four more of the torch-bearers.

One of them, a slight man, made a step forward and said, "The Queen hath dropped her kerchief. Mayhap the young gentlewoman will restore it ?"

"She will do more than that !" said Antony, drawing her into the midst of them. "Dost not know her, Langston ? She is her sacred Majesty's own born, true, and faithful subject, the Lady ——"

"Hush, my friend; thou art ever over outspoken with thy names," returned the other, evidently annoyed at Babington's imprudence.

"I tell thee, she is one of us," replied Antony impatiently. "How is the Queen to know of her friends if we name them not to her ?"

"Are these her friends?" asked Cicely, looking round on the five figures in the leathern coats and yeomen's heavy buskins and shoes, and especially at the narrow face and keen pale eyes of Langston.

"Ay, verily," said one, whom Cicely could see even under his disguise to be a slender, graceful youth. "By John Eyre's favour have we come together here to gaze on the true and lawful mistress of our hearts, the champion of our faith, in her martyrdom." Then taking the kerchief from Langston's hand, Babington kissed it reverently, and tore it into five pieces, which he divided among himself and his fellows, saying, "This fair mistress shall bear witness to her sacred Majesty that we—Antony Babington, Chidiock Tichborne, Cuthbert Langston, John Charnock, John Savage —regard her as the sole and lawful Queen of England and Scotland, and that as we have gone for her sake into the likeness of the valley of the shadow of death, so will we meet death itself and stain this linen with our best heart's blood rather than not bring her again to freedom and the throne!"

Then with the most solemn oath each enthusiastically kissed the white token, and put it in his breast, but Langston looked with some alarm at the girl, and said to Babington, "Doth this young lady understand that you have put our lives into her hands?"

"She knows! she knows! I answer for her with my life," said Antony.

"Let her then swear to utter no word of what she has seen save to the Queen," said Langston, and Cicely detected a glitter in that pale eye, and with a horrified leap of thought, recollected how easy it would be to drag her away into one of those black pools, beyond all ken.

"Oh save me, Antony!" she cried, clinging to his arm.

"Let her then swear to utter no word of what she has seen save to the Queen."

H*

"No one shall touch you. I will guard you with my life!" exclaimed the impulsive young man, feeling for the sword that was not there.

"Who spoke of hurting the foolish wench?" growled Savage; but Tichborne said, "No one would hurt you, madam; but it is due to us all that you should give us your word of honour not to disclose what has passed, save to our only true mistress."

"Oh yes! yes!" cried Cicely hastily, scarcely knowing what passed her lips, and only anxious to escape from that gleaming eye of Langston, which had twice before filled her with a nameless sense of the necessity of terrified obedience. "Oh! let me go. I hear my father's voice."

She sprang forward with a cry between joy and terror, and darted up to Richard Talbot, while Savage, the man who looked most entirely unlike a disguised gentleman, stepped forward, and in a rough, north country dialect, averred that the young gentlewoman had lost her way.

"Poor maid," said kind Richard, gathering the two trembling little hands into one of his own broad ones. "How was it? Thanks, good fellow," and he dropped a broad piece into Savage's palm; "thou hast done good service. What, Cis, child, art quaking?"

"Hast seen any hobgoblins, Cis?" said Diccon, at her other side. "I'm sure I heard them laugh."

"Whist, Dick," said his father, putting a strong arm round the girl's waist. "See, my wench, yonder is the goodly light of day. We shall soon be there."

With all his fatherly kindness, he helped the agitated girl up the remaining ascent, as the lovely piece of blue sky between the retreating rocks grew wider, and the archway higher above them. Cis felt that infinite repose and reliance that none else could give, yet the repose was disturbed by the pang of recollection that the secret laid on her was their first severance. It was unjust to his kindness; strange, doubtful, nay grisly, to her foreboding mind, and she shivered alike from that and the chill of the damp cavern, and then he drew her cloak more closely about her, and halted to ask for the flask of wine which one of the adventurous spirits had brought, that Queen Elizabeth's health might be drunk by her true subjects in the bowels of the earth. The wine was, of course, exhausted; but Dr. Jones bustled forward with some cordial waters which he had provided in case of anyone being struck with the chill of the cave, and Cicely was made to swallow some.

By this time she had been missed, and the little party were met by some servants sent by the Earl at the instance of the much-alarmed Queen to inquire for her. A little farther on came Mistress Talbot, in much anxiety and distress, though as Diccon ran forward to meet her, and she saw Cicely on her husband's arm, she resumed her calm and staid demeanour, and when assured that the maiden had suffered no damage, she made no special demonstrations of joy or affection. Indeed, such would have been deemed unbecoming in the presence of strangers, and disrespectful to the Queen and the Earl, who were not far off.

Mary, on the other hand, started up, held out her arms, received the truant with such vehement kisses, as might almost have betrayed their real relationship, and then reproached her, with all sorts of endearing terms, for having so terrified them all; nor would she let the girl go from her side, and kept her hand in her own.

Diccon meanwhile had succeeded in securing his

father's attention, which had been wholly given to Cicely till she was placed in the women's hands. " Father," he said, " I wis that one of the knaves with the torches who found our Cis was the woman with the beads and bracelets, ay, and Tibbott, too."

" Belike, belike, my son," said Richard. " There are folk who can take as many forms as a barnacle goose. Keep thou a sharp eye as the fellows pass out, and pull me by the cloak if thou seest him."

Of course he was not seen, and Richard, who was growing more and more cautious about bringing vague or half-proved suspicions before his Lord, decided to be silent and to watch, though he sighed to his wife that the poor child would soon be in the web.

Cis had not failed to recognise that same identity, and to feel a half-realised conviction that the Queen had not chosen to confide to her that the two female disguises both belonged to Langston. Yet the contrast between Mary's endearments and the restrained manner of Susan so impelled her towards the veritable mother, that the compunction as to the concealment she had at first experienced passed away, and her heart felt that its obligations were towards her veritable and most loving parent. She told the Queen the whole story at night, to Mary's great delight. She said she was sure her little one had something on her mind, she had so little to say of her adventure, and the next day a little privy council was contrived, in which Cicely was summoned again to tell her tale. The ladies declared they had always hoped much from their darling page, in whom they had kept up the true faith, but Sir Andrew Melville shook his head and said : " I'd misdoot ony plot where the little finger of him was. What garred the silly loon call in the young leddy ere he kenned whether she wad keep counsel ?"

CHAPTER XVII.

THE EBBING WELL.

CICELY'S thirst for adventures had received a check, but the Queen, being particularly well and in good spirits, and trusting that this would be her last visit to Buxton, was inclined to enterprise, and there were long rides and hawking expeditions on the moors.

The last of these, ere leaving Buxton, brought the party to the hamlet of Barton Clough, where a loose horseshoe of the Earl's caused a halt at a little wayside smithy. Mary, always friendly and free-spoken, asked for a draught of water, and entered into conversation with the smith's rosy-cheeked wife who brought it to her, and said it was sure to be good and pure for the stream came from the Ebbing and Flowing Well, and she pointed up a steep path. Then, on a further question, she proceeded, "Has her ladyship never heard of the Ebbing Well that shows whether true love is soothfast?"

"How so?" asked the Queen. "How precious such a test might be. It would save many a maiden a broken heart, only that the poor fools would ne'er trust it."

"I have heard of it," said the Earl, "and Dr. Jones would demonstrate to your Grace that it is but a

superstition of the vulgar regarding a natural pheno-
menon."

"Yea, my Lord," said the smith, looking up from
the horse's foot; "'tis the trade of yonder philosophers
to gainsay whatever honest folk believed before them.
They'll deny next that hens lay eggs, or blight rots
wheat. My good wife speaks but plain truth, and we
have seen it o'er and o'er again."

"What have you seen, good man?" asked Mary
eagerly, and ready answer was made by the couple,
who had acquired some cultivation of speech and
manners by their wayside occupation, and likewise as
cicerones to the spring.

"Seen, quoth the lady?" said the smith. "Why,
he that is a true man and hath a true maid can quaff
a draught as deep as his gullet can hold—or she that
is true and hath a true love—but let one who hath a
flaw in the metal, on the one side or t'other, stoop to
drink, and the water shrinks away so as there's not
the moistening of a lip."

"Ay: the ladies may laugh," added his wife, "but
'tis soothfast for all that."

"Hast proved it, good dame?" asked the Queen
archly, for the pair were still young and well-looking
enough to be jested with.

"Ay! have we not, madam?" said the dame.
"Was not my man yonder, Rob, the tinker's son, whom
my father and brethren, the smiths down yonder at
Buxton, thought but scorn of, but we'd taken a sup
together at the Ebbing Well, and it played neither of us
false, so we held out against 'em all, and when they saw
there was no help for it, they gave Rob the second
best anvil and bellows for my portion, and here we
be."

" Living witnesses to the Well," said the Queen
merrily. " How say you, my Lord ? I would fain see
this marvel. Master Curll, will you try the venture ?"

" I fear it not, madam," said the secretary, looking
at the blushing Barbara.

Objections did not fail to arise from the Earl as to
the difficulties of the path and the lateness of the hour
but Rob Smith, perhaps wilfully, discovered another
of my Lord's horseshoes to be in a perilous state,
and his good wife, Dame Emmott, offered to conduct
the ladies by so good a path that they might think
themselves on the Queen's Walk at Buxton itself.

Lord Shrewsbury, finding himself a prisoner, was
obliged to yield compliance, and leaving Sir Andrew
Melville, with the grooms and falconers, in charge of
the horses, the Queen, the Earl, Cicely, Mary Seaton,
Barbara Mowbray, the two secretaries, and Richard
Talbot and young Diccon, started on the walk, together with Dr. Bourgoin, her physician, who was
eager to investigate the curiosity, and make it a subject of debate with Dr. Jones.

The path was a beautiful one, through rocks and
brushwood, mountain ash bushes showing their coral
berries amid their feathery leaves, golden and white
stars of stonecrop studding every coign of vantage,
and in more level spots the waxy bell-heather beginning to come into blossom. Still it was rather over
praise to call it as smooth as the carefully-levelled
and much-trodden Queen's path at Buxton, considering
that it ascended steeply all the way, and made the
solemn, much-enduring Earl pant for breath; but the
Queen, her rheumatics for the time entirely in abey-
ance, bounded on with the mountain step learned in
early childhood, and closely followed the brisk Em-

mott. The last ascent was a steep pull, taking away
the disposition to speak, and at its summit Mary stood
still holding out one hand, with a finger of the other
on her lips as a sign of silence to the rest of the
suite and to Emmott, who stood flushed and angered ;
for what she esteemed her lawful province seemed to
have been invaded from the other side of the country.

They were on the side of the descent from the
moorlands connected with the Peak, on a small
esplanade in the midst of which lay a deep clear
pool, with nine small springs or fountains discharging
themselves, under fern and wild rose or honeysuckle,
into its basin. Steps had been cut in the rock leading to the verge of the pool, and on the lowest of
these, with his back to the new-comers, was kneeling
a young man, his brown head bare, his short cloak laid
aside, so that his well-knit form could be seen ; the
sword and spurs that clanked against the rock, as well
as the whole fashion and texture of his riding-dress,
showing him to be a gentleman.

" We shall see the venture made," whispered Mary
to her daughter, who, in virtue of youth and lightness
of foot, had kept close behind her. Grasping the girl's
arm and smiling, she heard the young man's voice cry
aloud to the echoes of the rock, " Cis !" then stoop
forward and plunge face and head into the clear trans-
lucent water.

"Good luck to a true lover !" smiled the Queen.
" What ! starting, silly maid ? Cisses are plenty in these
parts as rowan berries."

" Nay, but——" gasped Cicely, for at that moment
the young man, rising from his knees, his face still
shining with the water, looked up at his unsuspected
spectators. An expression of astonishment and ecstasy

lighted up his honest sunburnt countenance as Master
Richard, who had just succeeded in dragging the portly
Earl up the steep path, met his gaze. He threw up
his arms, made apparently but one bound, and was
kneeling at the captain's feet, embracing his knees.

"My son! Humfrey! Thyself!" cried Richard.
"See! see what presence we are in."

"Your blessing, father, first," cried Humfrey, "ere
I can see aught else."

And as Richard quickly and thankfully laid his
hand on the brow, so much fairer than the face, and
then held his son for one moment in a close embrace,
with an exchange of the kiss that was not then only
a foreign fashion, Queen and Earl said to one another
with a sigh, that happy was the household where the
son had no eyes for any save his father.

Mary, however, must have found it hard to continue her smiles when, after due but hurried obeisance
to her and to his feudal chief, Humfrey turned to the
little figure beside her, all smiling with startled shyness,
and in one moment seemed to swallow it up in a huge
overpowering embrace, fraternal in the eyes of almost
all the spectators, but not by any means so to those
of Mary, especially after the name she had heard.
Diccon's greeting was the next, and was not quite so
visibly rapturous on the part of the elder brother, who
explained that he had arrived at Sheffield yesterday,
and finding no one to welcome him but little Edward,
had set forth for Buxton almost with daylight, and
having found himself obliged to rest his horse, he had
turned aside to————.   And here he recollected just in
time that Cis was in every one's eyes save his father's,
his own sister, and lamely concluded "to take a
draught of water," blushing under his brown skin as

he spoke. Poor fellow! the Queen, even while she wished him in the farthest West Indian isle, could not help understanding that strange doubt and dread that come over the mind at the last moment before a longed-for meeting, and which had made even the bold young sailor glad to rally his hopes by this divination. Fortunately she thought only herself and one or two of the foremost had heard the name he gave, as was proved by the Earl's good-humoured laugh, as he said,

"A draught, quotha? We understand that, young sir. And who may this your true love be?"

"That I hope soon to make known to your Lordship," returned Humfrey, with a readiness which he certainly did not possess before his voyage.

The ceremony was still to be fulfilled, and the smith's wife called them to order by saying, "Good luck to the young gentleman. He is a stranger here, or he would have known he should have come up by our path! Will you try the well, your Grace?"

"Nay, nay, good woman, my time for such toys is over!" said the Queen smiling, "but moved by such an example, here are others to make the venture, Master Curll is burning for it, I see."

"I fear no such trial, an't please your Grace," said Curll, bowing, with a bright defiance of the water, and exchanging a confident smile with the blushing Mistress Barbara—then kneeling by the well, and uttering her name aloud ere stooping to drink. He too succeeded in obtaining a full draught, and came up triumphantly.

"The water is a flatterer!" said the Earl. "It favours all."

The French secretary, Monsieur Nau, here came forward and took his place on the steps. No one heard, but every one knew the word he spoke was "Bessie," for

Elizabeth Pierrepoint had long been the object of his affections. No doubt he hoped that he should obtain some encouragement from the water, even while he gave a little laugh of affected incredulity as though only complying with a form to amuse the Queen. Down he went on his knees, bending over the pool, when behold he could not reach it! The streams that fed it were no longer issuing from the rock, the water was subsiding rapidly. The farther he stooped, the more it retreated, till he had almost fallen over, and the guide screamed out a note of warning, "Have a care, sir! If the water flees you, flee it will, and ye'll not mend matters by drowning yourself."

How he was to be drowned by water that fled from him was not clear, but with a muttered malediction he arose and glanced round as if he thought the mortification a trick on the part of the higher powers, since the Earl did not think him a match for the Countess's grandchild, and the Queen had made it known to him that she considered Bess Pierrepoint to have too much of her grandmother's conditions to be likely to be a good wife. There was a laugh too, scarce controlled by some of the less well-mannered of the suite, especially as the Earl, wishing to punish his presumption, loudly set the example.

There was a pause, as the discomfited secretary came back, and the guide exclaimed, "Come, my masters, be not daunted! Will none of you come on? Hath none of you faith in your love? Oh, fie!"

"We are married men, good women," said Richard, hoping to put an end to the scene, "and thus can laugh at your well."

"But will not these pretty ladies try it? It speaks as sooth to lass as to lad."

"I am ready," said Barbara Mowbray, as Curll
gave her his hand to bound lightly down the steps.
And to the general amazement, no sooner had "Gilbert"
echoed from her lips than the fountains again burst
forth, the water rose, and she had no difficulty in
reaching it, while no one could help bursting forth in
applause.   Her Gilbert fervently kissed the hand she
gave him to aid her steps up the slope, and Dame
Emmott, in triumphant congratulation, scanned them
over and exclaimed, "Ay, trust the well for knowing
true sweetheart and true maid.   Come you next, fair
mistress?"   Poor Mary Seaton shook her head, with
a look that the kindly woman understood, and she
turned towards Cicely, who had a girl's unthinking
impulse of curiosity, and had already put her hand
into Humfrey's, when his father exclaimed, "Nay, nay,
the maid is yet too young!" and the Queen added,
"Come back, thou silly little one, these tests be not
for babes like thee."

She was forced to be obedient, but she pouted a
little as she was absolutely held fast by Richard
Talbot's strong hand.   Humfrey was disappointed too;
but all was bright with him just then, and as the party
turned to make the descent, he said to her, "It matters
not, little Cis!   I'm sure of thee with the water or
without, and after all, thou couldst but have whispered
my name, till my father lets us speak all out!"

They were too much hemmed in by other people
for a private word, and a little mischievous banter was
going on with Sir Andrew Melville, who was supposed
to have a grave elderly courtship with Mistress Kennedy.   Humfrey was left in the absolute bliss of
ignorance, while the old habit and instinct of joy and
gladness in his presence reasserted itself in Cis, so

that, as he handed her down the rocks, she answered
in the old tone all his inquiries about his mother,
and all else that concerned them at home, Diccon
meantime risking his limbs by scrambling outside
the path, to keep abreast of his brother, and to put in
his word whenever he could.

On reaching the smithy, Humfrey had to go round
another way to fetch his horse, and could hardly hope
to come up with the rest before they reached Buxton.
His brother was spared to go with him, but his father
was too important a part of the escort to be spared.
So Cicely rode near the Queen, and heard no more
except the Earl's version of Dr. Jones's explanation of
the intermitting spring. They reached home only just
in time to prepare for supper, and the two youths
appeared almost simultaneously, so that Mistress Talbot, sitting at her needle on the broad terrace in front
of the Earl's lodge, beheld to her amazement and
delight the figure that, grown and altered as it was,
she recognised in an instant. In another second
Humfrey had sprung from his horse, rushed up the
steps, he knew not how, and the Queen, with tears
trembling in her eyes was saying, " Ah, Melville ! see
how sons meet their mothers !"

The great clock was striking seven, a preposterously
late hour for supper, and etiquette was stronger than
sentiment or perplexity. Every one hastened to assume an evening toilette, for a riding-dress would have
been an insult to the Earl, and the bell soon clanged
to call them down to their places in the hall. Even
Humfrey had brought in his cloak-bag wherewithal
to make himself presentable, and soon appeared, a well-
knit and active figure, in a plain dark blue jerkin, with
white slashes, and long hose knitted by his mother's

dainty fingers, and well-preserved shoes with blue
rosettes, and a flat blue velvet cap, with an exquisite
black and sapphire feather in it fastened by a curious
brooch. His hair was so short that its naturally strong
curl could hardly be seen, his ruddy sunburnt face
could hardly be called handsome, but it was full of
frankness and intelligence, and beaming with honest
joy, and close to him moved little Diccon, hardly able
to repress his ecstasy within company bounds, and letting it find vent in odd little gestures, wriggling with
his body, playing tunes on his knee, or making dancing-
steps with his feet.

Lord Shrewsbury welcomed his young kinsman as
one who had grown from a mere boy into a sturdy and
effective supporter. He made the new-comer sit near
him, and asked many questions, so that Humfrey was
the chief speaker all supper time, with here and there
a note from his father, the only person who had made
the same voyage. All heard with eager interest of the
voyage, the weeds in the Gulf Stream, the strange
birds and fishes, of Walter Raleigh's Virginian colony
and its ill success, of the half-starved men whom Sir
Richard Grenville had found only too ready to leave
Roanoake, of dark-skinned Indians, of chases of Spanish
ships, of the Peak of Teneriffe rising white from the
waves, of phosphorescent seas, of storms, and of shark-
catching.

Supper over, the audience again gathered round the
young traveller, a perfect fountain of various and wonderful information to those who had for the most part
never seen a book of travels. He narrated simply and
well, without his boyish shy embarrassment and awk-
wardness, and likewise, as his father alone could judge,
without boasting, though, if to no one else, to Diccon

and Cis, listening with wide open eyes, he seemed a
hero of heroes.   In the midst of his narration a message
came that the Queen of Scots requested the presence of
Mistress Cicely.   Humfrey stared in discomfiture, and
asked when she would return.

"Not to-night," faltered the girl, and the mother
added, for the benefit of the bystanders, "For lack of
other ladies of the household, much service hath of late
fallen to Cicely and myself, and she shares the Queen's
chamber."

Humfrey had to submit to exchange good-nights
with Cicely, and she made her way less willingly than
usual to the apartments of the Queen, who was being
made ready for her bed.   "Here comes our truant,"
she exclaimed as the maiden entered.   "I sent to rescue
thee from the western seafarer who had clawed thee
in his tarry clutch.   Thou didst act the sister's part
passing well.   I hear my Lord and all his *meiné* have
been sitting, open-mouthed, hearkening to his tales of
savages and cannibals."

"O madam, he told us of such lovely isles," said
Cis.   "The sea, he said, is blue, bluer than we can
conceive, with white waves of dazzling surf, breaking
on islands fringed with white shells and coral, and
with palms, their tops like the biggest ferns in the
brake, and laden with red golden fruit as big as
goose eggs.   And the birds!   O madam, my mother,
the birds!   They are small, small as our butterflies
and beetles, and they hang hovering and quivering
over a flower so that Humfrey thought they were
moths, for he saw nothing but a whizzing and a whirr-
ing till he smote the pretty thing dead, and then he
said that I should have wept for pity, for it was a
little bird with a long bill, and a breast that shines

red in one light, purple in another, and flame-coloured
in a third. He has brought home the little skin and
feathers of it for me."

"Thou hast supped full of travellers' tales, my
simple child."

"Yea, madam, but my Lord listened, and made
Humfrey sit beside him, and made much of him—my
Lord himself! I would fain bring him to you, madam.
It is so wondrous to hear him tell of the Red Men
with crowns of feathers and belts of beads. Such
gentle savages they be, and their chiefs as courteous
and stately as any of our princes, and yet those cruel
Spaniards make them slaves and force them to dig in
mines, so that they die and perish under their hands."

"And better so than that they should not come to
the knowledge of the faith," said Mary.

"I forgot that your Grace loves the Spaniards,'
said Cis, much in the tone in which she might have
spoken of a taste in her Grace for spiders, adders, or
any other noxious animal.

"One day my child will grow out of her little
heretic prejudices, and learn to love her mother's staunch
friends, the champions of Holy Church, and the repre-
sentatives of true knighthood in these degenerate days.
Ah, child! couldst thou but see a true Spanish cabal-
lero, or again, could I but show thee my noble cousin of
Guise, then wouldst thou know how to rate these gross
clownish English mastiffs who now turn thy silly little
brain. Ah, that thou couldst once meet a true prince!"

"The well," murmured Cicely.

"Tush, child," said the Queen, amused. "What
of that? Thy name is not Cis, is it? 'Tis only the
slough that serves thee for the nonce. The good youth
will find himself linked to some homely, housewifely

Cis in due time, when the Princess Bride is queening
it in France or Austria, and will own that the well was
wiser than he."

Poor Cis! If her inmost heart declared Humfrey
Talbot to be prince enough for her, she durst not entertain the sentiment, not knowing whether it were unworthy, and while Marie de Courcelles read aloud a
French legend of a saint to soothe the Queen to sleep,
she lay longing after the more sympathetic mother, and
wondering what was passing in the hall.

Richard Talbot had communed with his wife's eyes,
and made up his mind that Humfrey should know the
full truth before the Queen should enjoin his being put
off with the story of the parentage she had invented
for Bride Hepburn; and while some of the gentlemen
followed their habit of sitting late over the wine cup,
he craved their leave to have his son to himself a little
while, and took him out in the summer twilight on the
greensward, going through the guards, for whom he, as
the gentleman warder, had the password of the night.
In compliment to the expedition of the day it had been
made " True love and the Flowing Well." It sounded
agreeable in Humfrey's ears; he repeated it again, and
then added " Little Cis! she hath come to woman's
estate, and she hath caught some of the captive lady's
pretty tricks of the head and hands. How long hath
she been so thick with her ?"

" Since this journey. I have to speak with thee, my
son."

" I wait your pleasure, sir," said Humfrey, and as
his father paused a moment ere communicating his
strange tidings, he rendered the matter less easy by
saying, " I guess your purpose. If I may at once wed
my little Cis I will send word to Sir John Norreys that

I am not for this expedition to the Low Countries,
though there is good and manly work to be done there,
and I have the offer of a command, but I gave not
my word till I knew your will, and whether we might
wed at once."

"Thou hast much to hear, my son."

"Nay, surely no one has come between!" exclaimed Humfrey. "Methought she was less frank
and more coy than of old. If that sneaking traitor
Babington hath been making up to her I will slit his
false gullet for him."

"Hush, hush, Humfrey! thy seafaring boasts skill
not here. No *man* hath come between thee and
yonder poor maid."

"Poor! You mean not that she is sickly. Were
she so, I would so tend her that she should be well for
mere tenderness. But no, she was the very image of
health. No man, said you, father? Then it is a
woman. Ah! my Lady Countess is it, bent on making
her match her own way? Sir, you are too good and
upright to let a tyrannous dame like that sever
between us, though she be near of kin to us. My
mother might scruple to cross her, but you have seen
the world, sir."

"My lad, you are right in that it is a woman who
stands between you and Cis, but it is not the Countess.
None would have the right to do so, save the maiden's
own mother."

"Her mother! You have discovered her lineage!
Can she have ought against me?—I, your son, sir, of
the Talbot blood, and not ill endowed?"

"Alack, son, the Talbot may be a good dog, but the
lioness will scarce esteem him her mate. Riddles
apart, it is proved beyond question that our little maid

is of birth as high as it is unhappy. Thou canst be
secret, I know, Humfrey, and thou must be silent as
the grave, for it touches my honour and the poor child's
liberty."

"Who is she, then?" demanded Humfrey sharply.

His father pointed to the Queen's window. Humfrey stared at him, and muttered an ejaculation, then
exclaimed, "How and when was this known?"

Richard went over the facts, giving as few names
as possible, while his son stood looking down and
drawing lines with the point of his sword.

"I hoped," ended the father, "that these five years'
absence might have made thee forget thy childish
inclination;" and as Humfrey, without raising his face,
emphatically shook his head, he went on to add—"So,
my dear son, meseemeth that there is no remedy, but
that, for her peace and thine own, thou shouldest accept
this offer of brave Norreys, and by the time the
campaign is ended, they may be both safe in Scotland,
out of reach of vexing thy heart, my poor boy."

"Is it so sure that her royal lineage will be
owned?" muttered Humfrey. "Out on me for saying
so! But sure this lady hath made light enough of her
wedlock with yonder villain."

"Even so, but that was when she deemed its
offspring safe beneath the waves. I fear me that, however our poor damsel be regarded, she will be treated
as a mere bait and tool. If not bestowed on some
foreign prince (and there hath been talk of dukes and
archdukes), she may serve to tickle the pride of some
Scottish thief, such as was her father."

"Sir! sir! how can you speak patiently of such
profanation and cruelty? Papist butchers and Scottish
thieves, for the child of your hearth! Were it not

better that I stole her safely away and wedded her in secret, so that at least she might have an honest husband ?"

" Nay, his honesty would scarce be thus manifest," said Richard, " even if the maid would consent, which I think she would not. Her head is too full of her new greatness to have room for thee, my poor lad. Best that thou shouldest face the truth. And, verily, what is it but her duty to obey her mother, her true and veritable mother, Humfrey? It is but making her case harder, and adding to her griefs, to strive to awaken any inclination she may have had for thee ; and therefore it is that I counsel thee, nay, I might command thee, to absent thyself while it is still needful that she remain with us, passing for our daughter."

Humfrey still traced lines with his sword in the dust. He had always been a strong-willed though an obedient and honourable boy, and his father felt that these five years had made a man of him, whom, in spite of mediæval obedience, it was not easy to dispose of arbitrarily.

" There's no haste," he muttered. " Norreys will not go till my Lord of Leicester's commission be made out. It is five years since I was at home."

" My son, thou knowest that I would not send thee from me willingly. I had not done so ere now, but that it was well for thee to know the world and men, and Sheffield is a mere nest of intrigue and falsehood, where even if one keeps one's integrity, it is hard to be believed. But for my Lord, thy mother, and my poor folk, I would gladly go with thee to strike honest downright blows at a foe I could see and feel, rather than be nothing better than a warder, and be driven

distracted with women's tongues.   Why, they have
even set division between my Lord and his son Gilbert,
who was ever the dearest to him.   Young as he is,
methinks Diccon would be better away with thee than
where the very air smells of plots and lies."

"I trow the Queen of Scots will not be here much
longer," said Humfrey.   "Men say in London that Sir
Ralf Sadler is even now setting forth to take charge of
her, and send my Lord to London."

"We have had such hopes too often, my son," said
Richard.   "Nay, she hath left us more than once, but
always to fall back upon Sheffield like a weight to the
ground.   But she is full of hope in her son, now that
he is come of age, and hath put to death her great foe,
the Earl of Morton."

"The poor lady might as well put her faith in—
in a jelly-fish," said Humfrey, falling on a comparison
perfectly appreciated by the old sailor.

"Heh?   She will get naught but stings.   How
knowest thou?"

"Why, do none know here that King James is in
the hands of him they call the Master of Gray?"

"Queen Mary puts in him her chief hope."

"Then she hath indeed grasped a jelly-fish.   Know
you not, father, those proud and gay ones, with rose-
coloured bladders and long blue beards—blue as the
azure of a herald's coat?"

"Ay, marry I do.   I remember when I was a lad,
in my first voyage, laying hold on one.   I warrant
you I danced about till I was nearly overboard, and
my arm was as big as two for three days later.   Is
the fellow of that sort?   The false Scot."

"Look you, father, I met in London that same
Johnstone who was one of this lady's gentlemen at

one time. You remember him. He breakfasted at
Bridgefield once or twice ere the watch became more
strict."

"Yea, I remember him. He was an honest fellow
for a Scot."

"When he made out that I was the little lad he
remembered, he was very courteous, and desired his
commendations to you and to my mother. He had
been in Scotland, and had come south in the train of
this rogue, Gray. I took him to see the old *Pelican*,
and we had a breakfast aboard there. He asked much
after his poor Queen, whom he loves as much as ever,
and when he saw I was a man he could trust, your
true son, he said that he saw less hope for her than
ever in Scotland——her friends have been slain or
exiled, and the young generation that has grown up
have learned to dread her like an incarnation of the
scarlet one of Babylon. Their preachers would hail her
as Satan loosed on them, and the nobles dread nothing
so much as being made to disgorge the lands of the
Crown and the Church, on which they are battening.
As to her son, he was fain enough to break forth from
one set of tutors, and the messages of France and Spain
tickled his fancy——but he is nought. He is crammed
with scholarship, and not without a shrewd apprehen-
sion ; but, with respect be it spoken, more the stuff
that court fools are made of than kings. It may be,
as a learned man told Johnstone, that the shock the
Queen suffered when the brutes put Davy to death
before her eyes, three months ere his birth, hath damaged his constitution, for he is at the mercy of whoso-
ever chooses to lead him, and hath no will of his own.
This Master of Gray was at first inclined to the
Queen's party, thinking more might be got by a reversal

of all things, but now he finds the king's men so strong
in the saddle, and the Queen's French kindred like to
be too busy at home to aid her, what doth he do, but
list to our Queen's offers, and this ambassage of his,
which hath a colour of being for Queen Mary's release,
is verily to make terms with my Lord Treasurer and
Sir Francis Walsingham for the pension he is to have
for keeping his king in the same mind."

"Turning a son against a mother! I marvel that
honourable counsellors can bring themselves to the
like."

"Policy, sir, policy," said Humfrey. "And this
Gray maketh a fine show of chivalry and honour, in-
somuch that Sir Philip Sidney himself hath desired his
friendship; but, you see, the poor lady is as far from
freedom as she was when first she came to Sheffield."

"She is very far from believing it, poor dame. I
am sorry for her, Humfrey, more sorry than I ever
thought I could be, now I have seen more of her.
My Lord himself says he never knew her break a
promise. How gracious she is there is no telling."

"That we always knew," said Humfrey, looking
somewhat amazed, that his honoured father should
have fallen under the spell of the "siren between the
cold earth and moon."

"Yes, gracious, and of a wondrous constancy of
mind, and evenness of temper," said Richard. "Now
that thy mother and I have watched her more closely,
we can testify that, weary, worn, and sick of body and
of heart as she is, she never letteth a bitter or a chiding word pass her lips towards her servants. She hath
nothing to lose by it. Their fidelity is proven. They
would stand by her to the last, use them as she would,
but assuredly their love must be doubly bound up in

her when they see how she regardeth them before herself. Let what will be said of her, son Humfrey, I
shall always maintain that I never saw woman, save
thine own good mother, of such evenness of condition,
and sweetness of consideration for all about her, ay,
and patience in adversity, such as, Heaven forbid,
thy mother should ever know."

"Amen, and verily amen," said Humfrey. "Deem
you then that she hath not worked her own woe?"

"Nay, lad, what saith the Scripture, 'Judge not,
and ye shall not be judged'? How should I know
what hath passed seventeen years back in Scotland?"

"Ay, but for present plots and intrigues, judge
you her a true woman?"

"Humfrey, thou hadst once a fox in a cage. When
it found it vain to dash against the bars, rememberest
thou how it scratched away the earth in the rear, and
then sat over the hole it had made, lest we should see
it?"

"The fox, say you, sir? Then you cannot call her
ought but false."

"They tell me," said Sir Richard, "that ever since an
Italian named Machiavel wrote his Book of the Prince,
statecraft hath been craft indeed, and princes suck in
deceit with the very air they breathe. Ay, boy, it is
what chiefly vexes me in the whole I cannot doubt
that she is never so happy as when there is a plot or
scheme toward, not merely for her own freedom, but
the utter overthrow of our own gracious Sovereign,
who, if she hath kept this lady in durance, hath
shielded her from her own bloodthirsty subjects. And
for dissembling, I never saw her equal. Yet she, as
thy mother tells me, is a pious and devout woman, who
bears her troubles thus cheerfully and patiently, be-

I

cause she deems them a martyrdom for her religion. Ay, all women are riddles, they say, but this one the most of all !"

"Thinkest thou that she hath tampered with— with that poor maiden's faith ?" asked Humfrey huskily.

"I trow not yet, my son," replied Richard ; "Cis is as open as ever to thy mother, for I cannot believe she hath yet learnt to dissemble, and I greatly suspect that the Queen, hoping to return to Scotland, may be willing to keep her a Protestant, the better to win favour with her brother and the lords of his council ; but if he be such a cur as thou sayest, all hope of honourable release is at an end. So thou seest, Humfrey, how it lies, and how, in my judgment, to remain here is but to wring thine own heart, and bring the wench and thyself to sore straits. I lay not my commands on thee, a man grown, but such is my opinion on the matter."

"I will not disobey you, father," said Humfrey, "but suffer me to consider the matter."

CHAPTER XVIII.

CIS OR SISTER.

Buxtona, quæ calidæ celebraris nomine lymphæ
Forte mihi post hac non adeunda, Vale.[1]

THUS wrote Queen Mary with a diamond upon her
window pane, smiling as she said, " There, we will
leave a *memento* over which the admirable Dr. Jones
will gloat his philosophical soul. Never may I see
thee more, Buxton, yet never thought I to be so happy
as I have here been."

She spoke with the tenderness of farewell to the
spot which had always been the pleasantest abode of
the various places of durance which had been hers in
England. Each year she had hoped would be her last
of such visits, but on this occasion everything seemed
to point to a close to the present state of things, since
not only were the negotiations with Scotland apparently prosperous, but Lord Shrewsbury had obtained
an absolute promise from Elizabeth that she would at
all events relieve him from his onerous and expensive
charge. Thus there was general cheerfulness, as the
baggage was bestowed in carts and on beasts of burthen,
and Mary, as she stood finishing her inscription on

---

[1] Buxton, of whose warm waters all men tell,
Perchance I ne'er shall see thee more, Farewell.

the window, smiled sweetly and graciously on Mistress Talbot, and gave her joy of the arrival of her towardly and hopeful son, adding, " We surprised him at the well ! May his Cis, who is yet to be found, I trow, reward his lealty ! "

That was all the notice Mary deigned to take of the former relations between her daughter and young Talbot. She did not choose again to beg for secrecy when she was sure to hear that she had been forestalled, and she was too consummate a judge of character not to have learnt that, though she might despise the dogged, simple straightforwardness of Richard and Susan Talbot, their honour was perfectly trustworthy. She was able for the present to keep her daughter almost entirely to herself, since, on the return to Sheffield, the former state of things was resumed. The Bridgefield family was still quartered in the Manor-house, and Mistress Talbot continued to be, as it were, Lady Warder to the captive in the place of the Countess, who obstinately refused to return while Mary was still in her husband's keeping. Cicely, as Mary's acknowledged favourite, was almost always in her apartments, except at the meals of the whole company of Shrewsbury kinsfolk and retainers, when her place was always far removed from that of Humfrey. In truth, if ever an effort might have obtained a few seconds of private conversation, a strong sense of embarrassment and perplexity made the two young people fly apart rather than come together. They knew not what they wished. Humfrey might in his secret soul long for a token that Cis remembered his faithful affection, and yet he knew that to elicit one might do her life-long injury. So, however he might crave for word or look when out of

sight of her, an honourable reluctance always withheld
him from seeking any such sign in the short intervals
when he could have tried to go beneath the surface.
On the other hand, this apparent indifference piqued
her pride, and made her stiff, cold, and almost disdainful whenever there was any approach between
them. Her vanity might be flattered by the knowledge that she was beyond his reach; but it would
have been still more gratified could she have discovered any symptoms of pining and languishing after
her. She might peep at him from under her eye-
lashes in chapel and in hall; but in the former place
his gaze always seemed to be on the minister, in the
latter he showed no signs of flagging as a trencher
companion. Both mothers thought her marvellously
discreet; but neither beheld the strange tumult in her
heart, where were surging pride, vanity, ambition, and
wounded affection.

In a few days, Sir Ralf Sadler and his son-in-law Mr.
Somer arrived at Sheffield in order to take the charge
of the prisoner whilst Shrewsbury went to London.
The conferences and consultations were endless and
harassing, and it was finally decided that the Earl
should escort her to Wingfield, and, leaving her there
under charge of Sadler, should proceed to London.
She made formal application for Mistress Cicely Talbot
to accompany her as one of her suite, and her supposed parents could not but give their consent, but
six gentlewomen had been already enumerated, and
the authorities would not consent to her taking any
more ladies with her, and decreed that Mistress Cicely
must remain at home.

"This unkindness has made the parting from this
place less joyous than I looked for," said Mary, " but

courage, *ma mignonne*.   Soon shall I send for thee to
Scotland, and there shalt thou burst thine husk, and
show thyself in thy true colours;" and turning to
Susan, "Madam, I must commit my treasure to her
who has so long watched over her."

"Your Grace knows that she is no less my treasure,"
said Susan.

"I should have known it well," returned the
Queen, "from the innocence and guilelessness of the
damsel.   None save such a mother as Mistress Talbot
could have made her what she is.   Credit me, madam,
I have looked well into her heart, and found nought
to undo there.   You have bred her up better than her
poor mother could have done, and I gladly entrust her
once more to your care, assured that your well-tried
honour will keep her in mind of what she is, and to
what she may be called."

"She shall remember it, madam," said Susan.

"When I am a Queen once more," said Mary, "all
I can give will seem too poor a meed for what you
have been to my child.   Even as Queen of Scotland
or England itself, my power would be small in comparison with my will.   My gratitude, however, no
bounds can limit out to me."

And with tears of tenderness and thankfulness she
kissed the cheeks and lips of good Mistress Talbot,
who could not but likewise weep for the mother thus
compelled to part with her child.

The night was partly spent in caresses and promises
of the brilliant reception preparing in Scotland, with
auguries of the splendid marriage in store, with a
Prince of Lorraine, or even with an Archduke.

Cis was still young enough to dream of such a lot
as an opening to a fairy land of princely glories.   If

her mother knew better, she still looked tenderly back on her *beau pays de France* with that halo of brightness which is formed only in childhood and youth. Moreover, it might be desirable to enhance such aspiration as might best secure the young princess from anything derogatory to her real rank, while she was strongly warned against betraying it, and especially against any assumption of dignity should she ever hear of her mother's release, reception, and recognition in Scotland. For whatever might be the maternal longings, it would be needful to feel the way and prepare the ground for the acknowledgment of Bothwell's daughter in Scotland, while the knowledge of her existence in England would almost surely lead to her being detained as a hostage. She likewise warned the maiden never to regard any letter or billet from her as fully read till it had been held—without witnesses—to the fire.

Of Humfrey Talbot, Queen Mary scorned to say anything, or to utter a syllable that she thought a daughter of Scotland needed a warning against a petty English sailor. Indeed, she had confidence that the youth's parents would view the attachment as quite as undesirable for him as for the young princess, and would guard against it for his sake as much as for hers.

The true parting took place ere the household was astir. Afterwards, Mary, fully equipped for travelling, in a dark cloth riding-dress and hood, came across to the great hall of the Manor-house, and there sat while each one of the attendants filed in procession, as it were, before her. To each lady she presented some small token wrought by her own hands. To each gentleman she also gave some trinket, such as the elaborate dress of the time permitted, and to each serving man or maid a

piece of money.   Of each one she gravely but gently
besought pardon for all the displeasures or offences she
might have caused them, and as they replied, kissing
her hand, many of them with tears, she returned a kiss
on the brow to each woman and an entreaty to be remembered in their prayers, and a like request, with a
pressure of the hand, to each man or boy.

It must have been a tedious ceremony, and yet to
every one it seemed as if Mary put her whole heart
into it, and to any to whom she owed special thanks
they were freely paid.

The whole was only over by an hour before noon.
Then she partook of a manchet and a cup of wine,
drinking, with liquid eyes, to the health and prosperity
of her good host, and to the restoration of his family
peace, which she had so sorely, though unwittingly,
disturbed.

Then she let him hand her out, once more kissing
Susan Talbot and Cis, who was weeping bitterly, and
whispering to the latter, " Not over much grief, *ma
petite ;* not more than may befit, *ma mignonne*."

Lord Shrewsbury lifted her on her horse, and, with
him on one side and Sir Ralf Sadler on the other, she
rode down the long avenue on her way to Wingfield.

The Bridgefield family had already made their
arrangements, and their horses were waiting for them
amid the jubilations of Diccon and Ned.   The Queen
had given each of them a fair jewel, with special
thanks to them for being good brothers to her dear
Cis.   " As if one wanted thanks for being good to
one's own sister," said Ned, thrusting the delicate little
ruby brooch on his mother to be taken care of till his
days of foppery should set in, and he would need it
for cap and plume.

"Come, Cis, we are going home at last," said
Diccon. "What! thou art not breaking thine heart
over yonder Scottish lady—when we are going home,
home, I say, and have got rid of watch and ward for
ever? Hurrah!" and he threw up his cap, and was
joined in the shout by more than one of the youngsters
around, for Richard and most of the elders were
escorting the Queen out of the park, and Mistress Susan
had been summoned on some question of household
stuff. Cis, however, stood leaning against the balustrade, over which she had leant for the last glance
exchanged with her mother, her face hidden in her
hands and kerchief, weeping bitterly, feeling as if all
the glory and excitement of the last few weeks had
vanished as a dream and left her to the dreary dulness of common life, as little insignificant Cis Talbot
again.

It was Humfrey who first came near, almost timidly
touched her hand, and said, "Cheer up. It is but for
a little while, mayhap. She will send for thee.
Come, here is thine old palfrey—poor old Dapple.
Let me put thee on him, and for this brief time let us
feign that all is as it was, and thou art my little sister
once more."

"I know not which is truth and which is dreaming,"
said Cis, waking up through her tears, but resigning
her hand to him, and letting him lift her to her seat
on the old pony which had been the playfellow of both.

If it had been an effort to Humfrey to prolong the
word Cis into sister, he was rewarded for it. It gave
the key-note to their intercourse, and set her at ease
with him; and the idea that her present rustication
was but a comedy instead of a reality was consoling in
her present frame of mind. Mistress Susan, surrounded

ɪ*

with importunate inquirers as to household matters, and unable to escape from them, could only see that Humfrey had taken charge of the maiden, and trusted to his honour and his tact.   This was, however, only the beginning of a weary and perplexing time.   Nothing could restore Cis to her old place in the Bridgefield household, or make her look upon its tasks, cares, and joys as she had done only a few short months ago. Her share in them could only be acting, and she was too artless and simple to play a part.   Most frequently she was listless, dull, and pining, so much inclined to despise and neglect the ordinary household occupations which befitted the daughter of the family, that her adopted mother was forced, for the sake of her incognito, to rouse, and often to scold her when any witnesses were present who would have thought Mrs. Talbot's toleration of such conduct in a daughter suspicious and unnatural.

Such reproofs were dangerous in another way, for Humfrey could not bear to hear them, and was driven nearly to the verge of disrespect and perilous approaches to implying that Cis was no ordinary person to be sharply reproved when she sat musing and sighing instead of sewing Diccon's shirts.

Even the father himself could not well brook to hear the girl blamed, and both he and Humfrey could not help treating her with a kind of deference that made the younger brothers gape and wonder what had come to Humfrey on his travels " to make him treat our Cis as a born princess."

" You irreverent varlets," said Humfrey, " you have yet to learn that every woman ought to be treated as a born princess."

" By cock and pie," said spoilt Ned, " that beats all !   One's own sister !"

Whereupon Humfrey had the opportunity of vent-
ing a little of his vexation by thrashing his brother for
his oath, while sharp Diccon innocently asked if men
never swore by anything when at sea, and thereby
nearly got another castigation for irreverent mocking
of his elder brother's discipline.

At other times the girl's natural activity and high
spirits gained the upper hand, and she would abandon
herself without reserve to the old homely delights of
Bridgefield.   At the apple gathering, she was running
about, screaming with joy, and pelting the boys with
apples, more as she had done at thirteen than at
seventeen, and when called to order she inconsistently
pleaded, " Ah, mother! it is for the last time.   Do but
let me have my swing!" putting on a wistful and
caressing look, which Susan did not withstand when
the only companions were the three brothers, since
Humfrey had much of her own unselfishness and self-
command, resulting in a discretion that was seldom
at fault.

And that discretion made him decide at a fortnight's
end that his father had been right, and that it would
be better for him to absent himself from where he
could do no good, but only added to the general perplexity, and involved himself in the temptation of
betraying the affection he knew to be hopeless.

Before, however, it was possible to fit out either
Diccon or the four men who were anxious to go under
the leadership of Master Humfrey of Bridgefield, the
Earl and Countess of Shrewsbury were returning fully
reconciled.   Queen Elizabeth had made the Cavendishes ask pardon on their knees of the Earl for their
slanders ; and he, in his joy, had freely forgiven all.
Gilbert Talbot and his wife had shared in the general

reconciliation. His elder brother's death had made him the heir apparent, and all were coming home again, including the little Lady Arbell, once more to fill the Castle and the Manor-house, and to renew the free hospitable life of a great feudal chief, or of the Queen's old courtier, with doors wide open, and no ward or suspicion.

Richard rejoiced that his sons, before going abroad, should witness the return to the old times which had been at an end before they could remember Sheffield distinctly. The whole family were drawn up as usual to receive them, when the Earl and Countess arrived first of all at the Manor-house.

The Countess looked smaller, thinner, older, perhaps a trifle more shrewish, but she had evidently suffered much, and was very glad to have recovered her husband and her home.

" So, Susan Talbot," was her salutation, "you have thriven, it seems. You have been playing the part of hostess, I hear."

" Only so far as might serve his Lordship, madam."

" And the wench, there, what call you her ? Ay, Cicely. I hear the Scottish Queen hath been cockering her up and making her her bedfellow, till she hath spoilt her for a reasonable maiden. Is it so ? She looks it."

" I trust not, madam," said Susan.

" She grows a strapping wench, and we must find her a good husband to curb her pride. I have a young man already in my eye for her."

" So please your Ladyship, we do not think of marrying her as yet," returned Susan, in consternation.

" Tilly vally, Susan Talbot, tell me not such folly as that. Why, the maid is over seventeen at the very least! Save for all the coil this Scottish woman and her crew have made, I should have seen her well mated a year ago."

Here was a satisfactory prospect for Mistress Susan, bred as she had been to unquestioning submission to the Countess. There was no more to be said on that occasion, as the great lady passed on to bestow her notice on others of her little court.

Humfrey meantime had been warmly greeted by the younger men of the suite, and one of them handed him a letter which filled him with eagerness. It was from an old shipmate, who wrote, not without sanction, to inform him that Sir Francis Drake was fitting out an expedition, with the full consent of the Queen, to make a descent upon the Spaniards, and that there was no doubt that if he presented himself at Plymouth, he would obtain either the command, or at any rate the lieutenancy, of one of the numerous ships which were to be commissioned. Humfrey was before all else a sailor. He had made no engagement to Sir John Norreys, and many of the persons engaged on this expedition were already known to him. It was believed that the attack was to be upon Spain itself, and the notion filled him with ardour and excitement that almost drove Cicely out of his mind, as he laid the proposal before his father.

Richard was scarcely less excited. "You young lads are in luck," he said. "I sailed for years and never had more than a chance brush with the Don; never the chance of bearding him on his own shores!"

"Come with us, then, father," entreated Humfrey. "Sir Francis would be overjoyed to see you. You would get the choicest ship to your share."

"Nay, nay, my boy, tempt me not; I cannot leave

your mother to meet all the coils that may fall in her
way! No; I'm too old. I've lost my sea legs. I
leave thee to win the fame, son Humfrey!"

The decision was thus made, and Humfrey and
Diccon were to start together for London first, and then
for Plymouth, the second day after a great festival for
the wedding of the little Alethea, daughter of Gilbert,
Lord Talbot—still of very tender age—to the young
heir of Arundel. The Talbot family had been pre-
cluded from holding festival for full fourteen years,
or indeed from entertaining any guests, save the Commissioners sent down to confer from time to time with
the captive Queen, so that it was no wonder that they
were in the highest possible spirits at their release, and
determined to take the first opportunity of exercising
the gorgeous hospitality of the Tudor times.

Posts went out, riding round all the neighbourhood
with invitations. The halls were swept and adorned
with the best suit of hangings. All the gentlemen,
young and old, all the keepers and verdurers, were put
in requisition to slaughter all the game, quadruped and
biped, that fell in their way, the village women and
children were turned loose on the blackberries, cranberries, and bilberries, and all the ladies and serving-
women were called on to concoct pasties of many stories
high, subtilties of wonderful curiosity, sweetmeats and
comfits, cakes and marchpanes worthy of Camacho's
wedding, or to deck the halls with green boughs, and
weave garlands of heather and red berries.

Cis absolutely insisted, so that the heads of the
household gave way, on riding out with Richard and
Humfrey when they had a buck to mark down in
Rivelin Chase. And she set her heart on going out to
gather cranberries in the park, flinging herself about

with petulant irritation when Dame Susan showed herself unwilling to permit a proceeding which was thought scarcely becoming in any well-born damsel of the period. "Ah, child, child! thou wilt have to bear worse restraints than these," she said, "if ever thou comest to thy greatness."

Cis made no answer, but threw herself into a chair and pouted.

The next morning she did not present herself at the usual hour; but just as the good mother was about to go in quest of her to her chamber, a clear voice came singing up the valley—

"Berries to sell! berries to sell!
Berries fresh from moorland fell!"

And there stood a girl in peasant dress, with short petticoats, stout shoes soaked in dew, a round face under black brows, and cheeks glowing in morning freshness; and a boy swung the other handle of the basket overflowing with purple berries.

It was but a shallow disguise betrayed by the two roguish faces, and the good mother was so pleased to see Cis smile merrily again, that she did not scold over the escapade.

Yet the inconsistent girl hotly refused to go up to the castle and help to make pastry for her mother's bitter and malicious foe, and Sir Richard shook his head and said she was in the right on't, and should not be compelled. So Susan found herself making lame excuses, which did not avert a sharp lecture from the Countess on the cockering of her daughter.

CHAPTER XIX.

THE CLASH OF SWORDS.

FESTIVALS in the middle ages were conducted by day rather than by night, and it was a bright noonday sun that shone upon the great hall at Sheffield, bedecked with rich tapestry around the dais, where the floor was further spread with Eastern carpets. Below, the garniture of the walls was of green boughs, interspersed between stag's antlers, and the floor was strewn, in ancient fashion, with the fragrant rush.

All the tables, however, were spread with pure white napery, the difference being only in texture, but the higher table rejoiced in the wonderful extravagance of silver plates, while the lower had only trenchers. As to knives, each guest brought his or her own, and forks were not yet, but bread, in long fingers of crust, was provided to a large amount to supply the want. Splendid salt-cellars, towering as landmarks to the various degrees of guests, tankards, gilt and parcel gilt or shining with silver, perfectly swarmed along the board, and the meanest of the guests present drank from silver-rimmed cups of horn, while for the very greatest were reserved the tall, slender, opal Venice glasses, recently purchased by the Countess in London.

The pies, the glory of Yorkshire, surpassed them-

selves.   The young bride and bridegroom had the
felicity of contemplating one whose crust was elevated
into the altar of Hymen, with their own selves united
thereat, attended by numerous Cupids, made chiefly in
paste and sugar, and with little wings from the
feathers of the many slaughtered fowl within.   As to
the jellies, the devices and the subtilties, the pen refuses to describe them!   It will be enough to say that
the wedding itself was the least part of the entertainment.   It was gone through with very few spectators
in the early morning, and the guests only assembled
afterwards to this mighty dinner at a somewhat earlier
hour than they would now to a wedding breakfast.
The sewer marshalled all the guests in pairs according
to their rank, having gone through the roll with his
mistress, just as the lady of the house or her aide-de-
camp pairs the guests and puts cards in their plates in
modern times.   Every one was there who had any
connection with the Earl; and Cis, though flashes of
recollection of her true claims would come across her
now and then, was unable to keep from being eager
about her first gaiety.   Perhaps the strange life she
had led at Buxton, as it receded in the distance,
became more and more unreal and shadowy, and
she was growing back into the simple Cicely she had
always believed herself.   It was with perfectly girlish
natural pleasure that she donned the delicate sky-blue
farthingale, embroidered with white lilies by the skilful
hands of the captive Queen, and the daintily-fashioned
little cap of Flanders lace, and practised the pretty
dancing steps which the Queen had amused herself with
teaching her long ere they knew they were mother and
daughter.

As Talbots, the Bridgefield family were spectators

of the wedding, after which, one by one, the seneschal
paired them off. Richard was called away first, then
a huge old Yorkshire knight came and bore away
Mrs. Susan, and after an interval, during which the
young people entertained hopes of keeping together in
enviable obscurity, the following summons to the board
was heard in a loud voice—

"Master Antony Babington, Esquire, of Dethick ¡
Mistress Cicely Talbot, of Bridgefield."

Humfrey's brow grew dark with disappointment,
but cleared into a friendly greeting, as there advanced
a tall, slender gentleman, of the well-known fair, pink
and white colouring, and yellow hair, apparelled point
device in dark green velvet, with a full delicately
crimped ruff, bowing low as he extended his hand to
take that of the young lady, exchanging at the same
time a friendly greeting with his old comrade, before
leading Cis to her place.

On the whole, she was pleased. *Tête-à-têtes* with
Humfrey were dreadfully embarrassing, and she felt life
so flat without her nocturnal romance that she was
very glad to have some one who would care to talk to
her of the Queen. In point of fact, such conversation
was prohibited. In the former days, when there had
been much more intercourse between the Earl's household and the neighbourhood, regular cautions had been
given to every member of it not to discuss the prisoner
or make any communication about her habits. The
younger generation who had grown up in the time of
the closer captivity had never been instructed in these
laws, for the simple reason that they hardly saw any one.
Antony and Cicely were likewise most comfortably
isolated, for she was flanked by a young esquire, who
had no eyes nor ears save for the fair widow of sixteen

whom he had just led in, and Antony, by a fat and
deaf lady, whose only interest was in tasting as many
varieties of good cheer as she could, and trying to
discover how and of what they were compounded.
Knowing Mistress Cicely to be a member of the family,
she once or twice referred the question to her across
Antony, but getting very little satisfaction, she gave up
the young lady as a bad specimen of housewifery, and
was forced to be content with her own inductions.

There was plenty of time for Antony to begin with,
" Are there as many conies as ever in the chase ?" and
to begin on a discussion of all the memories connected
with the free days of childhood, the blackberry and
bilberry gatherings, the hide-and-seek in the rocks and
heather, the consternation when little Dick was lost,
the audacious comedy with the unsuspected spectators,
and all the hundred and one recollections, less memorable perhaps, but no less delightful to both. It was
only thus gradually that they approached their recent
encounter in the Castleton Cavern, and Antony explained how he had burnt to see his dear Queen and
mistress once again, and that his friends, Tichborne and
the rest, were ready to kiss every footstep she had
taken, and almost worshipped him and John Eyre for
contriving this mode of letting them behold the hitherto
unknown object of their veneration.

All that passionate, chivalrous devotion, which in
Sidney, Spenser, and many more attached itself to their
great Gloriana, had in these young men, all either
secretly or openly reconciled to Rome, found its object
in that rival in whom Edmund Spenser only beheld
his false Duessa or snowy Florimel. And, indeed,
romance had in her a congenial heroine, who needed
little self-blinding so to appear. Her beauty needed

no illusion to be credited. Even at her age, now over forty, the glimpse they had had in the fitful torchlight of the cavern had been ravishing, and had confirmed all they had ever heard of her witching loveliness; nor did they recollect how that very obscurity might have assisted it.

To their convictions, she was the only legitimate sovereign in the island, a confessor for their beloved Church, a captive princess and beauty driven from her throne, and kept in durance by a usurper. Thus every generous feeling was enlisted in her cause, with nothing to counterbalance them save the English hatred of the Spaniard, with whom her cause was inextricably linked; a dread of what might be inflicted on the country in the triumph of her party; and in some, a strange inconsistent personal loyalty to Elizabeth; but all these they were instructed to believe mere temptations and delusions that ought to be brushed aside as cobwebs.

Antony's Puritan tutor at Cambridge had, as Richard Talbot had foreboded, done little but add to his detestation of the Reformation, and he had since fallen in with several of the seminary priests who were circulating in England. Some were devoted and pious men, who at the utmost risk went from house to house to confirm the faith and constancy of the old families of their own communion. The saintly martyr spirit of one of these, whom Antony met in the house of a kinsman of his mother, had so wrought on him as to bring him heart and soul back to his mother's profession, in which he had been secretly nurtured in early childhood, and which had received additional confirmation at Sheffield, where Queen Mary and her ladies had always shown that they regarded him as one

of themselves, sure to return to them when he was his
own master.   It was not, however, of this that he
spoke to Cis, but whatever she ventured to tell him of
the Queen was listened to with delight as an extreme
favour, which set her tongue off with all the eager
pleasure of a girl, telling what she alone can tell.

All through the banquet they talked, for Babington
had much to ask of all the members of the household
whom he had known.   And after the feast was over
and the hall was cleared for dancing, Antony was
still, by etiquette, her partner for the evening.   The
young bride and bridegroom had first to perform a
stately pavise before the whole assembly in the centre
of the floor, in which, poor young things, they acquitted
themselves much as if they were in the dancing-
master's hands.   Then her father led out his mother,
and *vice versâ*.   The bridegroom had no grandparents,
but the stately Earl handed forth his little active wiry
Countess, bowing over her with a grand stiff devotion
as genuine and earnest as at their wedding twenty
years previously, for the reconciliation had been complete, and had restored all her ascendency over him.
Theirs, as Mistress Susan exultingly agreed with a
Hardwicke kinsman not seen for many years, was the
grandest and most featly of all the performances.   All
the time each pair were performing, the others were
awaiting their turn, the ladies in rows on benches or
settles, the gentlemen sometimes standing before them,
sometimes sitting on cushions or steps at their feet,
sometimes handing them comfits of sugar or dried fruits.

The number of gentlemen was greatly in excess,
so that Humfrey had no such agreeable occupation,
but had to stand in a herd among other young men,
watching with no gratified eye Antony Babington, in a

graceful attitude at Cicely's feet, while she conversed with him with untiring animation.

Humfrey was not the only one to remark them. Lady Shrewsbury nodded once or twice to herself as one who had discovered what she sought, and the next morning a mandate arrived at Bridgefield that Master Richard and his wife should come to speak with my Lady Countess.

Richard and his son were out of reach, having joined a party of the guests who had gone out hunting. Susan had to go alone, for she wished to keep Cicely as much as possible out of her Ladyship's sight, so she left the girl in charge of her keys, so that if father brought home any of the hunters to the midday meal, tankards and glasses might not be lacking.

The Countess's summons was to her own bower, a sort of dressing-room, within her great state bed-room, and with a small glazed window looking down into the great hall where her ladies sat at work, whence she could on occasion call down orders or directions or reproofs. Susan had known what it was to stand in dread of such a window at Chatsworth or Hardwicke, whence shrill shrieks of objurgation, followed sometimes by such missiles as pincushions, shoes, or combs. However the window was now closed, and my Lady sat in her arm-chair, as on a throne, a stool being set, to which she motioned her kinswoman.

"So! Susan Talbot," she said, "I have sent for you to do you a good turn, for you are mine own kins-woman of the Hardwicke blood, and have ever been reasonably humble and dutiful towards me and my Lord."

Mrs. Talbot did not by any means view this speech as the insult it would in these days appear to a lady of her birth and position, but accepted it as the compliment it was intended to be.

"Thus," continued Lady Shrewsbury, "I have always cast about how to marry that daughter of yours fitly. It would have been done ere now, had not that Scottish woman's tongue made mischief between me and my Lord, but I am come home to rule my own house now, and mine own blood have the first claim on me."

The alarm always excited by a summons to speak with my Lady Countess began to acquire definite form, and Susan made answer, "Your Ladyship is very good, but I doubt me whether my husband desires to bestow Cicely in marriage as yet."

"He hath surely received no marriage proposals for her without my knowledge or my Lord's," said Bess of Hardwicke, who was prepared to strain all feudal claims to the uttermost.

"No, madam, but——"

"Tell me not that you or he have the presumption to think that my son William Cavendish or even Edward Talbot will ever cast an eye on a mere portionless country maid, not comely, nor even like the Hardwickes or the Talbots. If I thought so for a moment, never shouldst thou darken these doors again, thou ungrateful, treacherous woman."

"Neither of us ever had the thought, far less the wish," said Susan most sincerely.

"Well, thou wast ever a simple woman, Susan Talbot," said the great lady, thereby meaning truthful, "so I will e'en take thy word for it, the more readily that I made contracts for both the lads when I was at court. As to Dick Talbot not being fain to bestow her, I trow that is because ye have spent too much on

your long-legged sons to be able to lay down a portion
for her, though she be your only daughter.   Anan ?"

For though this was quite true, Susan feeling that
it was not the whole truth, made but faint response.
However, the Countess went on, expecting to over-
power her with gratitude.   "The gentleman I mean is
willing to take her in her smock, and moreover his
wardship and marriage were granted to my Lord by her
Majesty.   Thou knowest whom I mean."

She wanted to hear a guess, and Susan actually
foreboded the truth, but was too full of dismay and
perplexity to do anything but shake her head as one
puzzled.

"What think'st thou of Mr. Babington ?" triumphantly exclaimed the Countess.

"Mr. Babington !" returned Susan.   "But he is no
longer a ward !"

"No.   We had granted his marriage to a little
niece of my Lord Treasurer's, but she died ere coming
to age.   Then Tom Ratcliffe's wife would have him for
her daughter, a mere babe.   But for that thou and
thine husband have done good service while evil
tongues kept me absent, and because the wench comes
of our own blood, we are willing to bestow her upon
him, **he** showing himself willing and content, as befits
a lad bred in our own household."

"Madam, we are much beholden to you and my
Lord, but sure Mr. Babington is more inclined to the
old faith."

"Tush, woman, what of that ?   Thou mayst say
the same of half our Northern youth !   They think it
grand to dabble with seminary priests in hiding, and
talk big about their conscience and the like, but when
they've seen a neighbour or two pay down a heavy

fine for recusancy, they think better of it, and a good wife settles their brains to jog to church to hear the parson with the rest of them."

"I fear me Cis is over young to settle any one's mind," said Susan.

"She is seventeen if she is a day," said my Lady, "and I was a wedded wife ere I saw my teens. Moreover, I will say for thee, Susan, that thou hast bred the girl as becomes one trained in my household, and unless she have been spoiled by resort to the Scottish woman, she is like to make the lad a moderately good wife, having seen nought of the unthrifty modes of the fine court dames, who queen it with standing ruffs a foot high, and coloured with turmeric, so please you, but who know no more how to bake a marchpane, or roll puff paste, than yonder messan dog !"

"She is a good girl," said Susan, "but——"

"What has the foolish wife to object now ?" said the Countess. "I tell you I marked them both last eve, and though I seldom turn my mind to such follies, I saw the plair tokens of love in every look and gesture of the young springald. Nay, 'twas his countenance that put it into my mind, for I am even too good - natured — over good - natured, Susan Talbot. How now," at some sound below, springing to the little window and flinging it back, "you lazy idle wenches —what are you doing there ? Is my work to stand still while you are toying with yon vile whelp ? He is tangling the yarn, don't you see, thou purblind Jane Dacre, with no eyes but for ogling. There ! there ! Round the leg of the chair, don't you see !" and down flew a shoe, which made the poor dog howl, and his mistress catch him up. "Put him down ! put him down this instant ! Thomas ! Davy ! Here, hang him up, I say," cried this over good-natured lady, interspersing her commands with a volley of sixteenth century Billingsgate, and ending by declaring that nothing fared well without her, and hurrying off to pounce down on the luckless damsels who had let their dog play with the embroidery yarn destined to emblazon the tapestry of Chatsworth with the achievements of Juno. The good nature was so far veritable that when she found little harm done, and had vented her wrath in strong language and boxes on the ear, she would forget her sentence upon the poor little greyhound, which Mrs. Jane Dacre had hastily conveyed out of sight during her transit downstairs. Susan was thus, to her great relief, released for the present, for guests came in before my Lady had fully completed her objurgations on her ladies, the hour of noon was nigh at hand, sounds in the court betokened the return of the huntsmen, and Susan effected her escape to her own sober old palfrey—glad that she would at least be able to take counsel with her husband on this most inconvenient proposition.

He came out to meet her at the court door, having just dismounted, and she knew by his face that she had not to give him the first intelligence of the difficulty in which they stood.

My Lord had himself spoken to him, like my Lady expecting him to be enchanted at the prospect of so good a match for his slenderly-portioned daughter, for Dethick was a fair estate, and the Babington family, though not ennobled, fully equal to a younger branch of the Talbots. However, Richard had had a less uncomfortable task than his wife, since the Earl was many degrees more reasonable than the Countess. He had shown himself somewhat offended at not meeting more

alacrity in the acceptance of his proposal, when Richard
had objected on account of the young gentleman's
Popish proclivities; but boldly declared that he was
quite certain that the stripling had been entirely cured.

This point of the narrative had just been reached
when it was interrupted by a scream, and Cicely came
flying into the hall, crying, "O father, father, stop
them! Humfrey and Mr. Babington! They are
killing one another."

"Where?" exclaimed Richard, catching up his
sword.

"In the Pleasance, father! Oh, stop them! They
will slay one another! They had their swords!" and
as the father was already gone, she threw herself into
the mother's arms, hid her face and sobbed with fright
as scarce became a princess for whom swords were for
the first time crossed. "Fear not! Father will stop
them," said the mother, with confidence she could only
keep up outwardly by the inward cry, "God protect
my boy. Father will come ere they can hurt one
another."

"But how came it about?" she added, as with an
arm round the trembling girl, she moved anxiously forward to know the issue.

"Oh! I know not. 'Twas Humfrey fell on him.
Hark!"

"'Tis father's voice," said Susan. "Thank God! I
know by the sound no harm is done! But how was
it, child?"

Cis told with more coherence now, but the tears in
her eyes and colour deepening: "I was taking in
Humfrey's kerchiefs from the bleaching on the grass,
when Master Babington—he had brought me a plume
of pheasant's feathers from the hunting, and he began.

O mother, is it sooth? He said my Lord had sent him."

"That is true, my child, but you know we have no choice but to refuse thee."

"Ay, mother, and Antony knows."

"Not thy true birth, child?"

"Not that, but the other story. So he began to say that if I were favourable — Mother, do men always do like that?" Hiding her face against the trusty breast, "And when I drew back, and said I could not and would not hearken to such folly———"

"That was well, dear child."

"He *would* have it that I should have to hear him, and he went down on his knee, and snatched at my hand. And therewith came a great howl of rage like an angry lion, and Humfrey bounded right over the sweetbrier fence, and cried out, 'Off, fellow! No Papist traitor knave shall meddle with her.' And then Antony gave him back the lie for calling him traitor, and they drew their swords, and I ran away to call father, but oh! mother, I heard them clash!" and she shuddered again.

"See," said Susan, as they had reached the corner of a thick screen of yew-trees, "all is safe. There they stand, and father between them speaking to them. No, we will not go nearer, since we know that it is well with them. Men deal with each other better out of women's earshot. Ah, see, there they are giving one another their hands. All is over now."

"Humfrey stands tall, grave, and stiff! He is only doing it because father bids him," said Cicely. "Antony is much more willing."

"Poor Humfrey! he knows better than Antony how vain any hope must be of my silly little princess," said Susan, with a sigh for her boy. " Come in, child, and set these locks in order. The hour of noon hath long been over, and father hath not yet dined."

So they flitted out of sight as Richard and his son turned from the place of encounter, the former saying, " Son Humfrey, I had deemed thee a wiser man."

" Sir, how could a man brook seeing that fellow on his knee to her ? Is it not enough to be debarred from my sweet princess myself, but I must see her beset by a Papist and traitor, fostered and encouraged too ?"

" And thou couldst not rest secure in the utter impossibility of her being given to him ? He is as much out of reach of her as thou art."

" He has secured my Lord and my Lady on his side !" growled Humfrey.

" My Lord is not an Amurath, nor my Lady either," said Richard, shortly. "As long as I pass for her father I have power to dispose of her, and I am not going to give another woman's daughter away without her consent."

" Yet the fellow may have her ear," said Humfrey. " I know him to be popishly inclined, and there is a web of those Romish priests all over the island, whereof this Queen holds the strands in her fingers, captive though she be. I should not wonder if she had devised this fellow's suit."

" This is the very madness of jealousy, Humfrey," said his father. " The whole matter was, as thy mother and thy Lord have both told me, simply a device of my Lady Countess's own brain."

" Babington took to it wondrous naturally," muttered Humfrey.

" That may be ; but as for the lady at Wingfield, her talk to our poor maid hath been all of archdukes

and dukes. She is far too haughty to think for a
moment of giving her daughter to a mere Derbyshire
esquire, not even of noble blood. You may trust her
for that."

This pacified Humfrey for a little while, especially
as the bell was clanging for the meal which had been
unusually deferred, and he had to hurry away to remove
certain marks, which were happily the result of the
sweetbrier weapons instead of that of Babington.

That a little blood had been shed was shown by
the state of his sword point, but Antony had disclaimed
being hurt when the master of the house came up, and
in the heat of the rebuke the father and son had hardly
noticed that he had thrown a kerchief round his left
hand ere he moved away.

Before dinner was over, word was brought in from
the door that Master Will Cavendish wanted to speak
to Master Humfrey. The ladies' hearts were in their
mouths, as it were, lest it should be to deliver a cartel,
and they looked to the father to interfere, but he sat
still, contenting himself with saying, as his son craved
license to quit the board, " Use discretion as well as
honour."

They were glad that the next minute Humfrey came
back to call his father to the door, where Will Cavendish sat on horseback. He had come by desire of
Babington, who had fully intended that the encounter
should be kept secret, but some servant must have been
aware of it either from the garden or the park, and the
Countess had got wind of it. She had summoned
Babington to her presence, before the castle barber
had finished dealing with the cut in his hand, and
the messenger reported that " my Lady was in one of
her raging fits," and talked of throwing young Hum-

frey into a dungeon, if not having him hung for his insolence.

Babington, who had talked to his friends of a slip with his hunting-knife while disembowelling a deer, was forced to tell the fact in haste to Cavendish, the nearest at hand, begging him to hurry down and advise Humfrey to set forth at once if he did not wish his journey to be unpleasantly delayed.

" My Lord is unwilling to cross my mother at the present," said young Cavendish with half a smile ; " and though it be not likely that much harm should come of the matter, yet if she laid hands on Humfrey at the present moment, there might be hindrance and vexation, so it may be well for him to set forth, in case Tony be unable to persuade my Lady that it is nought."

Will Cavendish had been a friendly comrade of both Humfrey and Antony in their boyish days, and his warning was fully to be trusted.

" I know not why I should creep off as though I had done aught that was evil," said Humfrey, drawing himself up.

" Well," said Will, " my Lord is always wroth at brawling with swords amongst us, and he might——my mother egging him on——lay you by the heels in the strong room for a week or so. Nay, for my part, methinks 'twas a strange requital of poor Babington's suit to your sister! Had she been your love instead of your sister there might have been plainer excuse, but sure you wot not of aught against Tony to warrant such heat."

" He was importuning her when she would have none of him," said Humfrey, feeling the perplexity he had drawn on himself.

" Will says well," added the father, feeling that it

by all means behoved them all to avert inquiry into the cause of Humfrey's passion, since neither Cicely's birth nor Antony's perilous inclinations could be pleaded. " To be detained a week or two might hinder thy voyage. So we will speed thee on thy way instantly."

" Tell me not where he halts for the night," said Cavendish significantly. " Fare thee well, Humfrey. I would return ere I am missed. I trust thou wilt have made the Spaniard's ships smoke, and weighted thy pouch with his dollars, before we see thee again."

" Fare thee well, Will, and thank thee kindly," returned Humfrey, as they wrung each other's hands. " And tell Antony that I thank him heartily for his thought, and owe him a good turn."

" That is well, my son," said Richard, as Cavendish rode out of the court. " Babington is both hot and weak-headed, and I fear me is in the toils of the Scottish lady; but he would never do aught that he held as disloyal by a comrade. I wish I could say the same of him anent the Queen."

" And you will guard her from him, sir ? " earnestly said Humfrey.

" As I would from—I would have said Frenchman or Spaniard, but, poor maid, that may only be her hap, if her mother should come to her throne again ; " and as Humfrey shrugged his shoulders at the improbability, " But we must see thee off, my boy. Poor mother ! this hurries the parting for her. So best, mayhap."

It was hastily arranged that Humfrey should ride off at once, and try to overtake a squire who had been at the festival, and had invited him to turn a little out of his road and spend a day or two at his house when leaving home. Humfrey had then declined, but hospitality in those days was elastic, and he had no doubt of a welcome. His father would bring Diccon and his baggage to join him there the next day.

Thus there were only a very few minutes for adieux, and, as Richard had felt, this was best for all, even the anxious mother. Cicely ran about with the rest in the stress of preparation, until Humfrey, hurrying upstairs, met her coming down with a packet of his lace cuffs in her hands.

He caught the hand on the balusters, and cried, "My princess, my princess, and art thou doing this for me?"

"Thou hast learnt fine compliments, Humfrey," said Cis, trying to do her part with quivering lips.

"Ah, Cis! thou knowest but too well what hath taught me no fine words but plain truth. Fear me not, I know what is due to thee. Cis, we never used to believe the tales and ballads that told of knights worshipping princesses beyond their reach, without a hope of more than a look—not even daring to wish for more; Cis, it is very truth. Be thou where thou wilt, with whom thou wilt, there will be one ready to serve thee to the uttermost, and never ask aught— aught but such remembrance as may befit the brother of thy childhood——"

"Mistress Cis," screamed one of the maids, "madam is waiting for those cuffs."

Cis ran down, but the squeeze and kiss on the hand remained, as it were, imprinted on it, far more than the last kiss of all, which he gave, as both knew and felt, to support his character as a brother before the assembled household.

K

CHAPTER XX.

WINGFIELD MANOR.

THE drawing of swords was not regarded as a heinous offence in Elizabethan days. It was not likely, under ordinary circumstances, to result in murder, and was looked on much as boxing is, or was recently, in public schools, as an evidence of high spirit, and a means of working off ill-blood.

Lady Shrewsbury was, however, much incensed at such a presumptuous reception of the suitor whom she had backed with her would-be despotic influence; and in spite of Babington's making extremely light of it, and declaring that he had himself been too forward in his suit, and the young lady's apparent fright had made her brother interfere over hastily for her protection, four yeomen were despatched by her Ladyship with orders instantly to bring back Master Humfrey Talbot to answer for himself.

They were met by Mr. Talbot with the sober reply that Master Humfrey was already set forth on his journey. The men, having no orders, never thought of pursuing him, and after a short interval Richard thought it expedient to proceed to the Manor-house to explain matters.

The Countess swooped upon him in one of her

ungovernable furies—one of those of which even
Gilbert Talbot avoided writing the particulars to his
father—abusing his whole household in general, and
his son in particular, in the most outrageous manner,
for thus receiving the favour she had done to their
beggarly, ill-favoured, ill-nurtured daughter. Richard
stood still and grave, his hat in his hand, as unmoved
and tranquil as if he had been breasting a stiff breeze
on the deck of his ship, with good sea-room and confidence in all his tackle, never even attempting to
open his lips, but looking at the Countess with a
steady gaze which somehow disconcerted her, for she
demanded wherefore he stared at her like one of his
clumsy hinds.

"Because her Ladyship does not know what she is
saying," he replied.

"Darest thou! Thou traitor, thou viper, thou
unhanged rascal, thou mire under my feet, thou blot
on the house! Darest thou beard me—me?" screamed
my Lady. "Darest thou—I say——"

If the sailor had looked one whit less calm and
resolute, my Lady would have had her clenched fist on
his ear, or her talons in his beard, but he was like a
rock against which the billows expended themselves,
and after more of the tempest than need stain these
pages, she deigned to demand what he meant or had
to say for his son.

"Solely this, madam, that my son had never even
heard of Babington's suit, far less that he had your
Ladyship's good-will. He found him kneeling to
Cicely in the garden, and the girl, distressed and dismayed at his importunity. There were hot words and
drawn blades. That was the whole. I parted them
and saw them join hands."

"So saith Master Babington. He is willing to overlook the insult, so will I and my Lord, if you will atone for it by instantly consenting to this espousal."

"That, madam, I cannot do."

She let him say no more, and the storm had begun to rage again, when Babington took advantage of an interval to take breath, and said, "I thank you, madam, and pray you peace. If a little space be vouchsafed me, I trust to show this worthy gentleman cause wherefore he should no longer withhold his fair damsel from me."

"Indeed!" said the Countess. "Art thou so confident? I marvel what better backer thou wouldst have than me! So conceited of themselves are young men now-a-days, they think, forsooth, their own merits and graces should go farther in mating them than the word and will of their betters. There, you may go! I wash my hands of the matter. One is as ingrate as the other."

Both gentlemen accepted this amiable dismissal, each hoping that the Countess might indeed have washed her hands of their affairs. On his departure Richard was summoned into the closet of the Earl, who had carefully kept out of the way during the uproar, only trusting not to be appealed to. "My good cousin," he asked, "what means this broil between the lads? Hath Babington spoken sooth?"

"He hath spoken well and more generously than, mayhap, I thought he would have done," said Richard.

"Ay; you have judged the poor youth somewhat hardly, as if the folly of pagedom never were outgrown," said the Earl. "I put him under governorship such as to drive out of his silly pate all the wiles that he was fed upon here. You will see him prove

himself an honest Protestant and good subject yet, and
be glad enough to give him your daughter. So he was
too hot a lover for Master Humfrey's notions, eh?" said
my Lord, laughing a little. "The varlet! He was over
prompt to protect his sister, yet 'twas a fault on the
right side, and I am sorry there was such a noise about
it that he should have gone without leave-takings."

"He will be glad to hear of your Lordship's goodness. I shall go after him to-morrow and take his
mails and little Diccon to him."

"That is well," said the Earl. "And give him
this, with his kinsman's good wishes that he may win
ten times more from the Don," pushing towards
Richard a packet of twenty broad gold pieces, stamped
with Queen Bess in all her glory; and then, after
receiving due thanks for the gift, which was meant half
as friendly feudal patronage from the head of the family,
half as a contribution to the royal service, the Earl
added, " I would crave of thee, Richard, to extend thy
journey to Wingfield. Here are some accounts of which
I could not sooner get the items, to be discharged between me and the lady there—and I would fain send
thee as the man whom I can most entirely trust. I
will give thee a pass, and a letter to Sadler, bidding
him admit thee to her presence, since there are matters
here which can sooner be discharged by one word of
mouth than by many weary lines of writing."

Good Master Richard's conscience had little occasion to wince, yet he could not but feel somewhat
guilty when this opportune commission was given to
him, since the Earl gave it unaware of his secret
understanding with the captive. He accepted it,
however, without hesitation, since he was certainly
not going to make a mischievous use of it, and bent

all his mind to understand the complicated accounts
that he was to lay before the Queen or her comptroller
of the household.

He had still another interview to undergo with
Antony Babington, who overtook him on his way
home through the crackling leaves that strewed the
avenue, as the October twilight fell. His recent conduct towards Humfrey gave him a certain right to
friendly attention, though, as the frank-hearted mariner
said to himself, it was hard that a plain man, who
never told a lie, nor willingly had a concealment of his
own, should be involved in a many-sided secret like
this, a sort of web, where there was no knowing
whether straining the wrong strand might not amount
to a betrayal, all because he had rescued an infant, and
not at once proclaimed her an alien.

"Sir," said Antony, "if my impatience to accost the
maiden we wot of, when I saw her alone, had not misled me, I should have sought you first to tell you that
no man knows better than I that my Lady Countess's
good will is not what is wanting to forward my suit."

"Knowing then that it is not in my power or right
to dispose of her, thine ardent wooing was out of place,"
said Richard.

"I own it, sir, though had I but had time I should
have let the maiden know that I sought her subject to
other approval, which I trust to obtain so as to satisfy
you."

"Young man," said Richard, "listen to friendly
counsel, and meddle not in perilous matters. I ask
thee not whether Dethick hath any commerce with
Wingfield; but I warn thee earnestly to eschew beginning again that which caused the trouble of thy childhood. Thou mayst do it innocently, seeking the con-

sent of the lady to this courtship of thine ; but I tell
thee, as one who knows more of the matter than thou
canst, that thou wilt only meet with disappointment."

"Hath the Queen other schemes for her?" asked
Babington, anxiously; and Richard, thinking of the
vista of possible archdukes, replied that she had ; but
that he was not free to speak, though he replied to
Babington's half-uttered question that his son Humfrey
was by no means intended.

"Ah!" cried Antony, "you give me hope, sir. I
will do her such service that she shall refuse me
nothing ! Sir! do you mock me !" he added, with a
fierce change of note.

"My poor lad, I could not but laugh to think what
a simple plotter you are, and what fine service you will
render if thou utterest thy vows to the very last person
who should hear them ! Credit me, thou wast never
made for privy schemes and conspiracies, and a Queen
who can only be served by such, is no mistress for thee.
Thou wilt but run thine own neck into the noose, and
belike that of others."

"That will I never do," quoth Antony. "I may
peril myself, but no others."

"Then the more you keep out of secrets the better.
Thou art too open-hearted and unguarded for them !
So speaks thy well-wisher, Antony, whose friendship
thou hast won by thine honourable conduct towards
my rash boy ; though I tell thee plainly, the maiden is
not for thee, whether as Scottish or English, Cis or Bride."

So they parted at the gate of the park, the younger
man full of hope and confidence, the elder full of
pitying misgiving.

He was too kind-hearted not to let Cicely know
that he should see her mother, or to refuse to take a

billet for her,—a little formal note necessarily silent on the matter at issue, since it had to be laid before the Earl, who smiled at the scrupulous precaution, and let it pass.

Thus the good father parted with Humfrey and Diccon, rejoicing in his heart that they would fight with open foes, instead of struggling with the meshes of perplexity, which beset all concerned with Queen Mary, and then he turned his horse's head towards Wingfield Manor, a grand old castellated mansion of the Talbots, considered by some to excel even Sheffield. It stood high, on ground falling very steeply from the walls on three sides, and on the south well fortified, court within court, and each with a deep-arched and portcullised gateway, with loopholed turrets on either side, a porter's lodge, and yeomen guards.

Mr. Talbot had to give his name and quality, and show his pass, at each of these gates, though they were still guarded by Shrewsbury retainers, with the talbot on their sleeves. He was, however, received with the respect and courtesy due to a trusted kinsman of their lord; and Sir Ralf Sadler, a thin, elderly, careworn statesman, came to greet him at the door of the hall, and would only have been glad could he have remained a week, instead of for the single night he wished to spend at Wingfield.

Sadler was one of Mary's most gentle and courteous warders, and he spoke of her with much kindness, regretting that her health had again begun to suffer from the approach of winter, and far more from disappointment.

The negotiation with Scotland on her behalf was now known to have been abortive. James had fallen into the hands of the faction most hostile to her, and

though his mother still clung with desperate hope to
the trust that he, at least, was labouring on her behalf,
no one else believed that he cared for anything but his
own security, and even she had been forced to perceive
that her liberation was again adjourned.

"And what think you was her thought when she
found that road closed up?" said Sir Ralf. "Why, for
her people! Her gentlewoman, Mrs. Mowbray, hath, it
seems, been long betrothed."

"Ay, to Gilbert Curll, the long-backed Scotch
Secretary. They were to be wed at Stirling so soon as
she arrived there again."

"Yea; but when she read the letter that overthrew
her hopes, what did she say but that 'her servants
must not grow gray-headed with waiting till she was
set free'! So she would have me make the case known
to Sir Parson, and we had them married in the parish
church two days since, they being both good Protestants."

"There is no doubt that her kindness of heart is
true," said Richard. "The poor folk at Sheffield and
Ecclesfield will miss her plentiful almsgiving."

"Some say it ought to be hindered, for that it is
but a purchasing of friends to her cause," said Sadler;
"but I have not the heart to check it, and what could
these of the meaner sort do to our Queen's prejudice?
I take care that nothing goes among them that could
hide a billet, and that none of her people have private
speech with them, so no harm can ensue from her
bounty."

A message here came that the Queen was ready to
admit Mr. Talbot, and Richard found himself in her
presence chamber, a larger and finer room than that in
the lodge at Sheffield, and with splendid tapestry
hangings and plenishings; but the windows all looked

K*

into the inner quadrangle, instead of on the expanse
of park, and thus, as Mary said, she felt more entirely
the prisoner.   This, however, was not perceptible at
the time, for the autumn evening had closed in; there
were two large fires burning, one at each end of the
room, and tall tapestry-covered screens and high-backed
settles were arranged so as to exclude the draughts
around the hearth, where Mary reclined on a couch-
like chair.   She looked ill, and though she brightened
with her sweet smile to welcome her guest, there
were dark circles round her eyes, and an air of de-
jection in her whole appearance.   She held out her
hand graciously, as Richard approached, closely followed by his host; he put his knee to the ground
and kissed it, as she said, "You must pardon me,
Mr. Talbot, for discourtesy, if I am less agile than
when we were at Buxton.   You see my old foe lies in
wait to plague me with aches and pains so soon as the
year declines."

"I am sorry to see your Grace thus," returned
Richard, standing on the step.

"The while I am glad to see you thus well, sir.
And how does the good lady, your wife, and my sweet
playfellow, your daughter?"

"Well, madam, I thank your Grace, and Cicely has
presumed to send a billet by mine hand."

"Ah! the dear bairnie," and all the Queen's consummate art could not repress the smile of gladness
and the movement of eager joy with which she held out
her hand for it, so that Richard regretted its extreme
brevity and unsatisfying nature, and Mary, recollecting
herself in a second, added, smiling at Sadler, "Mr.
Talbot knows how a poor prisoner must love the pretty
playfellows that are lent to her for a time."

Sir Ralf's presence hindered any more intimate conversation, and Richard had certainly committed a solecism in giving Cicely's letter the precedence over the Earl's. The Queen, however, had recalled her caution, and inquired for the health of the Lord and Lady, and, with a certain sarcasm on her lips, trusted that the peace of the family was complete, and that they were once more setting Hallamshire the example of living together as household doves.

Her hazel eyes meantime archly scanned the face of Richard, who could not quite forget the very un-dovelike treatment he had received, though he could and did sturdily aver that "my Lord and my Lady were perfectly reconciled, and seemed most happy in their reunion."

Well-a-day, let us trust that there will be no further disturbances to their harmony," said Mary, " a prayer I may utter most sincerely. Is the little Arbell come back with them ? "

" Yea, madam."

" And is she installed in my former rooms, with the canopy over her cradle to befit her strain of royalty ? "

" I think not, madam. Meseems that my Lady Countess hath seen reason to be heedful on that score. My young lady hath come back with a grave *gouvernante*, who makes her read her primer and sew her seam, and save that she sat next my Lady at the wedding feast there is little difference made between her and the other grandchildren."

The Queen then inquired into the circumstances of the wedding festivities with the interest of one to whom most of the parties were more or less known, and who seldom had the treat of a little feminine gossip. She asked who had been " her little Cis's

partner," and when she heard of Babington, she said,
" Ah ha, then, the poor youth has made his peace with
my Lord ? "

" Certes, madam, he is regarded with high favour
by both my Lord and my Lady," said Richard, heartily
wishing himself rid of his host.

" I rejoice to hear it," said Mary ; " I was afraid
that his childish knight-errantry towards the captive
dame had damaged the poor stripling's prospects for
ever.   He is our neighbour here, and I believe Sir
Ralf regards him as somewhat perilous."

" Nay, madam, if my Lord of Shrewsbury be satisfied with him, so surely ought I to be," said Sir Ralf.

Nothing more of importance passed that night.
The packet of accounts was handed over to Sir
Andrew Melville, and the two gentlemen dismissed
with gracious good-nights.

Richard Talbot was entirely trusted, and when the
next morning after prayers, breakfast, and a turn among
the stables, it was intimated that the Queen was ready
to see him anent my Lord's business, Sir Ralf Sadler,
who had his week's report to write to the Council,
requested that his presence might be dispensed with,
and thus Mr. Talbot was ushered into the Queen's closet
without any witnesses to their interview save Sir
Andrew Melville and Marie de Courcelles.   The
Queen was seated in a large chair, leaning against
cushions, and evidently in a good deal of pain, but, as
Richard made his obeisance, her eyes shone as she
quoted two lines from an old Scotch ballad—

> " ' Madame, how does my gay goss hawk ?
> Madame, how does my doo ? '

Now can I hear what I hunger for ! "

"My gay gosshawk, madam, is flown to join Sir Francis Drake at Plymouth, and taken his little brother with him. I come now from speeding them as far as Derby."

"Ah! you must not ask me to pray for success to them, my good sir,—only that there may be a time when nations may be no more divided, and I fear me we shall not live to see it. And my doo—my little Cis, did she weep as became a sister for the bold laddies?"

"She wept many tears, madam, but we are sore perplexed by a matter that I must lay before your Grace. My Lady Countess is hotly bent on a match between the maiden and young Babington."

"Babington!" exclaimed the Queen, with the lioness sparkle in her eye. "You refused the fellow of course?"

"Flatly, madam, but your Grace knows that it is ill making the Countess accept a denial of her will."

Mary laughed "Ah ha! methought, sir, you looked somewhat as if you had had a recent taste of my Lord of Shrewsbury's dove. But you are a man to hold your own sturdy will, Master Richard, let Lord or Lady say what they choose."

"I trust so, madam, I am master of mine own house, and, as I should certainly not give mine own daughter to Babington, so shall I guard your Grace's."

"You would not give the child to him if she were your own?"

"No, madam."

"And wherefore not? Because he is too much inclined to the poor prisoner and her faith? Is it so, sir?"

"Your Grace speaks the truth in part," said Richard,

and then with effort added, "and likewise, madam, with your pardon, I would say that though I verily believe it is nobleness of heart and spirit that inclines poor Antony to espouse your Grace's cause, there is to my mind a shallowness and indiscretion about his nature, even when most in earnest, such as would make me loath to commit any woman, or any secret, to his charge."

"You are an honest man, Mr. Talbot," said Mary; "I am glad my poor maid is in your charge. Tell me, is this suit on his part made to your daughter or to the Scottish orphan?"

"To the Scottish orphan, madam. Thus much he knows, though by what means I cannot tell, unless it be through that kinsman of mine, who, as I told your Grace, saw the babe the night I brought her in."

"Doubtless," responded Mary. "Take care he neither knows more, nor hints what he doth know to the Countess."

"So far as I can, I will, madam," said Richard, "but his tongue is not easy to silence; I marvel that he hath not let the secret ooze out already."

"Proving him to have more discretion than you gave him credit for, my good sir," said the Queen, smiling. "Refuse him, however, staunchly, grounding your refusal, if it so please you, on the very causes for which I should accept him, were the lassie verily what he deems her, my ward and kinswoman. Nor do you accede to him, whatever word or token he may declare that he brings from me, unless it bear this mark," and she hastily traced a peculiar-twisted form of M. "You know it?" she asked.

"I have seen it, madam," said Richard, gravely,

for he knew it as the letter which had been traced on the child's shoulders.

" Ah, good Master Richard," she said, with a sweet and wistful expression, looking up to his face in pleading, and changing to the familiar pronoun, " thou likest not my charge, and I know that it is hard on an upright man like thee to have all this dissembling thrust on thee, but what can a poor captive mother do but strive to save her child from an unworthy lot, or from captivity like her own ? I ask thee to say nought, that is all, and to shelter the maid, who hath been as thine own daughter, yet a little longer. Thou wilt not deny me, for her sake."

" Madam, I deny nothing that a Christian man and my Queen's faithful servant may in honour do. Your Grace has the right to choose your own daughter's lot, and with her I will deal as you direct me. But, madam, were it not well to bethink yourself whether it be not a perilous and a cruel policy to hold out a bait to nourish hope in order to bind to your service a foolish though a generous youth, whose devotion may, after all, work you and himself more ill than good ? "

Mary looked a good deal struck, and waved back her two attendants, who were both startled and offended at what Marie de Courcelles described as the Englishman's brutal boldness.

" Silence, dear friends," said she. " Would that I had always had counsellors who would deal with me with such honour and disinterestedness. Then should I not be here."

However, she then turned her attention to the accounts, where Sir Andrew Melville was ready to question and debate every item set down by Shrewsbury's steward ; while his mistress showed herself

liberal and open-handed. Indeed she had considerable
command of money from her French dowry, the proceeds
of which were, in spite of the troubles of the League,
regularly paid to her, and no doubt served her well in
maintaining the correspondence which, throughout her
captivity, eluded the vigilance of her keepers. On
taking leave of her, which Richard Talbot did before
joining his host at the mid-day meal, she reiterated her
thanks for his care of her daughter, and her charges to
let no persuasion induce him to consent to Babington's
overtures, adding that she hoped soon to obtain permission to have the maiden amongst her authorised
attendants. She gave him a billet, loosely tied with
black floss silk and unsealed, so that if needful, Sadler
and Shrewsbury might both inspect the tender, playful,
messages she wrote to her " *mignonne*," and which she
took care should not outrun those which she had often
addressed to Bessie Pierrepoint.

Cicely was a little disappointed when she first
opened the letter, but ere long she bethought herself
of the directions she had received to hold such notes
to the fire, and accordingly she watched, waiting even
till the next day before she could have free and solitary access to either of the two fires in the house,
those in the hall and in the kitchen.

At last, while the master was out farming, Ned at
school, and the mistress and all her maids engaged in
the unsavoury occupation of making candles, by repeated dipping of rushes into a caldron of melted
fat, after the winter's salting, she escaped under pretext of attending to the hall fire, and kneeling beside
the glowing embers, she held the paper over it, and soon
saw pale yellow characters appear and deepen into a sort
of brown or green, in which she read, " My little jewel

must share the ring with none less precious. Yet be
not amazed if commendations as from me be brought
thee. Jewels are sometimes useful to dazzle the eyes
of those who shall never possess them. Therefore
seem not cold nor over coy, so as to take away all
hope. It may be much for my service. Thou art
discreet, and thy good guardians will hinder all from
going too far. It might be well that he should deem
thee and me inclined to what *they* oppose. Be secret.
Keep thine own counsel, and let them not even guess
what thou hast here read. So fare thee well, with
my longing, yearning blessing."

Cicely hastily hid the letter in the large housewifely pocket attached to her girdle, feeling excited
and important at having a real secret unguessed by
any one, and yet experiencing some of the reluctance
natural to the pupil of Susan Talbot at the notion of
acting a part towards Babington. She really liked
him, and her heart warmed to him as a true friend of
her much-injured mother, so that it seemed the more
cruel to delude him with false hopes. Yet here was
she asked to do a real service to her mother !

Poor Cis, she knelt gazing perplexed into the
embers, now and then touching a stick to make them
glow, till Nat, the chief of "the old blue bottles of serving-
men," came in to lay the cloth for dinner, exclaiming,
" So, Mistress Cis ! Madam doth cocker thee truly,
letting thee dream over the coals, till thy face be as
red as my Lady's new farthingale, while she is toiling
away like a very scullion."

CHAPTER XXI.

A TANGLE.

IT was a rainy November afternoon. Dinner was over, the great wood fire had been made up, and Mistress Talbot was presiding over the womenfolk of her household and their tasks with needle and distaff. She had laid hands on her unwilling son Edward to show his father how well he could read the *pièce de resistance* of the family, Fabyan's Chronicle; and the boy, with an elbow firmly planted on either side of the great folio, was floundering through the miseries of King Stephen's time; while Mr. Talbot, after smoothing the head of his largest hound for some minutes, had leant back in his chair and dropped asleep. Cicely's hand tardily drew out her thread, her spindle scarcely balanced itself on the floor, and her maiden meditation was in an inactive sort of way occupied with the sense of dulness after the summer excitements, and wonder whether her greatness were all a dream, and anything would happen to recall her once more to be a princess. The kitten at her feet took the spindle for a lazily moving creature, and thought herself fascinating it, so she stared hard, with only an occasional whisk of the end of her striped tail; and Mistress Susan was only kept awake by her anxiety to adapt Diccon's last year's jerkin to Ned's use.

Suddenly the dogs outside bayed, the dogs inside pricked their ears, Ned joyfully halted, his father uttered the unconscious falsehood, " I'm not asleep, lad, go on," then woke up as horses' feet were heard ; Ned dashed out into the porch, and was in time to hold the horse of one of the two gentlemen, who, with cloaks over their heads, had ridden up to the door. He helped them off with their cloaks in the porch, exchanging greetings with William Cavendish and Antony Babington.

" Will Mrs. Talbot pardon our riding-boots ?" said the former. " We have only come down from the Manor-house, and we rode mostly on the grass."

Their excuses were accepted, though Susan had rather Master William had brought any other companion. However, on such an afternoon, almost any variety was welcome, especially to the younger folk, and room was made for them in the circle, and according to the hospitality of the time, a cup of canary fetched for each to warm him after the ride, while another was brought to the master of the house to pledge them in——a relic of the barbarous ages, when such a security was needed that the beverage was not poisoned.

Will Cavendish then explained that a post had come that morning to his stepfather from Wingfield, having been joined on the way by Babington (people always preferred travelling in companies for security's sake), and that, as there was a packet from Sir Ralf Sadler for Master Richard, he had brought it down, accompanied by his friend, who was anxious to pay his *devoirs* to the ladies, and though Will spoke to the mother, he smiled and nodded comprehension at the daughter, who blushed furiously, and set her spindle to twirl and leap so violently, as to make the kitten

believe the creature had taken fright, and was going to
escape. On she dashed with a sudden spring, in-
volving herself and it in the flax. The old watch-dog
roused himself with a growl to keep order, Cicely flung
herself on the cat, Antony hurried to the rescue to
help her disentangle it, and received a fierce scratch
for his pains, which made him start back, while Mrs.
Talbot put in her word. " Ah, Master Babington, it is
ill meddling with a cat in the toils, specially for men
folk ! Here, Cis, hold her fast and I will soon have
her free. Still, Tib !

Cicely's cheeks were of a still deeper colour as she
held fast the mischievous favourite, while the good
mother untwisted the flax from its little claws and
supple limbs, while it winked, twisted its head about
sentimentally, purred, and altogether wore an air of
injured innocence and forgiveness.

" I am afraid, sir, you receive nothing but damage
at our house," said Mrs. Talbot politely. " Hast drawn
blood ? Oh fie ! thou ill-mannered Tib ! Will you
have a tuft from a beaver to stop the blood ?"

" Thanks, madam, no, it is a small scratch. I
would, I would that I could face truer perils for this
lady's sake !"

" That I hope you will not, sir," said Richard, in a
serious tone, which conveyed a meaning to the ears of
the initiated, though Will Cavendish only laughed, and
said,

" Our kinsman takes it gravely ! It was in the
days of our grandfathers that ladies could throw a
glove among the lions, and bid a knight fetch it out
for her love."

" It has not needed a lion to defeat Mr. Babington,"
observed Ned, looking up from his book with a sober

twinkle in his eye, which set them all laughing, though
his father declared that he ought to have his ears
boxed for a malapert varlet.

Will Cavendish declared that the least the fair
damsel could do for her knight-errant was to bind up
his wounds, but Cis was too shy to show any disposition so to do, and it was Mrs. Talbot who salved the
scratch for him. She had a feeling for the motherless
youth, upon whom she foreboded that a fatal game
might be played.

When quiet was restored, Mr. Talbot craved license
from his guests, and opened the packet. There was a
letter for Mistress Cicely Talbot in Queen Mary's well-
known beautiful hand, which Antony followed with
eager eyes, and a low gasp of "Ah! favoured maiden,"
making the good mother, who overheard it, say to herself, "Methinks his love is chiefly for the maid as
something appertaining to the Queen, though he wots
not how nearly. His heart is most for the Queen herself, poor lad."

The maiden did not show any great haste to open
the letter, being aware that the true *gist* of it could
only be discovered in private, and her father was
studying his own likewise in silence. It was from
Sir Ralf Sadler to request that Mistress Cicely might
be permitted to become a regular member of the household. There was now a vacancy since, though Mrs.
Curll was nearly as much about the Queen as ever, it
was as the secretary's wife, not as one of the maiden
attendants; and Sir Ralf wrote that he wished the more
to profit by the opportunity, as he might soon be dis-
placed by some one not of a temper greatly to consider
the prisoner's wishes. Moreover, he said the poor lady
was ill at ease, and much dejected at the tenor of

her late letters from Scotland, and that she had said
repeatedly that nothing would do her good but the
presence of her pretty playfellow. Sir Ralf added
assurances that he would watch over the maiden like
his own daughter, and would take the utmost care
of the faith and good order of all within his household. Curll also wrote by order of his mistress a formal
application for the young lady, to which Mary had
added in her own hand, " I thank the good Master
Richard and Mrs. Susan beforehand, for I know they
will not deny me."

Refusal was, of course, impossible to a mother who
had every right to claim her own child ; and there was
nothing to be done but to fix the time for setting off :
and Cicely, who had by this time read her own letter,
or at least all that was on the surface, looked up tremulous, with a strange frightened gladness, and said,
" Mother, she needs me."

" I shall shortly be returning home," said Antony,
" and shall much rejoice if I may be one of the party
who will escort this fair maiden."

" I shall take my daughter myself on a pillion, sir,"
said Richard, shortly.

" Then, sir, I may tell my Lord that you purpose to
grant this request," said Will Cavendish, who had expected at least some time to be asked for deliberation,
and knew his mother would expect her permission to
be requested.

" I may not choose but do so," replied Richard ; and
then, thinking he might have said too much, he added,
" It were sheer cruelty to deny any solace to the poor
lady."

" Sick and in prison, and balked by her only son,"
added Susan, " one's heart cannot but ache for her."

"Let not Mr. Secretary Walsingham hear you say so, good madam," said Cavendish, smiling. In London they think of her solely as a kind of malicious fury shut up in a cage, and there were those who looked askance at me when I declared that she was a gentlewoman of great sweetness and kindness of demeanour. I believe myself they will not rest till they have her blood!"

Cis and Susan cried out with horror, and Babington with stammering wrath demanded whether she was to be assassinated in the Spanish fashion, or on what pretext a charge could be brought against her. "Well," Cavendish answered, "as the saying is, give her rope enough, and she will hang herself." Indeed, there's no doubt but that she tampered enough with Throckmorton's plot to have been convicted of misprision of treason, and so she would have been, but that her most sacred Majesty, Queen Elizabeth, would have no charge made against her.

"Treason from one sovereign to another, that is new law!" said Babington.

"So to speak," said Richard; "but if she claim to be heiress to the crown, she must also be a subject. Heaven forefend that she should come to the throne!"

To which all except Cis and Babington uttered a hearty amen, while a picture arose before the girl of herself standing beside her royal mother robed in velvet and ermine on the throne, and of the faces of Lady Shrewsbury and her daughter as they recognised her, and were pardoned.

Cavendish presently took his leave, and carried the unwilling Babington off with him, rightly divining that the family would wish to make their arrangements alone. To Richard's relief, Babington had brought

him no private message, and to Cicely's disappointment, there was no addition in sympathetic ink to her
letter, though she scorched the paper brown in trying
to bring one out. The Scottish Queen was much too
wary to waste and risk her secret expedients without
necessity.

To Richard and Susan this was the real resignation
of their foster-child into the hands of her own parent.
It was true that she would still bear their name, and
pass for their daughter, but that would be only so long
as it might suit her mother's convenience; and instead
of seeing her every day, and enjoying her full confidence (so far as they knew), she would be out of
reach, and given up to influences, both moral and
religious, which they deeply distrusted; also to a fate
looming in the future with all the dark uncertainty
that brooded over all connected with Tudor or Stewart
royalty.

How much good Susan wept and prayed that night,
only her pillow knew, not even her husband; and there
was no particular comfort when my Lady Countess
descended on her in the first interval of fine weather,
full of wrath at not having been consulted, and discharging it in all sorts of predictions as to Cis's future.
No honest and loyal husband would have her, after
being turned loose in such company; she would be
corrupted in morals and manners, and a disgrace to the
Talbots; she would be perverted in faith, become a
Papist, and die in a nunnery beyond sea; or she would
be led into plots and have her head cut off; or pressed
to death by the *peine forte et dure*.

Susan had nothing to say to all this, but that her
husband thought it right, and then had a little vigorous advice on her own score against tamely submitting

to any man, a weakness which certainly could not be laid to the charge of the termagant of Hardwicke.

Cicely herself was glad to go. She loved her mother with a romantic enthusiastic affection, missed her engaging caresses, and felt her Bridgefield home eminently dull, flat, and even severe, especially since she had lost the excitement of Humfrey's presence, and likewise her companion Diccon. So she made her preparations with a joyful alacrity, which secretly pained her good foster-parents, and made Susan almost ready to reproach her with ingratitude.

They lectured her, after the fashion of the time, on the need of never forgetting her duty to her God in her affection to her mother, Susan trusting that she would never let herself be led away to the Romish faith, and Richard warning her strongly against untruth and falsehood, though she must be exposed to cruel perplexities as to the right—" But if thou be true to man, thou wilt be true to God," he said. " If thou be false to man, thou wilt soon be false to thy God likewise."

" We will pray for thee, child," said Susan. " Do thou pray earnestly for thyself that thou mayest ever see the right."

" My queen mother is a right pious woman. She is ever praying and reading holy books," said Cis. " Mother Susan, I marvel you, who know her, can speak thus."

" Nay, child, I would not lessen thy love and duty to her, poor soul, but it is not even piety in a mother that can keep a maiden from temptation. I blame not her in warning thee."

Richard himself escorted the damsel to her new home. There was no preventing their being joined by

Babington, who, being well acquainted with the road, and being also known as a gentleman of good estate, was able to do much to make their journey easy to them, and secure good accommodation for them at the inns, though Mr. Talbot entirely baffled his attempts to make them his guests, and insisted on bearing a full share of the reckoning. Neither did Cicely fulfil her mother's commission to show herself inclined to accept his attentions. If she had been under contrary orders, there would have been some excitement in going as far as she durst, but the only effect on her was embarrassment, and she treated Antony with the same shy stiffness she had shown to Humfrey, during the earlier part of his residence at home. Besides, she clung more and more to her adopted father, who, now that they were away from home and he was about to part with her, treated her with a tender, chivalrous deference, most winning in itself, and making her feel herself no longer a child.

Arriving at last at Wingfield, Sir Ralf Sadler had hardly greeted them before a messenger was sent to summon the young lady to the presence of the Queen of Scots. Her welcome amounted to ecstasy. The Queen rose from her cushioned invalid chair as the bright young face appeared at the door, held out her arms, gathered her into them, and, covering her with kisses, called her by all sorts of tender names in French and Scottish.

" O *ma mie*, my lassie, *ma fille*, mine ain wee thing, how sweet to have one bairn who is mine, mine ain, whom they have not robbed me of, for thy brother, ah, thy brother, he hath forsaken me! He is made of the false Darnley stuff, and compacted by Knox and Buchanan and the rest, and he will not stand a blast

of Queen Elizabeth's wrath for the poor mother that
bore him. Ay, he hath betrayed me, and deluded
me, my child; he hath sold me once more to the
English loons! I am set faster in prison than ever,
the iron entereth into my soul. Thou art but daughter
to a captive queen, who looks to thee to be her one
bairn, one comfort and solace."

Cicely responded by caresses, and indeed felt herself more than ever before the actual daughter, as she
heard with indignation of James's desertion of his
mother's cause; but Mary, whatever she said herself,
would not brook to hear her speak severely of him.
"The poor laddie," she said, " he was no better than
a prisoner among those dour Scots lords," and she described in graphic terms some of her own experiences
of royalty in Scotland.

The other ladies all welcomed the new-comer as
the best medicine both to the spirit and body of their
Queen. She was regularly enrolled among the Queen's
maidens, and shared their meals. Mary dined and
supped alone, sixteen dishes being served to her, both
on "fish and flesh days," and the reversion of these as
well as a provision of their own came to the higher
table of her attendants, where Cicely ranked with the
two Maries, Jean Kennedy, and Sir Andrew Melville.
There was a second table, at which ate the two secretaries, Mrs. Curll, and Elizabeth Curll, Gilbert's sister,
a most faithful attendant on the Queen. As before,
she shared the Queen's chamber, and there it was that
Mary asked her, " Well, *mignonne*, and how fares it
with thine ardent suitor? Didst say that he rode
with thee?"

" As far as the Manor gates, madam."

" And what said he? Was he very pressing?"

"Nay, madam, I was ever with my father—Mr. Talbot."

"And he keeps the poor youth at arm's length. Thine other swain, the sailor, his son, is gone off once more to rob the Spaniards, is he not?—so there is the more open field."

"Ay! but not till he had taught Antony a lesson."

The Queen made Cis tell the story of the encounter, at which she was much amused. "So my princess, even unknown, can make hearts beat and swords ring for her. Well done! thou art worthy to be one of the maids in Perceforest or Amadis de Gaul, who are bred in obscurity, and set all the knights a sparring together. Tourneys are gone out since my poor gude-father perished by mischance at one, or we would set thee aloft to be contended for."

"O madame *mère*, it made me greatly afraid, and poor Humfrey had to go off without leave-taking, my Lady Countess was so wrathful."

"So my Lady Countess is playing our game, is she! Backing Babington and banishing Talbot? Ha, ha," and Mary again laughed with a merriment that rejoiced the faithful ears of Jean Kennedy, under her bedclothes, but somewhat vexed Cicely. "Indeed, madam mother," she said, "if I must wed under my degree, I had rather it were Humfrey than Antony Babington."

"I tell thee, simple child, thou shalt wed neither. A woman does not wed every man to whom she gives a smile and a nod. So long as thou bear'st the name of this Talbot, he is a good watch-dog to hinder Babington from winning thee: but if my Lady Countess choose to send the swain here, favoured by her to pay his court to thee, why then, she gives us the best chance we have had for many a long day of holding intercourse with our friends without, and a hope of thee will bind him the more closely."

"He is all yours, heart and soul, already, madam."

"I know it, child, but men are men, and no chains are so strong as can be forged by a lady's lip and eye, if she do it cunningly. So said my *belle mère* in France, and well do I believe it. Why, if one of the sour-visaged reformers who haunt this place chanced to have a daughter with sweetness enough to temper the acidity, the youth might be throwing up his cap the next hour for Queen Bess and the Reformation, unless we can tie him down with a silken cable while he is in the mind."

"Yea, madam, you who are beautiful and winsome, you can do such things, I am homely and awkward."

"*Mort de ma vie*, child! the beauty of the best of us is in the man's eyes who looks at us. 'Tis true, thou hast more of the Border lassie than the princess. The likeness of some ewe-milking, cheese-making sonsie Hepburn hath descended to thee, and hath been fostered by country breeding. But thou hast by nature the turn of the neck, and the tread that belong to our Lorraine blood, the blood of Charlemagne, and now that I have thee altogether, see if I train thee not so as to bring out the princess that is in thee; and so, good-night, my bairnie, my sweet child; I shall sleep to-night, now that I have thy warm fresh young cheek beside mine. Thou art life to me, my little one."

CHAPTER XXII.

TUTBURY.

JAMES VI. again cruelly tore his mother's heart and dashed her hopes by an unfeeling letter, in which he declared her incapable of being treated with, since she was a prisoner and deposed. The not unreasonable expectation, that his manhood might reverse the proceedings wrought in his name in his infancy, was frustrated. Mary could no longer believe that he was constrained by a faction, but perceived clearly that he merely considered her as a rival, whose liberation would endanger his throne, and that whatever scruples he might once have entertained had given way to English gold and Scottish intimidation.

"The more simple was I to look for any other in the son of Darnley and the pupil of Buchanan," said she, "but a mother's heart is slow to give up her trust."

"And is there now no hope?" asked Cicely.

"Hope, child? *Dum spiro, spero.* The hope of coming forth honourably to him and to Elizabeth is at an end. There is another mode of coming forth," she added with a glittering eye, "a mode which shall make them rue that they have driven patience to extremity."

"By force of arms? Oh, madam!" cried Cicely.

" And wherefore not?   My noble kinsman, Guise,
is the paramount ruler in France, and will soon have
crushed the heretics there ; Parma is triumphant in
the Low Countries, and has only to tread out the last
remnants of faction with his iron boot.   They wait only
the call, which my motherly weakness has delayed, to
bring their hosts to avenge my wrongs, and restore
this island to the true faith.   Then thou, child, wilt
be my heiress.   We will give thee to one who will
worthily bear the sceptre, and make thee blessed at
home.   The Austrians make good husbands, I am told.
Matthias or Albert would be a noble mate for thee ;
only thou must be trained to more princely bearing,
my little home-bred lassie."

In spite—nay, perhaps, in consequence—of these
anticipations, an entire change began for Cicely.   It
was as if all the romance of her princely station had
died out and the reality had set in.   Her freedom was
at an end.   As one of the suite of the Queen of Scots,
she was as much a prisoner as the rest ; whereas before,
both at Buxton and Sheffield, she had been like a dog
or kitten admitted to be petted and played with, but
living another life elsewhere, while now there was
nothing to relieve the weariness and monotony of the
restraint.

Nor was the petting what it was at first.   Mary
was far from being in the almost frolicsome mood which
had possessed her at Buxton ; her hopes and spirits
had sunk to the lowest pitch, and though she had an
admirably sweet and considerate temper, and was
scarcely ever fretful or unreasonable with her attendants, still depression, illness, and anxiety could not but
tell on her mode of dealing with her surroundings.
Sometimes she gave way entirely, and declared she

should waste away and perish in her captivity, and
that she only brought misery and destruction on all
who tried to befriend her; or, again, that she knew
that Burghley and Walsingham were determined to
have her blood.

It was in these moments that Cicely loved her most
warmly, for caresses and endearments soothed her, and
the grateful affection which received them would be
very sweet.   Or in a higher tone, she would trust
that, if she were to perish, she might be a martyr and
confessor for her Church, though, as she owned, the
sacrifice would be stained by many a sin; and she
betook herself to the devotions which then touched
her daughter more than in any other respect.

More often, however, her indomitable spirit resorted
to fresh schemes, and chafed fiercely and hotly at
thought of her wrongs; and this made her the more
critical of all that displeased her in Cicely.

Much that had been treated as charming and amusing when Cicely was her plaything and her visitor was
now treated as unbecoming English rusticity.   The
Princess Bride must speak French and Italian, perhaps
Latin; and the girl, whose literary education had
stopped short when she ceased to attend Master
Sniggius's school, was made to study her Cicero once
more with the almoner, who was now a French priest
named De Préaux, while Queen Mary herself heard
her read French, and, though always good-natured,
was excruciated by her pronunciation.

Moreover, Mary was too admirable a needlewoman
not to wish to make her daughter the same; whereas
Cicely's turn had always been for the department of
housewifery, and she could make a castle in pastry far
better than in tapestry; but where Queen Mary had

a whole service of cooks and pantlers of her own, this
accomplishment was uncalled for, and was in fact
considered undignified.　She had to sit still and learn
all the embroidery stitches and lace-making arts
brought by Mary from the Court of France, till her
eyes grew weary, her heart faint, and her young limbs
ached for the freedom of Bridgefield Pleasaunce and
Sheffield Park.

Her mother sometimes saw her weariness, and
would try to enliven her by setting her to dance, but
here poor Cicely's untaught movements were sure to
incur reproof; and even if they had been far more
satisfactory to the beholders, what refreshment were
they in comparison with gathering cranberries in the
park, or holding a basket for Ned in the apple-tree?
Mrs. Kennedy made no scruple of scolding her roundly
for fretting in a month over what the Queen had borne
for full eighteen years.

"Ah!" said poor Cicely, "but she had always been
a queen, and was used to being mewed up close!"

And if this was the case at Wingfield, how much
more was it so at Tutbury, whither Mary was removed
in January.　The space was far smaller, and the rooms
were cold and damp; there was much less outlet, the
atmosphere was unwholesome, and the furniture insufficient.　Mary was in bed with rheumatism almost
from the time of her arrival, but she seemed thus to
become the more vigilant over her daughter, and distressed by her shortcomings.　If the Queen did not
take exercise, the suite were not supposed to require
any, and indeed it was never desired by her elder
ladies, but to the country maiden it was absolute
punishment to be thus shut up day after day.　Neither
Sir Ralf Sadler nor his colleague, Mr. Somer, had

L

brought a wife to share the charge, so that there was
none of the neutral ground afforded by intercourse
with the ladies of the Talbot family, and at first the
only variety Cicely ever had was the attendance at
chapel on the other side of the court.

It was remarkable that Mary discouraged all
proselytising towards the Protestants of her train, and
even forbore to make any open attempt on her
daughter's faith. "*Celà viendrà*," she said to Marie
de Courcelles. "The sermons of M. le Pasteur will
do more to convert her to our side than a hundred
controversial arguments of our excellent Abbé ; and
when the good time comes, one High Mass will be
enough to win her over."

"Alas ! when shall we ever again assist at the
Holy Sacrifice in all its glory !" sighed the lady.

"Ah, my good Courcelles ! of what have you not
deprived yourself for me ! Sacrifice, ah ! truly you
share it ! But for the child, it would give needless
offence and difficulty were she to embrace our holy
faith at present. She is simple and impetuous, and
has not yet sufficiently outgrown the rude straight-
forward breeding of the good housewife, Madam Susan,
not to rush into open confession of her faith, and then !
oh the fracas ! The wicked wolves would have stolen
a precious lamb from M. le Pasteur's fold ! Master
Richard would be sent for ! Our restraint would be the
closer ! Moreover, even when the moment of freedom
strikes, who knows that to find her of their own religion may not win us favour with the English ?"

So, from whatever motive, Cis remained unmolested
in her religion, save by the weariness of the controversial sermons, during which the young lady contrived to abstract her mind pretty completely. If in

good spirits she would construct airy castles for her
Archduke; if dispirited, she yearned with a homesick
feeling for Bridgefield and Mrs. Talbot. There was
something in the firm sober wisdom and steady kindness of that good lady which inspired a sense of confidence, for which no caresses nor brilliant auguries
could compensate.

Weary and cramped she was to the point of having
a feverish attack, and on one slightly delirious night
she fretted piteously after " mother," and shook off the
Queen's hand, entreating that "mother, real mother,"
would come. Mary was much pained, and declared
that if the child were not better the next day she should
have a messenger sent to summon Mrs. Talbot. However, she was better in the morning; and the Queen,
who had been making strong representations of the
unhealthiness and other inconveniences of Tutbury,
received a promise that she should change her abode
as soon as Chartley, a house belonging to the young
Earl of Essex, could be prepared for her.

The giving away large alms had always been one
of her great solaces—not that she was often permitted
any personal contact with the poor: only to sit at a
window watching them as they flocked into the court,
to be relieved by her servants under supervision from
some officer of her warders, so as to hinder any surrep-
titious communication from passing between them.
Sometimes, however, the poor would accost her or her
suite as she rode out; and she had a great compassion
for them, deprived, as she said, of the alms of the
religious houses, and flogged or branded if hunger forced
them into beggary. On a fine spring day Sir Ralf
Sadler invited the ladies out to a hawking party on
the banks of the Dove, with the little sparrow hawks,

whose prey was specially larks.   Pity for the beautiful
soaring songster, or for the young ones that might be
starved in their nests, if the parent birds were killed,
had not then been thought of.   A gallop on the moors,
though they were strangely dull, gray, and stony,
was always the best remedy for the Queen's ailments ;
and the party got into the saddle gaily, and joyously
followed the chase, thinking only of the dexterity and
beauty of the flight of pursuer and pursued, instead
of the deadly terror and cruel death to which they
condemned the crested creature, the very proverb for
joyousness.

It was during the halt which followed the slaughter
of one of the larks, and the reclaiming of the hawk,
that Cicely strayed a little away from the rest of the
party to gather some golden willow catkins and sprays
of white sloe thorn wherewith to adorn a beaupot that
might cheer the dull rooms at Tutbury.

She had jumped down from her pony for the purpose, and was culling the branch, when from the copsewood that clothed the gorge of the river a ragged
woman, with a hood tied over her head, came forward
with outstretched hand asking for alms.

"You may have something from the Queen anon,
Goody, when I can get back to her," said Cis, not much
liking the looks or the voice of the woman.

"And have you nothing to cross the poor woman's
hand with, fair mistress ?" returned the beggar. "She
brought you fair fortune once ; how know you but she
can bring you more ?"

And Cicely recognised the person who had haunted
her at Sheffield, Tideswell, and Buxton, and whom she
had heard pronounced to be no woman at all.

"I need no fortune of your bringing," she said

proudly, and trying to get nearer the rest of the party, heartily wishing she was on, not off, her little rough pony.

"My young lady is proud," said her tormentor, fixing on her the little pale eyes she so much disliked. "She is not one of the maidens who would thank one who can make or mar her life, and cast spells that can help her to a princely husband or leave her to a prison."

"Let go," said Cicely, as she saw a retaining hand laid on her pony's bridle; "I will not be beset thus."

"And this is your gratitude to her who helped you to lie in a queen's bosom; ay, and who could aid you to rise higher or fall lower?"

"I owe nothing to you," said Cicely, too angry to think of prudence. "Let me go!"

There was a laugh, and not a woman's laugh. "You owe nothing, quoth my mistress? Not to one who saw you, a drenched babe, brought in from the wreck, and who gave the sign which has raised you to your present honours? Beware!"

By this time, however, the conversation had attracted notice, and several riders were coming towards them.

There was an immediate change of voice from the threatening tone to the beggar's whine; but the words were—"I must have my reward ere I speak out."

"What is this? A masterful beggar wife besetting Mistress Talbot," said Mr. Somer, who came first.

"I had naught to give her," said Cicely.

"She should have the lash for thus frightening you," said Somer. "Yonder lady is too good to such vagabonds, and they come about us in swarms. Stand back, woman, or it may be the worse for you. Let me help you to your horse, Mistress Cicely."

Instead of obeying, the seeming woman, to gain time perhaps, began a story of woe; and Mr. Somer, being anxious to remount the young lady, did not immediately stop it, so that before Cis was in her saddle the Queen had ridden up, with Sir Ralf Sadler a little behind her. There were thus a few seconds free, in which the stranger sprang to the Queen's bridle and said a few hasty words almost inaudibly, and as Cis thought, in French; but they were answered aloud in English—"My good woman, I know all that you can tell me, and more, of this young lady's fortune. Here are such alms as are mine to give; but hold your peace, and quit us now."

Sir Ralf Sadler and his son-in-law both looked suspicious at this interview, and bade one of the grooms ride after the woman and see what became of her, but the fellow soon lost sight of her in the broken ground by the river-side.

When the party reached home, there was an anxious consultation of the inner circle of confidantes over Cicely's story. Neither she nor the Queen had the least doubt that the stranger was Cuthbert Langston, who had been employed as an agent of hers for many years past; his insignificant stature and colourless features eminently fitting him for it. No concealment was made now that he was the messenger with the beads and bracelets, which were explained to refer to some ivory beads which had been once placed among some spars purchased by the Queen, and which Jean had recognised as part of a rosary belonging to poor Alison Hepburn, the nurse who had carried the babe from Lochleven. This had opened the way to the recovery of her daughter. Mary and Sir Andrew Melville had always held him to be devotedly faithful,

but there had certainly been something of greed, and
something of menace in his language which excited
anxiety. Cicely was sure that his expressions conveyed that he really knew her royal birth, and meant
to threaten her with the consequences, but the few
who had known it were absolutely persuaded that
this was impossible, and believed that he could only
surmise that she was of more importance than an
archer's daughter.

He had told the Queen in French that he was in
great need, and expected a reward for his discretion
respecting what he had brought her. And when he perceived the danger of being overheard, he had changed
it into a pleading, " I did but tell the fair young lady
that I could cast a spell that would bring her some
good fortune. Would her Grace hear it ? "

" So," said Mary, " I could but answer him as I
did, Sadler and Somer being both nigh. I gave him
my purse, with all there was therein. How much
was it, Andrew ? "

" Five golden pieces, besides groats and testers,
madam," replied Sir Andrew.

" If he come again, he must have more, if it can
be contrived without suspicion," said the Queen. " I
fear me he may become troublesome if he guess somewhat, and have to be paid to hold his tongue."

" I dread worse than that," said Melville, apart to
Jean Kennedy ; " there was a scunner in his een that
I mislikit, as though her Grace had offended him.
And if the lust of the penny-fee hath possessed him,
'tis but who can bid the highest, to have him fast
body and soul. Those lads ! those lads ! I've seen a
mony of them. They'll begin for pure love of the
Queen and of Holy Church, but ye see, 'tis lying and

falsehood and disguise that is needed, and one way
or other they get so in love with it, that they come at
last to lie to us as well as to the other side, and then
none kens where to have them! Cuthbert has been
over to that weary Paris, and once a man goes there,
he leaves his truth and honour behind him, and ye
kenna whether he be serving you, or Queen Elizabeth,
or the deil himsel'. I wish I could stop that loon's
thrapple, or else wot how much he kens anent our
Lady Bride."

CHAPTER XXIII.

THE LOVE TOKEN.

"YONDER woman came to tell this young lady's fortune," said Sir Ralf, a few days later. "Did she guess what I, an old man, have to bode for her!" and he smiled at the Queen. "Here is a token I was entreated by a young gentleman to deliver to this young lady, with his humble suit that he may pay his devoirs to her to-morrow, your Grace permitting."

"I knew not," said Mary, "that my women had license to receive visitors."

"Assuredly not, as a rule, but this young gentleman, Mr. Babington of Dethick, has my Lord and Lady of Shrewsbury's special commendation."

"I knew the young man," said Mary, with perfectly acted heedlessness. "He was my Lady Shrewsbury's page in his boyhood. I should have no objection to receive him."

"That, madam, may not be," returned Sadler. "I am sorry to say it is contrary to the orders of the council, but if Mr. and Mrs. Curll, and the fair Mistress Cicely, will do me the honour to dine with me to-morrow in the hall, we may bring about the auspicious meeting my Lady desires."

Cicely's first impulse had been to pout and say she

L*

wanted none of Mr. Babington's tokens, nor his company; but her mother's eye held her back, and besides
any sort of change of scene, or any new face, could not
but be delightful, so there was a certain leap of the
young heart when the invitation was accepted for her;
and she let Sir Ralf put the token into her hand, and
a choice one it was. Everybody pressed to look at it,
while she stood blushing, coy and unwilling to display
the small egg-shaped watch of the kind recently invented at Nuremberg. Sir Ralf observed that the
young lady showed a comely shamefast maidenliness,
and therewith bowed himself out of the room.

Cicely laughed with impatient scorn. " Well
spoken, reverend seignior," she said, as she found
herself alone with the Queen. " I wish my Lady
Countess would leave me alone. I am none of hers."

" Nay, mademoiselle, be not thus disdainful," said
the Queen, in a gay tone of banter; " give me here
this poor token that thou dost so despise, when many
a maiden would be distraught with delight and gratitude. Let me see it, I say."

And as Cicely, restraining with difficulty an impatient, uncourtly gesture, placed the watch in her hand,
her delicate deft fingers opened the case, disregarding
both the face and the place for inserting the key; but
dealing with a spring, which revealed that the case
was double, and that between the two thin plates of
silver which formed it, was inserted a tiny piece of
the thinnest paper, written from corner to corner with
the smallest characters in cipher. Mary laughed
joyously and triumphantly as she held it up. " There,
mignonne! What sayest thou to thy token now?
This is the first secret news I have had from the
outer world since we came to this weary Tutbury

And oh! the exquisite jest that my Lady and Sir
Ralf Sadler should be the bearers! I always knew
some good would come of that suitor of thine! Thou
must not flout him, my fair lady, nor scowl at him so
with thy beetle brows."

"It seems but hard to lure him on with false
hopes," said Cicely, gravely.

"Hoots, lassie," as Dame Jean would say, "'tis but
joy and delight to men to be thus tickled. 'Tis the
greatest kindness we can do them thus to amuse
them," said Mary, drawing up her head with the
conscious fascination of the serpent of old Nile, and
toying the while with the ciphered letter, in eagerness,
and yet dread, of what it might contain.

Such things were not easy to make out, even to
those who had the key, and Mary, unwilling to trust
it out of her own hands, leant over it, spelling it out
for many minutes, but at last broke forth into a clear
ringing burst of girlish laughter and clasped her hands
together, "Mignonne, mignonne, it is too rare a jest to
hold back. Deem not that your Highness stands first
here! Oh no! 'Tis a letter from Bernardo de Mendoza
with a proposition for whose hand thinkest thou? For
this poor old captive hand! For mine, maiden. Ay,
and from whom? From his Excellency, the Prince of
Parma, Lieutenant of the Netherlands. Anon will he be
here with 30,000 picked men and the Spanish fleet;
and then I shall ride once again at the head of my brave
men, hear trumpets bray, and see banners fly! We
will begin to work our banner at once, child, and let
Sir Ralf think it is a bed-quilt for her sacred Majesty,
Elizabeth. Thou look'st dismayed, little maiden."

"Spanish ships and men, madam, ah! and how would
it be with my father—Mr. and Mrs. Talbot, I mean?"

"Not a hair of their heads shall be touched, child.
We will send down a chosen troop to protect them,
with Babington at its head if thou wilt.   But,"
added the Queen, recollecting herself, and perceiving
that she had startled and even shocked her daughter,
"it is not to be to-morrow, nor for many a weary
month.   All that is here demanded is whether, all
being well, he might look for my hand as his guerdon.
Shall I propose thine instead ?"

"O madam, he is an old man and full of gout !"

"Well ! we will not pull caps for him just yet.
And see, thou must be secret as the grave, child, or
thou wilt ruin thy mother.   I ought not to have told
thee, but the surprise was too much for me, and thou
canst keep a secret.   Leave me now, child, and send
me Monsieur Nau."

The next time any converse was held between
mother and daughter, Queen Mary said, "Will it grieve
thee much, my lassie, to return this bauble, on the
plea of thy duty to the good couple at Bridgefield?"

After all Cicely had become so fond of the curious
and ingenious egg that she was rather sorry to part
with it, and there was a little dismal resignation in her
answer, "I will do your bidding, madam."

"Thou shalt have a better.   I will write to
Chateauneuf for the choicest that Paris can furnish,"
said Mary, "but seest thou, none other mode is so safe
for conveying an answer to this suitor of mine !   Nay,
little one, do not fear.   He is not at hand, and if he
be so gout-ridden and stern as I have heard, we will
find some way to content him and make him do the
service without giving thee a stepfather, even though
he be grandson to an emperor."

There was something perplexing and distressing to

Cis in this sudden mood of exultation at such a suitor.
However, Parma's proposal might mean liberty and a
recovered throne, and who could wonder at the joy
that even the faintest gleam of light afforded to one
whose captivity had lasted longer than Cicely's young
life ?—and then once more there was an alternation of
feeling at the last moment, when Cicely, dressed in
her best, came to receive instructions.

"I ken not, I ken not," said Mary, speaking the
Scottish tongue, to which she recurred in her moments
of deepest feeling, "I ought not to let it go. I ought
to tell the noble Prince to have naught to do with a
being like me. 'Tis not only the *jettatura* wherewith
the Queen Mother used to reproach me. Men need
but bear me good will, and misery overtakes them.
Death is the best that befalls them! The gentle
husband of my girlhood—then the frantic Chastelar,
my poor, poor good Davie, Darnley, Bothwell, Geordie
Douglas, young Willie, and again Norfolk, and the
noble and knightly Don John! One spark of love
and devotion to the wretched Mary, and all is over
with them! Give me back that paper, child, and
warn Babington against ever dreaming of aid to a
wretch like me. I will perish alone! It is enough!
I will drag down no more generous spirits in the
whirlpool around me."

"Madam! madam!" exclaimed De Préaux the
almoner, who was standing, "this is not like your
noble self. Have you endured so much to be faint-
hearted when the end is near, and you are made a
smooth and polished instrument, welded in the fire, for
the triumph of the Church over her enemies?"

"Ah, Father!" said the Queen, "how should not
my heart fail me when I think of the many high

spirits who have fallen for my sake? Ay, and when I look out on yonder peaceful vales and happy homesteads, and think of them ravaged by those furious Spaniards and Italians, whom my brother of Anjou himself called very fiends!"

"Fiends are the tools of Divine wrath," returned Préaux. "Look at the profaned sanctuaries and outraged convents on which these proud English have waxen fat, and say whether a heavy retribution be not due to them."

"Ah, father! I may be weak, but I never loved persecution. King Francis and I were dragged to behold the executions at Amboise. That was enough for us. His gentle spirit never recovered it, and I—I see their contorted visages and forms still in my restless nights; and if the Spanish dogs should deal with England as with Haarlem or Antwerp, and all through me!—Oh! I should be happier dying within these walls!"

"Nay, madam, as Queen you would have the reins in your own hand: you could exercise what wholesome severity or well-tempered leniency you chose," urged the almoner; "it were ill requiting the favour of the saints who have opened this door to you at last to turn aside now in terror at the phantasy that long weariness of spirit hath conjured up before you."

So Mary rallied herself, and in five minutes more was as eager in giving her directions to Cicely and to the Curlls as though her heart had not recently failed her.

Cis was to go forth with her chaperons, not by any means enjoying the message to Babington, and yet unable to help being very glad to escape for ever so short a time from the dull prison apartments. There

might be no great faith in her powers of diplomacy,
but as it was probable that Babington would have
more opportunity of conversing with her than with
the Curlls, she was charged to attend heedfully to
whatever he might say.

Sir Râlf's son-in-law, Mr. Somer, was sent to escort
the trio to the hall at the hour of noon; and there,
pacing the ample chamber, while the board at the
upper end was being laid, were Sir Ralf Sadler and
his guest Mr. Babington. Antony was dressed in
green velvet slashed with primrose satin, setting off his
good mien to the greatest advantage, and he came up
with suppressed but rapturous eagerness, bowing low
to Mrs. Curll and the secretary, but falling on his knee
to kiss the hand of the dark-browed girl. Her recent
courtly training made her much less rustically
awkward than she would have been a few months
before, but she was extremely stiff, and held her head
as though her ruff were buckram, as she began her
lesson. "Sir, I am greatly beholden to you for this
token, but if it be not sent with the knowledge and
consent of my honoured father and mother I may not
accept of it."

"Alas! that you will say so, fair mistress," said
Antony, but he was probably prepared for this re-
jection, for he did not seem utterly overwhelmed by it.

"The young lady exercises a wise discretion," said
Sir Ralf Sadler to Mrs. Curll. "If I had known that
mine old friend Mr. Talbot of Bridgefield was un-
favourable to the suit, I would not have harboured
the young spark, but when he brought my Lady
Countess's commendation, I thought all was well."

Barbara Curll had her cue, namely, to occupy Sir
Ralf so as to leave the young people to themselves, so

she drew him off to tell him in confidence a long and not particularly veracious story of the objections of the Talbots to Antony Babington; whilst her husband engaged the attention of Mr. Somer, and there was a space in which, as Antony took back the watch, he was able to inquire "Was the egg-shell opened?"

"Ay," said Cis, blushing furiously and against her will, "the egg was sucked and replenished."

"Take consolation," said Antony, and as some one came near them, "Duty and discretion shall, I trust, both be satisfied when I next sun myself in the light of those lovely eyes." Then, as the coast became more clear, "You are about shortly to move. Chartley is preparing for you."

"So we are told."

"There are others preparing," said Antony, bending over her, holding her hand, and apparently making love to her with all his might. "Tell me, lady, who hath charge of the Queen's buttery? Is it faithful old Halbert as at Sheffield?"

"It is," replied Cis.

"Then let him look well at the bottom of each barrel of beer supplied for the use of her household. There is an honest man, a brewer, at Burton, whom Paulett will employ, who will provide that letters be sent to and fro. Gifford and Langston, who are both of these parts, know him well." Cis started at the name. "Do you trust Langston then?" she asked.

"Wholly! Why, he is the keenest and ablest of us all. Have you not seen him and had speech with him in many strange shapes? He can change his voice, and whine like any beggar wife."

"Yea," said Cis, "but the Queen and Sir Andrew doubted a little if he meant not threats last time we met."

"All put on—excellent dissembling to beguile the keepers. He told me all," said Antony, "and how he had to scare thee and change tone suddenly. Why, he it is who laid this same egg, and will receive it. There is a sworn band, as you know already, who will let her know our plans, and be at her commands through that means. Then, when we have done service approaching to be worthy of her, *then* it may be that I shall have earned at least a look or sign."

"Alas! sir," said Cicely, "how can I give you false hopes?" For her honest heart burnt to tell the poor fellow that she would in case of his success be farther removed from him than ever.

"What would be false now *shall* be true then. I will wring love from thee by my deeds for her whom we both alike love, and then wilt thou be mine own, my true Bride!"

By this time other guests had arrived, and the dinner was ready. Babington was, in deference to the Countess, allowed to sit next to his lady-love. She found he had been at Sheffield, and had visited Bridge-field, vainly endeavouring to obtain sanction to his addresses from her adopted parents. He saw how her eyes brightened and heard how her voice quivered with eagerness to hear of what still seemed home to her, and he was pleased to feel himself gratifying her by telling her how Mrs. Talbot looked, and how Brown Dumpling had been turned out in the Park, and Mr. Talbot had taken a new horse, which Ned had insisted on calling "Fulvius," from its colour, for Ned was such a scholar that he was to be sent to study at Cambridge. Then he would have wandered off to little Lady Arbell's being put under Master Sniggius's

tuition, but Cicely would bring him back to Bridgefield, and to Ned's brothers.

No, the boasted expedition to Spain had not
begun yet. Sir Francis Drake was lingering about
Plymouth, digging a ditch, it was said, to bring water
from Dartmoor. He would never get license to attack
King Philip on his own shores. The Queen knew
better than to give it. Humfrey and Diccon would
get no better sport than robbing a ship or two on the
way to the Netherlands. Antony, for his part, could
not see that piracy on the high seas was fit work for
a gentleman.

"A gentleman loves to serve his queen and country
in all places," said Cicely.

"Ah!" said Antony, with a long breath, as though
making a discovery, "sits the wind in that quarter?"

"Antony," exclaimed she, in her eagerness calling
him by the familiar name of childhood, "you are in
error. I declare most solemnly that it is quite another
matter that stands in your way."

"And you will not tell me wherefore you are thus
cruel?"

"I cannot, sir. You will understand in time that
what you call cruelty is true kindness."

This was the gist of the interview. All the rest
only repeated it in one form or another; and when
Cis returned, it was with a saddened heart, for she
could not but perceive that Antony was well-nigh
crazed, not so much with love of her, as with the contemplation of the wrongs of the Church and the Queen,
whom he regarded with equally passionate devotion,
and with burning zeal and indignation to avenge
their sufferings, and restore them to their pristine
glory. He did, indeed, love her, as he professed to

have done from infancy, but as if she were to be his own personal portion of the reward. Indeed there was magnanimity enough in the youth almost to lose the individual hope in the dazzle of the great victory for which he was willing to devote his own life and happiness in the true spirit of a crusader. Cicely did not fully or consciously realise all this, but she had such a glimpse of it as to give her a guilty feeling in concealing from him the whole truth, which would have shown how fallacious were the hopes that her mother did not scruple, for her own purposes, to encourage. Poor Cicely! she had not had royal training enough to look on all subjects as simply pawns on the monarch's chess-board; and she was so evidently unhappy over Babington's courtship, and so little disposed to enjoy her first feminine triumph, that the Queen declared that Nature had designed her for the convent she had so narrowly missed; and, valuable as was the intelligence she had brought, she was never trusted with the contents of the correspondence. On the removal of Mary to Chartley the barrel with the false bottom came into use, but the secretaries Nau and Curll alone knew in full what was there conveyed. Little more was said to Cicely of Babington.

However, it was a relief when, before the end of this summer, Cicely heard of his marriage to a young lady selected by the Earl. She hoped it would make him forget his dangerous inclination to herself; but yet there was a little lurking vanity which believed that it had been rather a marriage for property's than for love's sake.

CHAPTER XXIV.

A LIONESS AT BAY.

It was in the middle of the summer of 1586 that Humfrey and his young brother Richard, in broad grass hats and long feathers, found themselves again in London, Diccon looking considerably taller and leaner than when he went away.   For when, after many months' delay, the naval expedition had taken place, he had been laid low with fever during the attack on Florida by Sir Francis Drake's little fleet; and the return to England had been only just in time to save his life.   Though Humfrey had set forth merely as a lieutenant, he had returned in command of a vessel, and stood in high repute for good discipline, readiness of resource, and personal exploits.   His ship had, however, suffered so severely as to be scarcely seaworthy when the fleet arrived in Plymouth harbour; and Sir Francis, finding it necessary to put her into dock and dismiss her crew, had chosen the young Captain Talbot to ride to London with his despatches to her Majesty.

The commission might well delight the brothers, who were burning to hear of home, and to know how it fared with Cicely, having been absolutely without intelligence ever since they had sailed from Plymouth

in January, since which they had plundered the
Spaniard both at home and in the West Indies, but
had had no letters.

They rode post into London, taking their last change
of horses at Kensington, on a fine June evening, when
the sun was mounting high upon the steeple of St.
Paul's, and speeding through the fields in hopes of
being able to reach the Strand in time for supper at
Lord Shrewsbury's mansion, which, even in the absence
of my Lord, was always a harbour for all of the name
of Talbot.   Nor, indeed, was it safe to be out after
dark, for the neighbourhood of the city was full of
roisterers of all sorts, if not of highwaymen and cut-
purses, who might come in numbers too large even for
the two young gentlemen and the two servants, who
remained out of the four volunteers from Bridgefield.

They were just passing Westminster where the
Abbey, Hall, and St. Stephen's Chapel, and their precincts, stood up in their venerable but unstained beauty
among the fields and fine trees, and some of the
Westminster boys, flat-capped, gowned, and yellow-
stockinged, ran out with the cry that always flattered
Diccon, not to say Humfrey, though he tried to be
superior to it, " Mariners ! mariners from the Western
Main !   Hurrah for gallant Drake !   Down with the
Don !"   For the tokens of the sea, in the form of
clothes and weapons, were well known and highly
esteemed.

Two or three gentlemen who were walking along
the road turned and looked up, and the young sailors
recognised in a moment a home face.   There was an
exclamation on either side of " Antony Babington !"
and " Humfrey Talbot !" and a ready clasp of the hand
in right of old companionship.

"Welcome home!" exclaimed Antony. "Is all well with you?"

"Royally well," returned Humfrey. "Know'st thou aught of our father and mother?"

"All was well with them when last I heard," said Antony.

"And Cis—my sister I mean?" said Diccon, putting, in his unconsciousness, the very question Humfrey was burning to ask.

"She is still with the Queen of Scots, at Chartley," replied Babington.

"Chartley, where is that? It is a new place for her captivity."

"'Tis a house of my Lord of Essex, not far from Lichfield," returned Antony. "They sent her thither this spring, after they had well-nigh slain her with the damp and wretched lodgings they provided at Tutbury."

"Who? Not our Cis?" asked Diccon.

"Nay," said Antony, "it hurt not her vigorous youth—but I meant the long-suffering princess."

"Hath Sir Ralf Sadler still the charge of her?" inquired Humfrey.

"No, indeed. He was too gentle a jailer for the Council. They have given her Sir Amias Paulett, a mere Puritan and Leicestrian, who is as hard as the nether millstone, and well-nigh as dull," said Babington, with a little significant chuckle, which perhaps alarmed one of his companions, a small slight man with a slight halt, clad in black like a lawyer. "Mr. Babington," he said, "pardon me for interrupting you, but we shall make Mr. Gage tarry supper for us."

"Nay, Mr. Langston," said Babington, who was in high spirits, "these are kinsmen of your own, sons of

Mr. Richard Talbot of Bridgefield, to whom you have often told me you were akin."

Mr. Langston was thus compelled to come forward, shake hands with the young travellers, welcome them home, and desire to be commended to their worthy parents; and Babington, in the exuberance of his welcome, named his other two companions—Mr. Tichborne, a fine, handsome, graceful, and somewhat melancholy young man; Captain Fortescue, a bearded moustached bravo, in the height of the fashion, a long plume in his Spanish hat, and his short gray cloak glittering with silver lace. Humfrey returned their salute, but was as glad as they evidently were when they got Babington away with them, and left the brothers to pursue their way, after inviting them to come and see him at his lodgings as early as possible.

"It is before supper," said Diccon, sagely, "or I should say Master Antony had been acquainted with some good canary."

"More likely he is uplifted with some fancy of his own. It may be only with the meeting of me after our encounter," said Humfrey. "He is a brave fellow and kindly, but never did craft so want ballast as does that pate of his!"

"Humfrey," said his brother, riding nearer to him, "did he not call that fellow in black, Langston?"

"Ay, Cuthbert Langston. I have heard of him. No good comrade for his weak brain."

"Humfrey, it is so, though father would not credit me. I knew his halt and his eye—just like the venomous little snake that was the death of poor Foster. He is the same with the witch woman Tibbott, ay, and with her with the beads and bracelets, who beset Cis and me at Buxton."

Young Diccon had proved himself on the voyage
to have an unerring eye for recognition, and his brother
gave a low whistle. " I fear me then Master Antony
may be running himself into trouble."

"See, they turn in mounting the steps to the upper
fence of yonder house with the deep carved balcony.
Another has joined them ! I like not his looks. He
is like one of those hardened cavaliers from the
Netherlands."

" Ay ! who seem to have left pity and conscience
behind them there," said Humfrey, looking anxiously
up at the fine old gabled house with its projecting
timbered front, and doubting inwardly whether it
would be wise to act on his old playfellow's invitation,
yet with an almost sick longing to know on what terms
the youth stood with Cicely.

In another quarter of an hour they were at the
gateway of Shrewsbury House, where the porter proved
to be one of the Sheffield retainers, and admitted them
joyfully. My Lord Earl was in Yorkshire, he said,
but my Lord and Lady Talbot were at home, and
would be fain to see them, and there too was Master
William Cavendish.

They were handed on into the courtyard, where
servants ran to take their horses, and as the news
ran that Master Richard's sons had arrived from the
Indies, Will Cavendish came running down the hall
steps to embrace them in his glee, while Lord Talbot
came to the door of the hall to welcome them. These
great London houses, which had not quite· lost their
names of hostels or inns, did really serve as free lodgings to all members of the family who might visit
town, and above all such travellers as these, bringing
news of grand national achievements.

Very soon after Gilbert's accession to the heirship, quarrels had begun between his wife and her mother the Countess.

Lord Talbot had much of his father's stately grace, and his wife was a finished lady. They heartily welcomed the two lads who had grown from boys to men. My lady smilingly excused the riding-gear, and as soon as the dust of travel had been removed they were seated at the board, and called on to tell of the gallant deeds in which they had taken part, whilst they heard in exchange of Lord Leicester's doings in the Netherlands, and the splendid exploits of the Stanleys at Zutphen.

Lord Talbot promised to take Humfrey to Richmond the next day, to be presented to her Majesty, so soon as he should be equipped, so as not to lose his character of mariner, but still not to affront her sensibilities by aught of uncourtly or unstudied in his apparel.

They confirmed what Babington had said of the Queen of Scots' changes of residence and of keepers. As to Cicely, they had been lately so little at Sheffield that they had almost forgotten her, but they thought that if she were still at Chartley, there could be no objection to her brothers having an interview with her on their way home, if they chose to go out of their road for it.

Humfrey mentioned his meeting with Babington in Westminster, and Lord Talbot made some inquiries as to his companions, adding that there were strange stories and suspicions afloat, and that he feared that the young man was disaffected and was consorting with Popish recusants. Diccon's tongue was on the alert with his observation, but at a sign from his brother, who did not wish to get Babington into trouble, he was silent. Cavendish, however, laughed and said he was for ever in Mr. Secretary's house, and even had a room there.

Very early the next morning the body servant of his Lordship was in attendance with a barber and the fashionable tailor of the Court, and in good time Humfrey and Diccon were arrayed in such garments as were judged to suit the Queen's taste, and to become the character of young mariners from the West. Humfrey had a dainty jewel of shell-work from the spoils of Carthagena, entrusted to him by Drake to present to the Queen as a foretaste of what was to come. Lady Talbot greatly admired its novelty and beauty, and thought the Queen would be enchanted with it, giving him a pretty little perfumed box to present it in.

Lord Talbot, well pleased to introduce his spirited young cousins, took them in his boat to Richmond, which they reached just as the evening coolness came on. They were told that her Majesty was walking in the Park, and thither, so soon as the ruffs had been adjusted and the fresh Spanish gloves drawn on, they resorted.

The Queen walked freely there without guards—. without even swords being worn by the gentlemen in attendance—loving as she did to display her confidence in her people. No precautions were taken, but they were allowed to gather together on the greensward to watch her, as among the beautiful shady trees she paced along.

The eyes of the two youths were eagerly directed towards her, as they followed Lord Talbot. Was she not indeed the cynosure of all the realm? Did she not hold the heart of every loyal Englishman by an invisible rein? Was not her favour their dream and

their reward ? She was a little in advance of her
suite. Her hair, of that light sandy tint which is slow
to whiten, was built up in curls under a rich stiff coif,
covered with silver lace, and lifted high at the temples.
From this a light gauze veil hung round her shoulders
and over her splendid standing ruff, which stood up
like the erected neck ornaments of some birds, opening
in front, and showing the lesser ruff or frill encircling
her throat, and terminating a lace tucker within her
low-cut boddice. Rich necklaces, the jewel of the
Garter, and a whole constellation of brilliants, decorated
her bosom, and the boddice of her blue satin dress and
its sleeves were laced with seed pearls. The waist, a
very slender one, was encircled with a gold cord and
heavy tassels, the farthingale spread out its magnificent
proportions, and a richly embroidered white satin
petticoat showed itself in front, but did not conceal
the active, well-shaped feet. There was something
extraordinarily majestic in her whole bearing, especially
the poise of her head, which made the spectator never
perceive how small her stature actually was. Her face
and complexion, too, were of the cast on which time is
slow to make an impression, being always pale and
fair, with keen and delicately-cut features; so that
her admirers had quite as much reason to be dazzled
as when she was half her present age ; nay, perhaps
more, for the habit of command had added to the
regality which really was her principal beauty. Sir
Christopher Hatton, with a handsome but very small
face at the top of a very tall and portly frame, dressed
in the extreme of foppery, came behind her, and then
a bevy of ladies and gentlemen.

As the Talbots approached, she was moving slowly
on, unusually erect even for her, and her face com-

posed to severe majesty, like that of a judge, the tawny eyes with a strange gleam in them fixed on some one in the throng on the grass near at hand. Lord Talbot advanced with a bow so low that he swept the ground with his plume, and while the two youths followed his example, Diccon's quick eye noted that she glanced for one rapid second at their weapons, then continued her steady gaze, never withdrawing it even to receive Lord Talbot's salutation as he knelt before her, though she said, " We greet you well, my good lord. Are not we well guarded, not having one man with a sword near me ? "

" Here are three good swords, madam," returned he, " mine own, and those of my two young kinsmen, whom I venture to present to your Majesty, as they bear greetings from your trusty servant, Sir Francis Drake."

While he spoke there had been a by-play unperceived by him, or by the somewhat slow and tardy Hatton. A touch from Diccon had made Humfrey follow the direction of the Queen's eye, and they saw it was fixed on a figure in a loose cloak strangely resembling that which they had seen on the stair of the house Babington had entered. They also saw a certain quailing and cowering of the form, and a scowl on the shaggy red eyebrows, and Irish features, and Humfrey at once edged himself so as to come between the fellow and the Queen, though he was ready to expect a pistol shot in his back, but better thus, was his thought, than that it should strike her,—and both laid their hands on their swords.

" How now ! " said Hatton, " young men, you are over prompt. Her Majesty needs no swords. You are out of rank. Fall in and do your obeisance."

Something in the Queen's relaxed gaze told Hum-

frey that the peril was over, and that he might kneel
as Talbot named him, explaining his lineage as Elizabeth always wished to have done. A sort of tremor
passed over her, but she instantly recalled her attention.
" From Drake !" she said, in her clear, somewhat shrill
voice. " So, young gentleman, you have been with
the pirate who outruns our orders, and fills our brother
of Spain with malice such that he would have our life
by fair or foul means."

" That shall he never do while your Grace has
English watch-dogs to guard you," returned Talbot.

" The Talbot is a trusty hound by water or by
land," said Elizabeth, surveying the goodly proportion
of the elder brother. " Whelps of a good litter, though
yonder lad be somewhat long and lean. Well, and
how fares Sir Francis ? Let him make his will, for
the Spaniards one day will have his blood."

" I have letters and a token from him for your
Grace," said Humfrey.

" Come then in," said the Queen. " We will see
it in the bower, and hear what thou wouldst say."

A bower, or small summer-house, stood at the end
of the path, and here she took her way, seating herself
on a kind of rustic throne evidently intended for her,
and there receiving from Humfrey the letter and the
gift, and asking some questions about the voyage ; but
she seemed preoccupied and anxious, and did not show
the enthusiastic approbation of her sailors' exploits
which the young men expected. After glancing over
it, she bade them carry the letter to Mr. Secretary
Walsingham the next day ; nor did she bid the party
remain to supper ; but as soon as half a dozen of her
gentlemen pensioners, who had been summoned by her
orders, came up, she rose to return to the palace.

Yet, to Talbot's surprise, she gave both the young men her hand to kiss, and even laid it upon Humfrey's freshly-trimmed head, saying, " You have done good service, my brave young spark. Use your eyes more than your tongue, and you will do well. We would not wish for stauncher bulwarks against traitor — Papist or Spaniard."

This was their dismissal. The audience was over, and they had to depart, Lord Talbot declaring that Humfrey had had marvellous good hap, and he had seldom seen her Majesty so gracious at a first presentation, unless a man was more comely than he could call his young cousins.

" Methinks she was glad to see our swords," said Diccon. " There was a scowling fellow she had her eye on, just as I have seen Sir Francis keep a whole troop of savage Indians in check as we landed on an island."

Lord Talbot laughed rather provokingly, and said, " The Queen hath swords enough at command without being beholden to thine, my doughty cousin!"

Diccon was suppressed, and mortified, but he thought the more. Humfrey owned his disappointment at more notice not having been taken of his commanders' exploits, and was answered, " Humour or policy, boy, policy or humour—one or both. One day, Drake and Hawkins and the rest will be her brave mariners, her golden boys ; another, mere pirates and robbers, bringing the Dons' wrath down upon us. You must take her as you find her, she is but a woman after all ; and even now there is said to be a plot—more deadly than ever before—which the Council are watching that they may lay the blame on the right shoulders.

Lord Talbot did not, however, know more than

that there were flying rumours of a fearful design, that
the Duke of Parma should land from the Netherlands,
the Queen be assassinated, and Mary of Scotland
liberated and proclaimed, all at once ; and he marvelled
at her residence at Chartley being permitted, since
it would not be difficult to set it on fire, and carry her
away in the confusion. He added that the whole of
the country, especially the Londoners, were declaring
that they should never sleep in peace while she lived,
and there was nothing but Queen Elizabeth's life
between her and the crown.

"And that knave meant mischief, and the Queen
knew it, and bore him down with her eye, just as
Drake did by the cannibal chief with the poisoned
arrow," thought Diccon, but Lord Talbot's previous
manner had silenced him effectually.

CHAPTER XXV.

PAUL'S WALK.

WILL CAVENDISH, who was in training for a statesman, and acted as a secretary to Sir Francis Walsingham, advised that the letters should be carried to him at once that same evening, as he would be in attendance on the Queen the next morning, and she would inquire for them.

The great man's house was not far off, and he walked thither with Humfrey, who told him what he had seen, and asked whether it ought not at once to be reported to Walsingham.

Will whistled. "They are driving it very close," he said. "Humfrey, old comrade, thy brains were always more of the order fit to face a tough breeze than to meddle with Court plots. Credit me, there is cause for what amazed thee. The Queen and her Council know what they are about. Risk a little, and put an end to all the plottings for ever! That's the word."

"Risk even the Queen's life?"

Will Cavendish looked sapient, and replied, "We of the Council Board know many a thing that looks passing strange."

Mr. Secretary Walsingham's town house was, like

Lord Talbot's, built round a court, across which Cavendish led the way, with the assured air of one used to
the service, and at home there. The hall was thronged
with people waiting, but Cavendish passed it, opened
a little wicket, and admitted his friends into a small
anteroom, where he bade them remain, while he
announced them to Sir Francis.

He disappeared, shutting a door behind him, and
after a moment's interval another person, with a brown
cloak round him, came hastily and stealthily across to
the door. He had let down the cloak which muffled his
chin, not expecting the presence of any one, and there
was a moment's start as he was conscious of the young
men standing there. He passed through the door
instantly, but not before Humfrey had had time to
recognise in him no other than Cuthbert Langston,
almost the last person he would have looked for at Sir
Francis Walsingham's. Directly afterwards Cavendish
returned.

"Sir Francis could not see Captain Talbot, and
prayed him to excuse him, and send in the letter."

"It can't be helped," said Cavendish, with his
youthful airs of patronage. "He would gladly
have spoken with you when I told him of you, but
that Maude is just come on business that may
not tarry. So you must e'en entrust your packet
to me."

"Maude," repeated Humfrey, "Was that man's
name Maude? I should have dared be sworn that he
was my father's kinsman, Cuthbert Langston."

"Very like," said Will, "I would dare be sworn to
nothing concerning him, but that he is one of the
greatest and most useful villains unhung."

So saying, Will Cavendish disappeared with the

M

letters. He probably had had a caution administered
to him, for when he returned he was evidently swelling with the consciousness of a State secret, which he
would not on any account betray, yet of the existence
of which he desired to make his old comrade aware.

Humfrey asked whether he had told Mr. Secretary
of the man in Richmond Park.

" Never fear ! he knows it," returned the budding
statesman. " Why, look you, a man like Sir Francis
has ten thousand means of intelligence that a simple
mariner like you would never guess at. I thought it
strange myself when I came first into business of State,
but he hath eyes and ears everywhere, like the Queen's
gown in her picture. Men of the Privy Council, you
see, must despise none, for the lewdest and meanest
rogues oft prove those who can do the best service,
just as the bandy-legged cur will turn the spit, or
unearth the fox when your gallant hound can do
nought but bay outside."

" Is this Maude, or Langston, such a cur ? "

Cavendish gave his head a shake that expressed
unutterable things, saying : " Your kinsman, said you ?
I trust not on the Talbot side of the house ? "

" No. On his mother's side. I wondered the more
to see him here as he got that halt in the Rising of
the North, and on the wrong side, and hath ever been
reckoned a concealed Papist."

" Ay, ay. Dost not see, mine honest Humfrey,
that's the very point that fits him for our purpose ? "

" You mean that he is a double traitor and informer."

" We do not use such hard words in the Privy
Council Board as you do on deck, my good friend,"
said Cavendish. " We have our secret intelligencers,
you see, all in the Queen's service. Foul and dirty

work, but you can't dig out a fox without soiling of fingers, and if there be those that take kindly to the work, why, e'en let them do it."

" Then there is a plot ?"

" Content you, Humfrey ! You'll hear enough of it anon. A most foul, bloody, and horrible plot, quite enough to hang every soul that has meddled in it, and yet safe to do no harm—like poor Hal's blunderbuss, which would never go off, except when it burst, and blew him to pieces."

Will felt that he had said quite enough to impress Humfrey with a sense of his statecraft and import-ance, and was not sorry for an interruption before he should have said anything dangerous. It was from Frank Pierrepoint, who had been Diccon's schoolmate, and was enchanted to see him. Humfrey was to stay one day longer in town in case Walsingham should wish to see him, and to show Diccon something of London, which they had missed on their way to Plymouth.

St. Paul's Cathedral was even then the sight that all Englishmen were expected to have seen, and the brothers took their way thither, accompanied by Frank Pierre-point, who took their guidance on his hands. Had the lads seen the place at the opening of the century they would have thought it a piteous spectacle, for desecra-tion and sacrilege had rioted there unchecked, the mag-nificent peal of bells had been gambled away at a single throw of the dice, the library had been utterly destroyed, the magnificent plate melted up, and what covetous fanaticism had spared had been further ravaged by a terrible fire. At this time Bishop Bancroft had done his utmost towards reparation, and the old spire had been replaced by a wooden one ; but there was much

of ruin and decay visible all around, where stood the
famous octagon building called Paul's Cross, where
outdoor sermons were preached to listeners of all ranks.
This was of wood, and was kept in moderately good
repair.　Beyond, the nave of the Cathedral stretched
its length, the greatest in England.　Two sets of doors
immediately opposite to one another on the north and
south sides had rendered it a thoroughfare in very early
times, in spite of the endeavours of the clergy ; and at
this time "Duke Humfrey's Walk," from the tomb of
Duke Humfrey Stafford, as the twelve grand Norman
bays of this unrivalled nave were called, was the prime
place for the humours of London ; and it may be feared
that this, rather than the architecture, was the chief
idea in the minds of the youths, as a babel of strange
sounds fell on their ears, " a still roar like a humming
of bees," as it was described by a contemporary, or, as
Humfrey said, like the sea in a great hollow cave.　A
cluster of choir-boys were watching at the door to fall
on any one entering with spurs on, to levy their spur
money, and one gentleman, whom they had thus
attacked, was endeavouring to save his purse by calling on the youngest boy to sing his gamut.

Near at hand was a pillar, round which stood a set
of men, some rough, some knavish-looking, with the
blue coats, badges, short swords, and bucklers carried
by serving-men.　They were waiting to be hired, as if
in a statute fair, and two or three loud-voiced bargains
were going on.　In the middle aisle, gentlemen in all
the glory of plumed hats, jewelled ears, ruffed necks,
Spanish cloaks, silken jerkins, velvet hose, and be-rosed
shoes, were marching up and down, some attitudinising
to show their graces, some discussing the news of the
day, for "Paul's Walk" was the Bond Street, the Row,

the Tattersall's, the Club of London. Twelve scriveners
had their tables to act as letter-writers, and sometimes
as legal advisers, and great amusement might be had
by those who chose to stand listening to the blundering
directions of their clients. In the side aisles, horse-
dealing, merchants' exchanges, everything imaginable in
the way of traffic was going on. Disreputable-looking
men, who there were in sanctuary from their creditors,
there lurked around Humfrey Stafford's tomb; and
young Pierrepoint's warning to guard their purses
was evidently not wasted, for a country fellow, who
had just lost his, was loudly demanding justice, and
getting jeered at for his simplicity in expecting to
recover it.

"Seest thou this?" said a voice close to Humfrey,
and he found a hand on his arm, and Babington, in
the handsome equipment of one of the loungers, close
to him.

"A sorry sight, that would grieve my good mother,"
returned Humfrey.

"My Mother, the Church, is grieved," responded
Antony. "This is what you have brought us to, for
your so-called *religion*," he added, ignorant or oblivious
that these desecrations had been quite as shocking
before the Reformation. "All will soon be changed,
however," he added.

"Sir Thomas Gresham's New Exchange has cleared
off some of the traffic, they say," returned Humfrey.

"Pshaw!" said Antony; "I meant no such folly.
That were cleansing one stone while the whole house
is foul with shame. No. There shall be a swift
vengeance on these desecrators. The purifier shall
come again, and the glory and the beauty of the true
Faith shall be here as of old, when our fathers bowed

before the Holy Rood, instead of tearing it down."
His eye glanced with an enthusiasm which Humfrey
thought somewhat wild, and he said, "Whist! these
are not things to be thus spoken of."

"All is safe," said Babington, drawing him within
shelter of the chantry of Sir John Beauchamp's tomb.
"Never heed Diccon—Pierrepoint can guide him,"
and Humfrey saw their figures, apparently absorbed in
listening to the bidding for a horse. "I have things
of moment to say to thee, Humfrey Talbot. We have
been old comrades, and had that childish emulation
which turns to love in manhood in the face of perils."

Humfrey, recollecting how they had parted, held
out his hand in recognition of the friendliness.

"I would fain save thee," said Babington. "Heretic
and rival as thou art, I cannot but love thee, and I
would have thee die, if die thou must, in honourable
fight by sea or land, rather than be overtaken by the
doom that will fall on all who are persecuting our
true and lawful confessor and sovereign."

"Gramercy for thy good will, Tony," said Humfrey,
looking anxiously to see whether his old companion
was in his right mind, yet remembering what had been
said of plots.

"Thou deem'st me raving," said Antony, smiling
at the perplexed countenance before him, "but thou
wilt see too late that I speak sooth, when the armies
of the Church avenge the Name that has been profaned among you!"

"The Spaniards, I suppose you mean," said Humfrey coolly. "You must be far gone indeed to hope
to see those fiends turned loose on this peaceful land,
but by God's blessing we have kept them aloof before,
I trust we may again."

"You talk of God's blessing. Look at His House,"
said Babington.

"He is more like to bless honest men who fight
for their Queen, their homes and hearths, than traitors
who would bring in slaughterers and butchers to work
their will!"

"His glory is worked through judgment, and thus
must it begin!" returned the young man. "But I
would save thee, Humfrey," he added. "Go thou
back to Plymouth, and be warned to hold aloof from
that prison where the keepers will meet their fit
doom! and the captive will be set free. Thou dost
not believe," he added. "See here," and drawing into
the most sheltered part of the chantry, he produced
from his bosom a picture in the miniature style of the
period, containing six heads, among which his own
was plainly to be recognised, and likewise a face which
Humfrey felt as if he should never forget, that which
he had seen in Richmond Park, quailing beneath the
Queen's eye. Round the picture was the motto—

" *Hi mihi sunt comites quos ipsa pericula jungunt.*"

"I tell thee, Humfrey, thou wilt hear—if thou dost
live to hear — of these six as having wrought the
greatest deed of our times!"

"May it only be a deed an honest man need not be
ashamed of," said Humfrey, not at all convinced of his
friend's sanity.

"Ashamed of!" exclaimed Babington. "It is blest,
I tell thee, blest by holy men, blest by the noble and
suffering woman who will thus be delivered from her
martyrdom."

"Babington, if thou talkest thus, it will be my duty
to have thee put in ward," said Humfrey.

Antony laughed, and there was a triumphant ring very like insanity in his laughter. Humfrey, with a moment's idea that to hint that the conspiracy was known would blast it at once, if it were real, said, " I see not Cuthbert Langston among your six. Know you, I saw him only yestereven going into Secretary Walsingham's privy chamber."

"Was he so?" answered Babington. " Ha! ha! he holds them all in play till the great stroke be struck! Why! am not I myself in Walsingham's confidence? He thinketh that he is about to send me to France to watch the League. Ha! ha!"

Here Humfrey's other companions turned back in search of him; Babington vanished in the crowd, he hardly knew how, and he was left in perplexity and extreme difficulty as to what was his duty as friend or as subject. If Babington were sane, there must be a conspiracy for killing the Queen, bringing in the Spaniards and liberating Mary, and he had expressly spoken of having had the latter lady's sanction, while the sight of the fellow in Richmond Park gave a colour of probability to the guess. Yet the imprudence and absurdity of having portraits taken of six assassins before the blow was struck seemed to contradict all the rest. On the other hand, Cavendish had spoken of having all the meshes of the web in the hands of the Council; and Langston or Maude seemed to be trusted by both parties.

Humfrey decided to feel his way with Will Cavendish, and that evening spoke of having met Babington and having serious doubts whether he were in his right mind. Cavendish laughed, " Poor wretch! I could pity him," he said, "though his plans be wicked enough to merit no compassion. Nay, never fear, Humfrey.

All were overthrown, did I speak openly. Nay, to utter
one word would ruin me for ever. 'Tis quite sufficient to say that he and his fellows are only at large
till Mr. Secretary sees fit, that so his grip may be the
more sure."

Humfrey saw he was to be treated with no confidence, and this made him the more free to act. There
were many recusant gentlemen in the neighbourhood of
Chartley, and an assault and fight there were not im-
probable, if, as Cavendish hinted, there was a purpose
of letting the traitors implicate themselves in the
largest numbers and as fatally as possible. On the
other hand, Babington's hot head might only fancy he
had authority from the Queen for his projects. If,
through Cicely, he could convey the information to
Mary, it might save her from even appearing to be
cognisant of these wild schemes, whatever they might
be, and to hint that they were known was the surest
way to prevent their taking effect. Any way, Humfrey's heart was at Chartley, and every warning he had
received made him doubly anxious to be there in person, to be Cicely's guardian in case of whatever danger
might threaten her. He blessed the fiction which still
represented him as her brother, and which must open a
way for him to see her, but he resolved not to take
Diccon thither, and parted with him when the roads
diverged towards Lichfield, sending to his father a
letter which Diccon was to deliver only into his own
hand, with full details of all he had seen and heard,
and his motives for repairing to Chartley.

"Shall I see my little Cis?" thought he. "And
even if she play the princess to me, how will she meet
me? She scorned me even when she was at home.
How will it be now when she has been for well-

M*

nigh a year in this Queen's training? Ah! she will
be taught to despise me! Heigh ho! At least she
may be in need of a true heart and strong arm to
guard her, and they shall not fail her."

Will Cavendish, in the plenitude of the official importance with which he liked to dazzle his old playfellow, had offered him a pass to facilitate his entrance,
and he found reason to be glad that he had accepted
it, for there was a guard at the gate of Chartley Park,
and he was detained there while his letter was sent up
for inspection to Sir Amias Paulett, who had for the
last few months acted as warder to the Queen.

However, a friendly message came back, inviting
him to ride up. The house—though called a castle—
had been rebuilt in hospitable domestic style, and
looked much less like a prison than Sheffield Lodge,
but at every enclosure stood yeomen who challenged the
passers-by, as though this were a time of alarm. However, at the hall-door itself stood Sir Amias Paulett,
a thin, narrow-browed, anxious-looking man, with the
stiffest of ruffs, over which hung a scanty yellow beard.

"Welcome, sir," he said, with a nervous anxious
distressed manner. "Welcome, most welcome. You
will pardon any discourtesy, sir, but these are evil
times. The son, I think, of good Master Richard
Talbot of Bridgefield? Ay, I would not for worlds
have shown any lack of hospitality to one of his family.
It is no want of respect, sir. No; nor of my Lord's
house; but these are ill days, and with my charge, sir
—if Heaven itself keep not the house—who knows
what may chance or what may be laid on me?"

"I understand," said Humfrey, smiling. "I was
bred close to Sheffield, and hardly knew what 'twas to
live beyond watch and ward."

"Yea!" said Paulett, shaking his head. "You
come of a loyal house, sir; but even the good Earl
was less exercised than I am in the charge of this
same lady. But I am glad, glad to see you, sir. And
you would see your sister, sir? A modest young lady,
and not indevout, though I have sometimes seen her
sleep at sermon. It is well that the poor maiden
should see some one well affected, for she sitteth in the
very gate of Babylon; and with respect, sir, I marvel
that a woman, so godly as Mistress Talbot of Bridgefield is reported to be, should suffer it. However, I do
my poor best, under Heaven, to hinder the faithful of
the household from being tainted. I have removed
Préaux, who is well known to be a Popish priest in
disguise, and thus he can spread no more of his errors.
Moreover, my chaplain, Master Blunden, with other
godly men, preaches three times a week against Romish
errors, and all are enforced to attend. May their ears
be opened to the truth! I am about to attend this
lady on a ride in the Park, sir. It might—if she be
willing—be arranged that your sister, Mistress Talbot,
should spend the time in your company, and methinks
the lady will thereto agree, for she is ever ready to
show a certain carnal and worldly complaisance to the
wishes of her attendants, and I have observed that she
greatly affects the damsel, more, I fear, than may be for
the eternal welfare of the maiden's soul."

CHAPTER XXVI.

IN THE WEB.

IT was a beautiful bright summer day, and Queen
Mary and some of her train were preparing for their
ride.   The Queen was in high spirits, and that wonderful and changeful countenance of hers was beaming
with anticipation and hope, while her demeanour was
altogether delightful to every one who approached her.
She was adding some last instructions to Nau, who was
writing a letter for her to the French ambassador, and
Cicely stood by her, holding her little dog in a leash,
and looking somewhat anxious and wistful.   There was
more going on round the girl than she was allowed to
understand, and it made her anxious and uneasy.   She
knew that the correspondence through the brewer was
actively carried on, but she was not informed of what
passed.   Only she was aware that some crisis must be
expected, for her mother was ceaselessly restless and
full of expectation.   She had put all her jewels and
valuables into as small a compass as possible, and
talked more than ever of her plans for giving her
daughter either to the Archduke Matthias, or to some
great noble, as if the English crown were already within
her grasp.   Anxious, curious, and feeling injured by
the want of confidence, yet not daring to complain,

Cicely felt almost fretful at her mother's buoyancy,
but she had been taught a good many lessons in the
past year, and one of them was that she might indeed
be caressed, but that she must show neither humour
nor will of her own, and the least presumption in inquiry or criticism was promptly quashed.

There was a knock at the door, and the usher
announced that Sir Amias Paulett prayed to speak
with her Grace.　Her eye glanced round with the
rapid emotion of one doubtful whether it were for weal
or woe, yet with undaunted spirit to meet either, and
as she granted her permission, Cis heard her whisper to
Nau, " A rider came up even now !　'Tis the tidings !
Are the Catholics of Derby in the saddle ?　Are the
ships on the coast ? "

In came the tall old man with a stiff reverence :
" Madam, your Grace's horses attend you, and I have
tidings "—(Mary started forward)—" tidings for this
young lady, Mistress Cicely Talbot.　Her brother is
arrived from the Spanish Main, and requests permission
to see and speak with her."

Radiance flashed out on Cicely's countenance as
excitement faded on that of her mother : " Humfrey !
O madam, let me go to him ! " she entreated, with a
spring of joy and clasped hands.

Mary was far too kind-hearted to refuse, besides
to have done so would have excited suspicion at a
perilous moment, and the arrangement Sir Amias proposed was quickly made.　Mary Seaton was to attend
the Queen in Cicely's stead, and she was allowed to
hurry downstairs, and only one warning was possible :
" Go then, poor child, take thine holiday, only bear in
mind what and who thou art."

Yet the words had scarce died on her ears before

she was oblivious of all save that it was a familiar
home figure who stood at the bottom of the stairs, one
of the faces she trusted most in all the world which
beamed out upon her, the hands which she knew
would guard her through everything were stretched
out to her, the lips with veritable love in them kissed
the cheeks she did not withhold.   Sir Amias stood by
and gave the kindest smile she had seen from him,
quite changing his pinched features, and he proposed
to the two young people to go and walk in the garden
together, letting them out into the square walled
garden, very formal, but very bright and gay, and
with a pleached alley to shelter them from the sun.

"Good old gentleman!" exclaimed Humfrey, holding the maiden's hand in his.   "It is a shame to win
such pleasure by feigning."

"As for that," sighed Cis, "I never know what
is sooth here, and what am I save a living lie myself?
O Humfrey! I am so weary of it all."

"Ah! would that I could bear thee home with
me," he said, little prepared for this reception.

"Would that thou couldst!   O that I were indeed
thy sister, or that the writing in my swaddling bands
had been washed out!—Nay," catching back her words,
"I meant not that!   I would not but belong to the
dear Lady here.   She says I comfort her more than
any of them, and oh! she is—she is, there is no telling how sweet and how noble.   It was only that the
sight of thee awoke the yearning to be at home with
mother and with father.   Forget my folly, Humfrey."

"I cannot soon forget that Bridgefield seems to
thee thy true home," he said, putting strong restraint on
himself to say and do no more, while his heart throbbed
with a violence unawakened by storm or Spaniard.

" Tell me of them all," she said. " I have heard
naught of them since we left Tutbury, where at least
we were in my Lord's house, and the dear old silver
dog was on every sleeve. Ah! there he is, the trusty
rogue."

And snatching up Humfrey's hat, which was
fastened with a brooch of his crest in the fashion of
the day, she kissed the familiar token. Then, however, she blushed and drew herself up, remembering
the caution not to forget who she was, and with an
assumption of more formal dignity, she said, " And how
fares it with the good Mrs. Talbot ?"

" Well, when I last heard," said Humfrey, " but I
have not been at home. I only know what Will
Cavendish and my Lord Talbot told me. I sent
Diccon on to Bridgefield, and came out of the way to
see you, lady," he concluded, with the same regard to
actual circumstances that she had shown.

" Oh, that was good !" she whispered, and they both
seemed to feel a certain safety in avoiding personal
subjects. Humfrey had the history of his voyage to
narrate—to tell of little Diccon's gallant doings, and
to exalt Sir Francis Drake's skill and bravery, and at
last to let it ooze out, under Cis's eager questioning,
that when his captain had died of fever on the His-
paniola coast, and they had been overtaken by a
tornado, Sir Francis had declared that it was Humfrey's skill and steadfastness which had saved the ship
and crew.

" And it was that tornado," he said, " which
stemmed the fever, and saved little Diccon's life.
Oh! when he lay moaning below, then was the time
to long for my mother."

Time sped on till the great hall clock made Cicely

look up and say she feared that the riders would soon return, and then Humfrey knew that he must make sure to speak the words of warning he came to utter. He told, in haste, of his message to Queen Elizabeth, and of his being sent on to Secretary Walsingham, adding, " But I saw not the great man, for he was closeted—with whom think you? No other than Cuthbert Langston, whom Cavendish called by another name. It amazed me the more, because I had two days before met him in Westminster with Antony Babington, who presented him to me by his own name."

" Saw you Antony Babington ?" asked Cis, raising her eyes to his face, but looking uneasy.

" Twice, at Westminster, and again in Paul's Walk. Had you seen him since you have been here ?"

" Not here, but at Tutbury. He came once, and 1 was invited to dine in the hall, because he brought recommendations from the Countess." There was a pause, and then, as if she had begun to take in the import of Humfrey's words, she added, " What said you ? That Mr. Langston was going between him and Mr. Secretary ?"

" Not exactly that," and Humfrey repeated with more detail what he had seen of Langston, forbearing to ask any questions which Cicely might not be able to answer with honour; but they had been too much together in childhood not to catch one another's mean-ing with half a hint, and she said, " I see why you came here, Humfrey. It was good and true and kind, befitting you. I will tell the Queen. If Langston be in it, there is sure to be treachery. But, indeed, I know nothing or well-nigh nothing."

" I am glad of it," fervently exclaimed Humfrey.

" No; I only know that she has high hopes, and

thinks that the term of her captivity is well-nigh over. But it is Madame de Courcelles whom she trusts, not me," said Cicely, a little hurt.

"So is it much better for thee to know as little as possible," said Humfrey, growing intimate in tone again in spite of himself. "She hath not changed thee much, Cis, only thou art more grave and womanly, ay, and thou art taller, yea, and thinner, and paler, as I fear me thou mayest well be."

"Ah, Humfrey, 'tis a poor joy to be a princess in prison! And yet I shame me that I long to be away. Oh no, I would not. Mistress Seaton and Mrs. Curll and the rest might be free, yet they have borne this durance patiently all these years—and I think—I think she loves me a little, and oh! she is hardly used. Humfrey, what think'st thou that Mr. Langston meant? I wot now for certain that it was he who twice came to beset us, as Tibbott the huckster, and with the beads and bracelets! They all deem him a true friend to my Queen."

"So doth Babington," said Humfrey, curtly.

"Ah!" she said, with a little terrified sound of conviction, then added, "What thought you of Master Babington?"

"That he is half-crazed," said Humfrey.

"We may say no more," said Cis, seeing a servant advancing from the house to tell her that the riders were returning. "Shall I see you again, Humfrey?"

"If Sir Amias should invite me to lie here to-night, and remain to-morrow, since it will be Sunday."

"At least I shall see you in the morning, ere you depart," she said, as with unwilling yet prompt steps she returned to the house, Humfrey feeling that she was indeed his little Cis, yet that some change had come over her, not so much altering her, as developing the capabilities he had always seen.

For herself, poor child, her feelings were in a strange turmoil, more than usually conscious of that dual existence which had tormented her ever since she had been made aware of her true birth. Moreover, she had a sense of impending danger and evil, and, by force of contrast, the frank, open-hearted manner of Humfrey made her the more sensible of being kept in the dark as to serious matters, while outwardly made a pet and plaything by her mother, " just like Bijou," as she said to herself.

" So, little one," said Queen Mary, as she returned, " thou hast been revelling once more in tidings of Sheffield ! How long will it take me to polish away the dulness of thy clownish contact ? "

" Humfrey does not come from home, madam, but from London. Madam, let me tell you in your ear——"

Mary's eye instantly took the terrified alert expression which had come from many a shock and alarm. " What is it, child ? " she asked, however, in a voice of affected merriment. " I wager it is that he has found his true Cis. Nay, whisper it to me, if it touch thy silly little heart so deeply."

Cicely knelt down, the Queen bending over her, while she murmured in her ear, " He saw Cuthbert Langston, by a feigned name, admitted to Mr. Secretary Walsingham's privy chamber."

She *felt* the violent start this information caused, but the command of voice and countenance was perfect. " What of that, *mignonne ?* " she said. " What knoweth he of this Langston, as thou callest him ? "

" He is my—no—his father's kinsman, madam,

and is known to be but a plotter. Oh, surely, he is
not in your secrets, madam, my mother, after that
day at Tutbury ? "

"Alack, my lassie, Gifford or Babington answered
for him," said the Queen, "and he kens more than I
could desire. But this Humfrey of thine ! How came
he to blunder out such tidings to thee ? "

"It was no blunder, madam. He came here of
purpose."

"Sure," exclaimed Mary, "it were too good to hope
that he hath become well affected. He—a sailor of
Drake's, a son of Master Richard ! Hath Babington
won him over ; or is it for thy sake, child ? For I
bestowed no pains to cast smiles to him at Sheffield,
even had he come in my way."

"I think, madam," said Cicely, "that he is too loyal-
hearted to bear the sight of treachery without a word
of warning."

"Is he so ? Then he is the first of his nation who
hath been of such a mind ! Nay, *mignonne*, deny not
thy conquest. This is thy work."

"I deny not that—that I am beloved by Humfrey,"
said Cicely, "for I have known it all my life ; but *that*
goes for naught in what he deems it right to do."

"There spoke so truly Mistress Susan's scholar that
thou makest me laugh in spite of myself and all the
rest. Hold him fast, my maiden ; think what thou
wilt of his service, and leave me now, and send Melville
and Curll to me."

Cicely went away full of that undefined discomfort
experienced by generous young spirits when their elders,
more worldly-wise (or foolish), fail even to comprehend
the purity or loftiness of motive in which they themselves thoroughly believe. Yet, though she had in-

finitely more faith in Humfrey's affection than she had
in that of Babington, she had not by any means the
same dread of being used to bait the hook for him,
partly because she knew his integrity too well to expect
to shake it, and partly because he was perfectly aware
of her real birth, and could not be gulled with such
delusive hopes as poor Antony might once have been.

Humfrey meantime was made very welcome by Sir
Amias Paulett, who insisted on his spending the next
day, Sunday, at Chartley, and made him understand
that he was absolutely welcome, as having a strong
arm, stout heart, and clear brain used to command.
" Trusty aid do I need," said poor Sir Amias, " if ever
man lacked an arm of flesh.   The Council is putting
more on me than ever man had to bear, in an open
place like this, hard to be defended, and they will
not increase the guard lest they should give the alarm,
forsooth ! "

" What   is   it   that   you   apprehend ? "   inquired
Humfrey.

" There's enough to apprehend when all the hot-
headed Papists of Stafford and Derbyshire are waiting
the signal to fire the outhouses and carry off this lady
under cover of the confusion.   Mr. Secretary swears
they will not stir till the signal be given, and that it
never will ; but such sort of fellows are like enough to
mistake the sign, and the stress may come through
their dillydallying to make all sure as they say, and
then, if there be any mischance, I shall be the one to
bear the blame.   Ay, if it be their own work ! " he
added, speaking to himself, " Murder under trust !
That would serve as an answer to foreign princes, and
my head would have to pay for it, however welcome it
might be !   So, good Mr. Talbot, supposing any alarm

should arise, keep you close to the person of this lady,
for there be those who would make the fray a colour
for taking her life, under pretext of hindering her from
being carried off."

It was no wonder that a warder in such circumstances looked harassed and perplexed, and showed
himself glad of being joined by any ally whom he could
trust.   In truth, harsh and narrow as he was, Paulett
was too good and religious a man for the task that had
been thrust on him, where loyal obedience, sense of
expediency, and even religious fanaticism, were all in
opposition to the primary principles of truth, mercy,
and honour.   He was, besides, in constant anxiety,
living as he did between plot and counterplot, and with
the certainty that emissaries of the Council surrounded
him who would have no scruple in taking Mary's life,
and leaving him to bear the blame, when Elizabeth
would have to explain the deed to the other sovereigns
of Europe.   He disclosed almost all this to Humfrey,
whose frank, trustworthy expression seemed to move
him to unusual confidence.

At supper-time another person appeared, whom
Humfrey thought he had once seen at Sheffield——a thin,
yellow-haired and bearded man, much marked with
smallpox, in the black dress of a lawyer, who sat above
the household servants, though below the salt. Paulett
once drank to him with a certain air of patronage,
calling him Master Phillipps, a name that came as a
revelation to Humfrey.   Phillipps was the decipherer
who had, he knew, been employed to interpret Queen
Mary's letters after the Norfolk plot.   Were there,
then, fresh letters of that unfortunate lady in his hands,
or were any to be searched for and captured ?

CHAPTER XXVII.

THE CASTLE WELL.

" What vantage or what thing
  Gett'st thou thus for to sting,
    Thou false and flatt'ring liar ?
  Thy tongue doth hurt, it's seen
  No less than arrows keen
    Or hot consuming fire."

So sang the congregation in the chapel at Chartley, in
the strains of Sternhold and Hopkins, while Humfrey
Talbot could not forbear from a misgiving whether
these falsehoods were entirely on the side to which
they were thus liberally attributed. Opposite to him
stood Cicely, in her dainty Sunday farthingale of white,
embroidered with violet buds, and a green and violet
boddice to match, holding herself with that unconscious
royal bearing which had always distinguished her, but
with an expression of care and anxiety drawing her
dark brows nearer together as she bent over her book.

She knew that her mother had left her bed with the
earliest peep of summer dawn, and had met the two
secretaries in her cabinet. There they were busy for
hours, and she had only returned to her bed just as the
household began to bestir itself.

" My child," she said to Cicely, " I am about to put

my life into thy keeping and that of this Talbot lad.
If what he saith of this Langston be sooth, I am again
betrayed, fool that I was to expect aught else. My
life is spent in being betrayed. The fellow hath been
a go-between in all that hath passed between Babington
and me. If he hath uttered it to Walsingham, all is
over with our hopes, and the window in whose sun-
light I have been basking is closed for ever! But something may yet be saved. Something? What do I
say?——The letters I hold here would give colour for
taking my life, ay, and Babington's and Curll's, and
many more. I trusted to have burnt them, but in this
summer time there is no coming by fire or candle
without suspicion, and if I tore them they might be
pieced together, nay, and with addition. They must
be carried forth and made away with beyond the ken
of Paulett and his spies. Now, this lad hath some
bowels of compassion and generous indignation. Thou
wilt see him again, alone and unsuspected, ere he departs.
Thou must deal with him to bear this packet away,
and when he is far out of reach to drop it into the
most glowing fire, or the deepest pool he can find.
Tell him it may concern thy life and liberty, and he
will do it, but be not simple enough to say ought of
Babington."

"He would be as like to do it for Babington as for
any other," said Cis.

The Queen smiled and said, "Nineteen years old,
and know thus little of men."

"I know Humfrey at least," said Cis.

"Then deal with him after thy best knowledge,
to make him convey away this perilous matter ere
a search come upon us. Do it we must, maiden,
not for thy poor mother's sake alone, but for that of

many a faithful spirit outside, and above all of poor
Curll. Think of our Barbara! Would that I could
have sent her out of reach of our alarms and shocks,
but Paulett is bent on penning us together like silly
birds in the net. Still proofs will be wanting if thou
canst get this youth to destroy this packet unseen.
Tell him that I know his parents' son too well to offer
him any meed save the prayers and blessings of a poor
captive, or to fear that he would yield it for the largest
reward Elizabeth's coffers could yield."

"It shall be done, madam," said Cicely.

But there was a strong purpose in her mind that
Humfrey should not be implicated in the matter.

When after dinner Sir Amias Paulett made his
daily visit of inspection to the Queen, she begged that
the young Talbots might be permitted another walk in
the garden; and when he replied that he did not
approve of worldly pastime on the Sabbath, she
pleaded the celebrated example of John Knox finding
Calvin playing at bowls on a Sunday afternoon at
Geneva, and thus absolutely prevailed on him to let
them take a short walk together in brotherly love,
while the rest of the household was collected in the
hall to be catechised by the chaplain.

So out they went together, but to Humfrey's surprise, Cicely walked on hardly speaking to him, so that
he fancied at first that she must have had a lecture on
her demeanour to him. She took him along the broad
terrace beside the bowling-green, through some yew-
tree walks to a stone wall, and a gate which proved
to be locked. She looked much disappointed, but
scanning the wall with her eye, said, "We have scaled
walls together before now, and higher than this. Humfrey, I cannot tell you why, but I must go over here."

The wall was overgrown with stout branches of
ivy, and though the Sunday farthingale was not very
appropriate for climbing, Cicely's active feet and
Humfrey's strong arm carried her safely to where she
could jump down on the other side, into a sort of
wilderness where thorn and apple trees grew among
green mounds, heaps of stones and broken walls, the
ruins of some old outbuilding of the former castle.
There was only a certain trembling eagerness about
her, none of the mirthful exultation that the recurrence
of such an escapade with her old companion would
naturally have excited, and all she said was, " Stand
here, Humfrey; an you love me, follow me not.   I will
return anon."

With stealthy step she disappeared behind a mound
covered by a thicket of brambles, but Humfrey was
much too anxious for her safety not to move quietly
onwards.   He saw her kneeling by one of those black
yawning holes, often to be found in ruins, intent upon
fastening a small packet to a stone ; he understood all
in a moment, and drew back far enough to secure that
no one molested her.   There was something in this
reticence of hers that touched him greatly ; it showed
so entirely that she had learnt the lesson of loyalty
which his father's influence had impressed, and likewise
one of self-dependence.   What was right for her to do
for her mother and Queen might not be right for him, as
an Englishman, to aid and abet ; and small as the deed
seemed in itself, her thus silently taking it on herself
rather than perplex him with it, added a certain esteem
and respect to the affection he had always had for her.

She came back to him with bounding steps, as if
with a lightened heart, and as he asked her what this
strange place was, she explained that here were said to

be the ruins of the former castle, and that beyond lay
the ground where sometimes the party shot at the butts.
A little dog of Mary Seaton's had been lost the last
time of their archery, and it was feared that he had
fallen down the old well to which Cis now conducted
Humfrey. There was a sound—long, hollow, rever-
berating, when Humfrey threw a stone down, and when
Cicely asked him, in an awestruck voice, whether he
thought anything thrown there would ever be heard of
more, he could well say that he believed not.

She breathed freely, but they were out of bounds,
and had to scramble back, which they did undetected,
and with much more mirth than the first time.   Cicely
was young enough to be glad to throw off her anxieties
and forget them.   She did not want to talk over the
plots she only guessed at; which were not to her exciting
mysteries, but gloomy terrors into which she feared
to look.   Nor was she free to say much to Humfrey of
what she knew.   Indeed the rebound, and the satisfaction of having fulfilled her commission, had raised
Cicely's spirits, so that she was altogether the bright
childish companion Humfrey had known her before he
went to sea, or royalty had revealed itself to her; and
Sir Amias Paulett would hardly have thought them
solemn and serious enough for an edifying Sunday talk
could he have heard them laughing over Humfrey's
adventures on board ship, or her troubles in learning to
dance in a high and disposed manner.   She came in so
glowing and happy that the Queen smiled and sighed,
and called her her little milkmaid, commending her
highly, however, for having disposed of the dangerous
parcel unknown (as she believed) to her companion.
" The fewer who have to keep counsel, the sickerer it
is," she said.

Humfrey meantime joined the rest of the household, and comported himself at the evening sermon
with such exemplary discretion as entirely to win the
heart of Sir Amias Paulett, who thought him listening
to Mr. Blunden's oft-divided headings, while he was in
fact revolving on what pretext he could remain to protect Cicely.   The Knight gave him that pretext, when
he spoke of departing early on Monday morning,
offering him, or rather praying him to accept, the command of the guards, whose former captain had been
dismissed as untrustworthy.   Sir Amias undertook
that a special messenger should be sent to take a letter
to Bridgefield, explaining Humfrey's delay, and asking
permission from his parents to undertake the charge,
since it was at this very crisis that he was especially
in need of God-fearing men of full integrity.   Then
moved to confidence, the old gentleman disclosed that
not only was he in fear of an attack on the house
from the Roman Catholic gentry in the neighbourhood,
which was to take place as soon as Parma's ships were
seen on the coast, but that he dreaded his own servants
being tampered with by some whom he would not mention to take the life of the prisoner secretly.

"It hath been mooted to me," he said, lowering his
voice to a whisper, "that to take such a deed on me
would be good service to the Queen and to religion,
but I cast the thought from me.   It can be nought but
a deadly sin—accursed of God—and were I to consent, I should be the first to be accused."

"It would be no better than the King of Spain
himself," exclaimed Humfrey.

"Even so, young man, and right glad am I to
find one who thinks with me.   For the other practices, they are none of mine, and is it not written ' In

the same pit which they laid privily is their foot taken'?"

"Then there are other practices?"

"Ask me no questions, Mr. Talbot. All will be known soon enough. Be content that I will lay nothing on you inconsistent with the honour of a Christian man, knowing that you will serve the Queen faithfully."

Humfrey gave his word, resolving that he would warn Cicely to reckon henceforth on nothing on his part that did not befit a man in charge.

CHAPTER XXVIII.

HUNTING DOWN THE DEER.

HUMFREY had been sworn in of the service of the Queen, and had been put in charge of the guard mustered at Chartley for about ten days, during which he seldom saw Cicely, and wondered much not to have heard from home : when a stag-hunt was arranged to take place at the neighbouring park of Tickhill or Tixall, belonging to Sir Walter Ashton.

The chase always invigorated Queen Mary, and she came down in cheerful spirits, with Cicely and Mary Seaton as her attendants, and with the two secretaries, Nau and Curll, heading the other attendants.

"Now," she said to Cicely, " shall I see this swain, or this brother of thine, who hath done us such good service, and I promise you there will be more in my greeting than will meet Sir Amias's ear."

But to Cicely's disappointment Humfrey was not among the horsemen mustered at the door to attend and guard the Queen.

"My little maid's eye is seeking for her brother," said Mary, as Sir Amias advanced to assist her to her horse.

"He hath another charge which will keep him at home," replied Paulett, somewhat gruffly, and they rode on.

It was a beautiful day in early August, the trees in full foliage, the fields seen here and there through them assuming their amber harvest tints, the twin spires of Lichfield rising in the distance, the park and forest ground through which the little hunting-party rode rich with purple heather, illuminated here and there with a bright yellow spike or star, and the rapid motion of her brisk palfrey animated the Queen.   She began to hope that Humfrey had after all brought a false alarm, and that either he had been mistaken or that Langston was deceiving the Council itself, and though Sir Amias Paulett's close proximity held her silent, those who knew her best saw that her indomitably buoyant spirits were rising, and she hummed to herself the refrain of a gay French hunting-song, with the more zest perhaps that her warder held himself trebly upright, stiff and solemn under it, as one who thought such lively tunes equally unbefitting a lady, a queen, and a captive.   So at least Cis imagined as she watched them, little guessing that there might be deeper reasons of compassion and something like compunction to add to the gravity of the old knight's face.

As they came in sight of the gate of Tickhill Park, they became aware of a company whose steel caps and shouldered arquebuses did not look like those of huntsmen.   Mary bounded in her saddle ; she looked round at her little suite with a glance of exultation in her eye, which said as plainly as words, " My brave friends, the hour has come !" and she quickened her steed, expecting, no doubt, that she might have to outride Sir Amias in order to join them.

One gentleman came forward from the rest.   He held a parchment in his hand, and as soon as he was alongside of the Queen thus read :—

"Mary, late Queen of Scots and Queen Dowager of France, I, Thomas Gorges, attaint thee of high treason and of compassing the life of our most Gracious Majesty Queen Elizabeth, in company with Antony Babington, John Ballard, Chidiock Tichborne, Robert Barnwell, and others."

Mary held up her hands, and raised her eyes to Heaven, and a protest was on her lips, but Gorges cut it short with, "It skills not denying it, madam. The proofs are in our hands. I have orders to conduct you to Tickhill, while seals are put on your effects."

"That there may be proofs of your own making," said the Queen, with dignity. "I have experience of that mode of judgment. So, Sir Amias Paulett, the chase you lured me to was truly of a poor hunted doe whom you think you have run down at last. A worthy chase indeed, and of long continuance!"

"I do but obey my orders, madam," said Paulett, gloomily.

"Oh ay, and so does the sleuth-hound," said Mary.

"Your Grace must be pleased to ride on with me," said Mr. Gorges, laying his hand on her bridle.

"What are you doing with those gentlemen?" cried Mary, sharply reining in her horse, as she saw Nau and Curll surrounded by the armed men.

"They will be dealt with after her Majesty's pleasure," returned Paulett.

Mary dropped her rein and threw up her hands with a gesture of despair, but as Gorges was leading her away, she turned on her saddle, and raised her voice to call out, "Farewell, my true and faithful servants! Betide what may, your mistress will remember you in her prayers. Curll, we will take care of your wife."

And she waved her hand to them as they were

made, with a strong guard, to ride off in the direction
of Lichfield.   All the way to Tickhill, whither she
was conducted with Gorges and Paulett on either side
of her horse, Cis could hear her pleading for consideration for poor Barbara Curll, for whose sake she forgot
her own dignity and became a suppliant.

Sir Walter Ashton, a dull heavy-looking country
gentleman of burly form and ruddy countenance, stood
at his door, and somewhat clownishly offered his services to hand her from her horse.

She submitted passively till she had reached the
upper chamber which had been prepared for her, and
there, turning on the three gentlemen, demanded the
meaning of this treatment.

" You will soon know, madam," said Paulett.   " I
am sorry that thus it should be."

" Thus !" repeated Mary, scornfully.   " What means
this ?"

" It means, madam," said Gorges, a ruder man of
less feeling even than Paulett, " that your practices
with recusants and seminary priests have been detected.
The traitors are in the Counter, and will shortly be
brought to judgment for the evil purposes which have
been frustrated by the mercy of Heaven."

" It is well if treason against my good sister's person
have been detected and frustrated," said Mary ; " but
how doth that concern me ?"

" That, madam, the papers at Chartley will show,"
returned Gorges.   " Meantime you will remain here,
till her Majesty's pleasure be known."

" Where, then, are my women and my servants ?"
inquired the Queen.

" Your Grace will be attended by the servants of
Sir Walter Ashton."

"Gentlemen, this is not seemly," said Mary, the colour coming hotly into her face. "I know it is not the will of my cousin, the Queen of England, that I should remain here without any woman to attend me, nor any change of garments. You are exceeding your commission, and she shall hear of it."

Sir Amias Paulett here laid his hand on Gorges' arm, and after exchanging a few words with him, said—

"Madam, this young lady, Mistress Talbot, being simple, and of a loyal house, may remain with you for the present. For the rest, seals are put on all your effects at Chartley, and nothing can be removed from thence, but what is needful will be supplied by my Lady Ashton. I bid your Grace farewell, craving your pardon for what may have been hasty in this."

Mary stood in the centre of the floor, full of her own peculiar injured dignity, not answering, but making a low ironical reverence. Mary Seaton fell on her knees, clung to the Queen's dress, and declared that while she lived, she would not leave her mistress.

"Endure this also, *ma mie*," said the Queen, in French. "Give them no excuse for using violence. They would not scruple——" and as a demonstration to hinder French-speaking was made by the gentlemen, "Fear not for me, I shall not be alone."

"I understand your Grace and obey," said Mary Seaton, rising, with a certain bitterness in her tone, which made Mary say—"Ah! why must jealousy mar the fondest affection? Remember, it is their choice, not mine, my Seaton, friend of my youth. Bear my loving greetings to all. And take care of poor Barbara!"

"Madam, there must be no private messages," said Paulett.

"I send no messages save what you yourself may

N

hear, sir," replied the Queen. " My greetings to my
faithful servants, and my entreaty that all care and
tenderness may be shown to Mrs. Curll."

" I will bear them, madam," said the knight, " and
so I commend you to God's keeping, praying that He
may send you repentance. Believe me, madam, I am
sorry that this has been put upon me."

To this Mary only replied by a gesture of dismissal.
The three gentlemen drew back, a key grated in the
lock, and the mother and daughter were left alone.

To Cicely it was a terrible hopeless sound, and even
to her mother it was a lower depth of wretchedness.
She had been practically a captive for nearly twenty
years. She had been insulted, watched, guarded, coerced,
but never in this manner locked up before.

She clasped her hands together, dropped on her
knees at the table that stood by her, and hid her face.
So she continued till she was roused by the sound of
Cicely's sobs. Frightened and oppressed, and new to
all terror and sorrow, the girl had followed her example
in kneeling, but the very attempt to pray brought on
a fit of weeping, and the endeavour to restrain what
might disturb the Queen only rendered the sobs more
choking and strangling, till at last Mary heard, and
coming towards her, sat down on the floor, gathered
her into her arms, and kissing her forehead, said,
" Poor bairnie, and did she weep for her mother ? Have
the sorrows of her house come on her ?"

" O mother, I could not help it ! I meant to have
comforted you," said Cicely, between her sobs.

" And so thou dost, my child. Unwittingly they
have left me that which was most precious to me."

There was consolation in the fondness of the loving
embrace, at least to such sorrows as those of the

maiden; and Queen Mary had an inalienable power of
charming the will and affections of those in contact
with her, so that insensibly there came into Cicely's
heart a sense that, so far from weeping, she should
rejoice at being the one creature left to console her
mother.

".And," she said by and by, looking up with a
smile, " they must go to the bottom of the old well to
find anything."

" Hush, lassie.   Never speak above thy breath in a
prison till thou know'st whether walls have ears.   And,
apropos, let us examine what sort of a prison they have
given us this time."

So saying Mary rose, and leaning on her daughter's
arm, proceeded to explore her new abode.   Like her
apartment at the Lodge, it was at the top of the
house, a fashion not uncommon when it was desirable
to make the lower regions defensible; but, whereas she
had always hitherto been placed in the castles of the
highest nobility, she was now in that of a country
knight of no great wealth or refinement, and, moreover,
taken by surprise.

So the plenishing was of the simplest.   The walls
were covered with tapestry so faded that the pattern
could hardly be detected.   The hearth yawned dark
and dull, and by it stood one chair with a moth-eaten
cushion.   A heavy oaken table and two forms were in
the middle of the room, and there was the dreary, fusty
smell of want of habitation.   The Queen, whose instincts
for fresh air were always a distress to her ladies, sprang
to the mullioned window, but the heavy lattice defied
all her efforts.

" Let us see the rest of our dominions," she said,
turning to a door, which led to a still more gloomy

bedroom, where the only articles of furniture were a
great carved bed, with curtains of some undefined dark
colour, and an oaken chest. The window was a
mere slit, and even more impracticable than that of
the outer room. However, this did not seem to hor-
rify Mary so much as it did her daughter. "They
cannot mean to keep us here long," she said; "perhaps
only for the day, while they make their search—their
unsuccessful search—thanks to—we know whom, little
one."

"I hope so! How could we sleep there?" said
Cicely, looking with a shudder at the bed.

"Tush! I have seen worse in Scotland, *mignonne*,
ay and when I was welcomed as liege lady, not as
a captive. I have slept in a box like a coffin with one
side open, and I have likewise slept on a plaidie on
the braw purple blossoms of freshly pulled heather!
Nay, the very thought makes this chamber doubly
mouldy and stifling! Let the old knight beware. If
he open not his window I shall break it! Soft. Here
he comes."

Sir Walter Ashton appeared, louting low, looking
half-dogged, half-sheepish, and escorting two heavy-
footed, blue-coated serving-men, who proceeded to lay
the cloth, which at least had the merit of being perfectly clean and white. Two more brought in covered
silver dishes, one of which contained a Yorkshire
pudding, the other a piece of roast-beef, apparently
calculated to satisfy five hungry men. A flagon of
sack, a tankard of ale, a dish of apples, and a large loaf
of bread, completed the meal; at which the Queen
and Cicely, accustomed daily to a first table of sixteen dishes and a second of nine, compounded by her
Grace's own French cooks and pantlers, looked with a

certain amused dismay, as Sir Walter, standing by the
table, produced a dagger from a sheath at his belt, and
took up with it first a mouthful of the pudding, then
cut off a corner of the beef, finished off some of the
bread, and having swallowed these, as well as a
draught of each of the liquors, said, " Good and sound
meats, not tampered with, as I hereby testify. You
take us suddenly, madam ; but I thank Heaven, none
ever found us unprovided. Will it please you to fall
to ? Your woman can eat after you."

Mary's courtesy was unfailing, and though she felt
all a Frenchwoman's disgust at the roast-beef of old
England, she said, " We are too close companions not
to eat together, and I fear she will be the best trencher
comrade, for, sir, I am a woman sick and sorrowful, and
have little stomach for meat."

As Sir Walter carved a huge red piece from the ribs,
she could not help shrinking back from it, so that he
said with some affront, " You need not be queasy,
madam, it was cut from a home-fed bullock, only killed
three days since, and as prime a beast as any in
Stafford."

" Ah ! yes, sir. It is not the fault of the beef, but
of my feebleness. Mistress Talbot will do it reason.
But I, methinks I could eat better were the windows
opened."

But Sir Walter replied that these windows were
not of the new-fangled sort, made to open, that honest
men might get rheums, and foolish maids prate therefrom. So there was no hope in that direction. He
really seemed to be less ungracious than utterly clownish,
dull, and untaught, and extremely shy and embarrassed
with his prisoner.

Cicely poured out some wine, and persuaded her to

dip some bread in, which, with an apple, was all she could
taste.   However, the fare, though less nicely served
than by good Mrs. Susan, was not so alien to Cicely,
and she was of an age and constitution to be made
hungry by anxiety and trouble, so that—encouraged by
the Queen whenever she would have desisted—she
ended by demolishing a reasonable amount.

Sir Walter stood all the time, looking on moodily
and stolidly, with his cap in his hand.   The Queen
tried to talk to him, and make inquiries of him, but
he had probably steeled himself to her blandishments,
for nothing but gruff monosyllables could be extracted
from him, except when he finally asked what she would
be pleased to have for supper.

" Mine own cook and pantler have hitherto provided for me.   They would save your household the
charge, sir," said Mary, " and I would be at charges
for them."

" Madam, I can bear the charge in the Queen's
service.   Your black guard are under ward.   And if
not, no French jackanapes shall ever brew his messes
in my kitchen !   Command honest English fare,
madam, and if it be within my compass, you shall
have it.   No one shall be stinted in Walter Ashton's
house ; but I'll not away with any of your outlandish
kickshaws.   Come, what say you to eggs and bacon,
madam ? "

"As you will, sir," replied Mary, listlessly.   And Sir
Walter, opening the door, shouted to his serving-man,
who speedily removed the meal, he going last and
making his clumsy reverence at the door, which he
locked behind him.

" So," said Mary, " I descend !   I have had the
statesman, the earl, the courtly knight, the pedantic

Huguenot, for my warders. Now am I come to the
clown. Soon will it be the dungeon and the
headsman."

"O dear madam mother, speak not thus," cried
Cicely. "Remember they can find nothing against
you."

"They can make what they cannot find, my poor
child. If they thirst for my blood, it will cost them
little to forge a plea. Ah, lassie! there have been
times when nothing but my cousin Elizabeth's conscience, or her pity, stood between me and doom. If
she be brought to think that I have compassed her
death, why then there is naught for it but to lay my
head on the same pillow as Norfolk and More and
holy Fisher, and many another beside. Well, be it so!
I shall die a martyr for the Holy Church, and thus
may I atone by God's mercy for my many sins! Yea, I
offer myself a sacrifice," she said, folding her hands and
looking upward with a light on her face. "O do Thou
accept it, and let my sufferings purge away my many
misdeeds, and render it a pure and acceptable offering
unto Thee. Child, child," she added, turning to Cicely,
"would that thou wert of my faith, then couldst thou
pray for me."

"O mother, mother, I can do that. I do pray for
thee."

And hand in hand, with tears often rising, they
knelt while Mary repeated in broken voice the
Miserere.

CHAPTER XXIX.

THE SEARCH.

HUMFREY had been much disappointed, when, instead of joining the hunt, Sir Amias Paulett bade him undertake the instruction of half a dozen extremely awkward peasants, who had been called in to increase the guard, but who did not know how to shoulder, load, or fire an arquebus, had no command of their own limbs, and, if put to stand sentry, would quite innocently loll in the nearest corner, and go to sleep. However, he reflected that if he were resident in the same house as Cicely he could not expect opportunities to be daily made for their meeting, and he addressed himself with all his might to the endeavour to teach his awkward squad to stand upright for five minutes together. Sturdy fellows as they were, he had not been able to hinder them from lopping over in all directions, when horses were heard approaching. Every man of them, regardless of discipline, lumbered off to stare, and Humfrey, after shouting at them in vain, and wishing he had them all on board ship, gave up the endeavour to recall them, and followed their example, repairing to the hall-door, when he found Sir Amias Paulett dismounting, together with a clerkly-looking personage, attended by Will Cavendish. Mary Seaton was being assisted from her horse, evidently in great grief; and others of the personal attendants of Mary were there, but neither herself, Cicely, nor the Secretaries.

Before he had time to ask questions, his old companion came up to him. "You here still, Humfrey! Well! You have come in for the outburst of the train you scented out when you were with us in London, though I could not then speak explicitly."

"What mean you? Where is Cicely? Where is the Queen of Scots?" asked Humfrey anxiously.

Sir Amias Paulett heard him, and replied, "Your sister is safe, Master Talbot, and with the Queen of Scots at Tixall Castle. We permitted her attendance, as being young, simple, and loyal; she is less like to serve for plots than her elders in that lady's service."

Sir Amias strode on, conducting with him his guest, whom Cavendish explained to be Mr. Wade, sworn by her Majesty's Council to take possession of Queen Mary's effects, and there make search for evidence of the conspiracy. Cavendish followed, and Humfrey took leave to do the same.

The doors of the Queen's apartment were opened at the summons of Sir Amias Paulett, and Sir Andrew Melville, Mistress Kennedy, Marie de Courcelles, and the rest, stood anxiously demanding what was become of their Queen. They were briefly and harshly told that her foul and abominable plots and conspiracies against the life of the Queen, and the peace of the Kingdom, had been brought to light, and that she was under secure ward.

Jean Kennedy demanded to be taken to her at once, but Paulett replied, "That must not be, madam. We have strict commands to keep her secluded from all."

N*

Marie de Courcelles screamed aloud and wrung her hands, crying, "If ye have slain her, only tell us quickly!" Sir Andrew Melville gravely protested against such a barbarous insult to a Queen of Scotland and France, and was answered, "No queen, sir, but a State criminal, as we shall presently show."

Here Barbara Curll pressed forward, asking wildly for her husband; and Wade replying, with brutal brevity, that he was taken to London to be examined for his practices before the Council, the poor lady, well knowing that examination often meant torture, fell back in a swoon.

"We shall do nothing with all these women crying and standing about," said Wade impatiently; "have them all away, while we put seals on the effects."

"Nay, sirs," said Jean Kennedy. "Suffer me first to send her Grace some changes of garments."

"I tell thee, woman," said Wade, "our orders are precise! Not so much as a kerchief is to be taken from these chambers till search hath been made. We know what practices may lurk in the smallest rag."

"It is barbarous! It is atrocious! The King of France shall hear of it," shrieked Marie de Courcelles.

"The King of France has enough to do to take care of himself, my good lady," returned Wade, with a sneer.

"Sir," said Jean Kennedy, with more dignity, turning to Sir Amias Paulett, "I cannot believe that it can be by the orders of the Queen of England, herself a woman, that my mistress, her cousin, should be deprived of all attendance, and even of a change of linen. Such unseemly commands can never have been issued from herself."

"She is not without attendance," replied the knight,

" the little Talbot wench is with her, and for the rest,
Sir Walter and Lady Ashton have orders to supply her
needs during her stay among them. She is treated
with all honour, and is lodged in the best chambers,"
he added, consolingly.

" We must dally no longer," called out Wade.
" Have away all this throng into ward, Sir Amias.
We can do nothing with them here."

There was no help for it. Sir Andrew Melville did
indeed pause to enter his protest, but that, of course,
went for nothing with the Commissioners, and Humfrey
was ordered to conduct them to the upper gallery, there
to await further orders. It was a long passage, in the
highly pointed roof, with small chambers on either
side which could be used when there was a press of
guests. There was a steep stair, as the only access,
and it could be easily guarded, so Sir Amias directed
Humfrey to post a couple of men at the foot, and to
visit and relieve them from time to time.

It was a sad procession that climbed up those
narrow stairs, of those faithful followers who were
separated from their Queen for the first time. The
servants of lower rank were merely watched in their
kitchen, and not allowed to go beyond its courtyard,
but were permitted to cook for and wait on the
others, and bring them such needful furniture as was
required.

Humfrey was very sorry for them, having had some
acquaintance with them all his life, and he was dismayed to find himself, instead of watching over Cicely,
separated from her and made a jailer against his will.
And when he returned to the Queen's apartments, he
found Cavendish holding a taper, while Paulett and
Wade were vigorously affixing cords, fastened at each

end by huge red seals bearing the royal arms, to every
receptacle, and rudely plucking back the curtains that
veiled the ivory crucifix. Sir Amias's zeal would have
"plucked down the idol," as he said, but Wade restrained him by reminding him that all injury or
damage was forbidden.

Not till all was sealed, and a guard had been
stationed at the doors, would the Commissioners taste
any dinner, and then their conversation was brief and
guarded, so that Humfrey could discover little. He
did, indeed, catch the name of Babington in connection
with the "Counter prison," and a glance of inquiry to
Cavendish, with a nod in return, showed him that his
suspicions were correct, but he learnt little or nothing
more till the two, together with Phillipps, drew together in the deep window, with wine, apples, and
pears on the ledge before them, for a private discussion.
Humfrey went away to see that the sentries at the
staircase were relieved, and to secure that a sufficient
meal for the unfortunate captives in the upper stories
had been allowed to pass. Will Cavendish went with
him. He had known these ladies and gentlemen far
more intimately than Humfrey had done, and allowed
that it was harsh measure that they suffered for their
fidelity to their native sovereign.

"No harm will come to them in the end," he said,
"but what can we do ? That very faithfulness would
lead them to traverse our purposes did we not shut
them up closely out of reach of meddling, and there is
no other place where it can be done."

"And what are these same purposes ?" asked
Humfrey, as, having fulfilled his commission, the two
young men strolled out into the garden and threw
themselves on the grass, close to a large mulberry-tree,

whose luscious fruit dropped round, and hung within
easy reach.

"To trace out all the coils of as villainous and
bloodthirsty a plot as ever was hatched in a traitor's
brain," said Will; "but they little knew that we over-
looked their designs the whole time. Thou wast
mystified in London, honest Humfrey, I saw it plainly;
but I might not then speak out," he added, with all his
official self-importance.

"And poor Tony hath brought himself within
compass of the law?"

"Verily you may say so. But Tony Babington
always was a fool, and a wrong-headed fool, who was
sure to ruin himself sooner or later. You remember
the decoy for the wild-fowl? Well, never was silly duck
or goose so ready to swim into the nets as was he!"

"He always loved this Queen, yea, and the old
faith."

"He sucked in the poison with his mother's milk,
you may say. Mrs. Babington was naught but a
concealed Papist, and, coming from her, it cost nothing
to this Queen to beguile him when he was a mere lad,
and make him do her errands, as you know full well.
Then what must my Lord Earl do but send him to
that bitter Puritan at Cambridge, who turned him all
the more that way, out of very contradiction. My
Lord thought him cured of his Popish inclinations, and
never guessed they had only led him among those who
taught him to dissemble."

"And that not over well," said Humfrey. "My
father never trusted him."

"And would not give him your sister. Yea,
but the counterfeit was good enough for my Lord
who sees nothing but what is before his nose, and

for my mother who sees nothing but what she
will see. Well, he had fallen in with those who
deem this same Mary our only lawful Queen, and
would fain set her on the throne to bring back fire
and faggot by the Spanish sword among us."

" I deemed him well-nigh demented with brooding
over her troubles and those of his church."

" Demented in verity. His folly was surpassing.
He put his faith in a recusant priest—one John
Ballard—who goes ruffling about as Captain Fortescue
in velvet hose and a silver-laced cloak."

" Ha !"

" Hast seen him ?"

" Ay, in company with Babington, on the day I
came to London, passing through Westminster."

" Very like. Their chief place of meeting was at a
house at Westminster belonging to a fellow named
Gage. We took some of them there. Well, this
Ballard teaches poor Antony, by way of gospel truth,
that 'tis the mere duty of a good Catholic to slay the
enemies of the church, and that he who kills our
gracious Queen, whom God defend, will do the holiest
deed ; just as they gulled the fellow, who murdered the
Prince of Orange, and then died in torments, deeming
himself a holy martyr."

" But it was not Babington whom I saw at Richmond."

" Hold, I am coming to that. Let me tell you the
Queen bore it in mind, and asked after you. Well,
Babington has a number of friends, as hot-brained and
fanatical as himself, and when once he had swallowed
the notion of privily murdering the Queen, he got so
enamoured of it, that he swore in five more to aid him
in the enterprise, and then what must they do but have

all their portraits taken in one picture with a Latin
motto around them.   What !   Thou hast seen it ?"

"He showed it to me in Paul's Walk, and said I
should hear of them, and I thought one of them marvellously like the fellow I had seen in Richmond Park."

"So thought her Majesty.   But more of that anon.
On the self-same day as the Queen was to be slain by
these sacrilegious wretches, another band was to fall
on this place, free the lady and proclaim her, while
the Prince of Parma landed from the Netherlands and
brought fire and sword with him."

"And Antony would have brought this upon us ?"
said Humfrey, still slow to believe it of his old comrade.

"All for the true religion's sake," said Cavendish.
"They were ringing bells and giving thanks, for the
discovery and baffling thereof, when we came down
from London."

"As well they might," said Humfrey.   "But how
was it detected and overthrown ?   Was it through
Langston ?"

"Ah, ha !   we had had the strings in our hands all
along.   Why, Langston, as thou namest him, though we
call him Maude, and a master spy called Gifford, have
kept us warned thoroughly of every stage in the business.   Maude even contrived to borrow the picture under
colour of getting it blessed by the Pope's agent, and
lent it to Mr. Secretary Walsingham, by whom it was
privily shown to the Queen.   Thereby she recognised
the rogue Barnwell, an Irishman it seems, when she
was walking in the Park at Richmond with only her
women and Sir Christopher Hatton, who is better at
dancing than at fighting.   Not a sign did she give, but
she kept him in check with her royal eye, so that he

durst not so much as draw his pistol from his cloak; but she owned afterwards to my Lady Norris that she could have kissed you when you came between, and all the more, when you caught her meaning and followed her bidding silently.   You will hear of it again, Humps."

" However that may be, it is a noble thing to have seen such courage in a woman and a queen.   But how could they let it go so near ?   I could shudder now to think of the risk to her person ! "

" There goes more to policy than you yet wot of," said Will, in his patronising tone.   " In truth, Barnwell had started off unknown to his comrades, hoping to have the glory of the achievement all to himself by forestalling them, or else Mr. Secretary would have been warned in time to secure the Queen."

" But wherefore leave these traitors at large to work mischief ? "

" See you not, you simple Humfrey, that, as I said methinks some time since, it is well sometimes to give a rogue rope enough and he will hang himself ?   Close the trap too soon, and you miss the biggest rat of all. So we waited until the prey seemed shy and about to escape.   Babington had, it seems, suspected Maude or Langston, or whatever you call him, and had ridden out of town, hiding in St. John's Wood with some of his fellows, till they were starved out, and trying to creep into some outbuildings at Harrow, were there taken, and brought into London the morning we came away. Ballard, the blackest villain of all, is likewise in ward, and here we are to complete our evidence."

" Nay, throughout all you have said, I have heard nothing to explain this morning's work."

Will laughed outright.   " And so you think all this

would have been done without a word from their liege
lady, the princess they all wanted to deliver from
captivity! No, no, sir! 'Twas thus. There's an
honest man at Burton, a brewer, who sends beer week
by week for this house, and very good ale it is, as I can
testify. I wish I had a tankard of it here to qualify
these mulberries. This same brewer is instructed by
Gifford, whose uncle lives in these parts, to fit a false
bottom to one of his barrels, wherein is a box fitted for
the receipt of letters and parcels. Then by some means,
through Langston I believe, Babington and Gifford
made known to the Queen of Scots and the French
ambassador that here was a sure way of sending and
receiving letters. The Queen's butler, old Hannibal,
was to look in the bottom of the barrel with the yellow
hoop, and one Barnes, a familiar of Gifford and Babington, undertook the freight at the other end. The
ambassador, M. de Chateauneuf, seemed to doubt at
first, and sent a single letter by way of experiment,
and that having been duly delivered and answered, the
bait was swallowed, and not a week has gone by but
letters have come and gone from hence, all being first
opened, copied, and deciphered by worthy Mr. Phillipps,
and every word of them laid before the Council."

" Hum! We should not have reckoned that fair play
when we went to Master Sniggius's," observed Humfrey, as he heard his companion's tone of exultation.

" Fair play is a jewel that will not pass current in
statecraft," responded Cavendish. " Moreover, that
the plotter should be plotted against is surely only his
desert. But thou art a mere sailor, my Talbot, and
these subtilties of policy are not for thee."

" For the which Heaven be praised!" said Humfrey.
" Yet having, as you say, read all these letters by the

way, I see not wherefore ye are come down to seek for more."

Will here imitated the Lord Treasurer's nod as well as in him lay, not perhaps himself knowing the darker recesses of this same plot. He did know so much as that every stage in it had been revealed to Walsingham and Burghley as it proceeded. He did not know that the entire scheme had been hatched, not by a blind and fanatical partisan of Mary's, doing evil that what he supposed to be good might come, but by Gifford and Morgan, Walsingham's agents, for the express purpose of causing Mary totally to ruin herself, and to compel Elizabeth to put her to death, and that the unhappy Babington and his friends were thus recklessly sacrificed. The assassin had even been permitted to appear in Elizabeth's presence in order to terrify her into the conviction that her life could only be secured by Mary's death. They, too, did evil that good might come, thinking Mary's death alone could ensure them from Pope and Spaniard; but surely they descended into a lower depth of iniquity than did their victims.

Will himself was not certain what was wanted among the Queen's papers, unless it might be the actual letters from Babington, copies of which had been given by Phillipps to the Council, so he only looked sagacious; and Humfrey thought of the Castle Well, and felt the satisfaction there is in seeing a hunted creature escape. He asked, however, about Cuthbert Langston, saying, "He is—worse luck, as you may have heard—akin to my father, who always pitied him as misguided, but thought him as sincere in his folly as ever was this unlucky Babington."

"So he seems to have been till of late. He hovered about in sundry disguises, as you know, much to the torment of us all; but finally he seems to have taken some umbrage at the lady, thinking she flouted his services, or did not pay him high enough for them, and Gifford bought him over easily enough; but he goes with us by the name of Maude, and the best of it is that the poor fools thought he was hoodwinking us all the time. They never dreamt that we saw through them like glass. Babington was himself, with Mr. Secretary only last week, offering to go to France on business for him—the traitor! Hark! there are more sounds of horse hoofs. Who comes now, I marvel!"

This was soon answered by a serving-man, who hurried out to tell Humfrey that his father was arrived, and in a few moments the young man was blessed and embraced by the good Richard, while Diccon stood by, considerably repaired in flesh and colour by his brief stay under his mother's care.

Mr. Richard Talbot was heartily welcomed by Sir Amias Paulett, who regretted that his daughter was out of reach, but did not make any offer of facilitating their meeting.

Richard explained that he was on his way to London on behalf of the Earl. Reports and letters, not very clear, had reached Sheffield of young Babington being engaged in a most horrible conspiracy against the Queen and country, and my Lord and my Lady, who still preserved a great kindness for their former ward, could hardly believe it, and had sent their useful and trustworthy kinsman to learn the truth, and to find out whether any amount of fine or forfeiture would avail to save his life.

Sir Amias thought it would be a fruitless errand, and so did Richard himself, when he had heard as much of the history as it suited Paulett and Wade to

tell, and though they esteemed and trusted him, they
did not care to go beneath that outer surface of the
plot which was filling all London with fury.

When, having finished their after-dinner repose, they
repaired to make farther search, taking Cavendish to
assist, they somewhat reluctantly thought it due to Mr.
Talbot to invite his presence, but he declined. He and
his son had much to say to one another, he observed,
and not long to say it in.

"Besides," he added, when he found himself alone
with Humfrey, having despatched Diccon on some errand
to the stables, "'tis a sorry sight to see all the poor
Lady's dainty hoards turned out by strangers. If it
must be, it must, but it would irk me to be an idle
gazer thereon."

"I would only," said Humfrey, "be assured that
they would not light on the proofs of Cicely's birth."

"Thou mayst be at rest on that score, my son.
The Lady saw them, owned them, and bade thy mother
keep them, saying ours were safer hands than hers. Thy
mother was sore grieved, Humfrey, when she saw thee
not; but she sends thee her blessing, and saith thou
dost right to stay and watch over poor little Cis."

"It were well if I were watching over her," said
Humfrey, "but she is mewed up at Tixall, and I am
only keeping guard over poor Mistress Seaton and the
rest."

"Thou hast seen her?"

"Yea, and she was far more our own sweet maid
than when she came back to us at Bridgefield."

And Humfrey told his father all he had to tell of
what he had seen and heard since he had been at
Chartley. His adventures in London had already been
made known by Diccon. Mr. Talbot was aghast, per-

haps most of all at finding that his cousin Cuthbert
was a double traitor. From the Roman Catholic point
of view, there had been no treason in his·former machi-
nations on behalf of Mary, if she were in his eyes his
rightful sovereign, but the betrayal of confidence reposed
in him was so horrible that the good Master Richard
refused to believe it, till he had heard the proofs again
and again, and then he exclaimed,

"That such a Judas should ever call cousin with
us !"

There could be little hope, as both agreed, of saving
the unfortunate victims; but Richard was all the more
bent on fulfilling Lord Shrewsbury's orders, and doing
his utmost for Babington. As to Humfrey, it would
be better that he should remain where he was, so that
Cicely might have some protector near her in case of
any sudden dispersion of Mary's suite.

"Poor maiden !" said her foster-father, "she is in a
manner ours, and we cannot but watch over her; but
after all, I doubt me whether it had not been better
for her and for us, if the waves had beaten the little
life out of her ere I carried her home."

"She hath been the joy of my life," said Humfrey,
low and hoarsely.

"And I fear me she will be the sorrow of it. Not
by her fault, poor wench, but what hope canst thou
have, my son ?"

"None, sir," said Humfrey, "except of giving up all
if I can so defend her from aught." He spoke in a quiet
matter-of-fact way that made his father look with some
inquiry at his grave settled face, quite calm, as if saying
nothing new, but expressing a long-formed quiet purpose.

Nor, though Humfrey was his eldest son and heir,
did Richard Talbot try to cross it.

He asked whether he might see Cicely before going on to London, but Sir Amias said that in that case she would not be allowed to return to the Queen, and that to have had any intercourse with the prisoners might overthrow all his designs in London, and he therefore only left with Humfrey his commendations to her, with a pot of fresh honey and a lavender-scented set of kerchiefs from Mistress Susan.

CHAPTER XXX.

TÊTE-À-TÊTE.

DURING that close imprisonment at Tixall Cicely learnt to know her mother both in her strength and weakness. They were quite alone, except that Sir Walter Ashton daily came to perform the office of taster and carver at their meals, and on the first evening his wife dragged herself upstairs to superintend the arrangement of their bedroom, and to supply them with toilette requisites according to her own very limited notions and possessions. The Dame was a very homely, hard-featured lady, deaf, and extremely fat and heavy, one of the old uncultivated rustic gentry who had lagged far behind the general civilisation of the country, and regarded all refinements as effeminate French vanities. She believed, likewise, all that was said against Queen Mary, whom she looked on as barely restrained from plunging a dagger into Elizabeth's heart, and letting Parma's hell-hounds loose upon Tixall. To have such a guest imposed on her was no small grievance, and nothing but her husband's absolute mandate could have induced her to come up with the maids who brought sheets for the bed, pillows, and the like needments. Mary tried to make her requests as moderate as necessity would permit; but when they

had been shouted into her ears by one of the maids,
she shook her head at most of them, as articles unknown
to her.   Nor did she ever appear again.   The arrangement of the bed-chamber was performed by two maid-
servants, the Knight himself meanwhile standing a
grim sentinel over the two ladies in the outer apartment to hinder their holding any communication through
the servants.   All requests had to be made to him, and
on the first morning Mary made a most urgent one
for writing materials, books, and either needlework or
spinning.

Pen and ink had been expressly forbidden, the only
book in the house was a thumbed and torn primer, but
Dame Joan, after much grumbling at fine ladies' whims,
vouchsafed to send up a distaff, some wool, a piece of
unbleached linen, and a skein of white thread.

Queen Mary executed therewith an exquisite piece
of embroidery, which having escaped Dame Joan's first
impulse to burn it on the spot, remained for many
years the show and the wonder of Tixall.   Save for
this employment, she said she should have gone mad
in her utter uncertainty about her own fate, or that of
those involved with her.   To ask questions of Ashton
was like asking them of a post.   He would give her
no notion whether her servants were at Chartley or
not, whether they were at large or in confinement, far
less as to who was accused of the plot, and what had
been discovered.   All that could be said for him was
that his churlishness was passive and according to his
ideas of duty.   He was a very reluctant and uncomfortable jailer, but he never insulted, nor wilfully ill-
used his unfortunate captive.

Thus Mary was left to dwell on the little she knew,
namely, that Babington and his fellows were arrested,

and that she was supposed to be implicated; but there her knowledge ceased, except that Humfrey's warning convinced her that Cuthbert Langston had been at least one of the traitors. He had no doubt been offended and disappointed at that meeting during the hawking at Tutbury.

"Yet I need scarcely seek the why or the wherefore," she said. "I have spent my life in a world of treachery. No sooner do I take a step on ground that seems ever so firm, than it proves a quicksand. They will swallow me at last."

Daily—more than daily—did she and Cicely go over together that hurried conversation on the moor, and try to guess whether Langston intended to hint at Cicely's real birth. He had certainly not disclosed her secret as yet, or Paulett would never have selected her as sprung of a loyal house, but he might guess at the truth, and be waiting for an opportunity to sell it dearly to those who would regard her as possessed of dangerous pretensions.

And far more anxiously did the Queen recur to examining Cicely on what she had gathered from Humfrey. This was in fact nothing, for he had been on his guard against either telling or hearing anything inconsistent with loyalty to the English Queen, and thus had avoided conversation on these subjects.

Nor did the Queen communicate much. Cicely never understood clearly what she dreaded, what she expected to be found among her papers, or what had been in the packet thrown into the well. The girl did not dare to ask direct questions, and the Queen always turned off indirect inquiries, or else assured her that she was still a simple happy child, and that it was better for her own sake that she should know nothing, then caressed

her, and fondly pitied her for not being admitted to her
mother's confidence, but said piteously that she knew
not what the secrets of Queens and captives were, not
like those of Mistress Susan about the goose to be
dressed, or the crimson hose to be knitted for a surprise
to her good husband.

But Cicely could see that she expected the worst,
and believed in a set purpose to shed her blood, and
she spent much time in devotion, though sorely distressed by the absence of all those appliances which
her Church had taught her to rest upon. And these
prayers, which often began with floods of tears, so that
Cicely drew away into the window with her distaff in
order not to seem to watch them, ended with rendering
her serene and calm, with a look of high resignation, as
having offered herself as a sacrifice and martyr for her
Church.

And yet was it wholly as a Roman Catholic that
she had been hated, intrigued against, and deposed
in her own kingdom? Was it simply as a Roman
Catholic that she was, as she said, the subject of a
more cruel plot than that of which she was accused?

Mysterious woman that she was, she was never
more mysterious than to her daughter in those seventeen days that they were shut up together! It did not
so much strike Cicely at the time, when she was carried
along with all her mother's impulses and emotions,
without reflecting on them, but when in after times
she thought over all that then had passed, she felt
how little she had understood.

They suffered a good deal from the heat and closeness of the rooms, for Mary was like a modern
Englishwoman in her craving for free air, and these
were the dog-days. They had contrived by the help

of a diamond that the Queen carried about with her,
after the fashion of the time, to extract a pane or two
from the lattices so ingeniously that the master of the
house never found it out. And as their two apartments looked out different ways, they avoided the full
sunshine, for they had neither curtains nor blinds to
their windows, by moving from one to the other; but
still the closeness was very oppressive, and in the heat
of the day, just after dinner, they could do nothing but
lie on the table, while the Queen told stories of her old
life in France, till sometimes they both went to sleep.
Most of her dainty needlework was done in the long
light mornings, for she hardly slept at all in the hot
nights. Cis scarcely saw her in bed, for she prayed
long after the maiden had fallen asleep, and was up
with the light and embroidering by the window.

She only now began to urge Cicely to believe as she
did, and to join her Church, taking blame to herself for
never having attempted it more seriously. She told of
the oneness and the glory of Roman Catholicism as
she had seen it in France, held out its promises and
professions, and dwelt on the comfort of the intercession
of the Blessed Virgin and the Saints; assuring Cicely
that there was nothing but sacrilege, confusion, and
cruelty on the other side.

Sometimes the maiden was much moved by the
tender manner and persuasive words, and she really
had so much affection and admiration for her mother as
to be willing to do all that she wished, and to believe her
the ablest and most clear-sighted of human beings; but
whenever Mary was not actually talking to her, there
was a curious swaying back of the pendulum in her mind
to the conviction that what Master Richard and Mistress
Susan believed must be the right thing, that led to

trustworthy goodness. She had an enthusiastic love for the Queen, but her faith and trust were in them and in Humfrey, and she could see religious matters from their point of view better than from that of her mother.

So, though the Queen often felt herself carrying her daughter along, she always found that there had been a slipping back to the old standpoint every time she began again. She was considering with some anxiety of the young maiden's future.

"Could I but send thee to my good sister, the Duchess of Lorraine, she would see thee well and royally married," she said. "Then couldst thou be known by thine own name, and rank as Princess of Scotland. If I can only see my Courcelles again, she would take thee safely and prove all—and thy hand will be precious to many. It may yet bring back the true faith to England, when my brave cousin of Guise has put down the Béarnese, and when the poor stumbling-block here is taken away."

"Oh speak not of that, dear madam, my mother."

"I must speak, child. I must think how it will be with thee, so marvellously saved, and restored to be my comfort. I must provide for thy safety and honour. Happily the saints guarded me from ever mentioning thee in my letters, so that there is no fear that Elizabeth should lay hands on thee, unless Langston should have spoken—the which can hardly be. But if all be broken up here, I must find thee a dwelling with my kindred worthy of thy birth."

"Mr. and Mrs. Talbot would take me home," murmured Cicely.

"Girl! After all the training I have bestowed on thee, is it possible that thou wouldst fain go back to make cheeses and brew small beer with those Yorkshire boors, rather than reign a princess? I thought thy heart was nobler."

Cicely hung her head ashamed. " I was very happy there," she said in excuse.

" Happy—ay, with the milkmaid's bliss. There may be fewer sorrows in such a life as that—just as those comely kine of Ashton's that I see grazing in the park have fewer sorrows than human creatures. But what know they of our joys, or what know the commonalty of the joy of ruling, calling brave men one's own, riding before one's men in the field, wielding counsels of State, winning the love of thousands? Nay, nay, I will not believe it of my child, unless 'tis the base Border blood that is in her which speaks."

Cicely was somewhat overborne by being thus accused of meanness of tastes, when she had heard the Queen talk enviously of that same homely life which now she despised so heartily. She faltered in excuse, " Methought, madam, you would be glad to think there was one loving shelter ever open to me."

" Loving! Ah! I see what it is," said the Queen, in a tone of disgust. " It is the sailor loon that has overthrown it all. A couple of walks in the garden with him, and the silly maid is ready to throw over all nobler thoughts."

" Madam, he spoke no such word to me."

" 'Twas the infection, child—only the infection."

" Madam, I pray you——"

" Whist, child. Thou wilt be a perilous bride for any commoner, and let that thought, if no other, keep thee from lowering thine eyes to such as he. Were I and thy brother taken out of the way, none would stand between thee and both thrones! What would English or Scots say to find thee a household Joan,

wedded to one of Drake's rude pirate fellows? I
tell thee it would be the worse for him. They have
made it treason to wed royal blood without Elizabeth's
consent. No, no, for his sake, as well as thine own,
thou must promise me never thus to debase thy royal
lineage."

" Mother; neither he nor I have thought or spoken
of such a matter since we knew how it was with
me."

" And you give me your word ? "

" Yea, madam," said Cicely, who had really never
entertained the idea of marrying Humfrey, implicit
as was her trust in him as a brother and protector.

" That is well. And so soon as I am restored to
my poor servants, if I ever am, I will take measures
for sending the French remnant to their own land; nor
shall my Courcelles quit thee till she hath seen thee
safe in the keeping of Madame de Lorraine or of Queen
Louise, who is herself a kinswoman of ours, and, they
say, is piety and gentleness itself."

" As you will, madam," said Cicely, her heart sinking at the thought of the strange new world before her,
but perceiving that she must not be the means of
bringing Humfrey into trouble and danger.

Perhaps she felt this the more from seeing how
acutely her mother suffered at times from sorrow for
those involved in her disaster. She gave Babington
and his companions, as well as Nau and Curll, up for
lost, as the natural consequence of having befriended
her; and she blamed herself remorsefully, after the
long experience of the fatal consequences of meddling
in her affairs, for having entered into correspondence
with the bright enthusiastic boy whom she remembered,
and having lured him without doubt to his death.

"Alack! alack!" she said, "and yet such is liberty, that I should forget all I have gone through, and do the like again, if the door seemed opened to me. At least there is this comfort, cruel child, thy little heart was not set on him, gracious and handsome though he were—and thy mother's most devoted knight! Ah! poor youth, it wrings my soul to think of him. But at least he is a Catholic, his soul will be safe, and I will have hundreds of masses sung for him. Oh that I knew how it goes with them! This torture of silent suspense is the most cruel of all."

Mary paced the room with impatient misery, and in such a round the weary hours dragged by, only mitigated by one welcome thunderstorm, for seventeen days, whose summer length made them seem the more endless. Cicely, who had never before in her life been shut up in the house so many hours, was pale, listless, and even fretful towards the Queen, who bore with her petulance so tenderly as more than once to make her weep bitterly for very shame. After one of these fits of tears, Mary pleaded earnestly with Sir Walter Ashton for permission for the maiden to take a turn in the garden every day, but though the good gentleman's complexion bore testimony that he lived in the fresh air, he did not believe in its efficacy; he said he had no orders, and could do nothing without warrant. But that evening at supper, the serving-maid brought up a large brew of herbs, dark and nauseous, which Dame Ashton had sent as good for the young lady's megrim.

"Will you taste it, sir?" asked the Queen of Sir Walter, with a revival of her lively humour.

"The foul fiend have me if a drop comes within my lips," muttered the knight. "I am not bound to

taste for a tirewoman !" he added, leaving it in doubt
whether his objection arose from distaste to his lady's
messes, or from pride ; and he presently said, perhaps
half-ashamed of himself, and willing to cast the blame
on the other side,

"It was kindly meant of my good dame, and if you
choose to flout at, rather than benefit by it, that is no
affair of mine."

He left the potion, and Cicely disposed of it by
small instalments at the windows ; and a laugh over
the evident horror it excited in the master, did the
captives at least as much good as the camomile,
centaury, wormwood, and other ingredients of the
bowl.

Happily it was only two days later that Sir Walter
announced that his custody of the Queen was over,
and Sir Amias Paulett was come for her. There was
little preparation to make, for the two ladies had worn
their riding-dresses all the time ; but on reaching the
great door, where Sir Amias, attended by Humfrey, was
awaiting them, they were astonished to see a whole
troop on horseback, all armed with head-pieces, swords
and pistols, to the number of a hundred and forty.

"Wherefore is this little army raised ?" she asked.

"It is by order of the Queen," replied Ashton, with
his accustomed surly manner, "and need enough in
the time of such treasons !"

The Queen turned to him with tears on her cheeks.
"Good gentlemen," she said, "I am not witting of
anything against the Queen. Am I to be taken to the
Tower ?"

"No, madam, back to Chartley," replied Sir Amias.

"I knew they would never let me see my cousin,"
sighed the Queen. "Sir," as Paulett placed her on

her horse, " of your pity tell me whether I shall find
all my poor servants there."

"Yea, madam, save Mr. Nau and Mr. Curll, who
are answering for themselves and for you. Moreover,
Curll's wife was delivered two days since."

This intelligence filled Mary with more anxiety
than she chose to manifest to her unsympathising
surroundings ; Cis meanwhile had been assisted to
mount by Humfrey, who told her that Mrs. Curll was
thought to be doing well, but that there were fears for
the babe. It was impossible to exchange many words,
for they were immediately behind the Queen and her
two warders, and Humfrey could only tell her that his
father had been at Chartley, and had gone on to London ;
but there was inexpressible relief in hearing the sound
of his voice, and knowing she had some one to think for
her and protect her. The promise she had made to the
Queen only seemed to make him more entirely her
brother by putting that other love out of the question.

There was a sad sight at the gate,—a whole multitude
of wretched-looking beggars, and poor of all ages and
degrees of misery, who all held out their hands and
raised one cry of "Alms, alms, gracious Lady, alms, for
the love of heaven !"

Mary looked round on them with tearful eyes, and
exclaimed, " Alack, good folk, I have nothing to give
you ! I am as much a beggar as yourselves !"

The escort dispersed them roughly, Paulett assuring
her that they were nothing but "a sort of idle folk,"
who were only encouraged in laziness by her bounty,
which was very possibly true of a certain proportion
of them, but it had been a sore grief to her that since
Cuthbert Langston's last approach in disguise she had
been prevented from giving alms.

o

In due time Chartley was reached, and the first thing the Queen did on dismounting was to hurry to visit poor Barbara Curll, who had—on her increasing illness—been removed to one of the guest-chambers, where the Queen now found her, still in much distress about her husband, who was in close imprisonment in Walsingham's house, and had not been allowed to send her any kind of message; and in still more immediate anxiety about her new-born infant, who did not look at all as if its little life would last many hours.

She lifted up her languid eyelids, and scarcely smiled when the Queen declared, " See, Barbara, I am come back again to you, to nurse you and my god-daughter into health to receive your husband again. Nay, have no fears for him. They cannot hurt him. He has done nothing, and is a Scottish subject beside. My son shall write to claim him," she declared with such an assumed air of confidence that a shade of hope crossed the pale face, and the fear for her child became the more pressing of the two griefs.

" We will christen her at once," said Mary, turning to the nearest attendant. " Bear a request from me to Sir Amias that his chaplain may come at once and baptize my god-child."

Sir Amias was waiting in the gallery in very ill-humour at the Queen's delay, which kept his supper waiting. Moreover, his party had a strong dislike to private baptism, holding that the important point was the public covenant made by responsible persons, and the notion of the sponsorship of a Roman Catholic likewise shocked him. So he made ungracious answer that he would have no baptism save in church before the congregation, with true Protestant gossips.

" So saith he ? " exclaimed Mary, when the reply

was reported to her. "Nay, my poor little one, thou shalt not be shut out of the Kingdom of Heaven for his churlishness." And taking the infant on her knee, she dipped her hand in the bowl of water that had been prepared for the chaplain, and baptized it by her own name of Mary.

The existing Prayer-book had been made expressly to forbid lay baptism and baptism by women, at the special desire of the reformers, and Sir Amias was proportionately horrified, and told her it was an offence for the Archbishop's court.

"Very like," said Mary. "Your Protestant courts love to slay both body and soul. Will it please you to open my own chambers to me, sir?"

Sir Amias handed the key to one of her servants, but she motioned him aside.

"Those who put me forth must admit me," she said.

The door was opened by one of the gentlemen of the household, and they entered. Every repository had been ransacked, every cabinet stood open and empty, every drawer had been pulled out. Wearing apparel and the like remained, but even this showed signs of having been tossed over and roughly rearranged by masculine fingers.

Mary stood in the midst of the room, which had a strange air of desolation, an angry light in her eyes, and her hands clasped tightly one into the other. Paulett attempted some expression of regret for the disarray, pleading his orders.

"It needs not excuse, sir," said Mary, "I understand to whom I owe this insult. There are two things that your Queen can never take from me—royal blood and the Catholic faith. One day some of you will be sorry for what you have now put upon me! I would be alone, sir," and she proudly motioned him to the door, with a haughty gesture, showing her still fully Queen in her own apartments. Paulett obeyed, and when he was gone, the Queen seemed to abandon the command over herself she had preserved all this time. She threw herself into Jean Kennedy's arms, and wept freely and piteously, while the good lady, rejoicing at heart to have recovered "her bairn," fondled and soothed her with soft Scottish epithets, as though the worn woman had been a child again. "Yea, nurse, mine own nurse, I am come back to thee; for a little while—only a little while, nurse, for they will have my blood, and oh! I would it were ended, for I am aweary of it all."

Jean and Elizabeth Curll tried to cheer and console her, alarmed at this unwonted depression, but she only said, "Get me to bed, nurse, I am sair forfaughten."

She was altogether broken down by the long suspense, the hardships and the imprisonment she had undergone, and she kept her bed for several days, hardly speaking, but apparently reposing in the relief afforded by the recovered care and companionship of her much-loved attendants.

There she was when Paulett came to demand the keys of the caskets where her treasure was kept. Melville had refused to yield them, and all the Queen said was, "Robbery is to be added to the rest," a sentence which greatly stung the knight, but he actually seized all the coin that he found, including what belonged to Nau and Curll, and, only retaining enough for present expenses, sent the rest off to London.

CHAPTER XXXI.

EVIDENCE.

In the meantime the two Richard Talbots, father and son, had safely arrived in London, and had been made welcome at the house of their noble kinsman.

Nau and Curll, they heard, were in Walsingham's house, subjected to close examination; Babington and all his comrades were in the Tower. The Council was continually sitting to deliberate over the fate of the latter unhappy men, of whose guilt there was no doubt; and neither Lord Talbot nor Will Cavendish thought there was any possibility of Master Richard gaining permission to plead how the unfortunate Babington had been worked on and deceived. After the sentence should be pronounced, Cavendish thought that the request of the Earl of Shrewsbury might prevail to obtain permission for an interview between the prisoner and one commissioned by his former guardian. Will was daily attending Sir Francis Walsingham as his clerk, and was not by any means unwilling to relate anything he had been able to learn.

Queen Elizabeth was, it seemed, greatly agitated and distressed. The shock to her nerves on the day when she had so bravely overawed Barnwell with the power of her eye had been such as not to be easily

surmounted. She was restless and full of anxiety,
continually starting at every sound, and beginning
letters to the Queen of Scots which were never finished.
She had more than once inquired after the brave sailor
youths who had come so opportunely to her rescue;
and Lord Talbot thought it would be well to present
Diccon and his father to her, and accordingly took
them with him to Greenwich Palace, where they had
the benefit of looking on as loyal subjects, while her
Majesty, in royal fashion, dined in public, to the sound
of drums, trumpets, fifes, and stringed instruments.
But though dressed with her usual elaborate care, she
looked older, paler, thinner, and more haggard than
when Diccon had seen her three weeks previously, and
neither her eye nor mouth had the same steadiness.
She did not eat with relish, but almost as if she were
forcing herself, lest any lack of appetite might be observed and commented upon, and her looks continually
wandered as though in search of some lurking enemy;
for in truth no woman, nor man either, could easily
forget the suggestion which had recently been brought
to her knowledge, that an assassin might "lurk in her
gallery and stab her with his dagger, or if she should
walk in her garden, he might shoot her with his dagg,
or if she should walk abroad to take the air, he might
assault her with his arming sword and make sure
work." Even though the enemies were safe in prison,
she knew not but that dagger, dagg, or arming sword
might still be ready for her, and she believed that any
fatal charge openly made against Mary at the trial might
drive her friends to desperation and lead to the use of
dagg or dagger. She was more unhinged than ever
before, and commanded herself with difficulty when
going through all the scenes of her public life as usual.

The Talbots soon felt her keen eye on them, and a look of recognition passed over her face as she saw Diccon. As soon as the meal was over, and the table of trestles removed, she sent a page to command Lord Talbot to present them to her.

"So, sir," she said, as Richard the elder knelt before her, "you are the father of two brave sons, whom you have bred up to do good service; but I only see one of them here. Where is the elder?"

"So please your Majesty, Sir Amias Paulett desired to retain him at Chartley to assist in guarding the Queen of Scots."

"It is well. Paulett knows a trusty lad when he sees him. And so do I. I would have the youths both for my gentlemen pensioners—the elder when he can be spared from his charge, this stripling at once."

"We are much beholden to your Majesty," said Richard, bending his head the lower as he knelt on one knee; for such an appointment gave both training and recommendation to young country gentlemen, and was much sought after.

"Methinks," said Elizabeth, who had the royal faculty of remembering faces, "you have yourself so served us, Mr. Talbot?"

"I was for three years in the band of your Majesty's sister, Queen Mary," said Richard, "but I quitted it on her death to serve at sea, and I have since been in charge at Sheffield, under my Lord of Shrewsbury."

"We have heard that he hath found you a faithful servant," said the Queen, "yea, so well affected as even to have refused your daughter in marriage to this same Babington. Is this true?"

"It is, so please your Majesty."

"And it was because you already perceived his villainy ?"

"There were many causes, Madam," said Richard, catching at the chance of saying a word for the unhappy lad, "but it was not so much villainy that I perceived in him as a nature that might be easily practised upon by worse men than himself."

"Not so much a villain ready made as the stuff villains are made of," said the Queen, satisfied with her own repartee.

"So please your Majesty, the metal that in good hands becomes a brave sword, in evil ones becomes a treacherous dagger."

"Well said, Master Captain, and therefore we must destroy alike the dagger and the hands that perverted it."

"Yet," ventured Richard, "the dagger attempered by your Majesty's clemency might yet do noble service."

Elizabeth, however, broke out fiercely with one of her wonted oaths.

"How now ?   Thou wouldst not plead for the rascal !   I would have you to know that to crave pardon for such a fellow is well-nigh treason in itself. You have license to leave us, sir."

"I should scarce have brought you, Richard," said Lord Talbot, as soon as they had left the presence chamber, "had I known you would venture on such folly.   Know you not how incensed she is ?   Naught but your proved loyalty and my father's could have borne you off this time, and it would be small marvel to me if the lad's appointment were forgotten."

"I could not choose but run the risk," said Richard. "What else came I to London for ?"

"Well," said his cousin, "you are a brave man, Richard Talbot. I know those who had rather scale a Spanish fortress than face Queen Elizabeth in her wrath. Her tongue is sharper than even my step-dame's, though it doth not run on so long."

Lord Talbot was not quite easy when that evening a gentleman, clad in rich scarlet and gold, and armed to the teeth, presented himself at Shrewsbury House and inquired for Mr. Talbot of Bridgefield. However, it proved to be the officer of the troop of gentlemen pensioners come to enroll Diccon, tell him the requirements, and arrange when he should join in a capacity something like that of an esquire to one of the seniors of the troop. Humfrey was likewise inquired for, but it was thought better on all accounts that he should continue in his present situation, since it was especially needful to have trustworthy persons at Chartley in the existing crisis. Master Richard was well satisfied to find that his son's immediate superior would be a gentleman of a good Yorkshire family, whose father was known to him, and who promised to have a care of Master Richard the younger, and preserve him, as far as possible, from the perils of dicing, drinking, and running into bad company.

Launching a son in this manner and equipping him for service was an anxious task for a father, while day after day the trial was deferred, the examinations being secretly carried on before the Council till, as Cavendish explained, what was important should be disclosed.

Of course this implied what should be fatal to Queen Mary. The priest Ballard was racked, but he was a man of great determination, and nothing was elicited from him. The other prisoners, and Nau and Curll, were questioned again and again under threats

o*

and promises before the Council, and the letters that
had been copied on their transit through the beer barrels
were read and made the subject of cross-examination—
still all in private, for, as Cavendish said, "perilous stuff
to the Queen's Majesty might come out."

He allowed, however, day after day, that though
there was quite enough to be fatal to Ballard, Babington, Savage, and Barnwell, whatever else was wanting
was not forthcoming.   At last, however, Cavendish
returned full of a certain exultation : "We have it,"
he said,—" a most undoubted treasonable letter, which
will catch *her* between the shoulders and the head."

He spoke to Lord Talbot and Richard, who were
standing together in a window, and who knew only too
well who was referred to, and what the expression
signified.   On a further query from his step-brother,
Cavendish explained that it was a long letter, dated
July 15, arranging in detail the plan for "the Lady's"
own rescue from Chartley at the moment of the landing
of the Spaniards, and likewise showing her privy to
the design of the six gentlemen against the life of the
Queen, and desiring to know their names.   Nau had,
he said, verified the cipher as one used in the correspondence, and Babington, when it was shown to him,
had declared that it had been given to him in the
street by a stranger serving-man in a blue coat, and
that it had removed all doubt from his mind, as it was
an answer to a letter of his, a copy of which had been
produced, but not the letter itself.

"Which we have not found," said Cavendish.

"Not for all that search of yours at Chartley ?" said
Richard.   "Methought it was thorough enough ! "

" The Lady must have been marvellously prudent as
to the keeping of letters," said Will, " or else she must

have received some warning; for there is absolutely
naught to be found in her repositories that will serve
our purpose."

"*Our* purpose!" repeated Richard, as he recollected
many little kindnesses that William Cavendish when a
boy had received from the prisoner at Sheffield.

"Yea, Master Richard," he returned, unabashed.
"It is absolutely needful that we should openly prove
this woman to be what we know her to be in secret.
Her Majesty's life will never be safe for a moment
while she lives; and what would become of us all did
she overlive the Queen!"

"Well, Will, for all your mighty word *we*, you are
but the pen in Mr. Secretary's hand, so there is no
need to argue the matter with you," said Richard.

The speech considerably nettled Master William,
especially as it made Lord Talbot laugh.

"Father!" said Diccon afterwards, "Humfrey tried
to warn Mr. 'Babington that we had seen this Langston, who hath as many metamorphoses as there be in
Ovidius Naso, coming privily forth from Sir Francis
Walsingham's closet, but he would not listen, and
declared that Langston was holding Mr. Secretary in
play."

"Deceiving and being deceived," sighed his father.
"That is ever the way, my son! Remember that if
thou playest false, other men will play falser with thee
and bring thee to thy ruin. I would not leave thee
here save that the gentlemen pensioners are a more
honest and manly sort of folk than yonder gentlemen
with their state craft, wherein they throw over all truth
and honour as well as mercy."

This conversation took place as the father and son
were making their way to a house in Westminster,

where Antony Babington's wife was with her mother,
Lady Ratcliffe. It had been a match made by Lady
Shrewsbury, and it was part of Richard's commission
to see and confer with the family. It was not a satisfactory interview. The wife was a dull childish little
thing, not yet sixteen; and though she cried, she had
plainly never lived in any real sympathy or companionship with her husband, who had left her with her
parents, while leading the life of mingled amusement
and intrigue which had brought him to his present
state; and the mother, a hard-featured woman, evidently
thought herself cheated and ill used. She railed at
Babington and at my Lady Countess by turns; at the
one for his ruinous courses and neglect of her daughter,
at the other for having cozened her into giving her poor
child to a treacherous Papist, who would be attainted in
blood, and thus bring her poor daughter and grandchild
to poverty. The old lady really seemed to have lost all
pity for her son-in-law in indignation on her daughter's
account, and to care infinitely less for the saving of his
life than for the saving of his estate. Nor did the
young wife herself appear to possess much real affection
for poor Antony, of whom she had seen very little.
There must have been great faults on his side; yet
certainly Richard felt that there was some excuse for
him in the mother-in-law, and that if the unfortunate
young man could have married Cicely his lot might
have been different. Yet the good Captain felt all
the more that if Cis had been his own he still would
never have given her to Babington.

CHAPTER XXXII.

WESTMINSTER HALL.

BENEATH the noble roof of Westminster Hall, with the morning sun streaming in high aloft, at seven in the morning of the 14th of September, the Court met for the trial of Antony Babington and his confederates. The Talbot name and recommendation obtained ready admission, and Lord Talbot, Richard, and his son formed one small party together with William Cavendish, who had his tablets, on which to take notes for the use of his superior, Walsingham, who was, however, one of the Commissioners.

There they sat, those supreme judges, the three Chief-Justices in their scarlet robes of office forming the centre of the group, which also numbered Lords Cobham and Buckhurst, Sir Francis Knollys, Sir Christopher Hatton, and most of the chief law officers of the Crown.

" Is Mr. Secretary Walsingham one of the judges here ?" asked Diccon.   " Methought he had been in the place of the accuser."

" Peace, boy, and listen," said his father ; " these things pass my comprehension."

Nevertheless Richard had determined that if the course of the trial should offer the least opportunity, he would come forward and plead his former knowledge of young Babington as a rash and weak-headed youth, easily played upon by designing persons, but likely to take to heart such a lesson as this, and become a true and loyal subject. If he could obtain any sort of mitigation for the poor youth, it would be worth the risk.

The seven conspirators were brought in, and Richard could hardly keep a rush of tears from his eyes at the sight of those fine, high-spirited young men, especially Antony Babington, the playfellow of his own children.

Antony was carefully dressed in his favourite colour, dark green, his hair and beard trimmed, and his demeanour calm and resigned. The fire was gone from his blue eye, and his bright complexion had faded, but there was an air of dignity about him such as he had never worn before. His eyes, as he took his place, wandered round the vast assembly, and rested at length on Mr. Talbot, as though deriving encouragement and support from the look that met his. Next to him was another young man with the same look of birth and breeding, namely Chidiock Tichborne; but John Savage, an older man, had the reckless bearing of the brutalised soldiery of the Netherlandish wars. Robert Barnwell, with his red, shaggy brows and Irish physiognomy, was at once recognised by Diccon. Donne and Salisbury followed; and the seventh conspirator, John Ballard, was carried in a chair. Even Diccon's quick eye could hardly have detected the ruffling, swaggering, richly-clad Captain Fortescue in this tonsured man in priestly garb, deadly pale, and unable to stand, from the effects of torture, yet with undaunted, penetrating eyes, all unsubdued.

After the proclamation, Oyez, Oyez, and the command to keep silence, Sandys, the Clerk of the Crown,

began the proceedings. "John Ballard, Antony Babington, John Savage, Robert Barnwell, Chidiock Tichborne, Henry Donne, Thomas Salisbury, hold up your
hands and answer." The indictment was then read
at great length, charging them with conspiring to slay
the Queen, to deliver Mary, Queen of Scots, from
custody, to stir up rebellion, to bring the Spaniards
to invade England, and to change the religion of the
country. The question was first put to Ballard, Was
he guilty of these treasons or not guilty?

Ballard's reply was, "That I procured the delivery
of the Queen of Scots, I am guilty; and that I went
about to alter the religion, I am guilty; but that I
intended to slay her Majesty, I am not guilty."

"Not with his own hand," muttered Cavendish,
"but for the rest——"

"Pity that what is so bravely spoken should be
false," thought Richard, "yet it may be to leave the
way open to defence."

Sandys, however, insisted that he must plead to the
whole indictment, and Anderson, the Chief-Justice of
Common Pleas, declared that he must deny the whole
generally, or confess it generally; while Hatton put in,
"Ballard, under thine own hand are all things confessed,
therefore now it is much vanity to stand vaingloriously
in denying it."

"Then, sir, I confess I am guilty," he said, with
great calmness, though it was the resignation of all
hope.

The same question was then put to Babington.
He, with "a mild countenance, sober gesture," and all
his natural grace, stood up and spoke, saying "that the
time for concealment was past, and that he was ready
to avow how from his earliest infancy he had believed

England to have fallen from the true religion, and had trusted to see it restored thereto. Moreover, he had ever a deep love and compassion for the Queen of Scots. Some," he said, " who are yet at large, and who are yet as deep in the matter as I——"

" Gifford, Morgan, and another," whispered Cavendish significantly.

" Have they escaped ?" asked Diccon.

" So 'tis said."

" The decoy ducks," thought Richard.

Babington was explaining that these men had proposed to him a great enterprise for the rescue and restoration of the Queen of Scots, and the re-establishment of the Catholic religion in England by the sword of the Prince of Parma. A body of gentlemen were to attack Chartley, free Mary, and proclaim her Queen, and at the same time Queen Elizabeth was to be put to death by some speedy and skilful method.

" My Lords," he said, " I swear that all that was in me cried out against the wickedness of thus privily slaying her Majesty."

Some muttered, " The villain ! he lies," but the kindly Richard sighed inaudibly, " True, poor lad ! Thou must have given thy conscience over to strange keepers to be thus led astray."

And Babington went on to say that they had brought this gentleman, Father Ballard, who had wrought with him to prove that his scruples were weak, carnal, and ungodly, and that it would be a meritorious deed in the sight of Heaven thus to remove the heretic usurper.

Here the judges sternly bade him not to blaspheme, and he replied, with that " soberness and good grace " which seems to have struck all the beholders, that he

craved patience and pardon, meaning only to explain how he had been led to the madness which he
now repented, understanding himself to have been in
grievous error, though not for the sake of any temporal
reward; but being blinded to the guilt, and assured that
the deed was both lawful and meritorious. He thus
had been brought to destruction through the persuasions
of this Ballard.

"A very fit author for so bad a fact," responded
Hatton.

"Very true, sir," said Babington; "for from so bad
a ground never proceed any better fruits. He it was
who persuaded me to kill the Queen, and to commit
the other treasons, whereof I confess myself guilty."

Savage pleaded guilty at once, with the reckless
hardihood of a soldier accustomed to look on death as
the fortune of war.

Barnwell denied any intention of killing the Queen
(much to Diccon's surprise), but pleaded guilty to the
rest. Donne said that on being told of the plot he had
prayed that whatever was most to the honour and
glory of Heaven might be done, and being pushed hard
by Hatton, turned this into a confession of being guilty.
Salisbury declared that he had always protested against
killing the Queen, and that he would not have done so
for a kingdom, but of the rest he was guilty. Tichborne showed that but for an accidental lameness he
would have been at his home in Hampshire, but he
could not deny his knowledge of the treason.

All having pleaded guilty, no trial was permitted,
such as would have brought out the different degrees
of guilt, which varied in all the seven.

A long speech was, however, made by the counsel
for the Crown, detailing the plot as it had been ar-

ranged for the public knowledge, and reading aloud a letter from Babington to Queen Mary, describing his plans both for her rescue and the assassination, saying, " he had appointed six noble gentlemen for the despatch of the wicked competitor."

Richard caught a look of astonishment on the unhappy young man's face, but it passed into hopeless despondency, and the speech went on to describe the picture of the conspirators and its strange motto, concluding with an accusation that they meant to sack London, burn the ships, and " cloy the ordnance."

A shudder of horror went through the assembly, and perhaps few except Richard Talbot felt that the examination of the prisoners ought to have been public. The form, however, was gone through of asking whether they had cause to render wherefore they should not be condemned to die.

The first to speak was Ballard. His eyes glanced round with an indomitable expression of scorn and indignation, which, as Diccon whispered, he could have felt to his very backbone. It was like that of a trapped and maimed lion, as the man sat in his chair with crushed and racked limbs, but with a spirit untamed in its defiance.

" Cause, my Lords ?" he replied. " The cause I have to render will not avail here, but it may avail before another Judgment-seat, where the question will be, who used the weapons of treason, not merely against whom they were employed. Inquiry hath not been made here who suborned the priest, Dr. Gifford, to fetch me over from Paris, that we might together overcome the scruples of these young men, and lead them forward in a scheme for the promotion of the true religion and the right and lawful succession. No question hath here

been put in open court, who framed the conspiracy, nor
for what purpose.   No, my Lords ; it would baffle the
end you would bring about, yea, and blot the reputation
of some who stand in high places, if it came to light
that the plot was devised, not by the Catholics who
were to be the instruments thereof, nor by the Lady in
whose favour all was to be done,—not by these, the
mere victims, but by him who by a triumph of policy
thus sent forth his tempters to enclose them all within
his net—above all the persecuted Lady whom all true
Catholics own as the only lawful sovereign within
these realms.   Such schemes, when they succeed, are
termed policy.   My Lords, I confess that by the justice
of England we have been guilty of treason against
Queen Elizabeth ; but by the eternal law of the justice
of God, we have suffered treachery far exceeding that
for which we are about to die."

"I marvel that they let the fellow speak so far,"
was Cavendish's comment.

"Nay, but is it so ?" asked Diccon with startled
eyes.

"Hush ! you have yet to learn statecraft," returned
his friend.

His father's monitory hand only just saved the boy
from bursting out with something that would have
rather astonished Westminster Hall, and caused him to
be taken out by the ushers.   It is not wonderful that
no report of the priest's speech has been preserved.

The name of Antony Babington was then called.
Probably he had been too much absorbed in the
misery of his position to pay attention to the preceding
speech, for his reply was quite independent of it.   He
prayed the Lords to believe, and to represent to her
Majesty, that he had received with horror the suggestion

of compassing her death, and had only been brought to believe it a terrible necessity by the persuasions of this Ballard.

On this Hatton broke forth in indignant com-passion,—"O Ballard! Ballard! what hast thou done? A sort of brave youth, otherwise endowed with good gifts, by thy inducement hast thou brought to their utter destruction and confusion!"

This apparently gave some hope to Babington, for he answered—"Yes, I protest that, before I met this Bal-lard, I never meant nor intended for to kill the Queen; but by his persuasions I was induced to believe that she being excommunicate it was lawful to murder her."

For the first time Ballard betrayed any pain. "Yes, Mr. Babington," he said, "lay all the blame upon me; but I wish the shedding of my blood might be the saving of your life. Howbeit, say what you will, I will say no more."

"He is the bravest of them all!" was Diccon's comment.

"Wot you that he was once *our* spy?" returned Cavendish with a sneer; while Sir Christopher, with the satisfaction of a little nature in uttering reproaches, returned—"Nay, Ballard, you must say more and shall say more, for you must not commit treasons and then huddle them up. Is this your *Religio Catholica?* Nay, rather it is *Diabolica.*"

Ballard scorned to answer this, and the Clerk passed on to Savage, who retained his soldierly fatalism, and only shook his head. Barnwell again denied any pur-pose of injuring the Queen, and when Hatton spoke of his appearance in Richmond Park, he said all had been for conscience sake. So said Henry Donne, but with far more piety and dignity, adding, "*Fiat voluntas*

Dei;" and Thomas Salisbury was the only one who made any entreaty for pardon.

Speeches followed from the Attorney-General, and from Sir Christopher Hatton, and then the Lord Chief Justice Anderson pronounced the terrible sentence.

Richard Talbot sat with his head bowed between his hands. His son had begun listening with wide-stretched eyes and mouth, as boyhood hearkens to the dreadful, and with the hardness of an unmerciful time, too apt to confound pity with weakness; but when his eye fell on the man he had followed about as an elder playmate, and realised all it conveyed, his cheek blanched, his jaw fell, and he hardly knew how his father got him out of the court.

There was clearly no hope. The form of the trial was such as to leave no chance of escape from the utmost penalty. No witnesses had been examined, no degrees of guilt acknowledged, no palliations admitted. Perhaps men who would have brought the Spanish havoc on their native country, and have murdered their sovereign, were beyond the pale of compassion. All London clearly thought so; and yet, as Richard Talbot dwelt on their tones and looks, and remembered how they had been deluded and tempted, and made to believe their deed meritorious, he could not but feel exceeding pity for the four younger men. Ballard, Savage, and Barnwell might be justly doomed; even Babington had, by his own admission, entertained a fearfully evil design; but the other three had evidently dipped far less deeply into the plot, and Tichborne had only concealed it out of friendship. Yet the ruthless judgment condemned all alike! And why? To justify a yet more cruel blow! No wonder honest Richard Talbot felt sick at heart.

CHAPTER XXXIII.

IN THE TOWER.

" HERE is a letter from Mr. Secretary to the Lieutenant of the Tower, Master Richard, bidding him
admit you to speech of Babington," said Will Cavendish.
" He was loath to give it, and nothing but my Lord
Shrewsbury's interest would have done it, on my oath
that you are a prudent and discreet man, who hath
been conversant in these matters for many years."

". Yea, and that long before you were, Master Will,"
said Richard, always a little entertained by the young
gentleman's airs of patronage. " However, I am beholden to you."

" That you may be, for you are the only person
who hath obtained admission to the prisoners."

" Not even their wives ? "

" Mrs. Tichborne is in the country—so best for
her—and Mrs. Babington hath never demanded it. I
trow there is not love enough between them to make
them seek such a meeting. It was one of my mother's
matches. Mistress Cicely would have cleaved to him
more closely, though I am glad you saw through the
fellow too well to give her to him. She would be a
landless widow, whereas this Ratcliffe wife has a fair
portion for her child."

" Then Dethick will be forfeited ? "

" Ay.　They say the Queen hath promised it to Raleigh."

" And there is no hope of mercy ? "

" Not a tittle for any man of them !　Nay, so far from it, her Majesty asked if there were no worse nor more extraordinary mode of death for them."

" I should not have thought it of her."

" Her Majesty hath been affrighted, Master Richard, sorely affrighted, though she put so bold a face upon it, and there is nothing a woman, who prides herself on her courage, can so little pardon."

So Richard, sad at heart, took boat and ascended the Thames for his melancholy visit.　The gateway was guarded by a stalwart yeoman, halbert in hand, who detained him while the officer of the guard was called. On showing the letter from Sir Francis Walsingham, Mr. Talbot was conducted by this personage across the first paved court to the lodgings of the Lieutenant under so close a guard that he felt as if he were about to be incarcerated himself, and was there kept waiting in a sort of guard-room while the letter was delivered.

Presently the Lieutenant, Sir Owen Hopton, a well-bred courteous knight, appeared and saluted him with apologies for his detention and all these precautions, saying that the orders were to keep a close guard and to hinder all communication from without, so that nothing short of this letter would have obtained entrance for the bearer, whom he further required to set down his name and designation in full.　Then, after asking how long the visitor wished to remain with the prisoners— for Tichborne and Babington were quartered together —he called a warder and committed Mr. Talbot to his guidance, to remain for two hours locked up in the cell.

"Sir," added Sir Owen, "it is superfluous to tell you that on coming out, you must either give me your word of honour that you convey nothing from the prisoners, or else submit to be searched."

Richard smiled, and observed that men were wont to trust his word of honour, to which the knight heartily replied that he was sure of it, and he then followed the warder up stone stairs and along vaulted passages, where the clang of their footsteps made his heart sink. The prisoners were in the White Tower, the central body of the grim building, and the warder, after unlocking the door, announced, with no unnecessary rudeness, but rather as if he were glad of any comfort to his charges, "Here, sirs, is a gentleman to visit you."

They had both risen at the sound of the key turning in the lock, and Antony Babington's face lighted up as he exclaimed, "Mr. Talbot! I knew you would come if it were possible."

"I come by my Lord's desire," replied Richard, the close wringing of his hand expressing feeling to which he durst not give way in words.

He took in at the moment that the room, though stern and strong, was not squalid. It was lighted fully by a window, iron-barred, but not small, and according to custom, the prisoners had been permitted to furnish, at their own expense, sufficient garniture for comfort, and as both were wealthy men, they were fairly provided, and they were not fettered. Both looked paler than when Richard had seen them in Westminster Hall two days previously. Antony was as usual neatly arrayed, with well-trimmed hair and beard, but Tichborne's hung neglected, and there was a hollow, haggard look about his eyes, as if of dismay at his approaching fate. Neither was, however, forgetful of courtesy, and as Babington presented Mr. Talbot to his friend, the greeting and welcome would have befitted the halls of Dethick or Tichborne.

"Sirs," said the young man, with a sad smile irradiating for a moment the restless despair of his countenance, " it is not by choice that I am an intruder on your privacy; I will abstract myself so far as is possible."

"I have no secrets from my Chidiock," cried Babington.

"But Mr. Talbot may," replied his friend, " therefore I will only first inquire whether he can tell us aught of the royal lady for whose sake we suffer. They have asked us many questions, but answered none."

Richard was able to reply that after the seclusion at Tixall she had been brought back to Chartley, and there was no difference in the manner of her custody, moreover, that she had recovered from her attack of illness, tidings he had just received in a letter from Humfrey. He did not feel it needful to inflict a pang on the men who were to die in two days' time by letting them know that she was to be immediately brought to trial on the evidence extracted from them. On hearing that her captivity was not straitened, both looked relieved, and Tichborne, thanking him, lay down on his own bed, turned his face to the wall, and drew the covering over his head.

"Ah!" sighed Babington, "is there no hope for him—he who has done naught but guard too faithfully my unhappy secret? Is he to die for his faith and honour?"

"Alas, Antony! I am forbidden to give thee hope

for any. Of that we must not speak. The time is short enough for what needs to be spoken."

"I knew that there was none for myself," said Antony, "but for those whom———" There was a gesture from Tichborne as if he could not bear this, and he went on, "Yea, there is a matter on which I must needs speak to you, sir, The young lady— where is she?"—he spoke earnestly, and lowering his voice as he bent his head.

"She is still at Chartley."

"That is well. But, sir, she must be guarded. I fear me there is one who is aware of her parentage."

"The Scottish archer?"

"No, the truth."

"You knew it?"

"Not when I made my suit to her, or I should never have dared to lift my eyes so far."

"I suppose your knowledge came from Langston," said Richard, more perturbed than amazed at the disclosure.

"Even so. Yet I am not certain whether he knows or only guesses; but at any rate be on your guard for her sake. He has proved himself so unspeakable a villain that none can guess what he will do next. He—he it is above all—yea, above even Gifford and Ballard, who has brought us to this pass."

He was becoming fiercely agitated, but putting a force upon himself said, "Have patience, good Mr. Talbot, of your kindness, and I will tell you all, that you may understand the coilings of the serpent who led me hither, and if possible save her from them."

Antony then explained that so soon as he had become his own master he had followed the inclinations which led him to the church of his mother and of Queen Mary, the two beings he had always regarded with the most fervent affection and love. His mother's kindred had brought him in contact with the Roman Catholic priests who circulated in England, at the utmost peril of their lives, to keep up the faith of the gentry, and in many cases to intrigue for Queen Mary. Among these plotters he fell in with Cuthbert Langston, a Jesuit of the third order, though not a priest, and one of the most active agents in corresponding with Queen Mary. His small stature, colourless complexion, and insignificant features, rendered him almost a blank block, capable of assuming any variety of disguise. He also knew several languages, could imitate different dialects, and counterfeit male and female voices so that very few could detect him. He had soon made himself known to Babington as the huckster Tibbott of days gone by, and had then disclosed to him that Cicely was certainly not the daughter of her supposed parents, telling of her rescue from the wreck, and hinting that her rank was exalted, and that he knew secrets respecting her which he was about to make known to the Queen of Scots. With this purpose among others, Langston had adopted the disguise of the woman selling spars with the password "Beads and Bracelets," and being well known as an agent of correspondence to the suite of the captive Queen, he had been able to direct Gorion's attention to the maiden, and to let him know that she was the same with the infant who had been put on board the *Bride of Dunbar* at Dunbar.

How much more did Langston guess ? He had told Babington the story current among the outer circle of Mary's followers of the maiden being the daughter of the Scotch archer, and had taught him her true

name, encouraging too, his aspirations towards her during the time of his courtship.   Babington believed
Langston to have been at that time still a sincere
partizan of Queen Mary, but all along to have entertained a suspicion that there was a closer relationship
between Bride Hepburn and the Queen than was
avowed, though to Babington himself he had only given
mysterious hints.

But towards the end of the captivity at Tutbury, he
had made some further discovery, which confirmed his
suspicions, and had led to another attempt to accost
Cicely, and to make the Queen aware of his knowledge,
perhaps in order to verify it, or it might be to gain power
over her, a reward for the introduction, or to extort
bribes to secrecy.   For looking back, Antony could now
perceive that by this time a certain greed of lucre had
set in upon the man, who had obtained large sums of
secret service money from himself ; and avarice, together
with the rebuff he had received from the Queen, had
doubtless rendered him accessible to the temptations of
the arch-plotters Gifford and Morgan.   Richard could
believe this, for the knowledge had been forced on him
that there were an incredible number of intriguers at
that time, spies and conspirators, often in the pay of
both parties, impartially betraying the one to the other,
and sometimes, through miscalculation, meeting the fate
they richly deserved.   Many a man who had begun
enthusiastically to work in underground ways for what
he thought the righteous cause, became so enamoured
of the undermining process, and the gold there to be
picked up, that from a wrong-headed partizan he became a traitor—often a double-faced one—and would
work secretly in the interest of whichever cause would
pay him best.

Poor Babington had been far too youthfully simple to guess what he now perceived, that he had been made the mere tool and instrument of these traitors. He had been instructed in Gifford's arrangement with the Burton brewer for conveying letters to Mary at Chartley, and had been made the means of informing her of it by means of his interview with Cicely, when he had brought the letter in the watch. The letter had been conveyed to him by Langston, the watch had been his own device. It was after this meeting, of which Richard now heard for the first time, that Langston had fully told his belief respecting the true birth of Bride Hepburn, and assured Babington that there was no hope of his wedding her, though the Queen might allow him to delude himself with the idea of her favour in order to bind him to her service.

It was then that Babington consented to Lady Shrewsbury's new match with the well-endowed Eleanor Ratcliffe. If he could not have Cicely, he cared not whom he had. He had been leading a wild and extravagant life about town, when (as poor Tichborne afterwards said on the scaffold) the flourishing estate of Babington and Tichborne was the talk of Fleet Street and the Strand, and he had also many calls for secret service money, so that all his thought was to have more to spend in the service of Queen Mary and her daughter.

"Oh, sir! I have been as one distraught all this past year," he said. "How often since I have been shut up here, and I have seen how I have been duped and gulled, have your words come back to me, that to enter on crooked ways was the way to destruction for myself and others, and that I might only be serving

worse men than myself! And yet they were priests
who misled me!"

" Even in your own religion there are many priests
who would withhold you from such crimes," said
Richard.

"There are! I know it! I have spoken with them.
They say no priest can put aside the eternal laws of God's
justice. So these others, Chidióck here, Donne and
Salisbury, always cried out against the slaying of the
Queen, though——wretch that I was——and gulled by
Ballard and Savage, I deemed the exploit so noble and
praiseworthy that I even joined Tichborne with me
in that accursed portraiture! Yea, you may well deem
me mad, but it was Gifford who encouraged me in
having it made, no doubt to assure our ruin. Oh, Mr.
Talbot! was ever man so cruelly deceived as me?"

" It is only too true. Antony. My heart is full of
rage and indignation when I think thereof. And yet,
my poor lad, what concerns thee most is to lay aside all
such thoughts as may not tend to repentance before
God."

" I know it, I know it, sir. All the more that we
shall die without the last sacraments. Commend us
to the prayers of our Queen, sir, and of *her*. But to
proceed with what imports you to know for her sake,
while I have space to speak."

He proceeded to tell how, between dissipation and
intrigue, he had lived in a perpetual state of excitement,
going backwards and forwards between London and
Lichfield to attend to the correspondence with Queen
Mary and the Spanish ambassador in France, and to
arrange the details of the plot; always being worked
up to the highest pitch by Gifford and Ballard, while
Langston continued to be the great assistant in all the

correspondence.   All the time Sir Francis Walsingham, who was really aware of all, if not the prime mover in the intrigue, appeared perfectly unsuspicious ; often received Babington at his house, and discussed a plan of sending him on a commission to France, while in point of fact every letter that travelled in the Burton barrels was deciphered by Phillipps, and laid before the Secretary before being read by the proper owners.   In none of these, however, as Babington could assure Mr. Talbot, had Cicely been mentioned,—the only danger to her was through Langston.

Things had come to a climax in July, when Babington had been urged to obtain from Mary such definite approbation of his plans as might satisfy his confederates, and had in consequence written the letter and obtained the answer, copies of which had been read to him at his private examination, and which certainly contained fatal matter to both him and the Queen.

They had no doubt been called forth with that intent, and a doubt had begun to arise in the victim's mind whether the last reply had been really the Queen's own.   It had been delivered to him in the street, not by the usual channel, but by a blue-coated serving-man.   Two or three days later Humfrey had told him of Langston's interview with Walsingham, which he had at the time laughed to scorn, thinking himself able to penetrate any disguise of that Proteus, and likewise believing that he was blinding Walsingham.

He first took alarm a few days after Humfrey's departure, and wrote to Queen Mary to warn her, convinced that the traitor must be Langston.   Ballard became himself suspected, and after lurking about in various disguises was arrested in Babington's own lodgings.   To

disarm suspicion, Antony went to Walsingham to talk
about the French Mission, and tried to resume his usual
habits, but in a tavern, he became aware that Langston,
under some fresh shape, was watching him, and hastily
throwing down the reckoning, he fled without his cloak
or sword to Gage's house at Westminster, where he took
horse, hid himself in St. John's Wood, and finally was
taken, half starved, in an outhouse at Harrow, belonging to a farmer, whose mercy involved him in the like
doom.

This was the substance of the story told by the
unfortunate young man to Richard Talbot, whom he
owned as the best and wisest friend he had ever had—
going back to the warnings twice given, that no cause is
served by departing from the right; no kingdom safely
won by worshipping the devil: "And sure I did worship him when I let myself be led by Gifford," he said.

His chief anxiety was not for his wife and her child,
who he said would be well taken care of by the Ratcliffe family, and who, alas! had never won his heart.
In fact he was relieved that he was not permitted to
see the young thing, even had she wished it; it could
do no good to either of them, though he had written a
letter, which she was to deliver, for the Queen, commending her to her Majesty's mercy.

His love had been for Cicely, and even that had
never been, as Richard saw, such purifying, restraining,
self-sacrificing affection as was Humfrey's. It was
half romance, half a sort of offshoot from his one great
and absorbing passion of devotion to the Queen of
Scots, which was still as strong as ever. He entrusted
Richard with his humblest commendations to her, and
strove to rest in the belief that as many a conspirator
before—such as Norfolk, Throckmorton, Parry—had

perished on her behalf while she remained untouched, that so it might again be, since surely, if she were to be tried, he would have been kept alive as a witness. The peculiar custom of the time in State prosecutions of hanging the witnesses before the trial had not occurred to him.

But how would it be with Cicely? "Is what this fellow guessed the very truth?" he asked.

Richard made a sign of affirmation, saying, "Is it only a guess on his part?"

Babington believed the man stopped short of absolute certainty, though he had declared himself to have reason to believe that a child must have been born to the captive queen at Lochleven; and if so, where else could she be? Was he waiting for clear proof to make the secret known to the Council? Did he intend to make profit of it and obtain in the poor girl a subject for further intrigue? Was he withheld by consideration for Richard Talbot, for whom Babington declared that if such a villain could be believed in any respect, he had much family regard and deep gratitude, since Richard had stood his friend when all his family had cast him off in much resentment at his change of purpose and opinion.

At any rate he had in his power Cicely's welfare and liberty, if not the lives of her adopted parents, since in the present juncture of affairs, and of universal suspicion, the concealment of the existence of one who stood so near the throne might easily be represented as high treason. Where was he?

No one knew. For appearance sake, Gifford had fled beyond seas, happily only to fall into a prison of the Duke of Guise: and they must hope that Langston might have followed the same course. Meantime,

P

Richard could but go on as before, Cicely being now
in her own mother's hands. The avowal of her
identity must remain for the present as might be determined by her who had the right to decide.

" I would I could feel hope for any I leave behind
me," said poor Antony. " I trow you will not bear the
maiden my message, for you will deem it a sin that I
have loved her, and only her, to the last, though I have
been false to that love as to all else beside. Tell
Humfrey how I long that I had been like him, though
he too must love on without hope."

He sent warm greetings to good Mistress Susan
Talbot and craved her prayers. He had one other
care, namely to commend to Mr. Talbot an old body
servant, Harry Gillingham by name, who had attended
on him in his boyhood at Sheffield, and had been with
him all his life, being admitted even now, under supervision from the warders, to wait on him when dressing
and at his meals. The poor man was broken-hearted,
and so near desperation that his master wished much
to get him out of London before the execution. So,
as Mr. Talbot meant to sail for Hull by the next day's
tide in the *Mastiff*, he promised to take the poor fellow
with him back to Bridgefield.

All this had taken much time. Antony did not
seem disposed to go farther into his own feelings in
the brief space that remained, but he took up a paper
from the table, and indicating Tichborne, who still
affected sleep, he asked whether it was fit that a man,
who could write thus, should die for a plot against
which he had always protested. Richard read these
touching lines :—

My prime of youth is but a frost of care,
  My feast of joy is but a dish of pain,
My crop of corn is but a field of tares,
  And all my goods is but vain hope of gain.
The day is fled, and yet I saw no sun ;
And now I live, and now my life is done.

My spring is past, and yet it hath not sprung ;
  The fruit is dead, and yet the leaves are green ;
My youth is past, and yet I am but young ;
  I saw the world, and yet I was not seen.
My thread is cut, and yet it is not spun ;
And now I live, and now my life is done.

I sought for death, and found it in the wombe ;
  I lookt for life, and yet it was a shade ;
I trode the ground, and knew it was my tombe,
  And now I dye, and now I am but made.
The glass is full, and yet my glass is run ;
And now I live, and now my life is done.

Little used to poetry, these lines made the good
man's eyes fill with tears as he looked at the two
goodly young men about to be cut off so early—one
indeed guilty, but the victim of an iniquitous act of
deliberate treachery.

He asked if Mr. Tichborne wished to entrust to
him aught that could be done by word of mouth, and
a few commissions were given to him. Then Antony
bethought him of thanks to Lord and Lady Shrewsbury for all they had done for him, and above all for
sending Mr. Talbot ; and a message to ask pardon for
having so belied the loyal education they had given
him. The divided religion of the country had been
his bane : his mother's charge secretly to follow her
faith had been the beginning, and then had followed
the charms of stratagem on behalf of Queen Mary.

Perhaps, after all, his death, as a repentant man still

single minded, saved him from lapsing into the double
vileness of the veteran intriguers whose prey he had
been.

"I commend me to the Mercy Master Who sees my
heart," he said.

Herewith the warder returned, and at his request
summoned Gillingham, a sturdy grizzled fellow, looking
grim with grief. Babington told him of the arrangement made, and that he was to leave London early in
the morning with Mr. Talbot, but the man immediately
dropped on his knees and swore a solemn oath that
nothing should induce him to leave the place while his
master breathed.

"Thou foolish knave," said Antony, "thou canst do
me no good, and wilt but make thyself a more piteous
wretch than thou art already. Why, 'tis for love of
thee that I would have thee spared the sight."

"Am I a babe to be spared?" growled the man.

And all that he could be induced to promise was
that he would repair to Bridgefield as soon as all was
over—"Unless," said he, "I meet one of those accursed
rogues, and then a halter would be sweet, if I had first
had my will of them."

"Hush, Harry, or Master Warder will be locking
thee up next," said Antony.

And then came the farewell. It was at last a long,
speechless, sorrowful embrace; and then Antony, slipping from it to his knees, said—"Bless me! Oh bless
me: thou who hast been mine only true friend. Bless
me as a father!"

"May God in Heaven bless thee!" said Richard,
solemnly laying his hand on his head. "May He, Who
knoweth how thou hast been led astray, pardon thee!
May He, Who hath felt the agonies and shame of the

Cross, redeem thee, and suffer thee not for any pains of death to fall from Him!"

He was glad to hear afterwards, when broken-hearted Gillingham joined him, that the last words heard from Antony Babington's lips were—" *Parce mihi, Domine* JESU !'

CHAPTER XXXIV.

FOTHERINGHAY.

"Is this my last journey?" said Queen Mary, with a strange, sad smile, as she took her seat in the heavy lumbering coach which had been appointed for her conveyance from Chartley, her rheumatism having set in too severely to permit her to ride.

"Say not so; your Grace has weathered many a storm before," said Marie de Courcelles. "This one will also pass over."

"Ah, my good Marie, never before have I felt this foreboding and sinking of the heart. I have always hoped before, but I have exhausted the casket of Pandora. Even hope is flown!"

Jean Kennedy tried to say something of "Darkest before dawn."

"The dawn, it may be, of the eternal day," said the Queen. "Nay, my friends, the most welcome tidings that could greet me would be that my weary bondage was over for ever, and that I should wreck no more gallant hearts. What, *mignonne*, art thou weeping? There will be freedom again for thee when that day comes."

"O madam, I want not freedom at such a price!" And yet Cicely had never recovered her

looks since those seventeen days at Tickhill. She still
looked white and thin, and her dark eyebrows lay in a
heavy line, seldom lifted by the merry looks and smiles
that used to flash over her face. Life had begun to
press its weight upon her, and day after day, as Humfrey watched her across the chapel, and exchanged a
word or two with her while crossing the yard, had he
grieved at her altered mien; and vexed himself with
wondering whether she had after all loved Babington,
and were mourning for him.

Truly, even without the passion of love, there had
been much to shock and appal a young heart in the
fate of the playfellow of her childhood, the suitor of
her youth. It was the first death among those she had
known intimately, and even her small knowledge of the
cause made her feel miserable and almost guilty, for
had not poor Antony plotted for her mother, and had
not she been held out to him as a delusive inducement?
Moreover, she felt the burden of a deep, pitying love
and admiration not wholly joined with perfect trust
and reliance. She had been from the first startled by
untruths and concealments. There was mystery all
round her, and the future was dark. There were terrible
forebodings for her mother; and if she looked beyond
for herself, only uncertainty and fear of being commanded to follow Marie de Courcelles to a foreign
court, perhaps to a convent; while she yearned with
an almost sick longing for home and kind Mrs. Talbot's
motherly tenderness and trustworthiness, and the very
renunciation of Humfrey that she had spoken so easily,
had made her aware of his full worth, and wakened
in her a longing for the right to rest on his stout arm
and faithful heart. To look across at him and know
him near often seemed her best support, and was she

to be cut off from him for ever ?   The devotions of the
Queen, though she had been deprived of her almoner,
had been much increased of late as one preparing for
death ; and with them were associated all her household of the Roman Catholic faith, leaving out Cicely
and the two Mrs. Curlls.   The long oft-repeated Latin
orisons, such as the penitential Psalms, would certainly
have been wearisome to the girl, but it gave her a pang
to be pointedly excluded as one who had no part nor
lot with her mother.   Perhaps this was done by calcu-
lation, in order to incline her to embrace her mother's
faith ; and the time was not spent very pleasantly, as
she had nothing but needlework to occupy her, and
no society save that of the sisters Curll.   Barbara's
spirits were greatly depressed by the loss of her infant
and anxiety for her husband.   His evidence might be
life or death to the Queen, and his betrayal of her confidence, or his being tortured for his fidelity, were terrible
alternatives for his wife's imagination.   It was hard to
say whether she were more sorry or glad when, on leaving Chartley, she was forbidden to continue her attendance on the Queen, and set free to follow him to London.
The poor lady knew nothing, and dreaded everything.
She could not help discussing her anxieties when alone
with Cicely, thus rendering perceptible more and more
of the ramifications of plot and intrigue — past and
present — at which she herself only guessed a part.
Assuredly the finding herself a princess, and sharing the
captivity of a queen, had not proved so like a chapter
of the *Morte d'Arthur* as it had seemed to Cicely at
Buxton.

It was as unlike as was riding a white palfrey
through a forest, guided by knights in armour, to the
being packed with all the ladies into a heavy jolting

conveyance, guarded before and behind by armed servants and yeomen, among whom Humfrey's form could only now and then be detected.

The Queen had chosen her seat where she could best look out from the scant amount of window. She gazed at the harvest-fields full of sheaves, the orchards laden with ruddy apples, the trees assuming their autumn tints, with lingering eyes, as of one who foreboded that these sights of earth were passing from her.

Two nights were spent on the road, one at Leicester ; and on the fourth day, the captain in charge of the castle for the governor Sir William Fitzwilliam, who had come to escort and receive her, came to the carriage window and bade her look up.   " This is Periho Lane," he said, " whence your Grace may have the first sight of the poor house which is to have the honour of receiving you."

" *Perio !* I perish," repeated Mary ; " an ominous road."

The place showed itself to be of immense strength. The hollow sound caused by rolling over a drawbridge was twice heard, and the carriage crossed two courts before stopping at the foot of a broad flight of stone steps, where stood Sir William Fitzwilliam and Sir Amias Paulett ready to hand out the Queen.

A few stone steps were mounted, then an enormous hall had to be traversed. The little procession had formed in pairs, and Humfrey was able to give his hand to Cicely and walk with her along the vast space, on which many windows emblazoned with coats of arms shed their light—the western ones full of the bright September sunshine.   One of these, emblazoned with the royal shield in crimson mantlings, cast a blood-red stain on the white stone pavement.   Mary, who was walking

P*

first, holding by the arm of Sir Andrew Melville, paused, shuddered, pointed, and said, " See, Andrew, there will my blood be shed."

" Madam, madam! speak not thus. By the help of the saints you will yet win through your troubles."

" Ay, Andrew, but only by one fate ; " and she looked upwards.

Her faithful followers could not but notice that there was no eager assurance that no ill was intended her, such as they had often heard from Shrewsbury and Sadler.

Cicely looked at Humfrey with widely-opened eyes, and the half-breathed question, " What does it mean ? "

He shook his head gravely and said, " I cannot tell," but he could not keep his manner from betraying that he expected the worst.

Meanwhile Mary was conducted on to her apartments, up a stair as usual, and forming another side of the inner court at right angles to the Hall. There was no reason to complain of these, Mary's furniture having as usual been sent forward with her inferior servants, and arranged by them. She was weary, and sat down at once on her chair, and as soon as Paulett had gone through his usual formalities with even more than his wonted stiffness, and had left her, she said, " I see what we are come here for. It is that yonder hall may be the place of my death."

Cheering assurances and deprecations of evil augury were poured on her, but she put them aside, saying, " Nay, my friends, trow you not that I rejoice in the close of my weary captivity ? "

She resumed her usual habits very calmly, as far as her increased rheumatism would permit, and showed anxiety that a large piece of embroidery should be completed, and thus about a fortnight passed. Then came the first token of the future. Sir Amias Paulett, Sir Walter Mildmay, and a notary, sought her presence and presented her with a letter from Queen Elizabeth, informing her that there were heavy accusations against her, and that as she was residing under the protection of the laws of England, she must be tried by those laws, and must make answer to the commissioners appointed for the purpose. Mary put on all her queenly dignity, and declared that she would never condescend to answer as a subject of the Queen of England, but would only consent to refer their differences to a tribunal of foreign princes. As to her being under the protection of English law, she had come to England of her own free will, and had been kept there a prisoner ever since, so that she did not consider herself *protected* by the law of England.

Meanwhile fresh noblemen commissioned to sit on the trial arrived day by day. There was trampling of horses and jingling of equipments, and the captive suite daily heard reports of fresh arrivals, and saw glimpses of new colours and badges flitting across the court, while conferences were held with Mary in the hope of inducing her to submit to the English jurisdiction. She was sorely perplexed, seeing as she did that to persist in her absolute refusal to be bound by English law would be prejudicial to her claim to the English crown, and being also assured by Burghley that if she refused to plead the trial would still take place, and she would be sentenced in her absence. Her spirit rose at this threat, and she answered disdainfully, but it worked with her none the less when the treasurer had left her.

" Oh," she cried that night, " would but Elizabeth

be content to let me resign my rights to my son, making them secure to him, and then let me retire to some convent in Lorraine, or in Germany, or wherever she would, so would I never trouble her more !"

"Will you not write this to her?" asked Cicely.

"What would be the use of it, child? They would tamper with the letter, pledging me to what I never would undertake. I know how they can cut and garble, add and take away! Never have they let me see or speak to her as woman to woman. All I have said or done has been coloured."

"Mother, I would that I could go to her; Humfrey has seen and spoken to her, why should not I?"

"Thou, poor silly maid! They would drive Cis Talbot away with scorn, and as to Bride Hepburn, why, she would but run into all her mother's dangers."

"It might be done, and if so I will do it," said Cicely, clasping her hands together.

"No, child, say no more. My worn-out old life is not worth the risk of thy young freedom. But I love thee for it, mine ain bairnie, *mon enfant à moi*. If thy brother had thy spirit, child——"

"I hate the thought of him! Call him not my brother!" cried Cicely hotly. "If he were worth one brass farthing he would have unfurled the Scottish lion long ago, and ridden across the Border to deliver his mother."

"And how many do you think would have followed that same lion?" said Mary, sadly.

"Then he should have come alone with his good horse and his good sword!"

"To lose both crowns, if not life! No, no, lassie; he is a pawky chiel, as they say in the north, and cares not to risk aught for the mother he hath never seen,

and of whom he hath been taught to believe strange
tales."

The more the Queen said in excuse for the indifference of her son, the stronger was the purpose
that grew up in the heart of the daughter, while
fresh commissioners arrived every day, and further
conversations were held with the Queen. Lord
Shrewsbury was known to be summoned, and Cicely
spent half her time in watching for some well-known
face, in the hope that he might bring her good foster-
father in his train. More than once she declared that
she saw a cap or sleeve with the well-beloved silver dog,
when it turned out to be a wyvern or the royal lion himself. Queen Mary even laughed at her for thinking her
mastiff had gone on his hind legs when she once even
imagined him in the Warwick Bear and ragged staff.

At last, however, all unexpectedly, while the Queen
was in conference with Hatton, there came a message
by the steward of the household, that Master Richard
Talbot had arrived, and that permission had been
granted by Sir Amias for him to speak with Mistress
Cicely. She sprang up joyously, but Mrs. Kennedy
demurred.

"Set him up!" quoth she. "My certie, things are
come to a pretty pass that any one's permission save
her Majesty's should be speired for one of her women,
and I wonder that you, my mistress, should be the
last to think of her honour!"

"O Mrs. Kennedy, dear Mrs. Jean," entreated
Cicely, "hinder me not. If I wait till I can ask her,
I may lose my sole hope of speaking with him. I
know she would not be displeased, and it imports,
indeed it imports."

"Come, Mrs. Kennett," said the steward, who by

no means shared his master's sourness, " if it were a
young gallant that craved to see thy fair mistress, I
could see why you should doubt; but being her father
and brother, there can surely be no objection."

" The young lady knows what I mean," said the
old gentlewoman with great dignity, " but if she will
answer it to the Queen——"

" I will, I will," cried Cicely, whose colour had
risen with eagerness, and she was immediately marshalled by the steward beyond the door that closed in
the royal captive's suite of apartments to a gallery.
At the door of communication three yeomen were
always placed under an officer. Humfrey was one of
those who took turns to command this guard, but he
was not now on duty. He was, however, standing
beside his father awaiting Cicely's coming.

Eagerly she moved up to Master Richard, bent her
knee for his blessing, and raised her face for his
paternal kiss with the same fond gladness as if she
had been his daughter in truth. He took one hand,
and Humfrey the other, and they followed the steward,
who had promised to procure them a private interview,
so difficult a matter, in the fulness of the castle, that
he had no place to offer them save the deep embrasure
of a great oriel window at the end of the gallery.
They would be seen there, but there was no fear of
their being heard without their own consent, and till
the chapel bell rang for evening prayers and sermon
there would be no interruption. And as Cicely found
herself seated between Master Richard and the window, with Humfrey opposite, she was sensible of a
repose and *bien être* she had not felt since she quitted
Bridgefield. She had already heard on the way that
all was well there, and that my Lord was not come,

though named in the commission as being Earl Marshal of England, sending his kinsman of Bridgefield in his stead with letters of excuse.

"In sooth he cannot bear to come and sit in judgment on one he hath known so long and closely," said Richard; "but he hath bidden me to come hither and remain so as to bring him a full report of all."

"How doth my Lady Countess take that?" asked Humfrey.

"I question whether the Countess would let him go if he wished it. She is altogether changed in mind, and come round to her first love for this Lady, declaring that it is all her Lord's fault that the custody was taken from them, and that she could. and would have hindered all this."

"That may be so," said Humfrey. "If all be true that is whispered, there have been dealings which would not have been possible at Sheffield."

"So it may be. In any wise my Lady is bitterly grieved, and they send for thy mother every second day to pacify her."

"Dear mother!" murmured Cis; "when shall I see her again?"

"I would that she had thee for a little space, my wench," said Richard; "thou hast lost thy round ruddy cheeks. Hast been sick?"

"Nay, sir, save as we all are—sick at heart! But all seems well now you are here. Tell me of little Ned. Is he as good scholar as ever?"

"Verily he is. We intend by God's blessing to bring him up for the ministry. I hope in another year to take him to Cambridge. Thy mother is knitting his hosen of gray and black already."

Other questions and answers followed about Bridgefield tidings, which still evidently touched Cicely as closely as if she had been a born Talbot. There was a kind of rest in dwelling on these before coming to the sadder, more pressing concern of her other life. It was not till the slow striking of the Castle clock warned them that they had less than an hour to spend together that they came to closer matters, and Richard transferred to Cicely those last sad messages to her Queen, which he had undertaken for Babington and Tichborne.

"The Queen hath shed many tears for them," she said, "and hath writ to the French and Spanish ambassadors to have masses said for them. Poor Antony ! Did he send no word to me, dear father ?"

The man being dead, Mr. Talbot saw no objection to telling her how he had said he had never loved any other, though he had been false to that love.

"Ah, poor Antony !" said Cis, with her grave simplicity. "But it would not have been right for me to be a hindrance to the marriage of one who could never have me."

"While he loved you it would," said Humfrey hastily. "Yea," as she lifted up her eyes to him, "it would so, as my father will tell you, because he could not truly love that other woman."

Richard smiled sadly, and could not but assent to his son's honest truth and faith.

"Then," said Cis, with the same straightforwardness, sprung of their old fraternal intercourse, "you must quit all love for me save a brother's, Humfrey ; for my Queen mother made me give her my word on my duty never to wed you."

"I know," returned Humfrey calmly. "I have known all that these two years ; but what has that to do with my love ?"

"Come, come, children," said Richard, hardening himself though his eyes were moist; "I did not come here to hear you two discourse like the folks in a pastoral! We may not waste time. Tell me, child, if thou be not forbidden, hath she any purpose for thee?"

"O sir, I fear that what she would most desire is to bestow me abroad with some of her kindred of Lorraine. But I mean to strive hard against it, and pray her earnestly. And, father, I have one great purpose. She saith that these cruel statesmen, who are all below in this castle, have hindered Queen Elizabeth from ever truly hearing and knowing all, and from speaking with her as woman to woman. Father, I will go to London, I will make my way to the Queen, and when she hears who I am—of her own blood and kindred—she must listen to me; and I will tell her what my mother Queen really is, and how cruelly she has been played upon, and entreat of her to see her face to face and talk with her, and judge whether she can have done all she is accused of."

"Thou art a brave maiden, Cis," exclaimed Humfrey with deep feeling.

"Will you take me, sir?" said Cicely, looking up to Master Richard.

"Child, I cannot say at once. It is a perilous purpose, and requires much to be thought over."

"But you will aid me?" she said earnestly.

"If it be thy duty, woe be to me if I gainsay thee," said Richard; "but there is no need to decide as yet. We must await the issue of this trial, if the trial ever take place."

"Will Cavendish saith," put in Humfrey, "that a trial there will be of some sort, whether the Lady consent to plead or not."

"Until that is ended we can do nothing," said his father. "Meantime, Cicely child, we shall be here at hand, and be sure that I will not be slack to aid thee in what may be thy duty as a daughter. So rest thee in that, my wench, and pray that we may be led to know the right."

And Richard spoke as a man of high moral courage in making this promise, well knowing that it might involve himself in great danger. The worst that could befall Cicely might be imprisonment, and a life of constraint, jealously watched; but his own long concealment of her birth might easily be construed into treason, and the horrible consequences of such an accusation were only too fresh in his memory. Yet, as he said afterwards to his son, "There was no forbidding the maiden to do her utmost for her own mother, neither was there any letting her run the risk alone."

To which Humfrey heartily responded.

"The Queen may forbid her, or the purpose may pass away," added Richard, "or it may be clearly useless and impossible to make the attempt; but I cannot as a Christian man strive to dissuade her from doing what she can. And as thou saidst, Humfrey, she is changed. She hath borne her modestly and discreetly, ay and truly, through all. The childishness is gone out of her, and I mark no lightness of purpose in her."

On that afternoon Queen Mary announced that she had yielded to Hatton's representations so far as to consent to appear before the Commissioners, provided her protest against the proceedings were put on record.

"Nay, blame me not, good Melville," she said. "I am wearied out with their arguments. What matters it how they do the deed on which they are bent? It was an ill thing when King Harry the Eighth brought

in this fashion of forcing the law to give a colour to
his will! In the good old times, the blow came without being first baited by one and another, and made a
spectacle to all men, in the name of justice, forsooth!"

Mary Seaton faltered something of her Majesty's
innocence shining out like the light of day.

"Flatter not thyself so far, *ma mie*," said Mary.
"Were mine innocence clearer than the sun they would
blacken it. All that can come of this same trial is
that I may speak to posterity, if they stifle my voice
here, and so be known to have died a martyr to my
faith. Get we to our prayers, girls, rather than feed
on vain hopes *De profundis clamavi.*"

CHAPTER XXXV.

BEFORE THE COMMISSIONERS.

WHO would be permitted to witness the trial? As small matters at hand eclipse great matters farther off, this formed the immediate excitement in Queen Mary's little household, when it was disclosed that she was to appear only attended by Sir Andrew Melville and her two Maries before her judges.

The vast hall had space enough on the ground for numerous spectators, and a small gallery intended for musicians was granted, with some reluctance, to the ladies and gentlemen of the suite, who, as Sir Amias Paulett observed, could do no hurt, if secluded there. Thither then they proceeded, and to Cicely's no small delight, found Humfrey awaiting them there, partly as a guard, partly as a master of the ceremonies, ready to explain the arrangements, and tell the names of the personages who appeared in sight.

"There," said he, " close below us, where you cannot see it, is the chair with a cloth of state over it."

" For our Queen?" asked Jean Kennedy.

" No, madam. It is there to represent the Majesty of Queen Elizabeth. That other chair, half-way down the hall, with the canopy from the beam over it, is for the Queen of Scots."

Jean Kennedy sniffed the air a little at this, but her attention was directed to the gentlemen who began to fill the seats on either side.   Some of them had be- fore had interviews with Queen Mary, and thus were known by sight to her own attendants ; some had been seen by Humfrey during his visit to London ; and even now at a great distance, and a different table, he had been taking his meals with them at the present juncture.

The seats were long benches against the wall, for the Earls on one side, the Barons on the other.   The Lord Chancellor Bromley, in his red and white gown, and Burghley, the Lord Treasurer, with long white beard and hard impenetrable face, sat with them.

"That a man should have such a beard, and yet dare to speak to the Queen as he did two days ago," whispered Cis.

"See," said Mrs. Kennedy, "who is that burly figure with the black eyes and grizzled beard ?"

"That, madam," said Humfrey, "is the Earl of Warwick."

"The brother of the minion Leicester ?" said Jean Kennedy.   "He hath scant show of his comeliness."

"Nay ; they say he is become the best favoured," said Humfrey ; "my Lord of Leicester being grown heavy and red-faced.   He is away in the Nether- lands, or you might judge of him."

"And who," asked the lady, "may be yon, with the strangely-plumed hat and long, yellow hair, like a half- tamed Borderer ?"

"He ?" said Humfrey.   "He is my Lord of Cum- berland.   I marvelled to see him back so soon.   He is here, there, and everywhere ; and when I was in Lon- don was commanding a fleet bearing victuals to relieve the Dutch in Helvoetsluys.   Had I not other work in

hand, I would gladly sail with him, though there be
something fantastic in his humour. But here come the
Knights of the Privy Council, who are to my mind
more noteworthy than the Earls."

The seats of these knights were placed a little below
and beyond those of the noblemen. The courteous Sir
Ralf Sadler looked up and saluted the ladies in the
gallery as he entered. " He was always kindly," said
Jean Kennedy, as she returned the bow. " I am glad
to see him here."

" But oh, Humfrey !" cried Cicely, " who is yonder,
with the short cloak standing on end with pearls, and
the quilted satin waistcoat, jewelled ears, and frizzed
head ? He looks fitter to lead off a dance than a
trial."

" He is Sir Christopher Hatton, her Majesty's Vice-
Chamberlain," replied Humfrey.

" Who, if rumour saith true, made his fortune by a
galliard," said Dr. Bourgoin.

" Here is a contrast to him," said Jean Kennedy.
" See that figure, as puritanical as Sir Amias himself, with
the long face, scant beard, black skull-cap, and plain
crimped ruff. His visage is pulled into so solemn a
length that were we at home in Edinburgh, I should
expect to see him ascend a pulpit, and deliver a screed
to us all on the iniquities of dancing and playing on
the lute !"

" That, madam," said Humfrey, " is Mr. Secretary,
Sir Francis Walsingham."

Here Elizabeth Curll leant forward, looked, and
shivered a little. " Ah, Master Humfrey, is it in that
man's power that my poor brother lies ?"

" 'Tis true, madam," said Humfrey," but indeed you
need not fear. I heard from Will Cavendish last night

that Mr. Curll is well. They have not touched either of the Secretaries to hurt them, and if aught have been avowed, it was by Monsieur Nau, and that on the mere threat. Do you see old Will yonder, Cicely, just within Mr. Secretary's call—with the poke of papers and the tablet?"

"Is that Will Cavendish? How precise and stiff he hath grown, and why doth he not look up and greet us? He knoweth us far better than doth Sir Ralf Sadler; doth he not know we are here?"

"Ay, Mistress Cicely," said Dr. Bourgoin from behind, "but the young gentleman has his fortune to make, and knows better than to look on the seamy side of Court favour."

"Ah! see those scarlet robes," here exclaimed Cis. "Are they the judges, Humfrey?"

"Ay, the two Chief-Justices and the Chief Baron of the Exchequer. There they sit in front of the Earls, and three more judges in front of the Barons."

"And there are more red robes at that little table in front, besides the black ones."

"Those are Doctors of Law, and those in black with coifs are the Attorney and Solicitor General. The rest are clerks and writers and the like."

"It is a mighty and fearful array," said Cicely with a long breath.

"A mighty comedy wherewith to mock at justice," said Jean.

"Prudence, madam, and caution," suggested Dr. Bourgoin. "And hush!"

"A crier here shouted aloud, "Oyez, oyez, oyez! Mary, Queen of Scotland and Dowager of France, come into the Court!"

Then from a door in the centre, leaning on Sir

Andrew Melville's arm, came forward the Queen, in a black velvet dress, her long transparent veil hanging over it from her cap, and followed by the two Maries, one carrying a crimson velvet folding-chair, and the other a footstool. She turned at first towards the throne, but she was motioned aside, and made to perceive that her place was not there. She drew her slender figure up with offended dignity. " I am a queen," she said ; " I married a king of France, and my seat ought to be there."

However, with this protest she passed on to her appointed place, looking sadly round at the assembled judges and lawyers.

" Alas !" she said, " so many counsellors, and not one for me."

Were there any Englishmen there besides Richard Talbot and his son who felt the pathos of this appeal ? One defenceless woman against an array of the legal force of the whole kingdom. It may be feared that the feelings of most were as if they had at last secured some wild, noxious, and incomprehensible animal in their net, on whose struggles they looked with the un- pitying eye of the hunter.

The Lord Chancellor began by declaring that the Queen of England convened the Court as a duty in one who might not bear the sword in vain, to examine into the practices against her own life, giving the Queen of Scots the opportunity of clearing herself.

At the desire of Burghley, the commission was read by the Clerk of the Court, and Mary then made her public protest against its legality, or power over her.

It was a wonderful thing, as those spectators in the gallery felt, to see how brave and how acute was the defence of that solitary lady, seated there with all those

learned men against her; her papers gone, nothing left
to her but her brain and her tongue. No loss of dignity nor of gentleness was shown in her replies; they
were always simple and direct. The difficulty for her
was all the greater that she had not been allowed to
know the form of the accusation, before it was hurled
against her in full force by Mr. Serjeant Gawdy, who
detailed the whole of the conspiracy of Ballard and
Babington in all its branches, and declared her to have
known and approved of it, and to have suggested the
manner of executing it.

Breathlessly did Cicely listen as the Queen rose up.
Humfrey watched her almost more closely than the
royal prisoner. When there was a denial of all knowledge or intercourse with Ballard or Babington, Jean
Kennedy's hard-lined face never faltered; but Cicely's
brows came together in concern at the mention of
the last name, and did not clear as the Queen explained that though many Catholics might indeed write
to her with offers of service, she could have no knowledge of anything they might attempt. To confute
this, extracts from their confessions were read, and
likewise that letter of Babington's which he had
written to her detailing his plans, and that lengthy
answer, brought by the blue-coated serving-man, in
which the mode of carrying her off from Chartley was
suggested, and which had the postscript desiring to
know the names of the six who were to remove the
usurping competitor.

The Queen denied this letter flatly, declaring that
it might have been written with her alphabet of
ciphers, but was certainly none of hers. " There may
have been designs against the Queen and for procuring
my liberty," she said, " but I, shut up in close prison.

was not aware of them, and how can I be made to answer for them ? Only lately did I receive a letter asking my pardon if schemes were made on my behalf without my privity, nor can anything be easier than to counterfeit a cipher, as was lately proved by a young man in France. Verily, I greatly fear that if these same letters were traced to their deviser, it would prove to be the one who is sitting here. Think you," she added, turning to Walsingham, " think you, Mr. Secretary, that I am ignorant of your devices used so craftily against me ? Your spies surrounded me on every side, but you know not, perhaps, that some of your spies have been false and brought intelligence to me. And if such have been his dealings, my Lords," she said, appealing to the judges and peers, " how can I be assured that he hath not counterfeited my ciphers to bring me to my death ? Hath he not already practised against my life and that of my son ?"

Walsingham rose in his place, and lifting up his hands and eyes declared, " I call God to record that as a private person I have done nothing unbeseeming an honest man, nor as a public person have I done anything to dishonour my place."

Somewhat ironically Mary admitted this disavowal, and after some unimportant discussion, the Court adjourned until the next day, it being already late, according to the early habits of the time.

Cicely had been entirely carried along by her mother's pleading. Tears had started as Queen Mary wept her indignant tears, and a glow had risen in her cheeks at the accusation of Walsingham. Ever and anon she looked to Humfrey's face for sympathy, but he sat gravely listening, his two hands clasped over the hilt of his sword, and his chin resting on them, as if to prevent a muscle of his face from moving. When they rose up to leave the galleries, and there was the power to say a word, she turned to him earnestly.

"A piteous sight," he said, "and a right gallant defence."

He did not mean it, but the words struck like lead on Cicely's heart, for they did not amount to an acquittal before the tribunal of his secret conviction, any more than did Walsingham's disavowal, for who could tell what Mr. Secretary's conscience *did* think unbecoming to his office?

Cicely found her mother on her couch giving a free course to her tears, in the reaction after the strain and effort of her defence. Melville and the Maries were assuring her that she had most bravely confuted her enemies, and that she had only to hold on with equal courage to the end. Mrs. Kennedy and Dr. Bourgoin came in to join in the same encouragements, and the commendation evidently soothed her. "However it may end," she said, "Mary of Scotland shall not go down to future ages as a craven spirit. But let us not discuss it further, my dear friends, my head aches, and I can bear no further word at present."

Dr. Bourgoin made her take some food and then lie down to rest, while in an outer room a lute was played and a low soft song was sung. She had not slept all the previous night, but she fell asleep, holding the hand of Cicely, who was on a cushion by her side. The girl, having been likewise much disturbed, slept too, and only gradually awoke as her mother was sitting up on her couch discussing the next day's defence with Melville and Bourgoin.

"I fear me, madam, there is no holding to the profession of entire ignorance," said Melville.

"They have no letters from Babington to me to show," said the Queen. "I took care of *that* by the help of this good bairn. I can defy them to produce the originals out of all my ransacked cabinets."

"They have the copies both of them and of your Majesty's replies, and Nau and Curll to verify them."

"What are copies worth, or what are dead and tortured men's confessions worth?" said Mary.

"Were your Majesty a private person they would never be accepted as evidence," said Melville; "but——"

"But because I am a Queen and a Catholic there is no justice for me," said Mary. "Well, what is the defence you would have me confine myself to, my sole privy counsellors?"

Here Cis, to show she was awake, pressed her mother's hand and looked up in her face, but Mary, though returning the glance and the pressure, did not send her away, while Melville recommended strongly that the Queen should continue to insist on the imperfection of the evidence adduced against her, which he said might so touch some of the lawyers, or the nobles, that Burghley and Walsingham might be afraid to proceed. If this failed her, she must allow her knowledge of the plot for her own escape and the Spanish invasion, but strenuously deny the part which concerned Elizabeth's life.

"That it is which they above all desire to fix on me," said the Queen.

Cicely's brain was in confusion. Surely she had heard those letters read in the hall. Were they false or genuine? The Queen had utterly denied them there. Now she seemed to think the only point was to prove that these were not the originals. Dr. Bourgoin seemed to feel the same difficulty.

" Madame will pardon me," he said; " I have not been of her secret councils, but can she not, if rightly dealt with, prove those two letters that were read to have been forged by her enemies ?"

" What I could do is this, my good Bourgoin," said Mary; " were I only confronted with Nau and Curll, I could prove that the letter I received from Babington bore nothing about the destroying the usurping competitor.   The poor faithful lad was a fool, but not so great a fool as to tell me such things. And, on the other hand, hath either of you, my friends, ever seen in me such symptoms of midsummer madness as that I should be asking the names of the six who were to do the deed ?   What cared I for their names ?   I—who only wished to know as little of the matter as possible !"

" Can your Majesty prove that you knew nothing ?" asked Melville.

Mary paused.   " They cannot prove by fair means that I knew anything," said she, " for I did not.   Of course I was aware that Elizabeth must be taken out of the way, or the heretics would be rallying round her ; but there is no lack of folk who delight in work of that sort, and why should I meddle with the knowledge ?   With the Prince of Parma in London, she, if she hath the high courage she boasteth of, would soon cause the Spanish pikes to use small ceremony with her !   Why should I concern myself about poor Antony and his five gentlemen ?   But it is the same as it was twenty years ago.   What I know will have to be, and yet choose not to hear of, is made the head and front of mine offending, that the real actors may go free ! And because I have writ naught that they can bring against me, they take my letters and add to and garble

them, till none knows where to have them. Would
that we were in France! There it was a good sword-cut
or pistol-shot at once, and one took one's chance of a
return, without all this hypocrisy of law and justice to
weary one out and make men double traitors."

"Methought Walsingham winced when your Majesty went to the point with him," said Bourgoin.

"And you put up with his explanation?" said
Melville.

"Truly I longed to demand of what practices Mr.
Secretary *in his office,*—not as a private person—
would be ashamed; but it seemed to me that they
might call it womanish spite, and to that the Queen of
Scots will never descend!"

"Pity but that we had Babington's letter! Then
might we put him to confusion by proving the addi-
tions," said Melville.

"It is not possible, my good friend. The letter is
at the bottom of the Castle well; is it not, *mignonne?*
Mourn for it not, Andrew. It would have been of
little avail, and it carried with it stuff that Mr. Secretary would give almost his precious place to possess,
and that might be fatal to more of us. I hoped that
there might have been safety for poor Babington in
the destruction of that packet, never guessing at the
villainy of yon Burton brewer, nor of those who set
him on. Come, it serves not to fret ourselves any
more. I must answer as occasion serves me; speaking
not so much to Elizabeth's Commission, who have fore-
doomed me, as to all Christendom, and to the Scots
and English of all ages, who will be my judges."

Her judges? Ay! but how? With the same
enthusiastic pity and indignation, mixed with the same
misgiving as her own daughter felt. Not wholly inno-

cent, not wholly guilty, yet far less guilty than those who had laid their own crimes on her in Scotland, or who plotted to involve her in meshes partly woven by herself in England. The evil done to her was frightful, but it would have been powerless had she been wholly blameless. Alas! is it not so with all of us?

The second day's trial came on. Mary Seaton was so overpowered with the strain she had gone through that the Queen would not take her into the hall, but let Cicely sit at her feet instead. On this day none of the Crown lawyers took part in the proceedings; for, as Cavendish whispered to Humfrey, there had been high words between them and my Lord Treasurer and Mr. Secretary; and they had declared themselves incapable of conducting a prosecution so inconsistent with the forms of law to which they were accustomed. The pedantic fellows wanted more direct evidence, he said, and Humfrey honoured them.

Lord Burghley then conducted the proceedings, and they had thus a more personal character. The Queen, however, acted on Melville's advice, and no longer denied all knowledge of the conspiracy, but insisted that she was ignorant of the proposed murder of Elizabeth, and argued most pertinently that a copy of a deciphered cipher, without the original, was no proof at all, desiring further that Nau and Curll should be examined in her presence. She reminded the Commissioners how their Queen herself had been called in question for Wyatt's rebellion, in spite of her innocence. "Heaven is my witness," she added, "that much as I desire the safety and glory of the Catholic religion, I would not purchase it at the price of blood. I would rather play Esther than Judith."

Her defence was completed by her taking off the

ring which Elizabeth had sent to her at Lochleven. "This," she said, holding it up, "your Queen sent to me in token of amity and protection. You best know how that pledge has been redeemed." Therewith she claimed another day's hearing, with an advocate granted to her, or else that, being a Princess, she might be believed on the word of a Princess.

This completed her defence, except so far that when Burghley responded in a speech of great length, she interrupted, and battled point by point, always keeping in view the strong point of the insufficient evidence and her own deprivation of the chances of confuting what was adduced against her.

It was late in the afternoon when he concluded. There was a pause, as though for a verdict by the Commissioners. Instead of this, Mary rose and repeated her appeal to be tried before the Parliament of England at Westminster. No reply was made, and the Court broke up.

CHAPTER XXXVI.

A VENTURE.

" MOTHER, dear mother, do but listen to me."

"I must listen, child, when thou callest me so from your heart; but it is of no use, my poor little one. They have referred the matter to the Star Chamber, that they may settle it there with closed doors and no forms of law. Thou couldst do nothing! And could I trust thee to go wandering to London, like a maiden in a ballad, all alone?"

"Nay, madam, I should not go alone. My father, I mean Mr. Talbot, would take me."

"Come, bairnie, that is presuming overmuch on the good man's kindness."

"I do not speak without warrant, madam. I told him what I longed to do, and he said it might be my duty, and if it were so, he would not gainsay me; but that he could not let me go alone, and would go with me. And he can get access for me to the Queen. He has seen her himself, and so has Humfrey; and Diccon is a gentleman pensioner."

"There have been ventures enough for me already," said Mary. "I will bring no more faithful heads into peril."

"Then will you not consent, mother? He will

Q

quit the castle to-morrow, and I am to see him in the
morning and give him an answer. If you would let
me go, he would crave license to take me home, saying
that I look paler than my wont."

"And so thou dost, child. If I could be sure of
ever seeing thee again, I should have proposed thy
going home to good Mistress Susan's tendance for a
little space. But it is not to be thought of. I could
not risk thee, or any honest loving heart, on so desperate a stake as mine! I love thee, mine ain, true,
leal lassie, all the more, and I honour him; but it may
not be! Ask me no more."

Mary was here interrupted by a request from Sir
Christopher Hatton for one of the many harassing
interviews that beset her during the days following the
trial, when judgment was withheld, according to the
express command of the vacillating Elizabeth, and the
case remitted to the Star Chamber. Lord Burghley
considered this hesitation to be the effect of judicial
blindness—so utterly had hatred and fear of the future
shut his eyes to all sense of justice and fair play.

Cicely felt all youth's disappointment in the rejec-
tion of its grand schemes. But to her surprise at night
Mary addressed her again, "My daughter, did that true-
hearted foster-father of thine speak in sooth?"

"He never doth otherwise," returned Cicely.

"For," said her mother, "I have thought of a way
of gaining thee access to the Queen, far less perilous to
him, and less likely to fail. I will give thee letters to
M. De Châteauneuf, the French Ambassador, whom I
have known in old times, with full credentials. It
might be well to have with thee those that I left with
Mistress Talbot. Then he will gain thee admittance,
and work for thee as one sent from France, and protected

by the rights of the Embassy.   Thus, Master Richard
need never appear in the matter at all, and at any
rate thou wouldst be secure.   Châteauneuf would find
means of sending thee abroad if needful."

"Oh! I would return to you, madam my mother,
or wait for you in London."

"That must be as the wills above decree," said Mary
sadly.   "It is folly in me, but I cannot help grasping at
the one hope held out to me.   There is that within me
that *will* hope and strive to the end, though I am using
my one precious jewel to weight the line I am casting
across the gulf.   At least they cannot do thee great
harm, my good child."

The Queen sat up half the night writing letters, one
to Elizabeth, one to Châteauneuf, and another to the
Duchess of Lorraine, which Cis was to deliver in case
of her being sent over to the Continent.   But the Queen
committed the conduct of the whole affair to M. De
Châteauneuf, since she could completely trust his discretion and regard for her; and, moreover, it was possible
that the face of affairs might undergo some great altera-
tion before Cicely could reach London.   Mr. Talbot must
necessarily go home first, being bound to do so by his
commission to the Earl.   "And, hark thee," said the
Queen, "what becomes of the young gallant?"

"I have not heard, madam," said Cicely, not liking
the tone.

"If my desires still have any effect," said Mary,
"he will stay here.   I will not have my damosel
errant squired by a youth under five-and-twenty."

"I promised you, madam, and he wots it," said
Cicely, with spirit.

"He wots it, doth he?" said the Queen, in rather a
provoking voice.   "No, no, *mignonne;* with all respect

to their honour and discretion, we do not put flint and
steel together, when we do not wish to kindle a fire.
Nay, little one, I meant not to vex thee, when thou
art doing one of the noblest deeds daughter ever did
for mother, and for a mother who sent thee away from
her, and whom thou hast scarce known for more than
two years!"

Cicely was sure to see her foster-father after morning prayers on the way from the chapel across the
inner court. Here she was able to tell him of the
Queen's consent, over which he looked grave, having
secretly persuaded himself that Mary would think the
venture too great, and not hopeful enough to be made.
He could not, however, wonder that the unfortunate
lady should catch at the least hope of preserving her
life; and she had dragged too many down in the whirlpool to leave room for wonder that she should consent
to peril her own daughter therein. Moreover, he
would have the present pleasure of taking her home
with him to his Susan, and who could say what would
happen in the meantime?

"Thou hast counted the cost?" he said.

"Yea, sir," Cis answered, as the young always do;
adding, "the Queen saith that if we commit all to the
French Ambassador, M. De Châteauneuf, who is her
very good friend, he will save you from any peril."

"Hm! I had rather be beholden to no Frenchman," muttered Richard, "but we will see, we will see.
I must now to Paulett to obtain consent to take thee
with me. Thou art pale and changed enough indeed
to need a blast of Hallamshire air, my poor maid."

So Master Richard betook him to the knight, a man
of many charges, and made known that finding his
daughter somewhat puling and sickly, he wished

having, as she told him, the consent of the Queen of Scots, to take her home with him for a time.

"You do well, Mr. Talbot," said Sir Amias. "In sooth, I have only marvelled that a pious and godly man like you should have consented to let her abide so long, at her tender age, among these papistical, idolatrous, and bloodthirsty women."

"I think not that she hath taken harm," said Richard.

"I have done my poor best; I have removed the priest of Baal," said the knight; "I have caused godly ministers constantly to preach sound doctrine in the ears of all who would hearken; and I have uplifted my testimony whensoever it was possible. But it is not well to expose the young to touching the accursed thing, and this lady hath shown herself greatly affected to your daughter, so that she might easily be seduced from the truth. Yet, sir, bethink you is it well to remove the maiden from witnessing that which will be a warning for ever of the judgment that falleth on conspiracy and idolatry?"

"You deem the matter so certain?" said Richard.

"Beyond a doubt, sir. This lady will never leave these walls alive. There can be no peace for England nor safety for our blessed and gracious Queen while she lives. Her guilt is certain; and as Mr. Secretary said to me last night, he and the Lord Treasurer are determined that for no legal quibbles, nor scruples of mercy from our ever-pitiful Queen, shall she now escape. Her Majesty, however her womanish heart may doubt now, will rejoice when the deed is done. Methinks I showed you the letter she did me the honour to write, thanking me for the part I took in conveying the lady suddenly to Tixall."

Richard had already read that letter three times, so he avowed his knowledge of it.

"You will not remove your son likewise?" added Sir Amias. "He hath an acquaintance with this lady's people, which is useful in one so thoroughly to be trusted ; and moreover, he will not be tampered with. For, sir, I am never without dread of some attempt being made to deal with this lady privily, in which case I should be the one to bear all the blame. Wherefore I have made request to have another honourable gentleman joined with me in this painful wardship."

Richard had no desire to remove his son. He shared Queen Mary's feelings on the inexpediency of Humfrey forming part of the escort of the young lady, and thought it was better for both to see as little of one another as possible.

Sir Amias accordingly, on his morning visit of inspection, intimated to the Queen that Mr. Talbot wished his daughter to return home with him for the recovery of her health. He spoke as if the whole suite were at his own disposal, and Mary resented it in her dignified manner.

"The young lady hath already requested license from us," she said, " and we have granted it. She will return when her health is fully restored."

Sir Amias had forbearance enough not to hint that unless the return were speedy, she would scarcely find the Queen there, and the matter was settled. Master Richard would not depart until after dinner, when other gentlemen were going, and this would enable Cicely to make up her mails, and there would still be time to ride a stage before dark. Her own horse was in the stables, and her goods would be bestowed in cloak bags on the saddles of the grooms who had accompanied Mr.

Talbot; for, small as was the estate of Bridgefield, for safety's sake he could not have gone on so long an expedition without a sufficient guard.

The intervening time was spent by the Queen in instructing her daughter how to act in various contingencies. If it were possible to the French Ambassador to present her as freshly come from the Soissons convent, where she was to have been reared, it would save Mr. Talbot from all risk; but the Queen doubted whether she could support the character, so English was her air, though there *were* Scottish and English nuns at Soissons, and still more at Louvaine and Douay, who *might* have brought her up.

" I cannot feign, madam," said Cicely, alarmed. "Oh, I hope I need only speak truth !" and her tone sounded much more like a confession of incapacity than a moral objection, and so it was received : " Poor child, I know thou canst not act a part, and thy return to the honest mastiffs will not further thee in it ; but I have bidden Châteauneuf to do what he can for thee— and after all the eyes will not be very critical."

If there still was time, Cicely was to endeavour first of all to obtain of Elizabeth that Mary might be brought to London to see her, and be judged before Parliament with full means of defence. If this were no longer possible, Cicely might attempt to expose Walsingham's contrivance ; but this would probably be too dangerous. Châteauneuf must judge. Or, as another alternative, Queen Mary gave Cicely the ring already shown at the trial, and with that as her pledge, a solemn offer was to be made on her behalf to retire into a convent in Austria, or in one of the Roman Catholic cantons of Switzerland, out of the reach of Spain and France, and there take the veil, resigning all her rights to her son. All her money had been taken away, but she told Cicely she had given orders to Châteauneuf to supply from her French dowry all that might be needed for the expenses that must be incurred.

Now that the matter was becoming so real, Cicely's heart quailed a little. Castles in the air that look heroic at the first glance would not so remain did not they show themselves terrible at a nearer approach, and the maiden wondered whether Queen Elizabeth would be much more formidable than my Lady Countess in a rage!

And what would become of herself? Would she be detained in the bondage in which the poor sisters of the Grey blood had been kept? Or would her mother carry her off to these strange lands? . . . It was all strange, and the very boldness of her offer, since it had been thus accepted, made her feel helpless and passive in the grasp of the powers that her simple wish had set moving.

The letters were sewn up in the most ingenious manner in her dress by Mary Seaton, in case any search should be made; but the only woman Sir Amias would be able to employ in such a matter was purblind and helpless, and they trusted much to his implicit faith in the Talbots.

There was only just time to complete her preparations before she was summoned; and with an almost convulsive embrace from her mother, and whispered benedictions from Jean Kennedy, she left the dreary walls of Fotheringhay.

Humfrey rode with them through the Chase. Both he and Cicely were very silent. When the time came for parting, Cicely said, as she laid her hand in his,

"Dear brother, for my sake do all thou canst for her with honour."

"That will I," said Humfrey. "Would that I were going with thee, Cicely!"

"So would not I," she returned; "for then there would be one true heart the less to watch over her."

"Come, daughter!" said Richard, who had engaged one of the gentlemen in conversation so as to leave them to themselves. "We must be jogging. Fare thee well, my son, till such time as thy duties permit thee to follow us."

Q*

CHAPTER XXXVII.

MY LADY'S REMORSE.

"And have you brought her back again! O my lass! my lass!" cried Mistress Susan, surprised and delighted out of her usual staid composure, as, going out to greet her husband, an unexpected figure was seen by his side, and Cicely sprang into her arms as if they were truly a haven of rest.

Susan looked over her head, even in the midst of the embrace, with the eyes of one hungering for her first-born son, but her husband shook his head. " No, mother, we have not brought thee the boy. Thou must content thyself with her thou hast here for a little space."

" I hope it bodes not ill," said Susan.

"It bodes," said Richard, "that I have brought thee back a good daughter with a pair of pale cheeks, which must be speedily coloured anew in our northern breezes."

" Ah, how sweet to be here at home," cried Cicely, turning round in rapturous greeting to all the serving men and women, and all the dogs. " We want only the boys! Where is Ned?"

Their arrival having been unannounced, Ned was with Master Sniggius, whose foremost scholar he now

was, and who kept him much later than the other lads
to prepare him for Cambridge ; but it was the return to
this tender foster-mother that seemed such extreme
bliss to Cicely. All was most unlike her reluctant
return two years previously, when nothing but her
inbred courtesy and natural sweetness of disposition
had prevented her from being contemptuous of the
country home. Now every stone, every leaf, seemed
precious to her, and she showed herself, even as she
ascended the steps to the hall, determined not to be
the guest but the daughter. There was a little movement on the parents' part, as if they bore in mind that
she came as a princess ; but she flew to draw up
Master Richard's chair, and put his wife's beside it, nor
would she sit, till they had prayed her to do so ; and
it was all done with such a graceful bearing, the noble
carriage of her head had become so much more remarkable, and a sweet readiness and responsiveness of manner
had so grown upon her, that Susan looked at her in
wondering admiration, as something more her own and
yet less her own than ever, tracing in her for the first
time some of the charms of the Queen of Scots.

All the household hovered about in delight, and
confidences could not be exchanged just then : the
travellers had to eat and drink, and they were only just
beginning to do so when Ned came home. He was of
slighter make than his brothers, and had a more
scholarly aspect : but his voice made itself heard before
him. " Is it true ? Is it true that my father is come ?
And our Cis too ? Ha !" and he rushed in, hardly
giving himself time for the respectful greeting to his
father, before he fell upon Cis with undoubting brotherly
delight.

" Is Humfrey come ?" he asked as soon as he could

take breath. " No ? I thought 'twas too good to be all true."

" How did you hear ?"

" Hob the hunter brought up word that the Queen's head was off. What ?" as Cicely gave a start and little scream. " Is it not so ?"

" No, indeed, boy," said his father. " What put that folly into his head ?"

" Because he saw, or thought he saw, Humfrey and Cis riding home with you, sir, and so thought all was over with the Queen of Scots. My Lady, they say, had one of her shrieking fits, and my Lord sent down to ask whether I knew aught; and when he found that I did not, would have me go home at once to bid you come up immediately to the Manor ; and before I had gotten out Dapple, there comes another message to say that, in as brief space as it will take to saddle them, there will be beasts here to bring up you and my mother and Cis, to tell my Lady Countess all that has befallen."

Cis's countenance so changed that kind Susan said, " I will make thine excuses to my Lady. Thou art weary and ill at ease, and I cannot have thee set forth at once again."

" The Queen would never have sent such sudden and hasty orders," said Cicely. " Mother, can you not stay with me ?—I have so much to say to you, and my time is short."

The Talbots were, however, too much accustomed to obedience to the peremptory commands of their feudal chiefs to venture on such disobedience. Susan's proposal had been a great piece of audacity, on which she would hardly have ventured but for her consciousness that the maiden was no Talbot at all.

Yet to Cis the dear company of her mother Susan, even in the Countess's society, seemed too precious to be resigned, and she had likewise been told that Lady Shrewsbury's mind had greatly changed towards Mary, and that since the irritation of the captive's presence had been removed, she remembered only the happier and kindlier portion of their past intercourse. There had been plenty of quarrels with her husband, but none so desperate as before, and at this present time the Earl and Countess were united against the surviving sons, who, with Gilbert at their head, were making large demands on them. Cicely felt grateful to the Earl for his absence from Fotheringhay, and, though disappointed of her peaceful home evening, declared she would come up to the Lodge rather than lose sight of "mother." The stable people, more considerate than their Lord and Lady, proved to have sent a horse litter for the conveyance of the ladies called out on the wet dark October evening, and here it was that Cis could enjoy her first precious moment of privacy with one for whom she had so long yearned. Susan rejoiced in the heavy lumbering conveyance as a luxury, sparing the maiden's fatigue, and she was commencing some inquiries into the indisposition which had procured this holiday, when Cicely broke in, "O mother, nothing aileth me. It is not for that cause—but oh! mother, I am to go to see Queen Elizabeth, and strive with her for her—for my mother's life and freedom."

"Thou! poor little maid. Doth thy father—what am I saying? Doth my husband know?"

"Oh yes. He will take me. He saith it is my duty."

"Then it must be well," said Susan in an altered voice on hearing this. "From whom came the proposal?"

"I made it," said Cicely in a low, feeble voice on the verge of tears. "Oh, dear mother, thou wilt not tell any one how faint of heart I am? I did mean it in sooth, but I never guessed how dreadful it would grow now I am pledged to it."

"Thou art pledged, then, and canst not falter?"

"Never," said Cicely; "I would not that any should know it, not even my father; but mother, mother, I could not help telling you. You will let no one guess? I know it is unworthy, but——"

"Not unworthy to fear, my poor child, so long as thou dost not waver."

"It *is*, it *is* unworthy of my lineage. My mother queen would say so," cried Cis, drawing herself up.

"Giving way would be unworthy," said Susan, "but turn thou to thy God, my child, and He will give thee strength to carry through whatever is the duty of a faithful daughter towards this poor lady; and my husband, thou sayest, holds that so it is?"

"Yea, madam; he craved license to take me home, since I have truly often been ailing since those dreadful days at Tixall, and he hath promised to go to London with me."

"And is this to be done in thine own true name?" asked Susan, trembling somewhat at the risk to her husband, as well as to the maiden.

"I trow that it is," said Cis, "but the matter is to be put into the hands of M. de Châteauneuf, the French Ambassador. I have a letter here," laying her hand on her bosom, "which, the Queen declares, will thoroughly prove to him who I am, and if I go as under his protection, none can do my father any harm."

Susan hoped so, but she trusted to understand all

better from her husband, though her heart failed her
as much as, or even perhaps more than, did that of
poor little Cis. Master Richard had sped on before
their tardy conveyance, and had had time to give the
heads of his intelligence before they reached the Manor-
house, and when they were conducted to my Lady's
chamber, they saw him, by the light of a large fire,
standing before the Earl and Countess, cap in hand,
much as a groom or gamekeeper would now stand
before his master and mistress.

The Earl, however, rose to receive the ladies; but
the Countess, no great observer of ceremony towards
other people, whatever she might exact from them
towards herself, cried out, "Come hither, come hither,
Cicely Talbot, and tell me how it fares with the poor
lady," and as the maiden came forward in the dim
light—"Ha! What! Is't she?" she cried, with a
sudden start. On my faith, what has she done to
thee? Thou art as like her as the foal to the mare."

This exclamation disconcerted the visitors, but
luckily for them the Earl laughed and declared that
he could see no resemblance in Mistress Cicely's dark
brows to the arched ones of the Queen of Scots, to
which his wife replied testily, "Who said there was?
The maid need not be uplifted, for there's nothing
alike between them, only she hath caught the trick of
her bearing so as to startle me in the dark, my head
running on the poor lady. I could have sworn 'twas
she coming in, as she was when she first came to our
care fifteen years agone. Pray Heaven she may not
haunt the place! How fareth she in health, wench?"

"Well, madam, save when the rheumatic pains take
her," said Cicely.

"And still of good courage?"

"That, madam, nothing can daunt."

Seats, though only joint stools, were given to the ladies, but Susan found herself no longer trembling at the effects of the Countess's insolence upon Cicely, who seemed to accept it all as a matter of course, and almost of indifference, though replying readily and with a gentle grace, most unlike her childish petulance.

Many close inquiries from the Earl and Countess were answered by Richard and the young lady, until they had a tolerably clear idea of the situation. The Countess wept bitterly, and to Cicely's great amazement began bemoaning herself that she was not still the poor lady's keeper. It was a shame to put her where there were no women to feel for her. Lady Shrewsbury had apparently forgotten that no one had been so virulent against the Queen as herself.

And when it was impossible to deny that things looked extremely ill, and that Burghley and Walsingham seemed resolved not to let slip this opportunity of ridding themselves of the prisoner, my Lady burst out with, "Ah! there it is! She will die, and my promise is broken, and she will haunt me to my dying day, all along of that venomous toad and spiteful viper, Mary Talbot."

A passionate fit of weeping succeeded, mingled with vituperations of her daughter Mary, far more than of herself, and amid it all, during Susan's endeavours at soothing, Cicely gathered that the cause of the Countess's despair was that in the time of her friendship and amity, she had uttered an assurance that the Queen need not fear death, as she would contrive means of safety. And on her own ground, in her own Castle or Lodge, there could be little doubt that she would have been able to have done so. The Earl, indeed, shook his head, but repented, for she laughed at him half angrily, half hysterically, for thinking he could have prevented anything that she was set upon.

And now she said and fully believed that the misunderstanding which had resulted in the removal of the prisoner had been entirely due to the slanders and deceits of her own daughter Mary, and her husband Gilbert, with whom she was at this time on the worst of terms.   And thus she laid on them the blame of the Queen's death (if that was really decreed), but though she outwardly blamed every creature save herself, such agony of mind, and even terror, proved that in very truth there must have been the conviction at the bottom of her heart that it was her own fault.

The Earl had beckoned away Master Richard, both glad to escape; but Cicely had to remain, and filled with compassion for one whom she had always regarded previously as an enemy, she could not help saying, " Dear madam, take comfort; I am going to bear a petition to the Queen's Majesty from the captive lady, and if she will hear me all will yet be well."

" How !   What ?   How !   Thou little moppet ! Knows she what she says, Susan Talbot ?"

Susan made answer that she had had time to hear no particulars yet, but that Cicely averred that she was going with her father's consent, whereupon Richard was immediately summoned back to explain.

The Earl and Countess could hardly believe that he should have consented that his daughter should be thus employed, and he had to excuse himself with what he could not help feeling were only half truths.

" The poor lady," he said, " is denied all power of sending word or letter to the Queen save through those whom she views as her enemies, and therefore she longed earnestly either to see her Majesty, or to hold communication with her through one whom she knoweth to be both simple and her own friend."

"Yea," said the Countess, "I could well have done this for her.could I but have had speech with her. Or she might have sent Bess Pierrepoint, who surely would have been a more fitting messenger."

"Save that she hath not had access to the Queen cf Scots of late," said Richard.

"Yea, and her father would scarcely be willing to risk the Queen's displeasure," said the Earl.

"Art thou ready to abide it, Master Richard?" said the Countess, "though after all it could do *you* little harm." And her tone marked the infinite distance she placed between him and Sir Henry Pierrepoint, the husband of her daughter.

"That is true, madam," said Richard; "and moreover, I cannot reconcile it to my conscience to debar the poor lady from any possible opening of safety."

"Thou art a good man, Richard," said the Earl, and therewith both he and the Countess became extremely, nay, almost inconveniently, desirous to forward the petitioner on her way. To listen to them that night, they would have had her go as an emissary of the house of Shrewsbury, and only the previous quarrel with Lord Talbot and his wife prevented them from proposing that she should be led to the foot of the throne by Gilbert himself.

Cicely began to be somewhat alarmed at plans that would disconcert all the instructions she had received, and only her old habits of respect kept her silent when she thought Master Richard not ready enough to refuse all these offers.

At last he succeeded in obtaining license to depart,

and no sooner was Cicely again shut up with Mistress
Susan in the litter than she exclaimed, " Now will it
be most hard to carry out the Queen's orders that I
should go first to the French Ambassador.   I would
that my Lady Countess would not think naught can
succeed without her meddling."

" Thou shouldst have let father tell thy purpose in
his own way," said Susan.

" Ah! mother, I am an indiscreet simpleton, not fit for
such a work as I have taken in hand," said poor Cis.
" Here hath my foolish tongue traversed it already !"

" Fear not," said Susan, as one who well knew the
nature of her kinswoman ; " belike she will have cooled
to-morrow, all the more because father said naught to
the nayward."

Susan was uneasy enough herself, and very desirous
to hear all from her husband in private.   And that
night he told her that he had very little hope of the
intercession being availing.   He believed that the
Treasurer and Secretary were absolutely determined on
Mary's death, and would sooner or later force consent
from the Queen ; but there was the possibility that
Elizabeth's feelings might be so far stirred that on a
sudden impulse she might set Mary at liberty, and
place her beyond their reach.

" And hap what may," he said, " when a daughter
offereth to do her utmost for a mother in peril of death,
what right have I to hinder her ?"

" May God guard the duteous !" said Susan.   " But
oh ! husband, is she worthy, for whom the child is thus
to lead you into peril ? "

" She is her mother," repeated Richard.   " Had I
erred—— "

" Which you never could do," broke in the wife.

"I am a sinful man," said he.

"Yea, but there are deeds you never could have done."

"By God's grace I trust not; but hear me out, wife. Mine errors, nay, my crimes, would not do away with the duty owed to me by my sons. How, then, should any sins of this poor Queen withhold her daughter from rendering her all the succour in her power? And thou, thou thyself, Susan, hast taken her for thine own too long to endure to let her undertake the matter alone and unaided."

"She would not attempt it thus," said Susan.

"I cannot tell; but I should thus be guilty of foiling her in a brave and filial purpose."

"And yet thou dost hold her poor mother a guilty woman?"

"Said I so? Nay, Susan, I am as dubious as ever I was on that head."

"After hearing the trial?"

"A word in thine ear, my discreet wife. The trial convinced me far more that place makes honest men act like cruel knaves than of aught else."

"Then thou holdest her innocent?"

"I said not so. I have known too long how she lives by the weaving of webs. I know not how it is, but these great folks seem not to deem that truth in word and deed is a part of their religion. For my part, I should distrust whatever godliness did not lead to truth, but a plain man never knows where to have them. That she and poor Antony Babington were in league to bring hither the Spaniards and restore the Pope, I have no manner of doubt on the word of both, but then they deem it—Heaven help them—a virtuous act; and it might be lawful in her, seeing that she has

always called herself a free sovereign unjustly detained.
What he stuck at and she denies, is the purpose of
murdering the Queen's Majesty."

"Sure that was the head and front of the poor
young man's offending."

"So it was, but not until he had been urged thereto
by his priests, and had obtained her consent in a letter.
Heaven forgive me if I misjudge any one, but my belief
is this—that the letters, whereof only the deciphered
copies were shown, did not quit the hands of either the
one or the other, such as we heard them at Fotheringhay.
So poor Babington said, so saith the Queen of Scots,
demanding vehemently to have them read in her presence before Nau and Curll, who could testify to them.
Cis deemeth that the true letter from Babington is in
a packet which, on learning from Humfrey his suspicion that there was treachery, the Queen gave her,
and she threw down a well at Chartley."

"That was pity."

"Say not so, for had the original letter been seized,
it would only have been treated in the same manner
as the copy, and never allowed to reach Queen Elizabeth."

"I am glad poor Cicely's mother can stand clear of
that guilt," said Susan. "I served her too long, and
received too much gentle treatment from her, to brook
the thought that she could be so far left to herself."

"Mind you, dame," said Richard, "I am not wholly
convinced that she was not aware that her friends would
in some way or other bring about the Queen's death,
and that she would scarce have visited it very harshly,
but she is far too wise—ay, and too tender-hearted, to
have entered into the matter beforehand. So I think
her not wholly guiltless, though the wrongs she hath

suffered have been so great that I would do whatever
was not disloyal to mine own Queen to aid her to
obtain justice."

"You are doing much, much indeed," said Susan ;
"and all this time you have told me nothing of my son,
save what all might hear.   How fares he ? is his heart
still set on this poor maid ?"

"And ever will be," said his father.   "His is not an
outspoken babbling love like poor Master Nau, who
they say was so inspired at finding himself in the same
city with Bess Pierrepoint that he could talk of nothing
else, and seemed to have no thought of his own danger
or his Queen's.   No, but he hath told me that he will
give up all to serve her, without hope of requital ; for
her mother hath made her forswear him, and though
she be not always on his tongue, he will do so, if I
mistake not his steadfastness."

Susan sighed, but she knew that the love, that had
begun when the lonely boy hailed the shipwrecked
infant as his little sister, was of a calm, but unquench-
able nature, were it for weal or woe.   She could not
but be thankful that the express mandate of both the
parents had withheld her son from sharing the danger
which was serious enough even for her husband's
prudence and coolness of head.

By the morning, as she had predicted, the ardour
of the Earl and Countess had considerably slackened ;
and though still willing to forward the petitioner on
her way, they did not wish their names to appear in
the matter.

They did, however, make an important offer.   The
Mastiff was newly come into harbour at Hull, and they
offered Richard the use of her as a conveyance.   He
gladly accepted it.   The saving of expense was a great

object; for he was most unwilling to use Queen Mary's
order on the French Ambassador, and he likewise
deemed it possible that such a means of evasion might
be very useful.

The *Mastiff* was sometimes used by some of the
Talbot family on journeys to London, and had a tolerably commodious cabin, according to the notions of the
time; and though it was late in the year, and poor Cis
was likely to be wretched enough on the voyage, the
additional security was worth having, and Cicely would
be under the care of Goatley's wife, who made all the
voyages with her husband. The Earl likewise charged
Richard Talbot with letters and messages of conciliation
to his son Gilbert, whose estrangement was a great
grief to him, arising as it did entirely from the quarrels
of the two wives, mother and daughter. He even
charged his kinsman with the proposal to give up
Sheffield to Lord and Lady Talbot and retire to Wingfield rather than continue at enmity. Mr. Talbot knew
the parties too well to have much hope of prevailing,
or producing permanent peace; but the commission
was welcome, as it would give a satisfactory pretext
for his presence in London.

A few days were spent at Bridgefield, Cicely making
herself the most loving, helpful, and charming of
daughters, and really basking in the peaceful atmosphere of Susan's presence; and then,—with many
prayers and blessings from that good lady,—they set
forth for Hull, taking with them two servants besides
poor Babington's man Gillingham, whose superior intelligence and knowledge of London would make him
useful, though there was a dark brooding look about
him that made Richard always dread some act of
revenge on his part toward his master's foes.

CHAPTER XXXVIII.

MASTER TALBOT AND HIS CHARGE.

THE afternoon on which they were to enter the old
town of Kingston-upon-Hull closed in with a dense
sea-fog, fast turning to drizzling rain. They could see
but a little distance on either side, and could not see
the lordly old church tower. The beads of dew on the
fringes of her pony's ears were more visible to Cicely
than anything else, and as she kept along by Master
Richard's side, she rejoiced both in the beaten, well-
trodden track, and in the pealing bells which seemed
to guide them into the haven ; while Richard was revolving, as he had done all through the journey, where
he could best lodge his companion so as to be safe, and
at the same time free from inconvenient curiosity.

The wetness of the evening made promptness of
decision the more needful, while the bad weather which
his experienced eye foresaw would make the choice
more important.

Discerning through the increasing gloom a lantern
moving in the street which seemed to him to light a sub-
stantial cloaked figure, he drew up and asked if he were
in the way to a well-known hostel. Fortune had favoured
him, for a voice demanded in return, " Do I hear the
voice of good Captain Talbot ?   At your service."

"Yea, it is I—Richard Talbot. Is it you, good Master Heatherthwayte?"

"It is verily, sir. Well do I remember you, good trusty Captain, and the goodly lady your wife. Do I see her here?" returned the clergyman, who had heartily grasped Richard's hand.

"No, sir, this is my daughter, for whose sake I would ask you to direct me to some lodging for the night."

"Nay, if the young lady will put up with my humble chambers, and my little daughter for her bed-fellow, I would not have so old an acquaintance go farther."

Richard accepted the offer gladly, and Mr. Heatherthwayte walked close to the horses, using his lantern to direct them, and sending flashes of light over the gabled ends of the old houses and the muffled passengers, till they came to a long flagged passage, when he asked them to dismount, bidding the servants and horses to await his return, and giving his hand to conduct the young lady along the narrow slippery alley, which seemed to have either broken walls or houses on either side.

He explained to Richard, by the way, that he had married the godly widow of a shipchandler, but that it had pleased Heaven to take her from him at the end of five years, leaving him two young children, but that her ancient nurse had the care of the house and the little ones.

Curates were not sumptuously lodged in those days. The cells which had been sufficient for monks commissioned by monasteries were no homes for men with families; and where means were to be had, a few rooms had been added without much grace, or old cottages

adapted— for indeed the requirements of the clergy of
the day did not soar above those of the farmer or petty
dealer.   Master Heatherthwayte pulled a string depending from a hole in a door, the place of which he
seemed to know by instinct, and admitted the new-
comers into a narrow paved entry, where he called
aloud, " Here, Oil! Dust! Goody! Bring a light!
Here are guests !"

A door was opened instantly into a large kitchen
or keeping room, bright with a fire and small lamp.
A girl of nine or ten sprang forward, but hung back at
the sight of strangers; a boy of twelve rose awkwardly
from conning his lessons by the low, unglazed lamp; an
old woman showed herself from some kind of pantry.

" Here," said the clergyman, " is my most esteemed
friend Captain Talbot of Bridgefield and his daughter,
who will do us the honour of abiding with us this night.
Do thou, Goody Madge, and thou, Oil-of-Gladness, make
the young lady welcome, and dry her garments, while
we go and see to the beasts.   Thou, Dust-and-Ashes,
mayest come with us and lead the gentleman's horse."

The lad, saddled with this dismal name, and arrayed
in garments which matched it in colour though not in
uncleanliness, sprang up with alacrity, infinitely prefer-
ring fog, rain, and darkness to his accidence, and never
guessing that he owed this relaxation to his father's
recollection of Mrs. Talbot's ways, and perception that
the young lady would be better attended to without his
presence.

Oil-of-Gladness was a nice little rosy girl in the
tightest and primmest of caps and collars, and with the
little housewifely hospitality that young mistresses of
houses early attain to.   There was no notion of equal
terms between the Curate's daughter and the Squire's :

the child brought a chair, and stood respectfully to receive the hood, cloak, and riding skirt, seeming delighted at the smile and thanks with which Cicely requited her attentions. The old woman felt the inner skirts, to make sure that they were not damp, and then the little girl brought warm water, and held the bowl while her guest washed face and hands, and smoothed her hair with the ivory comb which ladies always carried on a journey. The sweet power of setting people at ease was one Cis had inherited and cultivated by imitation, and Oil-of-Gladness was soon chattering away over her toilette. Would the lady really sleep with her in her little bed ? She would promise not to kick if she could help it. Then she exclaimed, " Oh! what fair thing was that at the lady's throat ? Was it a jewel of gold ? She had never seen one ; for father said it was not for Christian women to adorn themselves. Oh no ; she did not mean——" and, confused, she ran off to help Goody to lay the spotless tablecloth, Cis following to set the child at peace with herself, and unloose the tongue again into hopes that the lady liked conger pie ; for father had bought a mighty conger for twopence, and Goody had made a goodly pie of him.

By the time the homely meal was ready Mr. Talbot had returned from disposing of his horses and servants at a hostel, for whose comparative respectability Mr. Heatherthwayte had answered. The clergyman himself alone sat down to supper with his guests. He would not hear of letting either of his children do so ; but while Dust-and-Ashes retired to study his tasks for the Grammar School by firelight, Oil-of-Gladness assisted Goody in waiting, in a deft and ready manner pleasant to behold.

No sooner did Mr. Talbot mention the name Cicely

than Master Heatherthwayte looked up and said—
" Methinks it was I who spake that name over this
young lady in baptism."

"Even so," said Richard. "She knoweth all, but
she hath ever been our good and dutiful daughter, for
which we are the more thankful that Heaven hath
given us none other maid child."

He knew Master Heatherthwayte was inclined to
curiosity about other people's affairs, and therefore
turned the discourse on the doings of his sons, hoping
to keep him thus employed and avert all further conversation upon Cicely and the cause of the journey.
The good man was most interested in Edward, only he
exhorted Mr. Talbot to be careful with whom he bestowed the stripling at Cambridge, so that he might
shed the pure light of the Gospel, undimmed by
Popish obscurities and idolatries.

He began on his objections to the cross in baptism
and the ring in marriage, and dilated on them to his
own satisfaction over the tankard of ale that was
placed for him and his guest, and the apples and nuts
wherewith Cicely was surreptitiously feeding Oil-of-
Gladness and Dust-and-Ashes ; while the old woman
bustled about, and at length made her voice heard in
the announcement that the chamber was ready, and the
young lady was weary with travel, and it was time she
was abed, and Oil likewise.

Though not very young children, Oil and Dust, at
a sign from their father, knelt by his chair, and uttered
their evening prayers aloud, after which he blessed and
dismissed them—the boy to a shake-down in his own
room, the girl to the ecstasy of assisting the guest to
undress, and admiring the wonders of the very simple
toilette apparatus contained in her little cloak bag.

Richard meantime was responding as best he could to the inquiries he knew would be inevitable as soon as he fell in with the Reverend Master Heatherthwayte. He was going to London in the *Mastiff* on some business connected with the Queen of Scots, he said.

Whereupon Mr. Heatherthwayte quoted something from the Psalms about the wicked being taken in their own pits, and devoutly hoped she would not escape this time. His uncharitableness might be excused by the fact that he viewed it as an immediate possibility that the Prince of Parma might any day enter the Humber, when he would assuredly be burnt alive, and Oil-of-Gladness exposed to the fate of the children of Haarlem.

Then he added, " I grieved to hear that you and your household were so much exposed to the witchcrafts of that same woman, sir."

" I hope she hath done them little hurt," said Richard."

" Is it true," he added, " that the woman hath laid claim to the young lady now here as a kinswoman ?"

" It is true," said Richard, " but how hath it come to your knowledge, my good friend ? I deemed it known to none out of our house ; not even the Earl and Countess guess that she is no child of ours."

" Nay, Mr. Talbot, is it well to go on in a deceit ?"

" Call it rather a concealment," said Richard. " We have doubted it since, but when we began, it was merely that there was none to whom it seemed needful to explain that the babe was not the little daughter we buried here. But how did you learn it ? It imports to know."

" Sir, do you remember your old servant Colet, Gervas's wife ? It will be three years next Whitsuntide that hearing a great outcry as of a woman mal-

treated as I passed in the street, I made my way into
the house and found Gervas verily beating his wife with
a broomstick. After I had rebuked him and caused him
to desist, I asked him the cause, and he declared it to
be that his wife had been gadding to a stinking Papist
fellow, who would be sure to do a mischief to his noble
captain, Mr. Talbot. Thereupon Colet declares that she
had done no harm, the gentleman wist all before. She
knew him again for the captain's kinsman who was in
the house the day that the captain brought home the
babe."

"Cuthbert Langston!"

"Even so, sir. It seems that he had been with this
woman, and questioned her closely on all she remembered of the child, learning from her what I never knew
before, that there were marks branded on her shoulders
and a letter sewn in her clothes. Was it so, sir?"

"Ay, but my wife and I thought that even Colet
had never seen them."

"Nothing can escape a woman, sir. This man drew
all from her by assuring her that the maiden belonged
to some great folk, and was even akin to the King and
Queen of Scots, and that she might have some great
reward if she told her story to them. She even sold
him some three or four gold and ivory beads which she
says she found when sweeping out the room where the
child was first undressed."

"Hath she ever heard more of the fellow?"

"Nay, but Gervas since told me that he had met
some of my Lord's men who told him that your daughter
was one of the Queen of Scots' ladies, and said he, 'I
held my peace; but methought, It hath come of the
talebearing of that fellow to whom my wife prated.'"

"Gervas guessed right," said Richard. "That Langston did contrive to make known to the Queen of Scots such tokens as led to her owning the maiden as of near kin to her by the mother's side, and to her husband on the father's; but for many reasons she entreated us to allow the damsel still to bear our name, and be treated as our child."

"I doubt me whether it were well done of you, sir," said Mr. Heatherthwayte.

"Of that," said Richard, drawing up into himself, "no man can judge for another."

"She hath been with that woman; she will have imbibed her Popish vanities!" exclaimed the poor clergyman, almost ready to start up and separate Oil-of-Gladness at once from the contamination.

"You may be easy on that score," said Richard drily. "Her faith is what my good wife taught her, and she hath constantly attended the preachings of the chaplains of Sir Amias Paulett, who be all of your own way of thinking."

"You assure me?" said Mr. Heatherthwayte, "for it is the nature of these folk to act a part, even as did the parent the serpent."

Often as Richard had thought so himself, he was offended now, and rose, "If you think I have brought a serpent into your house, sir, we will take shelter elsewhere. I will call her."

Mr. Heatherthwayte apologised and protested, and showed himself willing to accept the assurance that Cicely was as simple and guileless as his own little maid; and Mr. Talbot, not wishing to be sent adrift with Cicely at that time of night, and certainly not to put such an affront on the good, if over-anxious father, was pacified, but the cordial tone of ease was at an end, and they were glad to separate and retire to rest.

Richard had much cause for thought. He perceived, what had always been a perplexity to him before, how Langston had arrived at the knowledge that enabled him to identify Cicely with the babe of Lochleven.

Mr. Talbot heard moanings and wailings of wind all night, which to his experience here meant either a three days' detention at Hull, or a land journey. With dawn there were gusts and showers. He rose betimes and went downstairs. He could hear his good host praying aloud in his room, and feeling determined not to vex that Puritan spirit by the presence of Queen Mary's pupil, he wrapped his cloak about him and went out to study the weather, and inquire for lodgings to which he might remove Cicely. He saw nothing he liked, and determined on consulting his old mate, Goatley, who generally acted as skipper, but he had first to return so as not to delay the morning meal. He found, on coming in, Cicely helping Oil-of-Gladness in making griddle cakes, and buttering them, so as to make Mr. Heatherthwayte declare that he had not tasted the like since Mistress Susan quitted Hull.

Moreover, he had not sat down to the meal more than ten minutes before he discovered, to his secret amusement, that Cicely had perfectly fascinated and charmed the good minister, who would have shuddered had he known that she did so by the graces inherited and acquired from the object of his abhorrence. Invitations to abide in their present quarters till it was possible to sail were pressed on them; and though Richard showed himself unwilling to accept them, they were so cordially reiterated, that he felt it wiser to accede to them rather than spread the mystery farther. He was never quite sure whether Mr. Heatherthwayte looked on the young lady as untainted, or whether he wished to secure her in his own instructions ; but he always described her as a modest and virtuous young lady, and so far from thinking her presence dangerous, only wished Oil to learn as much from her as possible.

Cicely was sorely disappointed, and wanted to ride on at once by land; but when her foster-father had shown her that the bad weather would be an almost equal obstacle, and that much time would be lost on the road, she submitted with the good temper she had cultivated under such a notable example.   She taught Oil-of-Gladness the cookery of one of her mothers and the stitchery of the other; she helped Dust-and-Ashes with his accidence, and enlightened him on the sports of the Bridgefield boys, so that his father looked round dismayed at the smothered laughter, when she assured him that she was only telling how her brother Diccon caught a coney, or the like, and in some magical way smoothed down his frowns with her smile.

Mistress Cicely Talbot's visit was likely to be an unforgotten era with Dust-and-Ashes and Oil-of-Glad-ness.   The good curate entreated that she and her father would lodge there on their return, and the invi-tation was accepted conditionally, Mr. Talbot writing to his wife, by the carriers, to send such a load of good cheer from Bridgefield as would amply compensate for the expenses of this hospitality.

R

CHAPTER XXXIX.

THE FETTERLOCK COURT.

PEOPLE did not pity themselves so much for suspense when, instead of receiving an answer in less than an hour, they had to wait for it for weeks if not months. Mrs. Talbot might be anxious at Bridgefield, and her son at Fotheringhay, and poor Queen Mary, whose life hung in the balance, more heartsick with what old writers well named *wanhope* than any of them; but they had to live on, and rise morning after morning without expecting any intelligence, unable to do anything but pray for those who might be in perils unknown.

After the strain and effort of her trial, Mary had become very ill, and kept her bed for many days. Humfrey continued to fulfil his daily duties as commander of the guards set upon her, but he seldom saw or spoke with any of her attendants, as Sir Andrew Melville, whom he knew the best of them, had on some suspicion been separated from his mistress and confined in another part of the Castle.

Sir Amias Paulett, too, was sick with gout and anxiety, and was much relieved when Sir Drew Drury was sent to his assistance. The new warder was a more courteous and easy-mannered person, and did not

fret himself or the prisoner with precautions like his
colleague; and on Sir Amias's reiterated complaint
that the guards were not numerous enough, he had
brought down five fresh men, hired in London, fellows
used to all sorts of weapons, and at home in military
discipline; but, as Humfrey soon perceived, at home
likewise in the license of camps, and most incongruous
companions for the simple village bumpkins, and the
precise retainers who had hitherto formed the garrison.
He did his best to keep order, but marvelled how Sir
Amias would view their excesses when he should come
forth again from his sick chamber.

The Queen was better, though still lame; and on
a fine November noontide she obtained, by earnest
entreaty, permission to gratify her longing for free air
by taking a turn in what was called the Fetterlock
Court, from the Yorkist badge of the falcon and fetterlock carved profusely on the decorations. This was the
inmost strength of the castle, on the highest ground,
an octagon court, with the keep closing one side of it,
and the others surrounded with huge massive walls,
shutting in a greensward with a well. There was
a broad commodious terrace in the thickness of the
walls, intended as a station whence the defenders could
shoot between the battlements, but in time of peace
forming a pleasant promenade sheltered from the wind,
and catching on its northern side the meridian rays of
this Martinmas summer day, so that physician as well
as jailer consented to permit the captive there to take
the air.

"Some watch there must be," said Paulett anxiously,
when his colleague reported the consent he had given.

"It will suffice, then," said Sir Drew Drury, "if
the officer of the guard—Talbot call you him?—stands

at the angle of the court, so as to keep her in his view. He is a well-nurtured youth, and will not vex her."

"Let him have the guard within call," said Paulett, and to this Drury assented, perhaps with a little amusement at the restless precautions of the invalid.

Accordingly, Humfrey took up his station, as unobtrusively as he could, at the corner of the terrace, and presently, through a doorway at the other end saw the Queen, hooded and cloaked, come forth, leaning heavily on the arm of Dr. Bourgoin, and attended by the two Maries and the two elder ladies. She moved slowly, and paused every few steps, gazing round her, inhaling the fresh air and enjoying the sunshine, or speaking a caressing word to little Bijou, who leaped about, and barked, and whined with delight at having her out of doors again. There was a seat in the wall, and her ladies spread cushions and cloaks for her to sit on it, warmed as it was by the sun; and there she rested, watching a starling running about on the turf, his gold-bespangled green plumage glistening. She hardly spoke; she seemed to be making the most of the repose of the fair calm day. Humfrey would not intrude by making her sensible of his presence, but he watched her from his station, wondering within himself if she cared for the peril to which she had exposed the daughter so dear to him.

Such were his thoughts when an angry bark from Bijou warned him to be on the alert. A man—ay, one of the new men-at-arms—was springing up the ramp leading to the summit of the wall almost immediately in front of the little group. There was a gleam of steel in his hand. With one long ringing whistle, Humfrey bounded from his place, and at the moment when the ruffian was on the point of assailing

the Queen, he caught him with one hand by the collar,
with the other tried to master the arm that held the
weapon. It was a sharp struggle, for the fellow was a
trained soldier in the full strength of manhood, and
Humfrey was a youth of twenty-three, and unarmed.
They went down together, rolling on the ground before
Mary's chair; but in another moment Humfrey was
the uppermost. He had his knee on the fellow's chest,
and held aloft, though in a bleeding hand, the dagger
wrenched from him. The victory had been won in a
few seconds, before the two men, whom his whistle had
brought, had time to rush forward. They were ready
now to throw themselves on the assailant. "Hold!"
cried Humfrey, speaking for the first time. "Hurt him
not! Hold him fast till I have him to Sir Amias!"

Each had an arm of the fallen man, and Humfrey
rose to meet the eyes of the Queen sparkling, as she
cried, "Bravely, bravely done, sir! We thank you.
Though it be but the poor remnant of a worthless life
that you have saved, we thank you. The sight of
your manhood has gladdened us."

Humfrey bowed low, and at the same time there
was a cry among the ladies that he was bleeding. It
was only his hand, as he showed them. The dagger
had been drawn across the palm before he could
capture it. The kerchiefs were instantly brought
forward to bind it up, Dr. Bourgoin saying that it
ought to have Master Gorion's attention.

"I may not wait for that, sir," said Humfrey. "I
must carry this villain at once to Sir Amias and
report on the affair."

"Nay, but you will come again to be tended,"
said the Queen, while Dr. Bourgoin fastened the
knot of the temporary bandage "Ah! and is it

Humfrey Talbot to whom I owe my life? There is one who will thank thee for it more than even I. But come back. Gorion must treat that hand, and then you will tell me what you have heard of her."

"Naught, alas, madam," said Humfrey with an expressive shake of the head, but ere he turned away Mary extended her hand to him, and as he bent his knee to kiss it she laid the other kindly on his dark curled head and said, "God bless thee, brave youth."

She was escorted to the door nearest to her apartments, and as she sank back on her day bed she could not help murmuring to Mary Seaton, "A brave laddie. Would that he had one drop of princely blood."

"The Talbot blood is not amiss," said the lady.

"True; and were it but mine own Scottish royalty that were in question I should see naught amiss, but with this English right that hath been the bane of us all, what can their love bring the poor children save woe?"

Meantime Humfrey was conducting his prisoner to Sir Amias Paulett. The man was a bronzed, tough-looking ruffian, with an air of having seen service, and a certain foreign touch in his accent. He glanced somewhat contemptuously at his captor, and said, "Neatly done, sir; I marvel if you'll get any thanks."

"What mean you?" said Humfrey sharply, but the fellow only shrugged his shoulders. The whole affair had been so noiseless, that Humfrey brought the first intelligence when he was admitted to the sick chamber, where Sir Amias sat in a large chair by the fire. He had left his prisoner guarded by two men at the door.

"How now! What is it?" cried Paulett at first sight of his bandaged hand. "Is she safe?"

"Even so, sir, and untouched," said Humfrey.

"Thanks be to God!" he exclaimed. "This is what I feared. Who was it?"

"One of the new men-at-arms from London— Peter Pierson he called himself, and said he had served in the Netherlands."

And after a few further words of explanation, Humfrey called in the prisoner and his guards, and before his face gave an account of his attempt upon the helpless Queen.

"Godless and murderous villain!" said Paulett, "what hast thou to say for thyself that I should not hang thee from the highest tower?"

"Naught that will hinder you, worshipful seignior," returned the man with a sneer. "In sooth I see no great odds between taking life with a dagger and with an axe, save that fewer folk are regaled with the spectacle."

"Wretch," said Paulett, "wouldst thou confound private murder with the open judgment of God and man?"

"Judgment hath been pronounced," said the fellow, "but it needs not to dispute the matter. Only if this honest youth had not come blundering in and cut his fingers in the fray, your captive would have been quietly rid of all her troubles, and I should have had my reward from certain great folk you wot of. Ay," as Sir Amias turned still yellower, "you take my meaning, sir."

"Take him away," said Paulett, collecting himself; "he would cloak his crime by accusing others of his desperate wickedness."

"Where, sir?" inquired Humfrey.

Sir Amias would have preferred hanging the fellow

without inquiry, but as Fotheringhay was not under martial law, he ordered him off to the dungeons for the present, while the nearest justice of the peace was sent for. The knight bade Humfrey remain while the prisoner was walked off under due guard, and made a few more inquiries, adding, with a sigh, " You must double the guard, Master Talbot, and get rid of all those London rogues—sons of Belial are they all, and I'll have none for whom I cannot answer—for I fear me 'tis all too true what the fellow says."

" Who would set him on ?"

" That I may not say. But would you believe it, Humfrey Talbot, I have been blamed—ay, rated like a hound, for that I will not lend myself to a privy murder."

" Verily, sir ?"

" Verily, and indeed, young man. 'Tis the part of a loyal subject, they say, to spare her Majesty's womanish feelings and her hatred of bloodshed, and this lady having been condemned, to take her off secretly so as to save the Queen the pain and heart-searchings of signing the warrant. You credit me not, sir, but I have the letter—to my sorrow and shame."

No wonder that the poor, precise, hard-hearted, but religious and high-principled man was laid up with a fit of the gout, after receiving the shameful letter which he described, which is still extant, signed by Walsingham and Davison.

" Strange loyalty," said Humfrey.

" And too much after the Spanish sort for an English Protestant," said Sir Amias. " I made answer that I would lay down my life to guard this unhappy woman to undergo the justice that is to be done upon her, but murder her, or allow her to be slain in my hands, I neither can nor will, so help me Heaven, as a true though sinful man."

"Amen," said Humfrey.

"And no small cause of thanks have I that in you, young sir, I have one who may be trusted for faith as well as courage, and I need not say discretion."

As he spoke, Sir Drew Drury, who had been out riding, returned, anxious to hear the details of this strange event. Sir Amias could not leave his room. Sir Drew accompanied Humfrey to the Queen's apartments to hear her account and that of her attendants. It was given with praises of the young gentleman which put him to the blush, and Sir Drew then gave permission for his hurt to be treated by Maître Gorion, and left him in the antechamber for the purpose.

Sir Amias would perhaps have done more wisely if he had not detained Humfrey from seeing the criminal guarded to his prison. For Sir Drew Drury, going from the Queen's presence to interrogate the fellow before sending for a magistrate, found the cell empty. It had been the turn of duty of one of the new London men-at-arms, and he had been placed as sentry at the door by the sergeant——the stupidest and trustiest of fellows——who stood gaping in utter amazement when he found that sentry and prisoner were both alike missing.

On the whole, the two warders agreed that it would be wiser to hush up the matter. When Mary heard that the man had escaped, she quietly said, " I understand. They know how to do such things better abroad."

Things returned to their usual state except that Humfrey had permission to go daily to have his hand

R*

attended to by M. Gorion, and the Queen never let pass this opportunity of speaking to him, though the very first time she ascertained that he knew as little as she did of the proceedings of his father and Cicely.

Now, for the first time, did Humfrey understand the charm that had captivated Babington, and that even his father confessed. Ailing, aging, and suffering as she was, and in daily expectation of her sentence of death, there was still something more wonderfully winning about her, a sweet pathetic cheerfulness, kindness, and resignation, that filled his heart with devotion to her. And then she spoke of Cicely, the rarest and greatest delight that he could enjoy. She evidently regarded him with favour, if not affection, because he loved the maiden whom she could not but deny to him. Would he not do anything for her? Ay, anything consistent with duty. And there came a twinge which startled him. Was she making him value duty less? Never. Besides, how few days he could see her. His hand was healing all too fast, and what might not come any day from London? Was Queen Mary's last conquest to be that of Humfrey Talbot?

CHAPTER XL.

THE SENTENCE.

THE tragedies of the stage compress themselves into a few hours, but the tragedies of real life are of slow and heavy march, and the heart-sickness of delay and hope and dread alike deferred is one of their chief trials.

Humfrey's hurt was quite well, but as he was at once trusted by his superiors, and acceptable to the captive, he was employed in many of those lesser communications between her and her keepers, for which the two knights did not feel it necessary to harass her with their presence. His post, for half the twenty-four hours, was on guard in the gallery outside her anteroom door; but he often knocked and was admitted as bearer of some message to her or her household; and equally often was called in to hear her requests, and sometimes he could not help believing because it pleased her to see him, even if there were nothing to tell her.

Nor was there anything known until the 19th of November, when the sound of horses' feet in large numbers, and the blast of bugles, announced the arrival of a numerous party. When marshalled into the ordinary dining-hall, they proved to be Lord Buckhurst, a dignified-looking nobleman, who bore a sad and grave countenance full of presage, with Mr. Beale, the Clerk of the Council, and two or three other officials and secretaries, among whom Humfrey perceived the inevitable Will Cavendish.

The two old comrades quickly sought each other out, Will observing, "So here you are still, Humfrey. We are like to see the end of a long story."

"How so?" asked Humfrey, with a thrill of horror, "is she sentenced?"

"By the Commissioners, all excepting my Lord Zouch, and by both houses of Parliament! We are come down to announce it to her. I'll have you into the presence-chamber if I can prevail. It will be a noteworthy thing to see how the daughter of a hundred kings brooks such a sentence."

"Hath no one spoken for her?" asked Humfrey, thinking at least as much of Cicely as of the victim.

"The King of Scots hath sent an ambassage," returned Cavendish, "but when I say 'tis the Master of Gray, you know what that means. King James may be urgent to save his mother—nay, he hath written more sharply and shrewishly than ever he did before; but as for this Gray, whatever he may say openly, we know that he has whispered to the Queen, 'The dead don't bite.'"

"The villain!"

"That may be, so far as he himself is concerned, but the counsel is canny, like the false Scot himself. What's this I hear, Humfrey, that you have been playing the champion, and getting wounded in the defence?"

"A mere nothing," said Humfrey, opening his hand, however, to show the mark. "I did but get my palm scored in hindering a villainous man-at-arms from slaying the poor lady."

"Yea, well are thy race named Talbot!" said

Cavendish. "Sturdy watch-dogs are ye all, with never a notion that sometimes it may be for the good of all parties to look the other way."

"If you mean that I am to stand by and see a helpless woman———"

"Hush! my good friend," said Will, holding up his hand. "I know thy breed far too well to mean any such thing. Moreover, thy precisian governor, old Paulett there, hath repelled, like instigations of Satan, more hints than one that pain might be saved to one queen and publicity to the other, if he would have taken a leaf from Don Philip's book, and permitted the lady to be dealt with secretly. Had he given an ear to the matter six months back, it would have spared poor Antony."

"Speak not thus, Will," said Humfrey, "or thou wilt make me believe thee a worse man than thou art, only for the sake of showing me how thou art versed in state policy. Tell me, instead, if thou hast seen my father."

"Thy father? yea, verily, and I have a packet for thee from him. It is in my mails, and I will give it thee anon. He is come on a bootless errand! As long as my mother and my sister Mall are both living, he might as well try to bring two catamounts together without hisses and scratches."

"Where is he lying?" asked Humfrey.

"In Shrewsbury House, after the family wont, and Gilbert makes him welcome enough, but Mall is angered with him for not lodging his daughter there likewise! I tell her he is afraid lest she should get hold of the wench, and work up a fresh web of tales against this lady, like those which did so much damage before. 'Twould be rare if she made out that Gravity himself, in the person of old Paulett, had been entranced by her."

"Peace with thy gibes," said Humfrey impatiently, "and tell me where my sister is."

"Where thinkest thou? Of all strange places in the world, he hath bestowed her with Madame de Salmonnet, the wife of one of the French Ambassador's following, to perfect her French, as he saith. Canst thou conceive wherefore he doth it? Hath he any marriage in view for her? Mall tried to find out, but he is secret. Tell me, Numps, what is it?"

"If he be secret, must not I be the same?" said Humfrey, laughing.

"Nay, thou owest me some return for all that I have told thee."

"Marry, Will, that is more like a maiden than a statesman! But be content, comrade, I know no more than thou what purposes there may be anent my sister's marriage," he added. "Only if thou canst give me my father's letter, I should be beholden to thee."

They were interrupted, however, by a summons to Humfrey, who was to go to the apartments of the Queen of Scots, to bear the information that in the space of half an hour the Lord Buckhurst and Master Beale would do themselves the honour of speaking with her.

"So," muttered Cavendish to himself as Humfrey went up the stairs, "there *is* then some secret. I marvel what it bodes! Did not that crafty villain Langston utter some sort of warning which I spurned, knowing the Bridgefield trustiness and good faith? This wench hath been mightily favoured by the lady. I must see to it."

Meantime Humfrey had been admitted to Queen

Mary's room, where she sat as usual at her needlework.
" You bring me tidings, my friend," she said, as he bent
his knee before her. " Methought I heard a fresh stir
in the Castle; who is arrived?"

" The Lord Buckhurst, so please your Grace, and
Master Beale. They crave an audience of your Grace
in half an hour's time."

" Yea, and I can well guess wherefore," said the
Queen. " Well, *Fiat voluntas tua!* Buckhurst? he is
kinsman of Elizabeth on the Boleyn side, methinks!
She would do me grace, you see, my masters, by sending
me such tidings by her cousin. They cannot hurt me!
I am far past that! So let us have no tears, my
lassies, but receive them right royally, as befits a message from one sovereign to another! Remember, it is
not before my Lord Buckhurst and Master Beale that
we sit, but before all posterities for evermore, who will
hear of Mary Stewart and her wrongs. Tell them I
am ready, sir. Nay but, my son," she added, with a
very different tone of the tender woman instead of the
outraged sovereign, " I see thou hast news for me. Is
it of the child?"

" Even so, madam. I wot little yet, but what I
know is hopeful. She is with Madame de Salmonnet,
wife of one of the suite of the French Ambassador."

" Ah! that speaketh much," said Mary, smiling,
" more than you know, young man. Salmonnet is
sprung of a Scottish archer, Jockie of the salmon net,
whereof they made in France M. de Salmonnet.
Châteauneuf must have owned her, and put her under
the protection of the Embassy. Hast thou had a letter
from thy father?"

" I am told that one is among Will Cavendish's
mails, madam, and I hope to have it anon."

"These men have all unawares brought with them that which may well bear me up through whatever may be coming."

A second message arrived from Lord Buckhurst himself, to say how grieved he was to be the bearer of heavy tidings, and to say that he would not presume to intrude on her Majesty's presence until she would notify to him that she was ready to receive him.

"They have become courteous," said Mary. "But why should we dally? The sooner this is over, the better."

The gentlemen were then admitted: Lord Buckhurst grave, sad, stately, and courteous; Sir Amias Paulett, as usual, grim and wooden in his puritanical stiffness; Sir Drew Drury keeping in the background as one grieved; and Mr. Beale, who had already often harassed the Queen before, eager, forward, and peremptory, as one whose exultation could hardly be repressed by respect for his superior, Lord Buckhurst.

Bending low before her, this nobleman craved her pardon for that which it was his duty to execute; and having kissed her hand, in token of her personal forgiveness, he bade Mr. Beale read the papers.

The Clerk of the Council stood forth almost without obeisance, till it was absolutely compelled from him by Buckhurst. He read aloud the details of the judgment, that Mary had been found guilty by the Commission, of conspiracy against the kingdom, and the life of the Queen, with the sentence from the High Court of Parliament that she was to die by being beheaded.

Mary listened with unmoved countenance, only she stood up and made solemn protest against the authority and power of the Commission either to try or condemn her. Beale was about to reply, but Lord Buckhurst checked him, telling him it was simply his business to record the protest; and then adding that he was charged to warn her to put away all hopes of mercy, and to prepare for death. This, he said, was on behalf of his Queen, who implored her to disburthen her conscience by a full confession. "It is not her work," added Buckhurst; "the sentence is not hers, but this thing is required by her people, inasmuch as her life can never be safe while your Grace lives, nor can her religion remain in any security."

Mary's demeanour had hitherto been resolute. Here a brightness and look of thankful joy came over her, as she raised her eyes to Heaven and joined her hands, saying, "I thank you, my lord; you have made it all gladness to me, by declaring me to be an instrument in the cause of my religion, for which, unworthy as I am, I shall rejoice to shed my blood."

"Saint and martyr, indeed!" broke out Paulett. "That is fine! when you are dying for plotting treason and murder!"

"Nay, sir," gently returned Mary, "I am not so presumptuous as to call myself saint or martyr; but though you have power over my body, you have none over my soul, nor can you prevent me from hoping that by the mercy of Him who died for me, my blood and life may be accepted by Him, as offerings freely made for His Church."

She then begged for the restoration of her Almoner De Préaux. She was told that the request would be referred to the Queen, but that she should have the attendance of an English Bishop and Dean. Paulett was so angered at the manner in which she had met the doom, that he began to threaten her

that she would be denied all that could serve to her
idolatries.

"Yea, verily," said she calmly, "I am aware that
the English have never been noted for mercy."

Lord Buckhurst succeeded in getting the knight
away without any more bitter replies. Humfrey and
Cavendish had, of course, to leave the room in their
train, and as it was the hour of guard for the former,
he had to take up his station and wait with what
patience he could until it should please Master William
to carry him the packet. He opened it eagerly, standing
close beneath the little lamp that illuminated his post,
to read it : but after all, it was somewhat disappointing,
for Mr. Talbot did not feel that absolute confidence in
the consciences of gentlemen-in-place which would
make him certain of that of Master Cavendish, supposing any notion should arise that Cicely's presence in
London could have any purpose connected with the
prisoner.

"To my dear son Humfrey, greeting—

"I do you to wit that we are here safely arrived
in London, though we were forced by stress of weather
to tarry seven days in Hull, at the house of good
Master Heatherthwayte, where we received good and
hospitable entertainment. The voyage was a fair one,
and the old *Mastiff* is as brave a little vessel as ever
she was wont to be ; but thy poor sister lay abed all
the time, and was right glad when we came into smooth
water. We have presented the letters to those whom
we came to seek, and so far matters have gone with
us more towardly than I had expected. There are
those who knew Cicely's mother at her years who say
there is a strange likeness between them, and who there•

fore received her the more favourably. I am lying at
present at Shrewsbury House, where my young Lord
makes me welcome, but it hath been judged meet that
thy sister should lodge with the good Madame de
Salmonnet, a lady of Scottish birth, who is wife to one
of the secretaries of M. de Châteauneuf, the French
Ambassador, but who was bred in the convent of
Soissons. She is a virtuous and honourable lady, and
hath taken charge of thy sister while we remain in
London. For the purpose for which we came, it goeth
forward, and those who should know assure me that
we do not lose time here. Diccon commendeth himself to thee; he is well in health, and hath much
improved in all his exercises. Mistress Curll is lodging
nigh unto the Strand, in hopes of being permitted to
see her husband; but that hath not yet been granted to
her, although she is assured that he is well in health,
and like ere long to be set free, as well as Monsieur
Nau.

"We came to London the day after the Parliament
had pronounced sentence upon the Lady at Fotheringhay. I promise you there was ringing of bells and
firing of cannon, and lighting of bonfires, so that we
deemed that there must have been some great defeat
of the Spaniards in the Low Countries; and when we
were told it was for joy that the Parliament had declared the Queen of Scots guilty of death, my poor
Cicely had well-nigh swooned to think that there
could be such joy for the doom of one poor sick lady.
There hath been a petition to the Queen that the
sentence may be carried out, and she hath answered in
a dubious and uncertain manner, which leaves ground
for hope; and the King of Scots hath written pressingly
and sent the Master of Gray to speak in his mother's

behalf; also M. de Châteauneuf hath both urged mercy on the Queen, and so written to France that King Henry is sending an Ambassador Extraordinary, M. de Bellièvre, to intercede for her.

"I send these presents by favour of Master Cavendish, who will tell thee more than I have here space to set down, and can assure thee that nothing hasty is like to be done in the business on which he hath come down with these gentlemen. And so no more at present from thy loving father,   RICHARD TALBOT."

Humfrey had to gather what he could from this letter, but he had no opportunity of speech with the prisoner on the remainder of that day, nor on the next, until after Lord Buckhurst and his followers had left Fotheringhay, bearing with them a long and most touching letter from the prisoner to Queen Elizabeth.

On that day, Paulett worked himself up to the strange idea that it was for the good of the unfortunate prisoner's soul, and an act of duty to his own sovereign, to march into the prison chamber and announce to Queen Mary that being a dead woman in the eye of the law, no royal state could be permitted her, in token of which he commanded her servants to remove the canopy over her chair. They all flatly refused to touch it, and the women began to cry "Out upon him," for being cowardly enough to insult their mistress; and she calmly said, "Sir, you may do as you please. My royal state comes from God, and is not yours to give or take away. I shall die a Queen, whatever you may do by such law as robbers in a forest might use with a righteous judge."

Intensely angered, Sir Amias came, hobbling and stumbling out to the door, pale with rage, and called

on Talbot to come and bring his men to tear down the
rag of vanity in which this contumacious woman put
her trust.

"The men are your servants, sir," said Humfrey,
with a flush on his cheek and his teeth set; "I am
here to guard the Queen of Scots, not to insult her."

"How, sirrah? Do you know to whom you speak?
Have you not sworn obedience to me?"

"In all things within my commission, sir; but this
is as much beyond it, as I believe it to be beyond
yours."

"Insolent, disloyal varlet! You are under ward
till I can account with and discharge you. To your
chamber!"

Humfrey could but walk away, grieved that his
power of bearing intelligence or alleviation to the
prisoner had been forfeited, and that he should probably
not even take leave of her. Was she to be left to all
the insults that the malice of her persecutor could
devise? Yet it was not exactly malice. Paulett would
have guarded her life from assassination with his own,
though chiefly for his own sake, and, as he said, for that
of "saving his poor posterity from so foul a blot;" but he
could not bear, as he told Sir Drew Drury, to see the
Popish, bloodthirsty woman sit queening it so calmly;
and when he tore down her cloth of state, and sat down
in her presence with his hat on, he did not so much
intend to pain the woman, Mary, as to express the
triumph of Elizabeth and of her religion. Humfrey believed his service over, and began to occupy himself with
putting his clothes together, while considering whether
to seek his father in London or to go home. After
about an hour, he was summoned to the hall, where
he expected to have found Sir Amias Paulett ready to

give him his discharge. He found, however, only Sir
Drew Drury, who thus accosted him—"Young man,
you had better return to your duty. Sir Amias is
willing to overlook what passed this morning."

"I thank you, sir, but I am not aware of having
done aught to need forgiveness," said Humfrey.

"Come, come, my fair youth, stand not on these
points. 'Tis true my good colleague hath an excess of
zeal, and I could wish he could have found it in his
heart to leave the poor lady these marks of dignity
that hurt no one. I would have no hand in it, and I
am glad thou wouldst not. He knoweth that he had
no power to require such service of thee. He will
say no more, and I trust that neither wilt thou; for it
would not be well to change warders at this time.
Another might not be so acceptable to the poor lady,
and I would fain save her all that I can."

Humfrey bowed, and thanked "him of milder
mood," nor was any further notice taken of this hasty
dismissal.

When next he had to enter the Queen's apartments,
the absence of all the tokens of her royal rank was to
him truly a shock, accustomed as he had been, from
his earliest childhood, to connect them with her, and
knowing what their removal signified.

Mary, who was writing, looked up as, with cap in
hand, he presented himself on one knee, his head bowed
lower than ever before, perhaps to hide the tear that
had sprung to his eye at sight of her pale, patient
countenance.

"How now, sir?" she said. "This obeisance is
out of place to one already dead in law. Don your
bonnet. There is no queen here for an Englishman."

"Ah! madam, suffer me. My reverence cannot

but be greater than ever," faltered Humfrey from his very heart, his words lost in the kiss he printed on the hand she granted him.

Mary bent "her gray discrowned head," crowned in his eyes as the Queen of Sorrows, and said to Marie de Courcelles, who stood behind her, "Is it not true, *ma mie*, that our griefs have this make-weight, namely, that they prove to us whose are the souls whose generosity is above all price! And what saith thy good father, my Humfrey?"

He had not ventured on bringing the letter into the apartments, but he repeated most of the substance of it, without, however, greatly raising the hopes of the Queen, though she was gratified that her cause was not neglected either by her son or by her brother-in-law.

"They, and above all my poor maid, will be comforted to have done their utmost," she said; "but I scarcely care that they should prevail. As I have written to my cousin Elizabeth, I am beholden to her for ending my long captivity, and above all for conferring on me the blessings and glories of one who dies for her faith, all unworthy as I am!" and she clasped her hands, while a rapt expression came upon her countenance.

Her chief desire seemed to be that neither Cicely nor her foster-father should run into danger on her account, and she much regretted that she had not been able to impress upon Humfrey messages to that effect before he wrote in answer to his father, sending his letter by Cavendish.

"Thou wilt not write again?" she asked.

"I doubt its being safe," said Humfrey. "I durst not speak openly even in the scroll I sent yesterday."

Then Mary recurred to the power which he possessed of visiting Sir Andrew Melville and the Almoner, the Abbé de Préaux, who were shut up in the Fetterlock tower and court, and requested him to take a billet which she had written to the latter. The request came like a blow to the young man. "With permission——" he began.

"I tell thee," said Mary, "this concerns naught but mine own soul. It is nothing to the State, but all and everything to me, a dying woman."

"Ah, madam! Let me but obtain consent."

"What! go to Paulett that he may have occasion to blaspheme my faith and insult me!" said the Queen, offended.

"I should go to Sir Drew Drury, who is of another mould," said Humfrey——

"But who dares not lift a finger to cross his fellow," said Mary, leaning back resignedly.

"And this is the young gentleman's love for your Grace!" exclaimed Jean Kennedy.

"Nay, madam," said Humfrey, stung to the quick, "but I am sworn!"

"Let him alone, Nurse Jeanie!" said Mary. "He is like the rest of the English. They know not how to distinguish between the spirit and the letter! I understand it all, though I had thought for a moment that in him there was a love for me and mine that would perceive that I could ask nothing that could damage his honour or his good faith. I—who had almost a mother's love and trust in him."

"Madam," cried Humfrey, "you know I would lay down my life for you, but I cannot break my trust."

"Your trust, fule laddie!" exclaimed Mrs. Kennedy. "Ane wad think the Queen speired of ye to carry a letter to Mendoza to burn and slay, instead of a bit scart of the pen to ask the good father for his prayers, or the like! But you are all alike; ye will not stir a hand to aid her poor soul."

"Pardon me, madam," entreated Humfrey. "The matter is, not what the letter may bear, but how my oath binds me! I may not be the bearer of aught in writing from this chamber. 'Twas the very reason I would not bring in my father's letter. Madam, say but you pardon me."

"Of course I pardon you," returned Mary coldly. "I have so much to pardon that I can well forgive the lukewarmness and precision that are so bred in your nature that you cannot help them. I pardon injuries, and I may well *try* to pardon disappointments. Fare you well, Mr. Talbot; may your fidelity have its reward from Sir Amias Paulett."

Humfrey was obliged to quit the apartment, cruelly wounded, sometimes wondering whether he had really acted on a harsh selfish punctilio in cutting off the dying woman from the consolations of religion, and thus taking part with the persecutors, while his heart bled for her. Sometimes it seemed to him as if he had been on the point of earning her consent to his marriage with her daughter, and had thrown it away, and at other moments a horror came over him lest he was being beguiled as poor Antony had been before him. And if he let his faith slip, how should he meet his father again? Yet his affection for the Queen repelled this idea like a cruel injury, while, day by day, it was renewed pain and grief to be treated by her with the gentlest and most studied courtesy, but no longer as almost one of her own inner circle of friends and confidants.

And as Sir Andrew Melville was in a few days more restored to her service, he was far less often required to bear messages, or do little services in the prison apartments, and he felt himself excluded, and cut off from the intimacy that had been very sweet, and even a little hopeful to him.

CHAPTER XLI.

HER ROYAL HIGHNESS.

CICELY had been living in almost as much suspense in
London as her mother at Fotheringhay.   For greater
security Mr. Talbot had kept her on board the *Mastiff*
till he had seen M. d'Aubépine Châteauneuf, and
presented to him Queen Mary's letter.   The Ambassador, an exceedingly polished and graceful Frenchman,
was greatly astonished, and at first incredulous ; but
he could not but accept the Queen's letter as genuine,
and he called into his counsels his Secretary De
Salmonnet, an elderly man, whose wife, a Scotswoman
by birth, preferred her husband's society to the
delights of Paris.   She was a Hamilton who had been
a *pensionnaire* in the convent at Soissons, and she
knew that it had been expected that an infant from
Lochleven might be sent to the Abbess, but that it
had never come, and that after many months of
waiting, tidings had arrived that the vessel which
carried the babe had been lost at sea.

M. de Châteauneuf thereupon committed the investigation to her and her husband.   Richard Talbot
took them first to the rooms where Mrs. Barbara Curll
had taken up her abode, so as to be near her husband,
who was still a prisoner in Walsingham's house.   She

fully confirmed all that Mr. Talbot said of the Queen's complete acceptance of Cis as her daughter, and moreover consented to come with the Salmonnets and Mr. Talbot, to visit the young lady on board the *Mastiff*.

Accordingly they went down the river together in Mr. Talbot's boat, and found Cicely, well cloaked and muffled, sitting under an awning, under the care of old Goatley, who treated her like a little queen, and was busy explaining to her all the different craft which filled the river.

She sprang up with the utmost delight at the sight of Mrs. Curll, and threw herself into her arms. There was an interchange of inquiries and comments that—unpremeditated as they were—could not but convince the auditor of the terms on which the young lady had stood with Queen Mary and her suite.

Afterwards Cicely took the two ladies to her cabin, a tiny box, but not uncomfortable according to her habits, and there, on Barbara's persuasion, she permitted Madame de Salmonnet to see the monograms on her shoulders. The lady went home convinced of her identity, and came again the next day with a gentleman in slouched hat, mask, and cloak.

As Cicely rose to receive him he uttered an exclamation of irrepressible astonishment, then added, " Your Highness will pardon me. Exactly thus did her royal mother stand when I took leave of her at Calais."

The Ambassador had thus been taken by storm, although the resemblance was more in figure and gesture than feature, but Mrs. Curll could aver that those who had seen Bothwell were at no loss to trace the derivation of the dark brows and somewhat homely features, in which the girl differed from the royal race of Scotland.

What was to be done ? Queen Mary's letter to

him begged him so far as was possible to give her
French protection, and avoid compromising "that excellent Talbot," and he thought it would be wisest for
her to await the coming of the Envoy Extraordinary,
M. de Pomponne Bellièvre, and be presented by him.
In the meantime her remaining on board ship in this
winter weather would be miserably uncomfortable, and
Richmond and Greenwich were so near that any intercourse with her would be dangerous, especially if
Langston was still in England. Lodgings or inns
where a young lady from the country could safely be
bestowed were not easily to be procured without
greater familiarity with the place than Mr. Talbot
possessed, and he could as little think of placing her
with Lady Talbot, whose gossiping tongue and shrewish
temper were not for a moment to be trusted. Therefore
M. de Châteauneuf's proposal that the young lady should
become Madame de Salmonnet's guest at the embassy
was not unwelcome. The lady was elderly, Scottish,
and, as M. de Châteauneuf with something of a
shudder assured Mr. Talbot, "most respectable." And
it was hoped that it would not be for long. So,
having seen her safely made over to the lady's care,
Richard ventured for the first time to make his presence in London known to his son, and to his kindred;
and he was the more glad to have her in these quarters
because Diccon told him that there was no doubt that
Langston was lurking about the town, and indeed he
was convinced that he had recognised that spy entering
Walsingham's house in the dress of a scrivener. He
would not alarm Cicely, but he bade her keep all
her goods in a state ready for immediate departure, in
case it should be needful to leave London at once after
seeing the Queen.

The French Ambassador's abode was an old con-
ventual building on the river-side, consisting of a
number of sets of separate chambers, like those of a
college, opening on a quadrangle in the centre, and
with one side occupied by the state apartments and
chapel.   This arrangement eminently suited the
French suite, every one of whom liked to have his
own little arrangements of cookery, and to look after
his own *marmite* in his own way, all being alike
horrified at the gross English diet and lack of vege-
tables.   Many tried experiments in the way of growing salads in little gardens of their own, with little
heed to the once beautiful green grass-plot which they
broke up.

Inside that gate it was like a new country, and as
all the shrill thin intonations of the French rang in
her ears, Cicely could hardly believe that she had—
she said—only a brick wall between her and old
England.

M. de Salmonnet was unmistakably a Scot by
descent, though he had never seen the land of his
ancestors.   His grandfather had been ennobled, but
only belonged to the lesser order of the *noblesse*, being
exempted from imposts, but not being above employment, especially in diplomacy.   He had acted as
secretary, interpreter, and general factotum, to a whole
succession of ambassadors, and thus his little *loge*, as
he called it, had become something of a home.   His
wife had once or twice before had to take charge of
young ladies, French or English, who were confided
to the embassy, and she had a guest chamber for
them, a small room, but with an oriel window over-
hanging the Thames and letting in the southern sun,
so as almost to compensate for the bareness of the rest,

where there was nothing but a square box-bed, a chest, and a few toilette essentials, to break upon the dulness of the dark wainscoted walls. Madame herself came to sleep with her guest, for lonely nights were regarded with dread in those times, and indeed she seemed to regard it as her duty never to lose sight of her charge for a moment.

Madame de Salmonnet's proper bed-chamber was the only approach to this little room, but that mattered the less as it was also the parlour! The bed, likewise a box, was in the far-off recesses, and the family were up and astir long before the November sun. Dressed Madame could scarcely be called—the costume in which she assisted Babette and queer wizened old Pierrot in doing the morning's work, horrified Cicely, used as she was to Mistress Susan's scrupulous neatness. Downstairs there was a sort of office room of Monsieur's, where the family meals were taken, and behind it an exceedingly small kitchen, where Madame and Pierrot performed marvels of cookery, surpassing those of Queen Mary's five cooks.

Cicely longed to assist in them, and after a slight demur, she was permitted to do so, chiefly because her duenna could not otherwise watch her and the confections at the same time. Cis could never make out whether it was as princess or simply as maiden that she was so closely watched, for Madame bristled and swelled like a mother cat about to spring at a strange dog, if any gentleman of the suite showed symptoms of accosting her. Nay, when Mr. Talbot once brought Diccon in with him, and there was a greeting, which to Cicely's mind was dismally cold and dry, the lady was so scandalised that Cicely was obliged formally to tell her that she would answer for it to the Queen. On Sunday, Mr. Talbot always

came to take her to church, and this was a terrible grievance to Madame, though it was to Cicely the one refreshment of the week. If it had been only the being out
of hearing of her hostess's incessant tongue, the walk
would have been a refreshment. Madame de Salmonnet
had been transported from home so young that she was
far more French than Scottish; she was a small woman
full of activity and zeal of all kinds, though perhaps
most of all for her *pot au feu*. She was busied about
her domestic affairs morning, noon, and night, and never
ceased chattering the whole time, till Cicely began to
regard the sound like the clack of the mill at Bridgefield. Yet, talker as she was, she was a safe woman,
and never had been known to betray secrets. Indeed,
much more of her conversation consisted of speculations
on the tenderness of the poultry, or the freshness of the
fish, than of anything that went much deeper. She
did, however, spend much time in describing the habits
and customs of the pensioners at Soissons; the *maigre*
food they had to eat; their tricks upon the elder and
graver nuns, and a good deal besides that was amusing
at first, but which became rather wearisome, and made
Cicely wonder what either of her mothers would have
thought of it.

The excuse for all this was to enable the maiden to
make her appearance before Queen Elizabeth as freshly
brought from Soissons by her mother's danger. Mary
herself had suggested this, as removing all danger from
the Talbots, and as making it easier for the French
Embassy to claim and protect Cis herself; and M. de
Châteauneuf had so far acquiesced as to desire Madame
de Salmonnet to see whether the young lady could be
prepared to assume the character before eyes that would
not be over qualified to judge. Cis, however, had

always been passive when the proposal was made, and
the more she heard from Madame de Salmonnet, the
more averse she was to it. The only consideration
that seemed to her in its favour was the avoidance of
implicating her foster-father, but a Sunday morning
spent with him removed the scruple.

" I know I cannot feign," she said. " They all used
to laugh at me at Chartley for being too much of the
downright mastiff to act a part."

" I am right glad to hear it," said Richard.

" Moreover," added Cicely, " if I did try to turn my
words with the Scottish or French ring, I wot that the
sight of the Queen's Majesty and my anxiety would
drive out from me all I should strive to remember, and
I should falter and utter mere folly; and if she saw
I was deceiving her, there would be no hope at all.
Nay, how could I ask God Almighty to bless my doing
with a lie in my mouth ?"

" There spake my Susan's own maid," said Richard.
" 'Tis the joy of my heart that they have not been able
to teach thee to lie with a good grace. Trust my
word, my wench, truth is the only wisdom, and one
would have thought they might have learnt it by this
time."

" I only doubted, lest it should be to your damage,
dear father. Can they call it treason ?"

" I trow not, my child. The worst that could hap
would be that I might be lodged in prison a while, or
have to pay a fine ; and liefer, far liefer, would I undergo the like than that those lips of thine should learn
guile. I say not that there is safety for any of us,
least of all for thee, my poor maid, but the danger is
tenfold increased by trying to deceive ; and, moreover,
it cannot be met with a good conscience."

s

"Moreover," said Cicely, "I have pleadings and promises to make on my mother-queen's behalf that would come strangely amiss if I had to feign that I had never seen her! May I not seek the Queen at once, without waiting for this French gentleman? Then would this weary, weary time be at an end! Each time I hear a bell, or a cannon shot, I start and think, Oh! has she signed the warrant? Is it too late?"

"There is no fear of that," said Richard; "I shall know from Will Cavendish the instant aught is done, and through Diccon I could get thee brought to the Queen's very chamber in time to plead. Meantime, the Queen is in many minds. She cannot bear to give up her kinswoman; she sits apart and mutters, '*Aut fer aut feri,*' and '*Ne feriare feri.*' Her ladies say she tosses and sighs all night, and hath once or twice awoke shrieking that she was covered with blood. It is Burghley and Walsingham who are forcing this on, and not her free will. Strengthen but her better will, and let her feel herself secure, and she will spare, and gladly."

"That do I hope to do," said Cicely, encouraged.

The poor girl had to endure many a vicissitude and heart-sinking before M. de Bellièvre appeared; and when he did come, he was a disappointment.

He was a most magnificent specimen of the *mignons* of Henri's court. The Embassy rang with stories of the number of mails he had brought, of the milk baths he sent for, the gloves he slept in, the valets who tweaked out superfluous hairs from his eyebrows, the delicacies required for his little dogs.

M. de Salmonnet reported that on hearing the story of "Mademoiselle," as Cicely was called in the Embassy, he had twirled the waxed ends of his moustaches into a satirical twist, and observed, "That is well found, and may serve as a last resource."

He never would say that he disbelieved what he was told of her; and when presented to her, he behaved with an exaggerated deference which angered her intensely, for it seemed to her mockery of her pretensions. No doubt his desire was that Mary's life should be granted to the intercession of his king rather than to any other consideration; and therefore once, twice, thrice, he had interviews with Elizabeth, and still he would not take the anxious suppliant, who was in an agony at each disappointment, as she watched the gay barge float down the river, and who began to devise setting forth alone, to seek the Queen at Richmond and end it all! She would have done so, but that Diccon told her that since the alarm caused by Barnwell, it had become so much more difficult to approach the Queen that she would have no hope.

But she was in a restless state that made Madame de Salmonnet's chatter almost distracting, when at last, far on in January, M. de Salmonnet came in.

"Well, mademoiselle, the moment is come. The passports are granted, but Monsieur the Ambassador Extraordinary has asked for a last private audience, and he prays your Highness to be ready to accompany him at nine of the clock to-morrow morning."

Cicely's first thought was to send tidings to Mr. Talbot, and in this M. de Salmonnet assisted her, though his wife thought it very superfluous to drag in the great, dull, heavy, English sailor. The girl longed for a sight and speech of him all that evening in vain, though she was sure she saw the *Mastiff's* boat pass down the river, and most earnestly did she wish she could have had her chamber to herself for the prayers

and preparations, on which Madame's tongue broke so
intolerably that she felt as if she should ere long be
wild and senseless, and unable to recollect anything.

She had only a little peace when Madame rose
early in the morning and left her, thinking her asleep,
for a brief interval, which gave her time to rally her
thoughts and commend herself to her only Guide.

She let Madame dress her, as had been determined,
in perfectly plain black, with a cap that would have
suited "a novice out of convent shade." It was certainly the most suitable garb for a petitioner for her
mother's life. In her hand she took the Queen's letter,
and the most essential proofs of her birth. She was
cloaked and hooded over all as warmly as possible to
encounter the cold of the river : and Madame de Salmonnet, sighing deeply at the cold, arranged herself to
chaperon her, and tried to make her fortify herself with
food, but she was too tremulous to swallow anything
but a little bread and wine. Poor child ! She felt
frightfully alone amongst all those foreign tongues,
above all when the two ambassadors crossed the court
to M. de Salmonnet's little door. Bellièvre, rolled up
in splendid sables from head to foot, bowed down to
the ground before her, almost sweeping the pavement
with his plume, and asked in his deferential voice of
mockery if her Royal Highness would do him the
honour of accepting his escort.

Cicely bent her head and said in French, " I thank
you, sir," giving him her hand ; and there was a grave
dignity in the action that repressed him, so that he did
not speak again as he led her to the barge, which was
covered in at the stern so as to afford a shelter from the
wind.

Her quick eye detected the *Mastiff's* boat as she

was handed down the stairs, and this was some relief, while she was placed in the seat of honour, with an ambassador on each side of her.

" May I ask," demanded Bellièvre, waving a scented handkerchief, " what her Highness is prepared to say, in case I have to confirm it ?"

" I thank your Excellency," replied Cicely, " but I mean to tell the simple truth; and as your Excellency has had no previous knowledge of me, I do not see how you can confirm it."

The two gentlemen looked at one another, and Châteauneuf said, " Do I understand her Royal Highness that she does not come as the *pensionnaire* from Soissons, as the Queen had recommended ?"

" No, sir," said Cicely; " I have considered the matter, and I could not support the character. All that I ask of your Excellencies is to bring me into the presence of Queen Elizabeth. I will do the rest myself, with the help of God."

" Perhaps she is right," said the one ambassador to the other. " These English are incomprehensible !"

CHAPTER XLII.

THE SUPPLICATION.

IN due time the boat drew up at the stairs leading to
the palace of Richmond.   Cicely, in the midst of her
trepidation, perceived that Diccon was among the
gentlemen pensioners who made a lane from the landing to receive them, as she was handed along by M. de
Bellièvre.   In the hall there was a pause, during
which the mufflings were thrown off, and Cicely
appeared in her simple black, a great contrast to her
cavalier, who was clad from neck to knee in pale pink
satin, quilted, and with a pearl at each intersection,
earrings in his ears, perfumed and long-fringed gloves
in his hand—a perfect specimen of the foppery of the
Court of France.   However, he might have been in
hodden gray without her perceiving it.   She had the
sensation of having plunged into deep, unknown waters,
without rope or plank, and being absolutely forced to
strike out for herself; yet the very urgency of the
moment, acting on her high blood and recent training,
made her, outwardly, perfectly self-possessed and calm.
She walked along, holding her head in the regal
manner that was her inheritance, and was so utterly
absorbed in the situation that she saw nothing, and
thought only of the Queen.

This was to be a private audience, and after a minute's demur with the clerk of the chamber, when Châteauneuf made some explanation, a door was opened, a curtain withdrawn, and the two ambassadors and the young lady were admitted to Elizabeth's closet, where she sat alone, in an arm-chair with a table before her. Cicely's first glance at the Queen reminded her of the Countess, though the face was older, and had an intellect and a grandeur latent in it, such as Bess of Hardwicke had never possessed; but it was haggard and worn, the eyelids red, either with weeping, or with sleeplessness, and there was an anxious look about the keen light hazel eyes which was sometimes almost pathetic, and gave Cicely hope. To the end of her days she never could recollect how the Queen was arrayed; she saw nothing but the expression in those falcon eyes, and the strangely sensitive mouth, which bewrayed the shrewish nose and chin, and the equally inconsistent firmness of the jaw.

The first glance Cicely encountered was one of utter amazement and wrath, as the Queen exclaimed, "Whom have you brought hither, Messieurs?"

Before either could reply, she, whom they had thought a raw, helpless girl, moved forward, and kneeling before Elizabeth said, "It is I, so please your Majesty, I, who have availed myself of the introduction of their Excellencies to lay before your Majesty a letter from my mother, the Queen of Scots."

Queen Elizabeth made so vehement and incredulous an exclamation of amazement that Cicely was the more reminded of the Countess, and this perhaps made her task the easier, and besides, she was not an untrained rustic, but had really been accustomed to familiar intercourse with a queen, who, captive as she was, maintained full state and etiquette.

She therefore made answer with dignity, " If it will please your Majesty to look at this letter, you will see the proofs of what I say, and that I am indeed Bride Hepburn, the daughter of Queen Mary's last marriage. I was born at Lochleven on the 20th of February of the year of grace 1567,[1] and thence secretly sent in the *Bride of Dunbar* to be bred up in France. The ship was wrecked, and all lost on board, but I was, by the grace of God, picked up by a good and gallant gentleman of my Lord of Shrewsbury's following, Master Richard Talbot of Bridgefield, who brought me up as his own daughter, all unknowing whence I came or who I was, until three years ago, when one of the secret agents who had knowledge of the affairs of the Queen of Scots made known to her that I was the babe who had been embarked in the *Bride of Dunbar*."

" Verily, thou must be a bold wench to expect me to believe such a mere minstrel's tale," said Elizabeth.

" Nevertheless, madam, it is the simple truth, as you will see if you deign to open this packet."

" And who or where is this same honourable gentleman who brought you up—Richard Talbot ? I have heard that name before ! "

" He is here, madam. He will confirm all I say."

The Queen touched a little bell, and ordered Master Talbot of Bridgefield to be brought to her, while, hastily casting her eyes on the credentials, she demanded of Châteauneuf, " Knew you aught of this, sir ? "

" I know only what the Queen of Scotland has written and what this Monsieur Talbot has told me,

---

[1] 1568 according to our Calendar.

madam," said Châteauneuf. "There can be no doubt
that the Queen of Scotland has treated her as a
daughter, and owns her for such in her letter to me,
as well as to your Majesty."

"And the letters are no forgery?"

"Mine is assuredly not, madam; I know the
private hand of the Queen of Scots too well to be
deceived. Moreover, Madame Curll, the wife of the
Secretary, and others, can speak to the manner in
which this young lady was treated."

"Openly treated as a daughter! That passes,
sir. My faithful subjects would never have left me
uninformed!"

"So please your Majesty," here the maiden ventured,
"I have always borne the name of Cicely Talbot, and
no one knows what is my real birth save those who
were with my mother at Lochleven, excepting Mrs.
Curll. The rest even of her own attendants only
understood me to be a Scottish orphan. My true
lineage should never have been known, were it not a
daughter's duty to plead for her mother."

By this time Mr. Talbot was at the door, and he
was received by the Queen with, "So ho! Master Talbot, how is this? You, that have been vaunted to us
as the very pink of fidelity, working up a tale that
smacks mightily of treason and leasing!"

"The truth is oft stranger than any playwright
can devise," said Richard, as he knelt.

"If it be truth, the worse for you, sir," said the
Queen, hotly. "What colour can you give to thus
hiding one who might, forsooth, claim royal blood,
tainted though it be?"

"Pardon me, your Grace. For many years I knew
not who the babe was whom I had taken from the

s*

wreck, and when the secret of her birth was discovered, I deemed it not mine own but that of the Queen of Scots."

"A captive's secrets are not her own, and are only kept by traitors," said Elizabeth, severely.

At this Cicely threw herself forward with glowing cheeks. "Madam, madam, traitor never was named in the same breath with Master Talbot's name before. If he kept the secret, it was out of pity, and knowing no hurt could come to your Majesty by it."

"Thou hast a tongue, wench, be thou who thou mayst," said Elizabeth sharply. "Stand back, and let him tell his own tale."

Richard very briefly related the history of the rescue of the infant, which he said he could confirm by the testimony of Goatley and of Heatherthwayte. He then explained how Langston had been present when she was brought home, and had afterwards made communications to the Queen of Scots that led to the girl, already in attendance on her, being claimed and recognised; after which he confessed that he had not the heart to do what might separate the mother and daughter by declaring their relationship. Elizabeth meanwhile was evidently comparing his narrative with the letters of the Queen of Scots, asking searching questions here and there.

She made a sound of perplexity and annoyance at the end, and said, "This must be further inquired into."

Here Cicely, fearing an instant dismissal, clasped her hands, and on her knees exclaimed, "Madam! it will not matter. No trouble shall ever be caused by my drop of royal blood; no one shall ever even know that Bride of Scotland exists, save the few who now know it, and have kept the secret most faithfully. I seek no state; all I ask is my mother's life. O madam, would you but see her, and speak with her, you would know how far from her thoughts is any evil to your royal person!"

"Tush, wench! we know better. Is this thy lesson?"

"None hath taught me any lesson, madam. I know what my mother's enemies have, as they say, proved against her, and I know they say that while she lives your Grace cannot be in security."

"That is what moves my people to demand her death," said Elizabeth.

"It is not of your own free will, madam, nor of your own kind heart," cried Cicely. "That I well know! And, madam, I will show you the way. Let but my mother be escorted to some convent abroad, in France or Austria, or anywhere beyond the reach of Spain, and her name should be hidden from everyone! None should know where to seek her. Not even the Abbess should know her name. She would be prisoned in a cell, but she would be happy, for she would have life and the free exercise of her religion. No English Papist, no Leaguer, none should ever trace her, and she would disquiet you no more."

"And who is to answer that, when once beyond English bounds, she should not stir up more trouble than ever?" demanded Elizabeth.

"That do I," said the girl. "Here am I, Bride Hepburn, ready to live in your Majesty's hands as a hostage, whom you might put to death at the first stirring on her behalf."

"Silly maid, we have no love of putting folk to death," said Elizabeth, rather hurt. "That is only for traitors, when they forfeit our mercy."

"Then, O madam, madam, what has been done
in her name cannot forfeit mercy for her! She was
shut up in prison; I was with her day and night, and
I know she had naught to do with any evil purpose
towards your Majesty. Ah! you do not believe me!
I know they have found her guilty, and *that* is not
what I came to say," she continued, getting bewildered
in her earnestness for a moment. "No. But, gracious
Queen, you have spared her often; I have heard her
say that you had again and again saved her life from
those who would fain have her blood."

"It is true," said Elizabeth, half softened.

"Save her then now, madam," entreated the girl.
"Let her go beyond their reach, yet where none shall
find her to use her name against you. Let me go to
her at Fotheringhay with these terms. She will consent
and bless and pray for you for ever; and here am I,
ready to do what you will with me!"

"To hang about Court, and be found secretly
wedded to some base groom!"

"No, madam. I give you my solemn word as a
Queen's daughter that I will never wed, save by your
consent, if my mother's life be granted. The King of
Scots knows not that there is such a being. He need
never know it. I will thank and bless you whether
you throw me into the Tower, or let me abide as the
humblest of your serving-women, under the name I
have always borne, Cicely Talbot."

"Foolish maid, thou mayest purpose as thou sayest,
but I know what wenches are made of too well to
trust thee."

"Ah madam, pardon me, but you know not how
strong a maiden's heart can be for a mother's sake.
Madam! you have never seen my mother. If you

but knew her patience and her tenderness, you would
know how not only I, but every man or woman in her
train, would gladly lay down life and liberty for her,
could we but break her bonds, and win her a shelter
among those of her own faith."

"Art a Papist?" asked the Queen, observing the
pronoun.

"Not so, an't please your Majesty. This gentleman bred me up in our own Church, nor would I
leave it."

"Strange—strange matters," muttered Elizabeth,
"and they need to be duly considered."

"I will then abide your Majesty's pleasure," said
Cicely, "craving license that it may be at Fotheringhay
with my mother. Then can I bear her the tidings,
and she will write in full her consent to these terms.
O madam, I see mercy in your looks. Receive a
daughter's blessing and thanks!"

"Over fast, over fast, maiden. Who told thee that
I had consented?"

"Your Majesty's own countenance," replied Cicely
readily. "I see pity in it, and the recollection that
all posterity for evermore will speak of the clemency
of Elizabeth as the crown of all her glories!"

"Child, child," said the Queen, really moved,
"Heaven knows that I would gladly practise clemency
if my people would suffer it, but they fear for my life,
and still more for themselves, were I removed, nor can
I blame them."

"Your Majesty, I know that. But my mother
would be dead to the world, leaving her rights solemnly
made over to her son. None would know where to
find her, and she would leave in your hands, and those
of the Parliament, a resignation of all her claims."

"And would she do this? Am I to take it on thy word, girl?"

"Your Majesty knows this ring, sent to her at Lochleven," said Cicely, holding it up. "It is the pledge that she binds herself to these conditions. Oh! let me but bear them to her, and you shall have them signed and sealed, and your Majesty will know the sweet bliss of pardoning. May I carry the tidings to her? I can go with this gentleman as Cis Talbot returning to her service."

Elizabeth bent her head as though assenting thoughtfully.

"How shall I thank you, gracious Queen?" cried Cicely, joining hands in a transport, but Elizabeth sharply cut her short.

"What means the wench? I have promised nothing. I have only said I will look into this strange story of thine, and consider this proposal—that is, if thy mother, as thou callest her, truly intend it—ay, and will keep to it."

"That is all I could ask of your Majesty," said Cicely. "The next messenger after my return shall carry her full consent to these conditions, and there will I abide your pleasure until the time comes for her to be conducted to her convent, if not to see your face, which would be best of all. O madam, what thanks will be worthy of such a grace?"

"Wait to see whether it is a grace, little cousin," said Elizabeth, but with a kiss to the young round cheek, and a friendliness of tone that surprised all. "Messieurs," she added to the ambassadors, "you came, if I mistake not, to bring me this young demoiselle."

"Who has, I hope, pleaded more effectually than I," returned Bellièvre.

" I have made no promises, sir," said the Queen, drawing herself up proudly.

" Still your Majesty forbids us not to hope," said Châteauneuf.

Wherewith they found themselves dismissed.

There was a great increase of genuine respect in the manner in which Bellièvre handed the young lady from the Queen's chamber through the gallery and hall, and finally to the boat. No one spoke, for there were many standing around, but Cicely could read in a glance that passed between the Frenchmen that they were astonished at her success. Her own brain was in a whirl, her heart beating high ; she could hardly realise what had passed, but when again placed in the barge the first words she heard were from Bellièvre. " Your Royal Highness will permit me to congratulate you." At the same time she saw, to her great joy, that M. de Châteauneuf had caused her foster-father to enter the barge with them. " If the Queen of Scotland were close at hand, the game would be won," said Bellièvre.

" Ah ! Milord Treasurer and M. le Secretaire are far too cunning to have let her be within reach," said Châteauneuf.

" Could we but have bound the Queen to anything," added Bellièvre.

" That she always knows how to avoid," said the resident ambassador.

" At least," said Cicely, " she has permitted that I should bear the terms to my mother at Fotheringhay."

" That is true," said Châteauneuf, " and in my opinion no time should be lost in so doing. I doubt," he added, looking at Richard, " whether, now that her Highness's exalted rank is known, the embassy will be permitted to remain a shelter to her, in case the Queen should demand her of me."

"Your Excellency speaks my thought," said Richard. "I am even disposed to believe that it would be wiser to begin our journey this very day."

"I grieve for the apparent inhospitality and disrespect to one whom I honour so highly," said Châteauneuf, "but I verily believe it would be the wiser plan. Look you, sir, the enemies of the unfortunate Queen of Scotland have done all in their power to hinder my colleague from seeing the Queen, but to-day the Lord Treasurer is occupied at Westminster, and Monsieur le Secretaire is sick. She sent for us in one of those wilful moods in which she chooses to assert herself without their knowledge, and she remains, as it were, stunned by the surprise, and touched by her Royal Highness's pleading. But let these gentlemen discover what has passed, or let her recover and send for them, and bah! they will inquire, and messengers will go forth at once to stop her Highness and yourself. All will be lost. But if you can actually be on the way to this castle before they hear of it—and it is possible you may have a full day in advance—they will be unable to hinder the conditions from being laid before the Queen of Scots, and we are witnesses of what they were."

"Oh, let us go! let us go at once, dear sir," entreated Cicely. "I burn to carry my mother this hope."

It was not yet noon, so early had been the audience, and dark and short as were the days, it was quite possible to make some progress on the journey before night. Cicely had kept the necessaries for her journey ready, and so had Mr. Talbot, even to the purchase of horses, which were in the Shrewsbury House stables.

The rest of the mails could be fetched by the *Mastiff's* crew, and brought to Hull under charge of Goatley. Madame de Salmonnet was a good deal scandalised at Son Altesse Royale going off with only a male escort, and to Cicely's surprise, wept over her, and prayed aloud that she might have good success, and bring safety and deliverance to the good and persecuted Queen for whom she had attempted so much.

" Sir," said Châteauneuf, as he stood beside Richard, waiting till the girl's preparations were over, " if there could have been any doubts of the royal lineage of your charge, her demeanour to-day would have disproved them. She stood there speaking as an equal, all undaunted before that Queen before whom all tremble, save when they can cajole her."

" She stood there in the strength of truth and inno- cence," said Richard.

Whereat the Frenchman again looked perplexed at these incomprehensible English.

Cicely presently appeared. It was wonderful to see how that one effort had given her dignity and womanhood. She thanked the two ambassadors for the countenance they had given to her, and begged them to continue their exertions in her mother's cause. " And," she added, " I believe my mother has already requested of you to keep this matter a secret."

They bowed, and she added, " You perceive, gentle- men, that the very conditions I have offered involve secrecy both as to my mother's future abode and my existence. Therefore, I trust that you will not consider it inconsistent with your duty to the King of France to send no word of this."

Again they assured her of their secrecy, and the promise was so far kept that the story was reserved for the private ear of Henri III. on Bellièvre's return, and never put into the despatches.

Two days later, Cicely enjoyed some of the happiest hours of her life. She stood by the bed where her mother was lying, and was greeted with the cry, " My child, my child! I thought I never should see thee more. *Domine, nunc dimittis!*"

" Nay, dearest mother, but I trust she will show mercy. I bring you conditions."

Mary laid her head on her daughter's shoulder and listened. It might be that she had too much experience of Elizabeth's vacillations to entertain much hope of her being allowed to retire beyond her grasp into a foreign convent, and she declared that she could not endure that her beloved, devoted child should wear away her life under Elizabeth's jealous eye ; but Cis put this aside, saying with a smile, " I think she will not be hard with me. She will be no worse than my Lady Countess, and I shall have a secret of joy within me in thinking of you resting among the good nuns."

And Mary caught hope from the anticipations she would not damp, and gave herself to the description of the peaceful cloister life, reviewing in turn the nunneries she had heard described, and talking over their rules. There would indeed be as little liberty as here, but she would live in the midst of prayer and praise, and be at rest from the plots and plans, the hopes and fears, of her long captivity, and be at leisure for penitence. " For, ah! my child, guiltless though I be of much that is laid to my charge, thy mother is a sinful woman, all unworthy of what her brave and innocent daughter has dared and done for her."

Almost equally precious with that mother's greeting

was the grave congratulating look of approval which
Cicely met in Humfrey's eyes when he had heard all
from his father.   He could exult in her, even while he
thought sadly of the future which she had so bravely
risked, watching over her from a distance in his silent,
self-restrained, unselfish devotion.

The Queen's coldness towards Humfrey had meantime diminished daily, though he could not guess
whether she really viewed his course as the right one, or
whether she forgave this as well as all other injuries
in the calm gentle state into which she had come, not
greatly moved by hope or fear, content alike to live
or die.

Richard, in much anxiety, was to remain another
day or two at Fotheringhay, on the plea of his wearied
horses and of the Sunday rest.

Meantime Mary diligently wrote the conditions,
but perhaps more to satisfy her daughter than with
much hope of their acceptance.

CHAPTER XLIII.

THE WARRANT.

"YEA, madam, they are gone! They stole away at once, and are far on the way to Fotheringhay, with these same conditions." So spoke Davison, under-secretary, Walsingham being still indisposed.

"And therefore will I see whether the Queen of Scots will ratify them, ere I go farther in the matter," returned Elizabeth.

"She will ratify them without question," said the Secretary, ironically, "seeing that to escape into the hands of one of your Majesty's enemies is just what she desires."

"She leaves her daughter as a pledge."

"Yea, a piece of tinsel to delude your Majesty."

Elizabeth swore an oath that there was truth in every word and gesture of the maiden.

"The poor wench may believe all she said herself," said Davison. "Nay, she is as much deluded as the rest, and so is that honest, dull-pated sailor, Talbot. If your Majesty will permit me to call in a fellow I have here, I can make all plain."

"Who is he? You know I cannot abide those foul carrion rascals you make use of," said Elizabeth, with an air of disgust.

" This man is gentleman born. Villain he may be,
but there is naught to offend your Majesty in him.
He is one Langston, a kinsman of this Talbot's; and
having once been a Papist, but now having seen the
error of his ways, he did good service in the unwinding
of the late horrible plot."

" Well, if no other way will serve you but I must
hear the fellow, have him in."

A neatly-dressed, small, elderly man, entirely arrayed
in black, was called in, and knelt most humbly before
the Queen. Being bidden to tell what he knew respecting the lady who had appeared before the Queen
the day before, calling herself Bride Hepburn, he returned for answer that he believed it to be verily her
name, but that she was the daughter of a man who had
fled to France, and become an archer of the Scottish guard.

He told how he had been at Hull when the infant
had been saved from the wreck, and brought home to
Mistress Susan Talbot, who left the place the next day,
and had, he understood, bred up the child as her own.
He himself, being then, as he confessed, led astray by
the delusions of Popery, had much commerce with the
Queen's party, and had learnt from some of the garrison
of Dunfermline that the child on board the lost ship
was the offspring of this same Hepburn, and of one of
Queen Mary's many namesake kindred, who had died
in childbirth at Lochleven. And now Langston professed bitterly to regret what he had done when, in
his disguise at Buxton, he had made known to some
of Mary's suite that the supposed Cicely Talbot was of
their country and kindred. She had been immediately
made a great favourite by the Queen of Scots, and the
attendants all knew who she really was, though she
still went by the name of Talbot. He imagined that

the Queen of Scots, whose charms were not so im-
perishable as those which dazzled his eyes at this
moment, wanted a fresh bait for her victims, since she
herself was growing old, and thus had actually succeeded in binding Babington to her service, though
even then the girl was puffed up with notions of her
own importance and had flouted him. And now, all
other hope having vanished, Queen Mary's last and
ablest resource had been to possess the poor maiden
with an idea of being actually her own child, and then
to work on her filial obedience' to offer herself as a
hostage, whom Mary herself could without scruple
leave to her fate, so soon as she was ready to head an
army of invaders.

Davison further added that the Secretary Nau could
corroborate that Bride Hepburn was known to the suite
as a kinswoman of the Queen, and that Mr. Cavendish,
clerk to Sir Francis Walsingham, knew that Babington
had been suitor to the young lady, and had crossed
swords with young Talbot on her account.

Elizabeth listened, and made no comment at the
time, save that she sharply questioned Langston; but
his tale was perfectly coherent, and as it threw the
onus of the deception entirely on Mary, it did not
conflict either with the sincerity evident in both Cicely
and her foster-father, or with the credentials supplied
by the Queen of Scots. Of the ciphered letter, and of
the monograms, Elizabeth had never heard, though, if
she had asked for further proof, they would have been
brought forward.

She heard all, dismissed Langston, and with some
petulance bade Davison likewise begone, being aware
that her ministers meant her to draw the moral that
she had involved herself in difficulties by holding a

private audience of the French Ambassadors without
their knowledge or presence. It may be that the very
sense of having been touched exasperated her the more.
She paced up and down the room restlessly, and her
ladies heard her muttering—"That she should cheat
me thus! I have pitied her often; I will pity her no
more! To breed up that poor child to be palmed on
me! I will make an end of it; I can endure this no
longer! These tossings to and fro are more than I
can bear, and all for one who is false, false, false, false!
My brain will bear no more. Hap what hap, an end
must be made of it. She or I, she or I must die; and
which is best for England and the faith? That girl had
well-nigh made me pity her, and it was all a vile cheat!"

Thus it was that Elizabeth sent for Davison, and
bade him bring the warrant with him.

And thus it was that in the midst of dinner in the
hall, on the Sunday, the 5th of February, the *meiné* of
the Castle were startled by the arrival of Mr. Beale,
the Clerk of the Council, always a bird of sinister
omen, and accompanied by a still more alarming figure,
a strong burly man clad in black velvet from head to
foot. Every one knew who he was, and a thrill of
dismay, that what had been so long expected had come
at last, went through all who saw him pass through
the hall. Sir Amias was summoned from table, and
remained in conference with the two arrivals all through
evening chapel time—an event in itself extraordinary
enough to excite general anxiety. It was Humfrey's
turn to be on guard, and he had not long taken his
station before he was called into the Queen's apartments, where she sat at the foot of her bed, in a large
chair with a small table before her. No one was with
her but her two mediciners, Bourgoin and Gorion.

"Here," she said, "is the list our good Doctor has writ of the herbs he requires for my threatened attack of rheumatism."

"I will endeavour, with Sir Amias's permission, to seek them in the park," said Humfrey.

"But tell me," said Mary, fixing her clear eyes upon him, "tell me truly. Is there not a surer and more lasting cure for all my ills in preparation ? Who was it who arrived to-night ?"

"Madame," said Humfrey, bowing his head low as he knelt on one knee, "it was Mr. Beale."

"Ay, and who besides ?"

"Madam, I heard no name, but"—as she waited for him to speak further, he uttered in a choked voice —"it was one clad in black."

"I perceive," said Mary, looking up with a smile. " A more effectual Doctor than you, my good Bourgoin. I thank my God and my cousin Elizabeth for giving me the martyr's hope at the close of the most mournful life that ever woman lived. Nay, leave me not as yet, good Humfrey. I have somewhat to say unto thee. I have a charge for thee." Something in her tone led him to look up earnestly in her face. "Thou lovest my child, I think," she added.

The young man's voice was scarcely heard, and he only said, "Yea, madam ;" but there was an intensity in the tone and eyes which went to her heart.

"Thou dost not speak, but thou canst do. Wilt thou take her, Humfrey, and with her, all the inheritance of peril and sorrow that dogs our unhappy race ?"

"Oh"—and there was a mighty sob that almost cut off his voice—" My life is already hers, and would be spent in her service wherever, whatever she was."

"I guessed it," said the Queen, letting her hand rest

on his shoulder. "And for her thou wilt endure, if needful, suspicion, danger, exile?"

"They will be welcome, so I may shield her."

"I trust thee," she said, and she took his firm strong hand into her own white wasted one. "But will thy father consent? Thou art his eldest son and heir."

"He loves her like his own daughter. My brother may have the lands."

"'Tis strange," said Mary, "that in wedding a princess, 'tis no crown, no kingdom, that is set before thee, only the loss of thine own inheritance. For now that the poor child has made herself known to Elizabeth, there will be no safety for her between these seas. I have considered it well. I had thought of sending her abroad with my French servants, and making her known to my kindred there. That would have been well if she could have accepted the true faith, or if— if her heart had not been thine; but to have sent her as she is would only expose her to persecution, and she hath not the mounting spirit that would cast aside love for the sake of rising. She lived too long with thy mother to be aught save a homely Cis. I would have made a princess of her, but it passes my powers. Nay, the question is, whether it may yet be possible to prevent the Queen from laying hands on her."

"My father is still here," said Humfrey, "and I deem not that any orders have come respecting her. Might not he crave permission to take her home, that is, if she will leave your Grace?"

"I will lay my commands on her! It is well thought of," said the Queen. "How soon canst thou have speech with him?"

"He is very like to come to my post," said Humfrey, "and then we can walk the gallery and talk unheard."

"It is well. Let him make his demand, and I will have her ready to depart as early as may be to-morrow morn. Bourgoin, I would ask thee to call the maiden hither."

Cicely appeared from the apartment where she had been sitting with the other ladies.

"Child," said the Queen, as she came in, "is thy mind set on wedding an archduke?"

"Marriage is not for me, madam," said Cicely, perplexed and shaken by this strange address and by Humfrey's presence.

"Nay, didst not once tell me of a betrothal now many years ago? What wouldst say if thine own mother were to ratify it?"

"Ah! madam," said Cicely, blushing crimson however, "but I pledged myself never to wed save with Queen Elizabeth's consent."

"On one condition," said the Queen. "But if that condition were not observed by the other party——"

"How—what, mother!" exclaimed Cicely, with a scream. "There is no fear — Humfrey, have you heard aught?"

"Nothing is certain," said Mary, calmly. "I ask thee not to break thy word. I ask thee, if thou wert free to marry, if thou wouldst be an Austrian or Lorraine duchess, or content thee with an honest English youth whose plighted word is more precious to him than gold."

"O mother, how can you ask?" said Cicely, dropping down, and hiding her face in the Queen's lap.

"Then, Humfrey Talbot, I give her to thee, my child, my Bride of Scotland. Thou wilt guard her, and shield her, and for thine own sake as well as hers, save her from the wrath and jealousy of Elizabeth.—

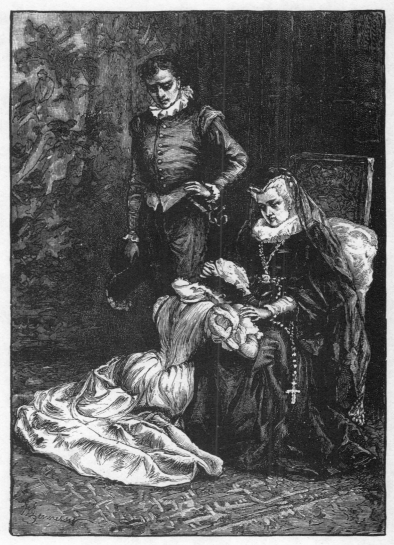

"O mother, how can you ask?"   PAGE 554.

Hark, hark! Rise, my child. They are presenting arms. We shall have Paulett in anon to convey my rere-supper."

They had only just time to compose themselves before Paulett came in, looking, as they all thought, grimmer and more starched than ever, and not well pleased to find Humfrey there, but the Queen was equal to the occasion.

"Here is Dr. Bourgoin's list of the herbs that he needs to ease my aches," she said. "Master Talbot is so good as to say that, being properly instructed, he will go in search of them."

"They will not be needed," said Paulett, but he spoke no farther to the Queen. Outside, however, he said to Humfrey, "Young man, you do not well to waste the Sabbath evening in converse with that blinded woman;" and meeting Mr. Talbot himself on the stair, he said, "You are going in quest of your son, sir. You would do wisely to admonish him that he will bring himself into suspicion, if not worse, by loitering amid the snares and wiles of the woman whom wrath is even now overtaking."

Richard found his son pacing the gallery, almost choked with agitation, and with the endeavour to conceal it from the two stolid, heavy yeomen who dozed behind the screen. Not till he had reached the extreme end did Humfrey master his voice enough to utter in his father's ear, "She has given her to me!"

Richard could not answer for a moment, then he said, "I fear me it will be thy ruin, Humfrey."

"Not ruin in love or faithfulness," said the youth. "Father, you know I should everywhere have followed her and watched over her, even to the death, even if she could never have been mine."

"I trow thou wouldst," said Richard.

"Nor would you have it otherwise—your child, your only daughter, to be left unguarded."

"Nay, I know not that I would," said Richard. "I cannot but care for the poor maid like mine own, and I would not have thee less true-hearted, Humfrey, even though it cost thee thine home, and us our eldest son."

"You have Diccon and Ned," said Humfrey. And then he told what had passed,-and his father observed that Beale had evidently no knowledge of Cicely's conference with the Queen, and apparently no orders to seize her. It had oozed out that a commission had been sent to five noblemen to come and superintend the execution, since Sir Amias Paulett had again refused to let it take place without witnesses, and Richard undertook to apply at once to Sir Amias for permission to remove his daughter, on the ground of saving her tender youth from the shock.

"Then," said he, "I will leave a token at Nottingham where I have taken her; whether home or at once to Hull. If I leave Brown Roundle at the inn for thee, then come home; but if it be White Blossom, then come to Hull. It will be best that thou dost not know while here, and I cannot go direct to Hull, because the fens at this season may not be fit for riding. Heatherthwayte will need no proofs to convince him that she is not thy sister, and can wed you at once, and you will also be able to embark in case there be any endeavour to arrest her."

"Taking service in Holland," said Humfrey, "until there may be safety in returning to England."

Richard sighed. The risk and sacrifice were great, and it was to him like the loss of two children, but

the die was cast; Humfrey never could be other than
Cicely's devoted champion and guardian, and it was
better that it should be as her husband. So he repaired to Sir Amias, and told him that he desired
not to expose his daughter's tender years and feeble
spirits to the sight of the Queen's death, and claimed
permission to take her away with him the next day,
saying that the permission of the Queen had already
been granted through his son, whom he would gladly
also take with him.

Paulett hemmed and hawed. He thought it a
great error in Mr. Talbot to avoid letting his daughter
be edified by a spectacle that might go far to moderate
the contagion of intercourse with so obstinate a Papist
and deceiver. Being of pitiless mould himself, he
was incapable of appreciating Richard's observation
that compassion would only increase her devotion to
the unfortunate lady. He would not, or could not,
part with Humfrey. He said that there would be
such a turmoil and concourse that the services of the
captain of his yeomen would be indispensable, but
that he himself, and all the rest, would be free on the
Thursday at latest.

Mr. Talbot's desire to be away was a surprise to
him, for he was in difficulties how, even in that
enormous hall, to dispose of all who claimed by right
or by favour to witness what he called the tardy
fulfilment of judgment. Yet though he thought it a
weakness, he did not refuse, and ere night Mr. Talbot
was able to send formal word that the horses would
be ready for Mistress Cicely at break of day the next
morning.

The message was transmitted through the ladies as
the Queen sat writing at her table, and she at once

gave orders to Elizabeth Curll to prepare the cloak bag with necessaries for the journey.

Cicely cried out, " O madam my mother, do not send me from you!"

" There is no help for it, little one. It is the only hope of safety or happiness for thee."

" But I pledged myself to await Queen Elizabeth's reply here!"

" She has replied," said Mary.

" How?" cried Cicely. " Methought your letter confirming mine offers had not yet been sent."

" It hath not, but she hath made known to me that she rejects thy terms, my poor maid."

" Is there then no hope?" said the girl, under her breath, which came short with dismay.

" Hope! yea," said Mary, with a ray of brightness on her face, " but not earthly hope. That is over, and I am more at rest and peace than I can remember to have been since I was a babe at my mother's knee. But, little one, I must preserve thee for thine Humfrey and for happiness, and so thou must be gone ere the hounds be on thy track."

" Never, mother, I cannot leave you. You bid no one else to go!" said Cis, clinging to her with a face bathed in tears.

" No one else is imperilled by remaining as thy bold venture has imperilled thee, my sweet maid. Think, child, how fears for thee would disturb my spirit, when I would fain commune only with Heaven. Seest thou not that to lose thy dear presence for the few days left to me will be far better for me than to be rent with anxiety for thee, and it may be to see thee snatched from me by these stern, harsh men?"

" To quit you now! It is unnatural! I cannot."

"You will go, child. As Queen and as mother alike, I lay my commands on you. Let not the last, almost the only commands I ever gave thee be transgressed, and waste not these last hours in a vain strife."

She spoke with an authority against which Cis had no appeal, save by holding her hand tight and covering it with kisses and tears. Mary presently released her hand and went on writing, giving her a little time to restrain her agony of bitter weeping. The first words spoken were, "I shall not name thee in my will, nor recommend thee to thy brother. It would only bring on thee suspicion and danger. Here, however, is a letter giving full evidence of thy birth, and mentioning the various witnesses who can attest it. I shall leave the like with Melville, but it will be for thy happiness and safety if it never see the light. Should thy brother die without heirs, then it might be thy duty to come forward and stretch out thy hand for these two crowns, which have more thorns than jewels in them. Alas! would that I could dare to hope they might be exchanged for a crown of stars! But lie down on the bed, my bairnie. I have much still to do, and thou hast a long journey before thee."

Cicely would fain have resisted, but was forced to obey, though protesting that she should not sleep; and she lay awake for a long time watching the Queen writing, until unawares slumber overpowered her eyes. When she awoke, the Queen was standing over her saying, "It is time thou wert astir, little one!"

"Oh! and have I lost all these hours of you?" cried Cicely, as her senses awoke to the remembrance of the situation of affairs. "Mother, why did you not let me watch with you?"

Mary only smiled and kissed her brow. The time

T

went by in the preparations, in all of which the Queen took an active part. Her money and jewels had been restored to her by Elizabeth's orders during her daughter's absence, and she had put twenty gold pieces in the silken and pearl purse which she always used. "More I may not give thee," she said. "I know not whether I shall be able to give my poor faithful servants enough to carry them to their homes. This thou must have to provide thee. And for my jewels, they should be all thine by right, but the more valuable ones, which bear tokens, might only bring thee under suspicion, poor child."

She wished Cicely to choose among them, but the poor girl had no heart for choice, and the Queen herself put in her hand a small case containing a few which were unobtrusive, yet well known to her, and among them a ring with the Hepburn arms, given by Bothwell. She also showed her a gold chain which she meant to give to Humfrey. In this manner time passed, till a message came in that Master Richard Talbot was ready.

"Who brought it?" asked the Queen, and when she heard that it was Humfrey himself who was at the door, she bade him be called in.

"Children," she said, "we were interrupted last night. Let me see you give your betrothal kiss, and bless you."

"One word, my mother," said Cicely. "Humfrey will not bear me ill-will if I say that while there can still be any hope that Queen Elizabeth will accept me for her prisoner in your stead, I neither can nor ought to wed him."

"Thou mayst safely accept the condition, my son," said Mary.

" Then if these messengers should come to conduct
my mother abroad, and to take me as her hostage,
Humfrey will know where to find me."

" Yea, thou art a good child to the last, my little
one," said Mary.

" You promise, Humfrey ?" said Cicely.

" I do," he said, knowing as well as the Queen how
little chance there was that he would be called on to
fulfil it, but feeling that the agony of the parting was
thus in some degree softened to Cicely.

Mary gave the betrothal ring to Humfrey, and she
laid her hands on their clasped ones. " My daughter
and my son," she said, " I leave you my blessing. If
filial love and unshaken truth can bring down blessings
from above, they will be yours. Think of your mother
in times to come as one who hath erred, but suffered
and repented. If your Church permits you, pray often
for her. Remember, when you hear her blamed, that
in the glare of courts, she had none to breed her up in
godly fear and simple truth like your good mother at
Bridgefield, but that she learnt to think what you view
in the light of deadly sin as the mere lawful instruments of government, above all for the weaker. Condemn her not utterly, but pray, pray with all your
hearts that her God and Saviour will accept her penitence, and unite her sufferings with those of her Lord,
since He has done her the grace of letting her die in
part for His Church. Now," she added, kissing each
brow, and then holding her daughter in her embrace,
" take her away, Humfrey, and let me turn my soul
from all earthly loves and cares !"

CHAPTER XLIV.

ON THE HUMBER.

MASTER TALBOT had done considerately in arranging that Cicely should at least begin her journey on a pillion behind himself, for her anguish of suppressed weeping unfitted her to guide a horse, and would have attracted the attention of any serving-man behind whom he could have placed her, whereas she could lay her head against his shoulder, and feel a kind of dreary repose there.

He would have gone by the more direct way to Hull, through Lincoln, but that he feared that February Fill-dyke would have rendered the fens impassable, so he directed his course more to the north-west. Cicely was silent, crushed, but more capable of riding than of anything else; in fact, the air and motion seemed to give her a certain relief.

He meant to halt for the night at a large inn at Nottingham. There was much stir in the court, and it seemed to be full of the train of some great noble. Richard knew not whether to be glad or sorry when he perceived the Shrewsbury colours and the silver mastiff badge, and was greeted by a cry of "Master Richard of Bridgefield!" Two or three retainers of higher degree came round him as he rode into the yard, and, while demanding his news, communicated their own, that my Lord was on his way to Fotheringhay to preside at the execution of the Queen of Scots.

He could feel Cicely's shudder as he lifted her off her horse, and he replied repressively, " I am bringing my daughter from thence."

" Come in and see my Lord," said the gentleman. " He is a woeful man at the work that is put on him."

Lord Shrewsbury did indeed look sad, almost broken, as he held out his hand to Richard, and said, " This is a piteous errand, cousin, on which I am bound. And thou, my young kinswoman, thou didst not succeed with her Majesty !"

" She is sick with grief and weariness," said Richard. " I would fain take her to her chamber."

The evident intimacy of the new-comers with so great a personage as my Lord procured for them better accommodation than they might otherwise have had, and Richard obtained for Cicely a tiny closet within the room where he was himself to sleep. He even contrived that she should be served alone, partly by himself, partly by the hostess, a kind motherly woman, to whom he committed her, while he supped with the Earl,- and was afterwards called into his sleeping chamber to tell him of his endeavours at treating with Lord and Lady Talbot, and also to hear his lamentations over the business he had been sent upon. He had actually offered to make over his office as Earl Marshal to Burghley for the nonce, but as he said, " that of all the nobles in England, such work should fall to the lot of him, who had been for fourteen years the poor lady's host, and knew her admirable patience and sweet conditions, was truly hard."

Moreover, he was joined in the commission with

the Earl of Kent, a sour Puritan, who would rejoice in making her drink to the dregs of the cup of bitterness! He was sick at heart with the thought. Richard represented that he would, at least, be able to give what comfort could be derived from mildness and compassion.

"Not I, not I!" said the poor man, always weak. "Not with those harsh yoke-fellows Kent and Paulett to drive me on, and that viper Beale to report to the Privy Council any strain of mercy as mere treason. What can I do?"

"You would do much, my Lord, if you would move them to restore—for these last hours—to her those faithful servants, Melville and De Préaux, whom Paulett hath seen fit to seclude from her. It is rank cruelty to let her die without the sacraments of her Church, when her conscience will not let her accept ours."

"It is true, Richard, over true. I will do what I can, but I doubt me whether I shall prevail, where Paulett looks on a Mass as mere idolatry, and will not brook that it should be offered in his house. But come you back with me, kinsman. We will send old Master Purvis to take your daughter safely home."

Richard of course refused, and at the same time, thinking an explanation necessary and due to the Earl, disclosed to him that Cicely was no child of his, but a near kinswoman of the Scottish Queen, whom it was desirable to place out of Queen Elizabeth's reach for the present, adding that there had been love passages between her and his son Humfrey, who intended to wed her and see some foreign service. Lord Shrewsbury showed at first some offence at having been kept in ignorance all these years of such a fact, and wondered what his Countess would say, marvelled too that his cousin should consent to his son's throwing himself away on a mere stranger, of perilous connection, and going off to foreign wars; but the good nobleman was a placable man, and always considerably influenced by the person who addressed him, and he ended by placing the *Mastiff* at Richard's disposal to take the young people to Scotland or Holland, or wherever they might wish to go.

This decided Mr. Talbot on making at once for the seaport; and accordingly he left behind him the horse, which was to serve as a token to his son that such was his course. Cicely had been worn out with her day's journey, and slept late and sound, so that she was not ready to leave her chamber till the Earl and his retinue were gone, and thus she was spared actual contact with him who was to doom her mother, and see that doom carried out. She was recruited by rest, and more ready to talk than on the previous day, but she was greatly disappointed to find that she might not be taken to Bridgefield.

" If I could only be with Mother Susan for one hour," she sighed.

" Would that thou couldst, my poor maid," said Richard. " The mother hath the trick of comfort."

" 'Twas not comfort I thought of. None can give me that," said the poor girl; " but she would teach me how to be a good wife to Humfrey."

These words were a satisfaction to Richard, who had begun to feel somewhat jealous for his son's sake, and to doubt whether the girl's affection rose to the point of requiting the great sacrifice made for his sake, though truly in those days parents were not wont to be solicitous as to the mutual attachment between a betrothed pair. However, Cicely's absolute resignation of herself and her fate into Humfrey's hands, without even a question, and with entire confidence and peace, was evidence enough that her heart was entirely his; nay, had been his throughout all the little flights of ambition now so entirely passed away, without apparently a thought on her part.

It was on the Friday forenoon, a day very unlike their last entrance into Hull, that they again entered the old town, in the brightness of a crisp frost; but poor Cicely could not but contrast her hopeful mood of November with her present overwhelming sorrow, where, however, there was one drop of sweetness. Her foster - father took her again to good Mr. Heather-thwayte's, according to the previous invitation, and was rejoiced to see that the joyous welcome of Oil-of-Gladness awoke a smile; and the little girl, being well trained in soberness and discretion, did not obtrude upon her grief.

Stern Puritan as he was, the minister himself contained his satisfaction that the Papist woman was to die and never reign over England until he was out of hearing of the pale maiden who had—strange as it seemed to him—loved her enough to be almost broken-hearted at her death.

Richard saw Goatley and set him to prepare the *Mastiff* for an immediate voyage. Her crew, somewhat like those of a few modern yachts, were permanently attached to her, and lived in the neighbourhood of the wharf, so that, under the personal superintendence of one who was as much loved and looked up to as Captain Talbot, all was soon in a state of forwardness, and Gillingham made himself very useful. When darkness put a stop to the work and supper was being made ready, Richard found time to explain matters to

Mr. Heatherthwayte, for his honourable mind would not permit him to ask his host unawares to perform an office that might possibly be construed as treasonable.   In spite of the preparation which he had already received through Colet's communications, the minister's wonder was extreme.   " Daughter to the Queen of Scots, say you, sir !   Yonder modest, shamefast maiden, of such seemly carriage and gentle speech ?"

Richard smiled and said—" My good friend, had you seen that poor lady—to whom God be merciful—as I have done, you would know that what is sweetest in our Cicely's outward woman is derived from her ; for the inner graces, I cannot but trace them to mine own good wife."

Mr. Heatherthwayte seemed at first hardly to hear him, so overpowered was he with the notion that the daughter of her, whom he was in the habit of classing with Athaliah and Herodias, was in his house, resting on the innocent pillow of Oil-of-Gladness.   He made his guest recount to him the steps by which the discovery had been made, and at last seemed to embrace the idea.   Then he asked whether Master Talbot were about to carry the young lady to the protection of her brother in Scotland ; and when the answer was that it might be poor protection even if conferred, and that by all accounts the Court of Scotland was by no means a place in which to leave a lonely damsel with no faithful guardian, the minister asked—

" How then will you bestow the maiden ?"

" In that, sir, I came to ask you to aid me.   My son Humfrey is following on our steps, leaving Fotheringhay so soon as his charge there is ended ; and I ask of you to wed him to the maid, whom we will then take to Holland, when he will take service with the States."

The amazement of the clergyman was redoubled, and he began at first to plead with Richard that a perilous overleaping ambition was leading him thus to mate his son with an evil, though a royal, race.

At this Richard smiled and shook his head, pointing out that the very last thing any of them desired was that Cicely's birth should be known; and that even if it were, her mother's marriage was very questionable. It was no ambition, he said, that actuated his son, " But you saw yourself how, nineteen years ago, the little lad welcomed her as his little sister come back to him. That love hath grown up with him. When, at fifteen years old, he learnt that she was a nameless stranger, his first cry was that he would wed her and give her his name. Never hath his love faltered ; and even when this misfortune of her rank was known, and he lost all hope of gaining her, while her mother bade her renounce him, his purpose was even still to watch over and guard her ; and at the end, beyond all our expectations, they have had her mother's dying blessing and entreaty that he would take her."

" Sir, do you give me your word for that ?"

" Yea, Master Heatherthwayte, as I am a true man. Mind you, worldly matters look as different to a poor woman who knoweth the headsman is in the house, as to one who hath her head on her dying pillow. This Queen had devised plans for sending our poor Cis abroad to her French and Lorraine kindred, with some of the French ladies of her train."

" Heaven forbid !" broke out Heatherthwayte, in horror. " The rankest of Papists——"

" Even so, and with recommendations to give her in marriage to some adventurous prince whom the Spaniards might abet in working woe to us in her

name. But when she saw how staunch the child is
in believing as mine own good dame taught her, she
saw, no doubt, that this would be mere giving her over
to be persecuted and mewed in a convent."

" Then the woman hath some bowels of mercy,
though a Papist."

" She even saith that she doubteth not that such as
live honestly and faithfully by the light that is in
them shall be saved. So when she saw she prevailed
nothing with the maid, she left off her endeavours.
Moreover, my son not only saved her life, but won her
regard by his faith and honour; and she called him
to her, and even besought him to be her daughter's
husband. I came to you, reverend sir, as one who
has known from the first that the young folk are no
kin to one another; and as I think the peril to you
is small, I deemed that you would do them this office.
Otherwise, I must take her to Holland and see them
wedded by a stranger there."

Mr. Heatherthwayte was somewhat touched, but he
sat and considered, perceiving that to marry the young
lady to a loyal Englishman was the safest way of
hindering her from falling into the clutches of a Popish
prince; but he still demurred, and asked how Mr.
Talbot could talk of the mere folly of love, and for its
sake let his eldest son and heir become a mere exile
and fugitive, cut off, it might be, from home.

" For that matter, sir," said Richard, " my son is
not one to loiter about, as the lubberly heir, cumbering
the land at home. He would, so long as I am spared
in health and strength, be doing service by land or
sea, and I trust that by the time he is needed at home,
all this may be so forgotten that Cis may return safely.
The maid hath been our child too long for us to risk

her alone. And for such love being weak and foolish, surely, sir, it was the voice of One greater than you or I that bade a man leave his father and mother and cleave unto his wife."

Mr. Heatherthwayte still murmured something about "youth" and "lightly undertaken," and Master Talbot observed, with a smile, that when he had seen Humfrey he might judge as to the lightness of purpose.

Richard meanwhile was watching somewhat anxiously for the arrival of his son, who, he had reckoned, would make so much more speed than was possible for Cis, that he might have almost overtaken them, if the fatal business had not been delayed longer than he had seen reason to anticipate. However, these last words had not long been out of his mouth when a man's footsteps, eager, yet with a tired sound and with the clank of spurs, came along the paved way outside, and there was a knock at the door. Some one else had been watching; for, as the street door was opened, Cicely sprang forward as Humfrey held out his arms; then, as she rested against his breast, he said, so that she alone could hear, "Her last words to me were, 'Give her my love and blessing, and tell her my joy is come—such joy as I never knew before.'"

Then they knew the deed was done, and Richard said, "God have mercy on her soul!" Nor did Mr. Heatherthwayte rebuke him. Indeed there was no time, for Humfrey exclaimed, "She is swooning." He gathered her in his arms, and carried her where they lighted him, laying her on Oil's little bed, but she was not entirely unconscious, and rallied her senses so as to give him a reassuring look, not quite a smile, and yet wondrously sweet, even in the eyes of others. Then, as the lamp flashed on his figure, she sprang to her feet, all else forgotten in the exclamation,

"O Humfrey, thou art hurt! What is it? Sit thee down."

They then saw that his face was, indeed, very pale and jaded, and that his dress was muddied from head to foot, and in some places there were marks of blood; but as she almost pushed him down on the chest beside the bed, he said, in a voice hoarse and sunk, betraying weariness—

"Naught, naught, Cis; only my beast fell with me going down a hill, and lamed himself, so that I had to lead him the last four or five miles. Moreover, this cut on my hand must needs break forth bleeding more than I knew in the dark, or I had not frighted thee by coming in such sorry plight;" and he in his turn gazed reassuringly into her eyes as she stood over him, anxiously examining, as if she scarce durst trust him, that if stiff and bruised at all, it mattered not. Then she begged a cup of wine for him, and sent Oil for water and linen, and Humfrey had to abandon his hand to her, to be cleansed and bound up, neither of them uttering a word more than needful, as she knelt by the chest performing this work with skilful hands, though there was now and then a tremor over her whole frame.

"Now, dear maid," said Richard, "thou must let him come with us and don some dry garments: then shalt thou see him again."

"Rest and food——he needs them," said Cis, in a voice weak and tremulous, though the self-restraint of her princely nature strove to control it. "Take him, father; methinks I cannot hear more to-night. He will tell me all when we are away together. I would be alone, and in the dark; I know he is come, and you are caring for him. That is enough, and I can still thank God."

Her face quivered, and she turned away; nor did
Humfrey dare to shake her further by another demonstration, but stumbled after his father to the minister's
chamber, where some incongruous clerical attire had
been provided for him, since he disdained the offer of
supping in bed.

Mr. Heatherthwayte was much struck with the
undemonstrativeness of their meeting, for there was
high esteem for austerity in the Puritan world, in contrast to the utter want of self-restraint shown by the
more secular characters.

When Humfrey presently made his appearance with
his father's cloak wrapped over the minister's clean
shirt and nether garments, Richard said,

"Son Humfrey, this good gentleman who baptized
our Cis would fain be certain that there is no lightness
of purpose in this thy design."

"Nay, nay, Mr. Talbot," broke in the minister, "I
spake ere I had seen this gentleman. From what I
have now beheld, I have no doubts that be she who
she may, it is a marriage made and blessed in heaven."

"I thank you, sir," said Humfrey, gravely; "it is
my one hope fulfilled.'

They spoke no more till he had eaten, for he was
much spent, having never rested more than a couple of
hours, and not slept at all since leaving Fotheringhay.
He had understood by the colour of the horse left at
Nottingham which road to take, and at the hostel at
Hull had encountered Gillingham, who directed him on
to Mr. Heatherthwayte's.

What he brought himself to tell of the last scene at
Fotheringhay has been mostly recorded by history, and
need not here be dwelt upon. When Bourgoin and
Melville fell back, unable to support their mistress

along the hall to the scaffold, the Queen had said to
him, "Thou wilt do me this last service," and had
leant on his arm along the crowded hall, and had
taken that moment to speak those last words for
Cicely. She had blessed James openly, and declared
her trust that he would find salvation if he lived well
and sincerely in the faith he had chosen. With him
she had secretly blessed her other child.

Humfrey was much shaken and could hardly command his voice to answer the questions of Master
Heatherthwayte, but he so replied to them that, one by
one, the phrases and turns were relinquished which the
worthy man had prepared for a Sunday's sermon on
" Go see now this accursed woman and bury her, for
she is a king's daughter," and he even began to consider of choosing for his text something that would
bid his congregation not to judge after the sight of
their eyes, nor condemn after the hearing of their ears.

When Humfrey had eaten and drunk, and the ruddy
hue was returning to his cheek, Mr. Heatherthwayte
discovered that he must speak with his churchwarden
that night. Probably the pleasure of communicating
the tidings that the deed was accomplished added
force to the consideration that the father and son
would rather be alone together, for he lighted his
lantern with alacrity, and carried off Dust-and-Ashes
with him.

Then Humfrey had more to tell which brooked no
delay. On the day after the departure of his father
and Cicely, Will Cavendish had arrived, and Humfrey
had been desired to demand from the prisoner an
immediate audience for that gentleman. Mary had
said, "This is anent the child. Call him in, Humfrey,"
and as Cavendish had passed the guard he had struck

his old comrade on the shoulder and observed, " What
gulls we have at Hallamshire."

He had come out from his conference fuming, and
desiring to hear from Humfrey whether he were aware
of the imposture that had been put on the Queen and
upon them all, and to which yonder stubborn woman
still chose to cleave—little Cis Talbot supposing herself a queen's daughter, and they all, even grave
Master Richard, being duped.   It was too much for
Will! A gentleman, so nearly connected with the
Privy Council, was not to be deceived like these simple
soldiers and sailors, though it suited Queen Mary's
purposes to declare the maid to be in sooth her
daughter, and to refuse to disown her.   He supposed
it was to embroil England for the future that she left
such a seed of mischief.

And old Paulett had been fool enough to let the
girl leave the Castle, whereas Cavendish's orders had
been to be as secret as possible lest the mischievous
suspicion of the existence of such a person should
spread, but to arrest her and bring her to London as
soon as the execution should be over; when, as he
said, no harm would happen to her provided she would
give up the pretensions with which she had been
deceived.

" It would have been safer for you both," said poor
Queen Mary to Humfrey afterwards, " if I had denied
her, but I could not disown my poor child, or prevent
her from yet claiming royal rights.   Moreover, I have
learnt enough of you Talbots to know that you would
not owe your safety to falsehood from a dying
woman."

But Will's conceit might be quite as effectual.
He was under orders to communicate the matter to no

one not already aware of it, and as above all things he desired to see the execution as the most memorable spectacle he was likely to behold in his life, and he believed Cicely to be safe at Bridgefield, he thought it unnecessary to take any farther steps until that should be over. Humfrey had listened to all with what countenance he might, and gave as little sign as possible.

But when the tragedy had been consummated, and he had seen the fair head fall, and himself withdrawn poor little Bijou from beneath his dead mistress's garment, handing him to Jean Kennedy, he had—with blood still curdling with horror—gone down to the stables, taken his horse, and ridden away.

There would no doubt be pursuit so soon as Richard and Cicely were found not to be at Bridgefield; but there was a space in which to act, and Mr. Talbot at once said, " The *Mastiff* is well-nigh ready to sail. Ye must be wedded to-morrow morn, and go on board without delay."

They judged it better not to speak of this to the poor bride in her heavy grief; and Humfrey, having heard from their little hostess that Mistress Cicely lay quite still, and sent him her loving greeting, consented to avail himself of the hospitable minister's own bed, hoping, as he confided to his father, that very weariness would hinder him from seeing the block, the axe, and the convulsed face, that had haunted him on the only previous time when he had tried to close his eyes.

Long before day Cicely heard her father's voice bidding her awake and dress herself, and handing in a light. The call was welcome, for it had been a night of strange dreams and sadder wakenings to the sense " it had come at last"—yet the one comfort, "Humfrey is near." She dressed herself in those plain black garments she had assumed in London, and in due time came down to where her father awaited her. She was pale, silent, and passive, and obeyed mechanically as he made her take a little food. She looked about as if for some one, and he said, "Humfrey will meet us anon." Then he himself put on her cloak, hood, and muffler. She was like one in a dream, never asking where they were going, and thus they left the house. There was light from a waning moon, and by it he led her to the church.

It was a strange wedding in that morning moonlight streaming in at the east window of that grand old church, and casting the shadows of the columns and arches on the floor, only aided by one wax light, which, as Mr. Heatherthwayte took care to protest, was not placed on the holy table out of superstition, but because he could not see without it. Indeed the table stood lengthways in the centre aisle, and would have been bare, even of a white cloth, had not Richard begged for a Communion for the young pair to speed them on their perilous way, and Mr. Heatherthwayte— almost under protest—consented, since a sea voyage and warlike service in a foreign land lay before them. But, except that he wore no surplice, he had resigned himself to Master Richard on that most unnatural morning, and stifled his inmost sighs when he had to pronounce the name Bride, given, not by himself, but by some Romish priest—when the bridegroom, with the hand wounded for Queen Mary's sake, gave a ruby ring, most unmistakably coming from that same perilous quarter, —and above all when the pair and the father knelt in deep reverence. Yet their devotion was evidently

so earnest and so heartfelt that he knew not how to
blame it, and he could not but bless them with his
whole heart as he walked down with them to the
wharf.   All were silent, except that Cicely once
paused and said she wanted to speak to " Father."
He came to her side, and she took his arm instead of
Humfrey's.

" Sir," she said ; " it has come to me that now my
sweet mother is left alone it would be no small joy to
her, and of great service to our good host's little daughter,
if Oil-of-Gladness could take my place at home for a
year or two."

" None will do that, Cis ; but there is much that
would be well in the notion, and I will consider of it.
She is a maid of good conditions, and the mother is
lonesome."

His consideration resulted in his making the proposal, much startling, though greatly gratifying, Master
Heatherthwayte, who thanked him, talked of his
honour for that discreet and godly woman Mistress
Susan, and said he must ponder and pray upon it,
and would reply when Mr. Talbot returned from his
voyage.

At the wharf lay the *Mastiff's* boat in charge of
Gervas and Gillingham.   All three stepped into it together, the most silent bride and bridegroom perhaps that
the Humber had ever seen.   Only each of the three wrung
the hand of the good clergyman.   At that moment all
the bells in Hull broke forth with a joyous peal, which
by the association made the bride look up with a smile.
Her husband forced one in return ; but his father's eyes,
which she could not see, filled with tears.   He knew
it was in exultation at her mother's death, and they
hurried into the boat lest she should catch the purport

of the shouts that were beginning to arise as the towns-
folk awoke to the knowledge that their enemy was
dead.

The fires of Smithfield were in the remembrance
of this generation. The cities of Flanders were writh-
ing under the Spanish yoke; "the richest spoils of
Mexico, the stoutest hearts of Spain," were already
mustering to reduce England to the condition of
Antwerp or Haarlem; and only Elizabeth's life had
seemed to lie between them and her who was bound
by her religion to bring all this upon the peaceful land.
No wonder those who knew not the tissue of cruel
deceits and treacheries that had worked the final ruin
of the captive, and believed her guilty of fearful crimes,
should have burst forth in a wild tumult of joy, such
as saddened even the Protestant soul of Mr. Heatherthwayte, as he turned homewards after giving his
blessing to the mournful young girl, whom the boat
was bearing over the muddy waters of the Hull.

They soon had her on board, but the preparations
were hardly yet complete, nor could the vessel make
her way down the river until the evening tide. It
was a bright clear day, and a seat on deck was arranged
for the lady, where she sat with Humfrey beside her,
holding her cloak round her, and telling her—strange
theme for a bridal day—all he thought well to tell
her of those last hours, when Mary had truly shown
herself purified by her long patience, and exalted by
the hope that her death had in it somewhat of martyrdom.

His father meantime superintended the work of
the crew, being extremely anxious to lose no time, and
to sail before night. Mr. Heatherthwayte's anxiety
brought him on board again, for he wanted to ask

more questions about the Bridgefield doings ere beginning his ponderings and his prayers respecting his
decision for his little daughter; nor had he taken his
final leave when the anchor was at length weighed,
and the ship had passed by the strange old gables,
timbered houses, and open lofts, that bounded the harbour out from the Hull river into the Humber itself,
while both the Talbots breathed more freely; but as
the chill air of evening made itself felt, they persuaded
Cicely to let her husband take her down to her
cabin.

It was at this moment, in the deepening twilight,
that the ship was hailed, and a boat came alongside,
and there was a summons, "In the Queen's name,"
and a slightly made lean figure in black came up the
side. He was accompanied by a stout man, apparently
a constable. There was a moment's pause, then the
new-comer said, "Kinsman Talbot——"

"I count no kindred with betrayers, Cuthbert
Langston," said Richard, drawing himself up with
folded arms.

"Scorn me not, Richard Talbot," was the reply;
"you stood my friend once when none other did so,
and for that cause have I hindered much hurt to you
and yours. But for me you had been in a London
jail for these three weeks past. Nor do I come to do
you evil now. Give up the wench, and your name
shall never be brought forward, since the matter is to
be private. Behold a warrant from the Council em-
powering me to bring before them the person of Bride
Hepburn, otherwise called Cicely Talbot."

"Man of treacheries and violence," said Mr.
Heatherthwayte, standing forward, an imposing figure
in his full black gown and white ruff, "go back! The

lady is not for thy double-dealing, nor is there now any such person as either Bride Hepburn or Cicely Talbot."

"I cry you mercy," sneered Langston. "I see how it is! I shall have to bear your reverence likewise away for a treasonable act in performing the office of matrimony for a person of royal blood without consent of the Queen. And your reverence knows the penalty."

At that instant there rang from the forecastle a never-to-be-forgotten howl of triumphant hatred and fury, and with a spring like that of a tiger, Gillingham bounded upon him with a shout, " Remember Babington!" and grappled with him, dragging him backwards to the bulwark. Richard and the constable both tried to seize the fiercely struggling forms, but in vain. They were over the side in a moment, and there was a heavy splash into the muddy waters of the Humber, thick with the downcome of swollen rivers, thrown back by the flowing tide.

Humfrey came dashing up from below, demanding who was overboard, and ready to leap to the rescue wherever any should point in the darkness, but his father withheld him, nor, indeed, was there sound or eddy to be perceived.

"It is the manifest judgment of God," said Mr. Heatherthwayte, in a low, awe-stricken voice.

But the constable cried aloud that a murder had been done in resisting the Queen's warrant.

With a ready gesture the minister made Humfrey understand that he must keep his wife in the cabin, and Richard at the same time called Mr. Heatherthwayte and all present to witness that, murder as it undoubtedly was, it had not been in resisting the

Queen's warrant, but in private revenge of the servant,
Harry Gillingham, for his master Babington, whom he
believed to have been betrayed by this gentleman.

It appeared that the constable knew neither the
name of the gentleman nor whom the warrant mentioned.　He had only been summoned in the Queen's
name to come on board the *Mastiff* to assist in securing the person of a young gentlewoman, but who she
was, or why she was to be arrested, the man did not
know.　He saw no lady on deck, and he was by no
means disposed to make any search, and the presence of
Master Heatherthwayte likewise impressed him much
with the belief that all was right with the gentlemen.

Of course it would have been his duty to detain
the *Mastiff* for an inquiry into the matter, but the
poor man was extremely ill at ease in the vessel and
among the retainers of my Lord of Shrewsbury ; and
in point of fact, they might all have been concerned in
a crime of much deeper dye without his venturing to
interfere.　He saw no one to arrest, the warrant was
lost, the murderer was dead, and he was thankful
enough to be returned to his boat with Master Richard
Talbot's assurance that it was probable that no inquiry
would be made, but that if it were, the pilot would be
there to bear witness of his innocence, and that he
himself should return in a month at latest with the
Mastiff.

Master Heatherthwayte consoled the constable
further by saying he would return in his boat, and
speak for him if there were any inquiry after the
other passenger.

"I must speak my farewells here," he said, "and
trust we shall have no coil to meet you on your
return, Master Richard."

"But for her," said Humfrey, "I could not let my father face it alone.   When she is in safety "——

"Tush, lad," said his father, "such plotters as yonder poor wretch had become are not such choice prizes as to be inquired for.   Men are only too glad to be rid of them when their foul work is done."

"So farewell, good Master Heatherthwayte," added Humfrey, "with thanks for this day's work.   I have read of good and evil geniuses or angels, be they which they may, haunting us for life, and striving for the mastery.   Methinks my Cis hath found both on the same Humber which brought her to us."

"Nay, go not forth with Pagan nor Popish follies on thy tongue, young man," said Heatherthwayte, "but rather pray that the blessing of the Holy One, the God of Abraham, Isaac, and Jacob, the God of thy father, may be with thee and thine in this strange land, and bring thee safely back in His own time.   And surely He will bless the faithful."

And Richard Talbot said Amen.

CHAPTER XLV.

TEN YEARS AFTER.

IT was ten years later in the reign of Elizabeth, when James VI. was under one of his many eclipses of favour, and when the united English and Dutch fleets had been performing gallant exploits at Cadiz and Tercera, that license for a few weeks' absence was requested for one of the lieutenants in her Majesty's guard, Master Richard Talbot.

"And wherefore?" demanded the royal lady of Sir Walter Raleigh, the captain of her guard, who made the request.

"To go to the Hague to look after his brother's widow and estate, so please your Majesty; more's the pity," said Raleigh.

"His brother's widow?" repeated the Queen.

"Yea, madam. For it may be feared that young Humfrey Talbot—I know not whether your Majesty ever saw him—but he was my brave brother Humfrey Gilbert's godson, and sailed with us to the West some sixteen years back. He was as gallant a sailor as ever trod a deck, and I never could see why he thought fit to take service with the States. But he did good work in the time of the Armada, and I saw him one of the foremost in the attack on Cadiz. Nay, he was one of those knighted by my Lord of Essex in the marketplace. Then he sailed with my Lord of Cumberland for the Azores, now six months since, and hath not since been heard of, as his brother tells me, and therefore doth Talbot request this favour of your Majesty."

"Send the young man to me," returned the Queen.

Diccon, to give him his old name, was not quite so unsophisticated as when his father had first left him in London. Though a good deal shocked by what a new arrival from Holland had just told him of the hopelessness of ever seeing the *Ark of Fortune* and her captain again, he was not so overpowered with grief as to prevent him from being full of excitement and gratification at the honour of an interview with the Queen, and he arranged his rich scarlet and gold attire so as to set himself off to the best advantage, that so he might be pronounced " a proper man."

Queen Elizabeth was now some years over sixty, and her nose and chin began to meet, but otherwise she was as well preserved as ever, and quite as alert and dignified. To his increased surprise, she was alone, and as she was becoming a little deaf, she made him kneel very near her chair.

"So, Master Talbot," she said, "you are the son of Richard Talbot of Bridgefield."

"An it so please your Majesty."

"And you request license from us to go to the Hague?"

"An it so please your Majesty," repeated Diccon, wondering what was coming next; and as she paused for him to continue—"There are grave rumours and great fears for my brother's ship—he being in the Dutch service—and I would fain learn the truth and see what may be done for his wife."

"Who is his wife?" demanded the Queen, fixing her keen glittering eyes on him, but he replied with readiness.

"She was an orphan brought up by my father and mother."

"Young man, speak plainly. No tampering serves here. She is the wench who came hither to plead for the Queen of Scots."

"Yea, madam," said Diccon, seeing that direct answers were required.

"Tell me truly," continued the Queen. "On your duty to your Queen, is she what she called herself?"

"To the best of my belief she is, madam," he answered.

"Look you, sir, Cavendish brought back word that it was all an ingenious figment which had deceived your father, mother, and the maid herself—and no wonder, since the Queen of Scots persisted therein to the last."

"Yea, madam, but my mother still keeps absolute proofs in the garments and the letter that were found on the child when recovered from the wreck. I had never known that she was not my sister till her journey to London; and when next I went to the north my mother told me the whole truth."

"I pray, then, how suits it with the boasted loyalty of your house that this brother of yours should have wedded the maid?"

"Madam; it was not prudent, but he had never a thought save for her throughout his life. Her mother committed her to him, and holding the matter a deep and dead secret, he thought to do your Majesty no wrong by the marriage. If he erred, be merciful, madam."

"Pah! foolish youth, to whom should I be merciful

since the man is dead? No doubt he hath left half a
score of children to be puffed up with the wind of
their royal extraction."

"Not one, madam. When last I heard they were
still childless."

"And now you are on your way to take on you
the cheering of your sister-in-law, the widow," said the
Queen, and as Diccon made a gesture of assent, she
stretched out her hand and drew him nearer. "She
is then alone in the world. She is my kinswoman, if
so be she is all she calls herself. Now, Master Talbot,
go not open-mouthed about your work, but tell this
lady that if she can prove her kindred to me, and
bring evidence of her birth at Lochleven, I will
welcome her here, treat her as my cousin the Princess
of Scotland, and, it may be, put her on her way to
higher preferment, so she prove herself worthy thereof.
You take me, sir?"

Diccon did take in the situation. He had understood how Cavendish, partly blinded by Langston,
partly unwilling to believe in any competitor who
would be nearer the throne than his niece Arabella
Stewart, and partly disconcerted by Langston's dis-
appearance, had made such a report to the Queen and
the French Ambassador, that they had thought that the
whole matter was an imposture, and had been so
ashamed of their acquiescence as to obliterate all
record of it. But the Queen's mind had since recurred
to the matter, and as in these later years of her reign
one of her constant desires was to hinder James from
making too sure of the succession, she was evidently
willing to play his sister off against him.

Nay, in the general uncertainty, dreams came over
Diccon of possible royal honours to Queen Bridget;

and then what glories would be reflected on the house of Talbot! His father and mother were too old, no doubt, to bask in the sunshine of the Court, and Ned—pity that he was a clergyman, and had done so dull a thing as marry that little pupil of his mother's, Lætitia, as he had rendered her Puritan name. But he might be made a bishop, and his mother's scholar would always become any station. And for Diccon himself—assuredly the *Mastiff* race would rejoice in a new coronet!

Seven weeks later, Diccon was back again, and was once more summoned to the Queen's apartment. He looked crestfallen, and she began,—

"Well, sir? Have you brought the lady?"

"Not so, an't please your Majesty."

"And wherefore? Fears she to come, or has she sent no message nor letter?"

"She sends her deep and humble thanks, madam, for the honour your Majesty intended her, but she———"

"How now? Is she too great a fool to accept of it?"

"Yea, madam. She prays your Grace to leave her in her obscurity at the Hague."

Elizabeth made a sound of utter amazement and incredulity, and then said, "This is new madness! Come, young man, tell me all! This is as good and new as ever was play. Let me hear. What like is she? And what is her house to be preferred to mine?"

Diccon saw his cue, and began—

"Her house, madam, is one of those tall Dutch mansions with high roof, and many small windows therein, with a stoop or broad flight of steps below, on the banks of a broad and pleasant canal, shaded with fine elm-trees. There I found her on the stoop, in the shade, with two or three children round her; for she

is a mother to all the English orphans there, and they
are but too many. They bring them to her as a matter
of course when their parents die, and she keeps them
till their kindred in England claim them. Madam,
her queenliness of port hath gained on her. Had she
come, she would not have shamed your Majesty; and
it seems that, none knowing her true birth, she is yet
well-nigh a princess among the many wives of officers
and merchants who dwell at the Hague, and doubly so
among the men, to whom she and her husband have
never failed to do a kindness. Well, madam, I weary
you. She greeted me as the tender sister she has ever
been, but she would not brook to hear of fears or compassion for my brother. She would listen to no word of
doubt that he was safe, but kept the whole household in
perfect readiness for him to come. At last I spake
your Majesty's gracious message; and, madam, pardon
me, but all I got was a sound rating, that I should
think any hope of royal splendour or preferment should
draw her from waiting for Humfrey. Ay, she knew
he would come! And if not, she would never be
more than his faithful widow. Had he not given up
all for her? Should she fail in patience because his
ship tarried awhile? No; he should find her ready
—in his home that he had made for her."

"Why, this is as good as the Globe Theatre!" cried
the Queen, but with a tear glittering in her eye.

"Your Majesty would have said so truly," said
Diccon; "for as I sat at evening, striving hard to
make her give over these fantastic notions and consult
her true interest, behold she gave a cry—'Tis his
foot!' Yea, and verily there was Humfrey, brown as
a berry, having been so far with his mate as to the
very mouth of the River Plate. He had, indeed, lost

his *Ark of Fortune,* but he has come home with a carrack that quadruples her burthen, and with a thousand bars of silver in her hold. And then, madam, the joy, the kisses, the embraces, and even more—the look of perfect content, and peace, and trust, were enough to make a bachelor long for a wife."

"Long to be a fool!" broke out the Queen sharply. "Look you, lad: there may be such couples as this Humfrey and—what call you her?—here and there."

"My father and mother are such."

"Yea, saucy cockerel as you are; but for one such, there are a hundred others who fret the yoke, and long to be free! Ay, and this brother of thine, what hath he got with this wife of his but banishment and dread of his own land?"

"Even so, madam; but they still count all they either could have had or hoped for, nought in comparison with their love to one another."

"After ten years! Ha! They are no subjects for this real world of ours; are they not rather swains in my poor Philip Sidney's Arcadia? No, no; 'twere pity to meddle with them. Leave them to their Dutch household and their carracks. Let them keep their own secret; I'll meddle in the matter no more."

And so, though after Elizabeth's death and James's accession, Sir Humfrey and Lady Talbot gladdened the eyes of the loving and venerable pair at Bridgefield, the Princess Bride of Scotland still remained in happy obscurity, "Unknown to History."

THE END.